DRAGON SAGA

BOOK FIVE

THE IMMORTAL VOW

NICOLETTE ANDREWS

Editing by Katie Crum & Charity Chimni
Case Laminate Art by Lauren Richelieu
Dust Jacket Art by Msriza
Exterior Design & Interior Formatting by Charity Chimni
Interior artwork by Nadica Borshkova

First Edition

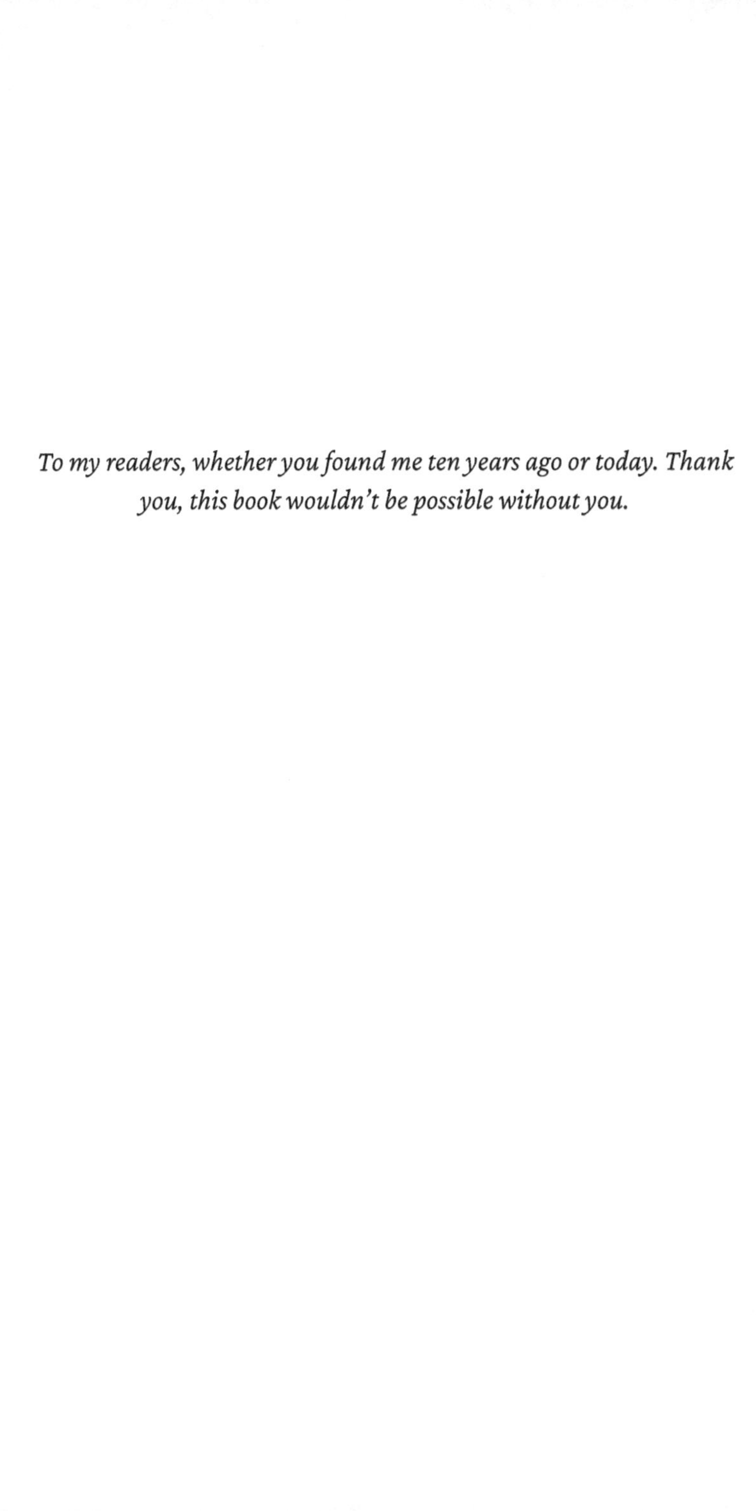

To my readers, whether you found me ten years ago or today. Thank you, this book wouldn't be possible without you.

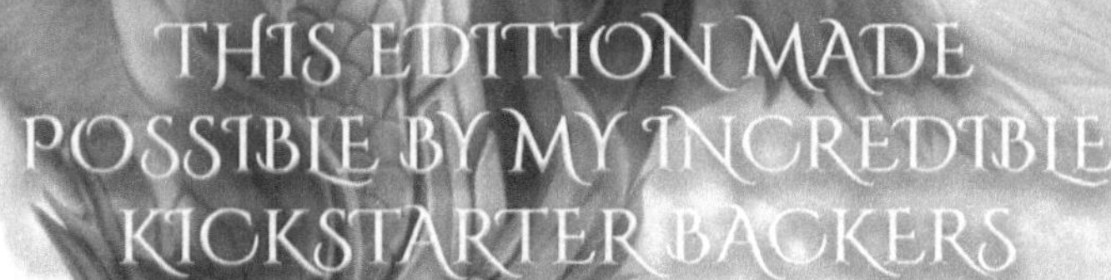

THIS EDITION MADE POSSIBLE BY MY INCREDIBLE KICKSTARTER BACKERS

EXTRA SPECIAL THANKS TO:

ALAINA CARGILL, AMBI CESE, ARIEL S., CAYLA H., CHEYENNE THOMPSON, LAUREN WAYMAN, LISA L., MARIA MEJIA, MARINA HATFIELD, MORGAN RANGLER, RACHEL, RACHEL RASMUSSEN

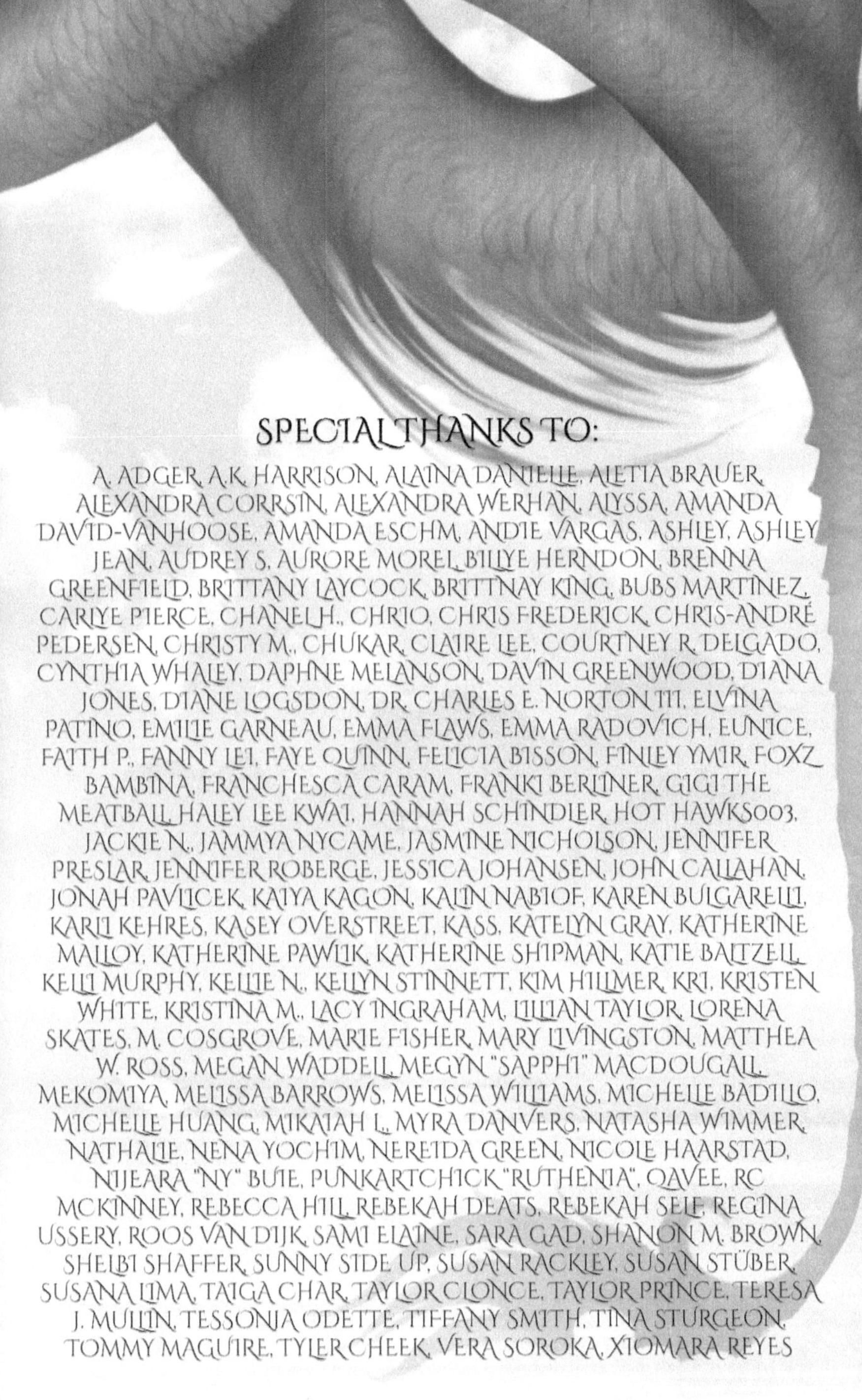

SPECIAL THANKS TO:

A. ADGER, A.K. HARRISON, ALAINA DANIELLE, ALETIA BRAUER, ALEXANDRA CORRSIN, ALEXANDRA WERHAN, ALYSSA, AMANDA DAVID-VANHOOSE, AMANDA ESCHM, ANDIE VARGAS, ASHLEY, ASHLEY JEAN, AUDREY S., AURORE MOREL, BILLYE HERNDON, BRENNA GREENFIELD, BRITTANY LAYCOCK, BRITTNAY KING, BUBS MARTINEZ, CARLYE PIERCE, CHANEL H., CHRIO, CHRIS FREDERICK, CHRIS-ANDRÉ PEDERSEN, CHRISTY M., CHUKAR, CLAIRE LEE, COURTNEY R. DELGADO, CYNTHIA WHALEY, DAPHNE MELANSON, DAVIN GREENWOOD, DIANA JONES, DIANE LOGSDON, DR. CHARLES E. NORTON III, ELVINA PATINO, EMILIE GARNEAU, EMMA FLAWS, EMMA RADOVICH, EUNICE, FAITH P., FANNY LEI, FAYE QUINN, FELICIA BISSON, FINLEY YMIR, FOXZ BAMBINA, FRANCHESCA CARAM, FRANKI BERLINER, GIGI THE MEATBALL, HALEY LEE KWAI, HANNAH SCHINDLER, HOT HAWKS003, JACKIE N., JAMMYA NYCAME, JASMINE NICHOLSON, JENNIFER PRESLAR, JENNIFER ROBERGE, JESSICA JOHANSEN, JOHN CALLAHAN, JONAH PAVLICEK, KAIYA KAGON, KALIN NABIOF, KAREN BULGARELLI, KARLI KEHRES, KASEY OVERSTREET, KASS, KATELYN GRAY, KATHERINE MALLOY, KATHERINE PAWLIK, KATHERINE SHIPMAN, KATIE BALTZELL, KELLI MURPHY, KELLIE N., KELLYN STINNETT, KIM HILLMER, KRI, KRISTEN WHITE, KRISTINA M., LACY INGRAHAM, LILLIAN TAYLOR, LORENA SKATES, M. COSGROVE, MARIE FISHER, MARY LIVINGSTON, MATTHEA W. ROSS, MEGAN WADDELL, MEGYN "SAPPHI" MACDOUGALL, MEKOMIYA, MELISSA BARROWS, MELISSA WILLIAMS, MICHELLE BADILLO, MICHELLE HUANG, MIKAIAH L., MYRA DANVERS, NATASHA WIMMER, NATHALIE, NENA YOCHIM, NEREIDA GREEN, NICOLE HAARSTAD, NIJEARA "NY" BUIE, PUNKARTCHICK "RUTHENIA", QAVEE, RC MCKINNEY, REBECCA HILL, REBEKAH DEATS, REBEKAH SELF, REGINA USSERY, ROOS VAN DIJK, SAMI ELAINE, SARA GAD, SHANON M. BROWN, SHELBI SHAFFER, SUNNY SIDE UP, SUSAN RACKLEY, SUSAN STÜBER, SUSANA LIMA, TAIGA CHAR, TAYLOR CLONCE, TAYLOR PRINCE, TERESA J. MULLIN, TESSONJA ODETTE, TIFFANY SMITH, TINA STURGEON, TOMMY MAGUIRE, TYLER CHEEK, VERA SOROKA, XIOMARA REYES

Lord of the
Sea's Palace
Namahane Village
Hidden Temple
Mt. Kiriyama
Moon Forest
Mt. Iwaki
Temple of
Mt. Iwaki
Kaedemori
Clan House
Mountain God's Shrine
Tengu Mountain
White Palace
Sun Temple
Osaka
Kaito's Palace

ONE

Suzume ran for her life. Her lungs burned with exertion as the wave crested behind her, knocking down trees and swallowing them up like a hungry, wet mouth. A root caught her ankle, and she tumbled to the ground, twisting as she fell so she faced the wall of water. Death loomed above her. There was no escaping it. She closed her eyes and braced for an impact that never came. A pillar of earth rose up from the ground, splitting the wave in two and sparing Suzume from the crushing pressure of water, instead merely sprinkling her with a fine mist.

Hikaru, whose earth power had created the pillar, offered her a hand and pulled her up. Their resonance thrummed through them at the touch, creating a jolt that made letting go difficult. He dropped her hand, and they turned to their opponent.

"Ready?" he asked.

Suzume nodded, fear making her tongue feel thick and words hard to form. The water receded, and Kazue strolled over, her head held high and defiant. This was the moment they'd been waiting for after months of careful planning and training.

Fire burned at her fingertips, and air coursed through her veins. She would get her revenge against Kazue for killing Souta. She'd end her and Hisato's reign of terror. Suzume formed a ball of flame in her hand, which swelled larger and larger, growing into a fiery tornado as she added in her new wind powers. Kazue similarly summoned another wave, and with a flick of her wrist, sent it careening toward Suzume and Hikaru.

The two opposing forces collided in a burst of steam, and in the ensuing chaos, she drew her staff. A song of sealing burst from her lips as she charged through the mist. But when she came through the other side, it wasn't Kazue she found but Souta, staring at her with large, soulful eyes. A wound bleeding on his chest.

She faltered, lowering her staff to her side. She tried to call out to him, but it felt like her mouth was full of cotton, and she couldn't make the words.

"Return to the beginning," the voice said.

A bright light flashed, and Suzume shielded her eyes to block it out. Fumbling about blind, she tumbled forward, falling down head over foot through a world of colors and sounds that passed by in a blur, evoking memories of Souta and Kazue's lives. She landed with a thud, the wind knocked out of her, and she lay stunned for a moment. Hundreds of shattered mirrors surrounded her that didn't reflect, but acted like windows through which she could peer through Kazue and Souta's eyes. Their lives compressed into brief fragments in time. Friends. Family. Lovers and enemies. All of it worming its way into her brain, blurring the lines between her memories and theirs.

Remembering those she'd lost made her want to weep, and the sudden rush of their pasts made her skull throb. How had she gotten here? Was this a dream or some sort of illusion? She tried covering her eyes to block them out, but the images continued playing behind her closed eyelids.

A boar yokai leered down at her with a cruel smile. Suzume remembered him as the forest guardian, Akio, whom Hisato had used against her in his twisted game. Noaki knelt beside him, head bowed, his expression blank, but she felt an aura of sadness emanating from him.

"He's yours now, Priestess. Now give me what I asked for." He held out a hoofed hand.

"First, his true name, then I'll give you the dragon," Kazue said.

"His name is—" Suzume didn't hear the name, because she jolted awake.

She shot up in bed, gasping for breath. Damp sweat coated her skin as she kicked off her blanket. She patted her body to make sure it was still hers, not Kazue's and not Souta's. Back in her own skin, her breathing less erratic, she reached for Kaito, but found his side of the futon empty. She'd fallen asleep waiting up late for him again.

Her skin twitched with restless energy as she fumbled in the dark to light the extinguished brazier. Before she could light one, however, the screen door crashed open, and Noaki burst in. His dark gaze swept over the room before coming to rest upon Suzume.

"Are you hurt?" he asked in a flat tone. The moon rose high above him and obscured his features. But her mind transplanted the sad, dejected version of him from her dreams into the flesh and blood version standing in front of her.

"It was nothing," she replied, hating how her voice shook.

She must have called out in her sleep, otherwise Noaki wouldn't have rushed in. The nightmares were happening with an alarming frequency as of late. She often dreamed of Souta, his life, his death. Kazue and Hikaru were a surprising new addition, as was Kazue's voice speaking to her and apparently showing her visions? Or was that wishful thinking on her part?

When Kaito was away, Noaki was the one who stood guard outside her door, and it was he who witnessed the shaking, terrified mess when a bad dream shook her. And she hated it. Maybe her guilty subconscious wanted a way to free him. If she knew his true, secret name, she could dissolve the bonds that tied them. A yokai's true name held power over them, and learning it could make them beholden to another.

Noaki motioned to close the door, satisfied after not finding any threats lurking in the shadows.

"Wait," Suzume said before she could second-guess herself.

Noaki turned back.

"Did Kazue trade sealing Kaito for your name?" she asked. She didn't want to give him false hope, but she needed to confirm the dream was one of Kazue's memories, not some fabrication of her psyche.

"Yes."

Her heart hurt as if the fragment of Kazue's guilt was a glass shard stabbed into her rib cage. Was Kazue trying to speak to her through her dreams again? Even after she'd faded away.

Was she back? Would she try to take over her body again? The implications both terrified and thrilled her.

Out loud she said, "If Kazue traded Kaito for you, how did he end up in the mountain shrine?"

"Because she betrayed Akio to have us both. Kazue always got what she wanted..."

"But why risk Kaito for you?"

Noaki raised a single eyebrow at her bluntness before saying, "Because I could help her capture the Eight."

He'd never mentioned it before, but Noaki was tight-lipped. The Eight were the most powerful kami in Akatsuki. They'd created the world and yokai. If Noaki had the strength to defeat them, then he was more powerful than she realized.

"And you're just telling me this now," Suzume mumbled under her breath.

Noaki didn't deign that with a response, and so she pushed forward.

"You told me once if I could learn your name, you'd be free from this." She gestured to the invisible bond which kept him more or less tethered to her.

Noaki didn't reply straight away. The wind rustled through the trees and leafless bushes outside the open door, facing the inner garden. A dusting of snow clung to the trees. The sound of the wind played through her mind like a melody. Ever since Souta had passed the wind of Kazue's soul onto Suzume, she'd noticed the wind's changing moods. The mournful cry of winter raised the hairs on the back of her arms, and Noaki's silence only made her anxiety rise. When they first met, he'd tried to kill her. Maybe freeing him wasn't the best idea. For all she knew, he was plotting revenge against her because Suzume allowed his children to be corrupted.

"Forget I said anything." She waved away the words as if she were swatting a moth.

"Did you learn my name?" Noaki asked, and it sent a chill down her spine.

She straightened her back and swallowed the lump in her throat. "No. Not yet. But I could find it. Somewhere... As long as you promise not to kill me once I do. I never wanted you to serve me..." A worm of guilt was twisting around in her gut. She was making promises she couldn't keep again and talking too much.

Before he could reply, the door slid open further, revealing Hikaru panting as if he'd run there from across the tengu compound. The memory of her nightmare overlayed with reality, and Suzume took an unconscious step before she stopped herself, wrapping her arms around her body as if she could shield her soul from the tug. The fragments of Kazue's soul tangled them together like thread.

"I woke from a nightmare and felt your panic. Is everything okay?" he said.

"You had a nightmare?" Suzume's skin prickled. It was probably just a coincidence. "Was I in it?"

Hikaru nodded slowly. "You, me, and Kazue. We were fighting, and then I lost you in the mist."

Suzume took another step. "And then, did you see a vision? Did the real Kazue speak to you in your dream, tell you to go back to the beginning?" She moved closer to him, felt the pulse of their power, drawing them together in the way the moon called to the tides.

"It wasn't Kazue I saw, but Hisato. He's calling out to me. I feel it even now." He reached out as if to touch Suzume's cheek.

"What's happened?" Rin said, arriving in time to interrupt what Hikaru was about to do.

Suzume leapt back as if burned while Rin threaded her fingers through Hikaru's in a possessive way. She pulled him out of the doorway, leaving Suzume feeling even more wretched.

"Everyone is barging into my room late at night, is all."

Pain contorted Hikaru's features, and she felt his anguish echo in her chest. Ever since she'd taken on Souta's soul fragment, their pull had only gotten stronger. The pieces of Kazue's soul were calling out to one another, yearning to be reunited. She wanted to know more about his dream, while simultaneously fearing the answer. She'd been avoiding him for weeks, fearing too much proximity would make them worse and hadn't tonight proved that? Now, they were sharing dreams. Was she projecting her subconscious onto him, or was this a new, strange dimension to resonance they couldn't have imagined? How much longer before she accidentally absorbed his fragment and killed him?

"Sorry," Hikaru said as he tore his gaze away from Suzume.

Rin looked at her husband, brows furrowed with concern. "It's alright. I know you can't help the draw that pulls you together."

It would be easier if Rin got jealous or angry. Instead, she looked at them both with this pitying gaze that made Suzume feel an inch tall.

Suzume cleared her throat. "If you don't mind, I'd prefer if you'd all clear out. Kaito will be back any second—"

And as if she'd spoken him into being, Kaito strolled up on their impromptu gathering in their room. His gaze darted between the four of them.

"Something wrong?" Kaito asked, his gaze fixed on her. His blue eyes scanned her up and down. A winter breeze followed him in. Kaito loved the cold. Being on this frigid mountain suited him and his icy power.

"It's nothing," Suzume said as Hikaru said, "She had a nightmare."

Suzume glared in his direction, and Hikaru wilted under her death glare and Noaki chose that moment to melt into the shadows.

"We should go. It's getting late," Rin said, tugging Hikaru away.

If he lingered a moment longer than necessary on the threshold, no one pointed it out. As they walked away, Suzume felt the ache of their parting as a dull throb in her chest. Kaito watched her with narrowed eyes. He knew her better than to believe, "it was nothing." He'd held her too many nights to count as she shivered from nightmares.

"Will you tell me what's really wrong, if I ask?" Kaito said.

"I told you, it's nothing," she replied in a tone that implied otherwise.

"Sure about that? You've got that wrinkle between your brows you get when you're thinking too hard." He pressed his thumb against the furrow of her brows, smoothing it with a gentle touch.

Lately, she melted when his hand brushed against her skin. But tonight, she was wound tight, and his touch sparked upon her skin, repelling him as it used to when they first met.

Kaito jerked his hand back and stared in disbelief for a moment.

"What were you and Noaki talking about? Another nightmare?"

She nodded. The words tangled up along with the rising, directionless anger that churned in her belly. Then he opened his arms to her with an unspoken invitation. She'd never admit to him out loud, but she found comfort in his embrace. And without a word, she fell into his arms and buried her head against his chest. When she was here, she could forget about all her worries. Wrapped in his arms, she could exist in this moment with him, listening to the reassuring rhythm of his heartbeat.

"I hope your dinner with the elder went well," she murmured against his haori.

The elder refused to allow her into the dining hall, and she pretended it didn't bother her because they needed the tengu's help in the war against Ai and Hisato. But the elder was unmoving as a mountain and refused to acknowledge the war or offer any aid to Kaito's cause. And so they'd been stuck on this mountain all winter playing politics. These sorts of negotiations were familiar to Suzume, and she was willing to wait. But she hated how frequently it took Kaito away from her. Often drinking late into the night to please the elder. But maybe the tengu elder had relented. Suzume could use good news for once.

"Are you changing the subject, then?"

"You can try wheedling it out of me, but we both know I'm too stubborn to answer, so let's skip it, and you tell me what happened and why you reek of sake?"

Kaito's chest rumbled with laughter, easing the tension. His palm slid across her lower back and grazed over the top of her rear, and butterflies took flight in her stomach. They'd been together for months, but feeling his hands rove across her body never got old. Kaito nibbled her ear, and she giggled in surprise.

"If you need a distraction, perhaps we should forget politics for tonight. And I get lost in your embrace and touch..." He kissed along her neck, which she arched, closing her eyes.

"I wouldn't protest," she murmured.

He kissed her, and for a moment, they were adrift in a world all their own, as her hands drifted across his chest, pulling back his haori, needing to be touching him skin to skin. Then Kaito pulled back and pressed his forehead against hers.

"The nightmares are getting worse..." he murmured against her hair.

"I know."

"Promise me you won't hide from me anymore. If something is wrong..."

"It's nothing I can't handle," Suzume said, stiffening in his grip. She didn't want to talk. She wanted to get back to kissing. At least, that was a pleasant diversion.

Kaito cupped her cheeks and tilted her head up to meet his gaze. "I can't lose you."

"You won't," she promised and sealed the vow with a kiss. All the while, her mind swirled with fears unspoken.

Two

A gentle snow fell on the mountaintop. The winter invigorated Kaito, whose veins ran with ice, but for his motley army, it had been a grueling few months. He'd answered the summons and come to the tengu's aid when Ai's army was attacking, and he thought the tengu would repay the favor in kind. Instead, he'd spent months deadlocked in a battle of wills with a doddering old fool who refused to release his people to fight alongside him. No matter how much they wished to. Mori, his one-time advisor and friend, had spent the better part of the last three months trying to convince his kin to join the fight. But they wouldn't move without the elder's say so.

At least once a day, Kaito strolled through the ramshackle encampment to visit with his army. Apart from a restless sense of boredom, they seemed content. The tengu weren't willing to provide an army, but they had supplied them with food and water, enough to keep his men contented. But he knew their generosity wouldn't last forever. Spring was inching up the mountain, and soon, the inclement weather wouldn't be reason enough to stay on the mountaintop.

Across the camp, Kaito noticed his general Shin, his mate, Akane, and Mori, the tengu elder's oldest son, talking together, their brows furrowed. Kaito strode over to them, and they all looked up at him. He could almost smell the bad news in the air.

"I take it there's bad news?" Kaito asked.

"Afraid so," Shin said.

Mori rubbed the back of his neck, avoiding Kaito's scrutinizing looks. He suspected he knew the source of the bad news.

"I take it we've worn out our welcome," Kaito addressed Mori.

His large, black wings twitched behind him as he nodded his head. "I've done my best to convince him. But the old man is stubborn," Mori said, head bowed.

Kaito curled a fist as he bit back the frustration threatening to claw its way out. It wasn't Mori's fault that his father was a fool.

"How long do we have?" Kaito asked in a clipped tone, ignoring the concerned look that passed between Shin and Akane.

"Until the first day of spring. The thaw won't happen for weeks. I could still try to change his mind," Mori said, but his tone implied he didn't think he'd succeed.

"Or you could defy your father's wishes and join me. Along with the others in your clan, awaiting you to take the lead."

"You know it's not as simple as that."

Kaito knew, but it didn't mean he liked it. But rather than take out his frustration on his old friend, he clapped him on the shoulder. "We'll prepare the army to move. Tell the elder I am grateful for his hospitality until now." He said the words through gritted teeth. Their time here had been wasted, months of planning and preparations that Kaito could've spent recruiting other clans, mustering armies amongst the lesser yokai. He'd gambled it all on the tengu, because no one else held as much strategic advantage. They were born fighters who lived and died by the blade, who could also fly.

There was no use waiting. Kaito excused himself and walked away from the camp. Whenever anger made his temper rise, he'd been trying to walk away rather than tear his subordinates to shreds. He'd say it was Suzume's influence on him, but she was often more bloodthirsty than him. Then, as if his subconscious had guided him to her, he found Suzume standing on the parapet facing the snowy mountain range.

The wind picked up and lifted strands of her sable hair, and he stood mesmerized by her beauty for a few heartbeats. A few yards of distance separated them, but it felt as if she were a thousand miles away, untouchable and remote. There'd been a subtle shift in her over the past few months, one he couldn't quite put his finger on. Though closer than they'd ever been, in moments like this, he felt invisible walls rising around her, blocking him out. Before she'd been an open book, easy to read. Now, he couldn't understand what thoughts were dancing behind those vacant gazes. It gave him an intense feeling of nostalgia and bitter loneliness. She must have sensed him staring, because she turned to look at him. In a blink, her image was overlaid with Kazue's, and he realized what felt so familiar about her mile-long stares. It felt like Kazue was staring out through Suzume's eyes. The thought made his stomach turn sour. He must be imagining it. Kazue was gone.

Kaito strode over to Suzume and grasped a hold of her, pulling her tight into his embrace.

"Stop, everyone is staring," Suzume squawked in protest, casting away any lingering doubts she was anyone but herself.

"You were deep in your own thoughts. If you think too hard, you might hurt yourself," he teased.

She hit him lightly on the chest and then tilted her head up to meet his gaze. "It's still me. You don't need to worry," she replied, as if reading his thoughts.

"Good, stay that way," Kaito said as he kissed the top of her head.

Despite her assurances, the chest-squeezing fear hadn't gone away. He'd known loss, and that fear always lingered, and it kept him fighting for a world where he and Suzume could be together. If he had to, he'd travel to the spirit realm and back to keep her soul planted in her body. They held onto one another for a few more minutes, even as Hana, one of his generals, came up to them and cleared her throat.

Reluctantly, he let go of Suzume, all the while keeping his palm pressed against her lower back. Being close to her comforted him; feeling her fire against his icy let him know she was still fighting to stay by his side.

"Sorry to interrupt," Hana said with a sly smile. "But there's an incident."

Kaito scowled. "If they're fighting again, put them through their drills. You know what to do," Kaito said, trying to dismiss her.

But Hana stood her ground. "We have a trio of outsiders looking for you. The tengu are holding them at arrow point. They say they have something important to tell you. You might want to investigate before the tengu decide their fate instead."

Kaito growled in frustration. Before turning to Suzume and saying. "I'll only be a moment."

Suzume nodded in understanding, stepping aside to allow him to follow Hana through the winding row of tents outside the compound to the edge of their encampment. Voices shouted excitedly as a ring of tengu soldiers surrounded a group of hollering, masked yokai.

"I must see the dragon. Bring us the dragon!" they shouted.

"I'm here. Tell me what you want before I decide you're too much trouble and let my friends finish you," Kaito drawled, looking over the furry, masked yokai before him. On first glance, they seemed somewhat familiar. But he couldn't quite place where he knew them from.

"Dragon!" the leader said in a booming voice, falling to his knees before him in the snow, half burying his face.

Kaito's lips twitched at the corner in amusement. They were dramatic, that was for sure. "Show yourself. Take off that mask," Kaito snarled.

The yokai removed it, revealing himself as a monkey yokai. "I've traveled a long way to meet you, your magnificence," the monkey yokai said.

"I can see that. Did you seek me out to be a nuisance?" Kaito asked.

"You do not remember us, my lord?" the monkey asked.

Before Kaito could answer, a ball of fire sizzled through the air, singeing the hairs on top of the monkey's head. It fell backward with an exaggerated yelp while his companions chattered in fear. Kaito glanced over his shoulder and saw Suzume striding up. Wind whipped her hair, and a ball of fire sat burning in her palm. It shouldn't have surprised him she'd followed. Telling her to stay back had been his first mistake. She'd only take it as a challenge.

"Was that really necessary?" he asked.

"These yokai kidnapped me last we saw them. I assumed this was their attempt at a trick." She shrugged.

"Not a trick!" the monkey yokai interjected.

"Who hasn't kidnapped you at this point?" Kaito murmured under his breath, and Suzume shot him one of her death glares, which was reassuring to see. Seeing her fired up was more assuring than words. She wasn't acting like herself unless she was flinging fire and spitting venom. "Did I ever tell you I love your fiery temper?" he asked.

"Now isn't the time for flirting," Suzume replied, her attention focused on the monkey yokai. "If you're not here to trick us. Why are you here? Weren't you working with Hisato before?" Suzume asked the monkey yokai.

"You are gracious and magnanimous to listen to this humble servant, dragon's lover."

Suzume wrinkled her nose at that. "I have a name, you know."

"A thousand pardons, your gloriousness, priestess of fire and wind. Forgive this worm's sudden and rude arrival. I wasn't sure how to best approach persons as glorious as you both. Even though our foolish elder brother tried to kidnap you and give you over to the one, the dark one. We had no choice, as we are weaker and inferior to you, but to grovel at your feet and beg your mercy."

"You did. Which begs the question, why would we listen to a word you say?"

"If I might be so bold as to say, you killed our kin in all your infinite wisdom."

"And what are you doing here? Back for revenge for killing your clansmen?" Kaito asked. Now, he remembered their brief run-in with these monkey yokai right after he'd met Suzume. They'd taken Suzume while a mimic had tried to convince him she was Kazue so she could drain all his spiritual energy from him.

"We're willing to forgive your past. Er... transgressions," the monkey yokai admitted.

"How generous of you," Kaito said, crossing his arms over his chest.

They groveled on their knees. There was only one reason someone blew smoke up your ass, and it was when they wanted something from you.

"Enough sniveling. What is it you want?" Kaito growled.

"You are clear and direct to the point. I appreciate that in a glorious leader," the monkey said.

Kaito rolled his eyes as he waved him to hurry.

"I've come seeking your help by giving you information that you seek."

"And that is?"

"Information about our mutual enemy," the monkey yokai said with more confidence, daring to raise his head and look Kaito in the eye.

"I bet they're working for Hisato still," Suzume interjected, glaring at the yokai.

The monkey yokai hissed at Hisato's name. A few beat their chests and howled like wild animals.

"Speak not his name. For he has caused great suffering among our people," the groveling monkey said.

"It would seem we've touched on a sore spot then," Kaito said, now that they'd caught his interest. He wasn't free of doubts, not yet. "What did he do that made you break your alliance with him, then?" Kaito asked.

It wasn't out of character for Hisato to betray an ally. He'd stabbed plenty of people in the back. It was just his way. But he was also clever enough to plan this sort of convoluted trick to lure them into a trap.

"That vile creature promised us power and influence, the likes our clan has never seen before. But he used us to create monstrosities. He sealed most of our clan in stone and then combined them with priests and priestesses to make monsters that are neither human nor yokai."

"I'm aware of hybrids. If that's all you came for, then I think we're done here." Kaito turned as if to walk away.

"Wait," the monkey yokai called out. "It wasn't just our clan that was affected. He's sealed others in stone as well, and we need your help to free them."

Kaito studied him for a moment. He needed to find yokai who could fight and defeat the hybrids, not waste time trying to save yokai, who'd likely already been turned. Without a way to reverse the hybrid's curse, they were useless to him.

"I can't help you. So you've wasted your time. I've got more important things to worry about. Besides, there's no way to save them once they're transformed."

"He hasn't transformed them yet. Just sealed a hundred, at least. Yokai are easy for him to find. Many join him of their own volition. But finding the priestesses and priests has proven more difficult for him. They're fighting back. If you broke their seals as you broke yours, you'd have an army loyal to you unto death," the monkey yokai pleaded, grabbing onto the hem of his hakama.

Kaito looked down at the monkey; maybe he'd gotten soft, or perhaps just desperate, because he didn't kick him away at the thought. If the tengu wouldn't help him, he needed an army. And the monkey was right; someone you'd rescued was the most grateful.

"And you know where to find them?" Kaito asked.

The monkey nodded. "I can take you to them straight away."

"Hana," Kaito said, and at his summons, she appeared at his side.

"Yes, my lord?"

"Follow the monkey, see if he's telling the truth, and then report back to me."

"Thank you, thank you." The monkey yokai bowed over and over.

"Your companions will remain here. And should you harm Hana and plot to trick me, it is your kin that will pay the price. Do you understand?"

The monkey nodded rapidly. "You can trust me, my lord."

"I hope so," Kaito said and dismissed them all to do his bidding as he strode over to the tengu compound. Suzume fell into step beside him, and he could feel her stare as they walked.

"And how do you plan on freeing those yokai? That's assuming it isn't a trap."

"Isn't that what you're best at, breaking seals?" Kaito teased.

Suzume thinned her lips in disapproval, but didn't outright refuse him. She'd been practicing all winter, and he knew she was capable of the task. A flurry of snow was falling on the ground between them.

"I'm sorry. I should've asked first..." he said.

She shook her head. "It's not that..." she trailed off. "I'll break all their seals. Whatever it takes to get your kingdom back, right?" The wry twist to her mouth and strange look in her eyes troubled him. Maybe it was because he'd been thinking of Kazue earlier, but he had this uncanny feeling churning in his gut. As if her specter were lingering between them. He wanted to reach out and assure Suzume that she came before his kingdom, before everything. Nothing mattered more to him than her. But the words lodged in his throat as he stood amidst the falling snow, watching her walk into the tengu compound, not once turning to look at him.

THREE

Ryuu, as former emperor, and sometimes shadow emperor, moved freely about the palace. It made him the obvious choice as a spy, given his access to places the average government official wouldn't have. Ryuu tried not to abuse his authority, however. Few in the palace knew his true identity, and given the shifting political climate with Izuki's recent return to the emperor's favor, he had to play his cards close to the chest. He'd spent most of the winter propping up those who supported the empress and the crown prince, while simultaneously trying to uncover Izuki's allies. It had been an exhausting season. Ryuu felt like they were caught in an endless game of go—each of them moving pieces on the board. Though their paths hardly crossed, he felt her hand moving the pieces on the board, just as he nudged his friends and allies into place from rooms at the Sun Temple.

Then, today, he'd received a cryptic summons from the current emperor, asking him to a private meeting. Afraid Izuki's spies would see him on the way, Ryuu had used secret back ways into the emperor's chambers and a bit of his dragon magic to get there unseen until he was standing in front of a befuddled eunuch who opened the doors, allowing him into the emperor's private rooms. The emperor was dressed down for their meeting. He looked rather humble in his simple white haori and hakama. Lacking the gilded trappings of an emperor, he was just another man. As were all his predecessors, Ryuu had to remind himself. Long ago, he'd hand-picked each ruler, guiding them, teaching them, and, at times, removing them from position. But it had been centuries since he'd gotten so involved. Now, he acted as a sometimes guide and distant observer, rarely involving himself in the affairs of running the country. Which was why the emperor's request and circumvention of ceremony surprised him.

"Master Ryuu, thank you for coming," the emperor said as he gestured to the seat across from him.

Ryuu took his seat, studying the man across from him, drawing out the awkward silence that hung between them. There was always an undercurrent of tension between him and the reigning emperors. Once they claimed their throne and the truth was revealed, many felt threatened by the existence of a living emperor, and feared he'd attempt to usurp them. Some trusted him by his word, while others tried to sever his claim to the throne with permanent solutions. Those never lasted long. Emperor Hisamune leaned upon Ryuu like an advisor at times and a distant rival at other times. They'd never spoken of it and never would, but Ryuu suspected the emperor knew about his affair with Izuki.

"It has been a long time since we spoke," the emperor said, folding his hands on the table between them.

"Indeed," Ryuu said calmly. He would reveal nothing at all.

The emperor poured them each a cup of tea from the kettle on the table. Thin tendrils of steam rose from the cup that Ryuu did not touch.

"I have concerns I fear only you can assuage, given your unique... heritage," he said before lifting the teacup to his mouth and taking a long sip.

"Oh?" Ryuu replied.

"I've received word of a yokai army on the move from Osaka, headed this way. They've been terrorizing villages and innocent humans. My governors think it's peasants panicking, making up stories. But I fear we both know the fairy tales are all real."

"And what is it you're asking me?" Ryuu asked.

"I need an army to fight against these yokai before they kill our people, and I think you can help me get them."

"Alas, I have no army of my own. As you know." Ryuu tipped his head at the emperor.

"Perhaps you don't, but you know someone who does: the dragon who has hold of my daughter, Suzume."

"I told you, Suzume is dead." The lie rolled easily off his tongue.

The emperor gave him a long, measuring look as if he'd seen through his lies. A cold chill ran down Ryuu's spine. But it was better he think his daughter and her power lost to him than let him continue chasing after her. Suzume had enough to worry about.

"I wish her no harm, and I know you correspond with her and

the dragon. I've seen the error of my ways and wish to offer a marital alliance in exchange for her help and the dragon's."

"That is an interesting offer indeed," Ryuu said. There was no point continuing the ruse. But he wasn't willing to agree to this strange arrangement. Suzume didn't need the emperor's permission to stay with the dragon.

"But you wish to decline. I can see it in your face."

Ryuu sincerely doubted his expression revealed anything, but either way, the emperor had anticipated his refusal.

"My goal has always been to protect the kingdom you created, but at times, I feel the constraints of my position hold me back. I am nothing more than a gilded figurehead sitting atop my golden throne." He looked at Ryuu imploringly.

Ryuu didn't see Hisamune as just another emperor sat upon his throne, but as a reflection of his past. No one knew the pressures of ruling and the loneliness better than Ryuu. He'd had spent his youth trying to become the very thing he'd later despise. He knew, and that commonality softened Ryuu to him, despite his better judgment.

"Why are you offering me this when you know you have nothing to offer in return?" Ryuu asked.

"Because I hope you can help me correct the mistake I made. I shouldn't have forgiven Izuki, or let her back into the White Palace. She's wormed her way into the hearts of my governors and gotten the empress and my oldest son banished for crimes they didn't commit."

Ryuu frowned. He hadn't heard of the empress and crown prince's banishment until now.

"It happened in secret. They fled this morning to avoid being arrested and tried. She plans to put our son on the throne in his place..." The emperor trailed off, seemingly conflicted. Ryuu knew that feeling. Knew what hold Izuki had.

"And you expect me to offer Suzume to the dragon who already has her?" The emperor surely had enough sense not to make an empty offer.

"I will help him find the man called Hisato. I know he is complicit in Izuki's rise to power. And I suspect the oncoming yokai army is his doing as well."

Ryuu's gut told him the same. Izuki had been too quiet this winter. He should have suspected the subtle power moves were a distraction, preparing her for this final blow.

"I'll bring them both here. That is all I can promise."

"Thank you," the emperor said as he sagged into his seat, like a great weight had been lifted off his shoulders.

Ryuu bowed before exiting. Then he moved unseen through the shadows back to his personal rooms at the Sun Temple. Their meeting weighed on him. He'd known Izuki was working to dethrone the crown prince. That came as no surprise. But the emperor's change of heart shocked him most of all. He hated yokai, and now he was begging one for aid? It seemed out of character, but maybe he'd changed.

When he returned to his room, the neko was waiting for him. He'd sent him out seeking information while he was gone. Normally, when he returned from an assignment, the neko would nap on his bed or eat his supper. But he wasn't up to his usual mischievous antics today. He was staring out into the villa garden, arms crossed with his tails lashing behind him.

"Did you miss me, or did something else put you in a foul mood?" Ryuu asked, while shuffling through the pile of documents on his desk. They were mostly invitations to events and letters from governors and petty government officials. All of it was of little importance, since he was leaving.

"The high priest is dead," the neko said bluntly.

Ryuu's head shot up. He'd seen him just that morning, and he'd seemed healthy for a man of his age.

Stranger still, the neko never delivered news this simply. Usually, he teased Ryuu with it first, drawing out the game of cat and mouse they often played. That, coupled with the news of the crown prince's exile, sent a shiver down his spine. Izuki was removing obstacles in her way, and he'd likely be next. He couldn't show his fear, not to the neko, not to anyone. And so, he shuffled through his papers as if he were unaffected.

"Why are you upset? I didn't think you particularly liked him."

"I don't. But there is a strange aura around the palace and the temple. I know you feel it too," he replied, glaring at Ryuu as if the aura were his fault.

Of course, Ryuu felt it. Hisato's slimy fingerprints were everywhere around the palace. As if his black tendrils were creeping invisibly over everything. But after three months of searching, he failed to find the shifter himself. He knew he was pulling the strings, but not where the puppet master resided.

"Well, good news is we're leaving."

"I give you a warning, and this is all I get?" the neko asked.

Ryuu sighed and shook his head. This was more typical of the neko's behavior. "What is it you want this time?"

"For starters, a large fish. And some time off. I risk my life for you. It's the least you can do. Unless you're finally ready to break our bond."

"I'll get you the fish then."

The neko lingered when, typically, he would slink off until he was summoned again.

"Is there anything else to report?"

"Careful you don't get entangled with her again."

"Wouldn't it be to your benefit if I fell to her assassin's knife?"

The neko stretched his arms over his head and yawned, once more taking on the persona of a lazy cat. "True. When you die, I will be free. But I'd rather you meet your end by my claws." He flexed his claws in a mock threat.

Ryuu simply rolled his eyes and waved a hand, dismissing the neko, who left with another flash of a predatory grin. Ryuu stayed at his desk a while longer, writing letters and tying up loose ends to prepare for his journey back to the tengu mountain. He couldn't quite put his finger on why he felt uneasy about the offer, but he knew that Kaito and Suzume would want to hear what he'd learned and decide for themselves. Before he left, he'd need to deal with the succession and prepare a funeral for the deceased high priest. As second-in-command, he by default became high priest, a position he had no desire to fill. This false life had been too short, but he didn't regret leaving it behind; better he leave now before he was inadvertently thrust into power. Ryuu was better suited to an absence entirely from governance.

By the time he finished, the sun had set, and his eyes were burning from squinting by candlelight. Someone knocked on the door, presumably one priest coming with more papers and preparations for the funeral. Rubbing his tired eyes, he moved to answer the door. He was certain that he was untouchable at the heart of the temple. That's why he hadn't bothered to check before opening the door. Izuki stood in his doorway, and the scent of alcohol wafting from her was a strong punch to the face.

"You took too long to answer." She laughed and tilted forward into his arms, forcing Ryuu to catch her or let her fall to the ground face-first.

It all happened so fast, he'd merely acted on instinct. Ryuu felt as if he was inside a hazy dream where they still trusted one another, and she'd show up at his door unannounced.

"What are you doing here?" he asked gruffly.

She wrapped her arms around his neck and smiled. "I missed you, that's all." She gave him a tilted smile. Not the polished courtier's smile, but the ghost of the young woman she'd been when he'd fallen in love with her.

She laughed again, and with a stumbling gait, walked over to his futon and collapsed upon it. He surveyed the area and found no one waiting in the shadows, coming to pounce upon him. She was alone and clearly intoxicated. Even she couldn't fake that with such conviction.

Ryuu stood at the foot of his unused futon and stared down at her. "You can't stay here. I'll bring you back to the palace."

He leaned down to haul her up by the armpits but when he tried, she grasped his face, squeezing his cheeks.

"No." She laughed. "I'm staying here tonight and if you try to move me, I will scream and cause a horrible scene."

With a sigh, Ryuu stepped back. He didn't doubt she'd do exactly that. This wasn't like her. Izuki was always in control of her alcohol consumption. It was one of her skills: she'd keep the sake flowing, partaking little herself, until her companions were spilling secrets that she stored away for future exploitation. He'd never seen her drunk before.

She rolled herself up in his blanket and started snoring gently. Ryuu sat back down at his desk and contemplated what to do. Letting your enemy into your room was probably not the wisest idea. But with her face relaxed in sleep, she looked rather harmless. The neko's warning echoed in his ears, and he could almost see his condescending smirk in his mind's eye.

He should call the palace guards and have her taken from his room. A voice at the back of his mind stalled his hand, and instead he stepped outside to stand guard as she slept. His trip could wait until she'd slept off the alcohol, and then he could get answers from her.

The night passed measured by each breath she took. Ryuu twitched when he heard the rustle of blankets as she tossed in her sleep, and the soft whimper that escaped her in the dark hours before dawn. Despite the temptation to step into the room and brush a cold hand against her brow, he resisted and stood sentry outside the door until the sun rose. When Ryuu heard her wake, he opened his door to find her artfully arranged in his bed, her composed mask back in place, like the carefree drunk who'd visited in the night, never existed. Ryuu offered her tea wordlessly, and she took it, sipping it daintily.

"Have you called for a palanquin yet?" she asked.

"Good morning to you, too," he replied, crossing his arms over his chest and leaning against the wall beside the door.

"It goes unsaid, but I hope this will stay between us." She rose as if she would simply waltz out without another word. But Ryuu threw out his arm to block her retreat.

"Do you think I'm going to let you leave without an explanation?"

"It was a lapse of judgment," she said coolly.

"You don't get drunk, no matter how much you drink."

"Is that what you really think?" she asked, her gaze flicking up to him, pinning him with an icy stare.

"You said you missed me." Ryuu knew he shouldn't have said it, but the words came out, anyway.

"Like I said, lapse of judgment."

Ryuu pressed his lips together. If her goal was to torture him, she was succeeding. He lowered his arm, allowing her to pass.

Izuki stepped out, then turned to face him.

"Remember your promise to me, Ryuu. She comes before everything else."

"Funny asking me that after everything you've done to her."

She lifted her head to meet his gaze. "You could never understand. I've done what I must to protect what matters most to me."

"Your power. I know."

"Keep her safe, Ryuu," she said.

For the briefest moment, he saw Izuki stripped of all her defenses and the woman she had been shining through, and he nearly wavered. His hand flinched as if he'd reach out and tuck that errant hair behind her ear. Why couldn't he escape her? Why was she in his veins, a slow-acting poison, without an antidote? If only he could walk away and forget her. If only her repeated betrayals and schemes were enough for him to hate her. If only. If only.

Then Izuki walked away from him, again.

FOUR

A cold wind howled across the mountaintop and dug icy fingers along the nape of Rin's neck as she wound her way through the rows of tents buried in snowdrifts. Kaito's ramshackle army huddled for warmth around their campfires as they dreamed of spring. The tengu guards on the walls, wings pulled in tight, gazed past the army just outside their walls, as if pretending the army wasn't there would make it go away. Kaito had summoned her to a meeting, and as she and Hikaru passed through the gates, she felt the tension in the air.

The tengu were cordial, but she felt their gazes sliding over her as if she were something filthy they didn't wish to linger on. Their distaste and Hikaru's increasing distance worried her. Shadows lingered in his eyes, and he was waking at night, haunted by his dreams. They talked of it often, but no amount of talking could fix the growing pull of resonance. Suzume and Hikaru were being drawn together, tighter and tighter like a pair of tangled threads, and Rin feared if she tugged too hard trying to hold him back, she'd strangle them both. She'd almost lost him once; she wasn't willing to lose him again.

They caught sight of Shin and his mate as they rounded the corner on their way to Kaito's chambers. Shin waved to them in greeting, and the four of them walked together to the meeting.

"Any idea why we were summoned?" Rin asked Shin.

Shin shook his head. "None. Which makes me uneasy."

Rin glanced at Hikaru. His attention was on the door, a vacant expression on his face as the bond called to him. She reached out, taking hold of his hand as if clinging to him would stop the slow decay of his mind. It worked, and Hikaru shook off the trance before looking at her with an apologetic smile. She squeezed his hand and looked back at Shin, who'd watched their brief exchange with a furrowed brow.

"Hana still hasn't returned with word about the hybrids?" Rin asked, partially to change the subject and partially because she was curious. The monkey yokai weren't a reliable source, but it was the best lead they'd gotten in months.

"Not yet. I talked to Mori on my way here; he's running behind, but he assured me nothing's changed with the tengu either. They still want us out by spring," Shin said, anticipating her next question.

There was no use speculating further, knowing Kaito would explain it all. A small part of Rin wanted to run away and spare Hikaru from his slow unraveling. Shin and Akane entered, and Rin fought her desires and followed them, squeezing Hikaru's hand once more for good measure. Suzume and Kaito sat side by side, awaiting them. Across from them, Ryuu spoke with his head tilted forward and his hands hidden in his billowing sleeves. The three of them turned as they entered, and Ryuu's head shot up, meeting her gaze with a guilty expression that reminded her of when he'd been a child.

His sudden arrival and guilty expression explained the urgent meeting. Whatever news he brought with him, it wasn't good. They took their places around the room and spoke of nothing in particular as they waited for the oni leader and Mori to join the meeting. The latter arrived many minutes after the rest of them, bowing in apology while blaming his father for keeping him longer than he expected. Once they'd all sat, Kaito cleared his throat to get their attention.

"Ryuu has a proposal from the human emperor. He gave us the briefest overview," Kaito gestured at himself and Suzume, "but I thought it best we discuss as a group." He motioned for Ryuu to speak.

Ryuu looked at everyone gathered there, but Rin noted he avoided looking at Suzume for long. Her expression was thunderous, but she'd held back from interjecting, so far.

"As Kaito inferred, the emperor wishes to ally with us, with a marital alliance..."

The only sign of Suzume's feelings was the smell of burning fibers and Hikaru's uncomfortable shifting in his seat. Rin held onto her husband tighter, hoping her touch would soothe him.

"A marital alliance between humans and yokai?" The oni leader laughed. His loud voice shook the rafters.

But no one found it as amusing as him. In fact, when his laughter died off, a deathly silence swelled in its place. They'd attempted to work with the humans in the past. And the emperor imprisoned Hikaru and sealed Rin in stone, while he used Suzume as a puppet in his war against the yokai.

"You can't be seriously considering this offer," Rin said, saying what she was sure was on everyone's minds.

"I know it's not ideal. But the emperor is offering us Hisato and a partner to destroy Ai."

"We don't need the emperor to help us find Hisato, though. We have the monkeys," Shin said.

"Can we trust the monkeys any more than we can the humans?" Kaito asked. "They tried to kidnap Suzume and plotted to murder me as well."

"And there's more. According to the emperor, Ai is on the move and headed for the palace. Izuki is plotting to usurp the emperor and place her son on the throne with Hisato's help. My spies have confirmed all this to be true. All evidence suggests this is a genuine offer."

"This could be our chance," Kaito said, turning to address the group. "A way for us to unite a force strong enough to defeat Hisato. If we have the humans at our back, neither Hisato nor Ai could stand against us."

The oni was grumbling, but everyone else was silent. Especially Suzume, who was uncharacteristically tight-lipped about the entire thing. Rin suspected she wasn't the only one with misgivings.

"What do you think, Suzume? It's your marriage that would seal the alliance."

Suzume looked at Rin with a mix of shock and gratitude.

"Honestly, I don't like it."

"Are you saying you'd rather not marry me?" Kaito said, his voice edging between teasing and serious.

They stared at one another long and hard, volumes spoken in that glance.

"Of course, I want to marry you," Suzume said after an overlong pause. "I don't like the emperor meddling in our relationship."

"Do you have any other suggestions, then?" Kaito asked, crossing his arms over his chest.

The tensions rose like the tide, and she'd need to intervene before they drowned in chaos.

"What if we wait until Hana returns? Assuming the monkey yokai are telling the truth, cutting off Hisato's army at its source would make him that much weaker."

Kaito crossed his arms over his chest and considered her for a moment.

"A priestess I know has been taking in refugees. Maybe she can give us information about their whereabouts," Akane suggested, and Rin resisted the urge to hug her.

"We could split up. You and Suzume go to the palace to negotiate with the emperor. Rin and I will investigate the hybrids," Hikaru added, looking at Rin for confirmation. His quick thinking filled her with pride.

She was glad he'd been the one to suggest it and not her.

"It would give us an advantage to divide and conquer. Myself and part of the army could seek Ai, scout out her army's movements," Shin said.

Kaito looked at Hikaru, then Rin, and after a few tense seconds, he nodded. "You're right. The more we learn about the hybrids and Ai's movements, the better. We'll go our separate ways and meet again on the next full moon."

The knot around her chest untangled at the thought. She'd needed a new goal and distance from the one thing that was slowly destroying Hikaru. Even if it was a temporary solution. Eventually, Hikaru's soul fragment, desperate to be reunited, would call him back here to Suzume.

Noaki found the tengu defenses impressive. Guards stationed along the perimeter walls patrolled on a rotating schedule that was impossible to predict unless you had insider knowledge, and two different protective barriers linked to two undisclosed members of the clan cloaked it all in a shroud of mist. If one fell, the other acted as a safety backup. Anytime Noaki arrived at a new location, his instinct was to check for vulnerabilities that might make his job of protecting his wards harder. This place seemed to lack defensive weak points. That fact alone was why he refused to let his guard down within its protective interior. Something was off about the tengu. But it wasn't his place to ask questions, just to guard.

Ryuu stepped out of the room, and as he passed, he gave Noaki the briefest nod. Noaki returned it with his own brief nod. He tried not to think about Kazue, but seeing her son walking around in the flesh brought back unpleasant memories. She'd broken her promises to him for that man, and left Noaki chained to that mountain alone, guarding her heart for centuries. His desire for revenge had driven him mad, or half-mad, by the time Suzume had found him. But the compulsion of Kazue's order brought him back from the brink once he realized she held a fragment of Kazue's soul. Since then, guarding her had given him a purpose and a means to channel the storming anger hidden behind the coldness of his exterior. Then she'd dangled his freedom in front of him, and the storm raged closer to the surface than it had in a year.

It'd been so long since he'd heard his true name spoken aloud, he wasn't even sure he would recognize it. He closed the lid on the thought. If he dwelled on it, resentment might pour out. Even if Suzume learned his name, there weren't any guarantees she'd set him free. Kazue had broken her promises, too, and hope was a dangerous addiction.

They filed out of the meeting room, and all that remained inside were Suzume and Kaito murmuring in low voices. When Kaito was with her, Noaki gave them more privacy, wandering the outer perimeters of the tengu clan. Noaki circled the inner hallways of the main building. He'd let his guard down with Tsuki and Akira, assuming danger would come from outside. But as he continued to learn, betrayal could come from close to home. His children were another wound that refused to heal. Their betrayal hurt, but worse was the phantom limb feeling he had when he looked for Tsuki's carefree smile when someone made a joke or Akira's sarcastic remarks when someone was being an ass. His time with his children had been brief, yet the ache of missing them ran much deeper than the time they'd had together. But like everything else that pained him, he shoved the feelings down deep. But that lid seemed harder to keep closed.

Noaki redoubled his focus on his patrol. Like the exterior, the interior rooms seemed built for defense and ease of maneuverability by winged yokai. The doors were wide enough for a tengu's wingspan, and the rooms were sparse and without interior decoration that a careless wing might knock over.

A shadow slunk past him and Noaki slashed at it with a sword but struck nothing. As he pivoted backward, he felt a blade pressed against his throat. He'd let his reflections on the past distract him and opened himself up to attack. A mistake he wouldn't make again. Noaki spun around, slashing at his attacker and scoring a line of blood onto the arm of Ryuu's neko servant. The neko often snuck in and out of Ryuu's rooms late at night and had learned to ignore his presence.

He narrowed his yellow eyes at Noaki as blood dripped from his wound. "Surprised I caught you unawares. Something on your mind?" the neko asked as he sheathed his dagger.

Noaki didn't bother answering but rested his hand upon the pommel of his sword in a silent threat. He hoped the neko would catch the hint and slink back into the shadows where he belonged.

A smile curved the neko's lips instead. "It's been a while since I've crossed swords with anyone. Shall we duel?"

"No," Noaki said, hoping to end the conversation. He didn't enjoy fighting. Swords were for killing and defense. Not for petty amusements. But he would not expand on his philosophies for the neko.

"No need to act so cold. We are both creators of the shadows. We could be friends. You know what a 'friend' is, don't you?" the neko said.

Noaki walked away from the neko, but while he'd turned his back, all his senses were on alert, expecting the neko's movements. He might be Ryuu's creature, but he saw the way he looked at Ryuu as if the moment he was off his leash, he'd slit his throat.

The neko chuckled as he walked away.

"I guess you've given up on finding the moon goddess then."

Noaki spun around, catching the neko by the throat before slamming him against the wall. "What do you know?" he snarled. It was a brash reaction. He'd let his feelings come too close to the surface, and it made him impulsive.

The neko's twin tails lashed behind him as a slow, triumphant smile spread across his face.

"Then you are chaffing at your bonds, as I do. I thought you were enjoying being the human's pet."

"Tell me what you know," he ground out.

The neko only laughed harder. "What will you give me for the information?"

Noaki loosed his grip and took a step back. He wasn't fool enough to make petty deals with devious yokai like him. Agree to whatever he'd offer him, and he'd likely send him off chasing shadows. Sayuri had disappeared, along with the rest of the Eight, when Kazue split her soul apart. For all he knew, she was dead. Even Tsuki and Akira couldn't find her.

"I won't help you free yourself of Ryuu," Noaki said, guessing the neko's motive.

His smirk fell. "Don't be so hasty in dismissing my offer. I was with my master as he searched for the trapped souls of the Eight. He didn't find them, but we found the pieces of Kazue's soul: Wind, Water, Fire, and Earth." He ticked each one off on his clawed fingers.

Noaki said nothing. It wasn't anything he hadn't heard before.

"Makes you wonder where they went. They couldn't have simply disappeared into nothing. Even the Great Dragon was sealed..." The neko disappeared in a puff of smoke but left his final words hanging in the air, conjuring up images in Noaki's mind.

He'd been there when Kazue had sealed them, all but Sayuri. Kazue dangled Sayuri like a prize to force his compliance. She promised him that once she had them all, once she'd made herself immortal, she'd set them free. Fool that he'd been, he believed her. He'd aided her in bringing down the gods themselves. Then Kazue had torn herself apart and awakened the darkness, who embraced her like a lover. Light and dark. To keep him bound, she needed the power of the Eight. And before he could do anything, she'd scattered them all. And Noaki knew nothing but centuries of loneliness until Suzume had arrived. He'd suspected their spirits were bound somewhere, but how was it that Ryuu found the pieces of Kazue's soul but not the rest? Did the neko know where Sayuri was?

Even if the neko did, Noaki couldn't act on his desires, no matter how enticing.

FIVE

They'd gathered for another evening meal. Another night where Suzume ate alone in their rooms. A slight he overlooked in hopes appeasing the elder would yield results. He'd left her with things unsaid, knowing that they should discuss their potential political marriage and how that affected their current relationship. That discussion would have to wait. The elder wanted to chase him and his army off the mountain, but he wouldn't let the last three months of effort go to waste. Kaito studied the elder from his honored spot among the dinner guests. The tengu were notoriously slow to act. But Kaito had been prepared to wait. His life stretched out unending, and a few months passed in an instant for him. Besides, winter wasn't an ideal time to wage war, and it gave his army time to heal and train before their campaign against Ai and Hisato. But then the elder had revoked his hospitality, and Kaito's threadbare patience was ready to rip apart. He'd never been the type to grovel before. The dragon who'd united the yokai against the Eight, whose power was unquestioned and fearsome, didn't grovel. But for months, he'd been bowing and scraping to the tengu, begging for scraps. Tonight, with the support of the White Palace behind him, he'd get their support at last.

Shin and the oni chief flanked him, and Mori sat across from him next to his younger brother and their mother. The tengu elder perched atop his teetering pile of cushions, his long, white beard coiled in his lap like a silvery snake that he stroked with a translucent, frail hand. Yokai lived forever but something was slowly draining the elder's life force. It was unheard of in Kaito's prime. But it'd become a common occurrence in the last few centuries. The elder's apparent illness was also why Mori suspected the elder was refusing to act. Death made fools of even immortals, it seemed.

A line of servants entered the room and set platters down before shuffling backward, their wings pinned behind their backs and their heads bowed. Everyone looked at the tengu elder for his signal to eat. Nothing in this damned palace happened without his word. But a rattling cough had taken hold of him and echoed across the room. Kaito drummed his fingers on his thigh as he waited, and his general Shin slid a sideways glance at him, a look that reminded him to behave himself.

As grating as the groveling was, it was necessary. The humans' help could be a boon. But he'd feel more confident with the aerial capabilities of the tengu at his back. Their involvement had turned the tide in the war against the Eight. Before he left, Kaito wanted to secure the elder's support.

When the tengu elder's coughing fit subsided, he gestured for them all to eat. They dug into their meals and the room was buzzing with subdued chatter. No one spoke to the elder unless he addressed them first, and it had been weeks since the elder had addressed Kaito. He had no appetite and instead focused on trying to get Mori's attention after their meeting. He'd implored him to speak with his father on his behalf. His tengu friend had danced around agreeing, but he hadn't said no either, and Kaito hoped he'd pull through. But in that moment, Mori turned away, chatting with his brother and mother, avoiding Kaito's insistent gaze. Kaito scooped up his soup bowl and gulped it down, narrowed gaze focused on the elder. How much longer would he pretend Kaito wasn't there, that he hadn't banished the very person who'd saved his people?

Servants presented the third course, and the elder hadn't looked up from his venison once. He might as well dine alone. And Kaito couldn't endure being overlooked for another moment. He set his chopsticks down with more force than necessary, and Shin's hand shot out to grab his elbow too late.

"Patience—" Shin tried to warn Kaito, but he was already standing.

A collective gasp filled the room as he approached the elder. Mori stood as if he'd restrain Kaito, but the elder made a slicing gesture which stopped Mori. The elder glared at Kaito without speaking, as if he expected the weight of his stare to convey his authority.

The tengu were slow to act, true, but even boulders rolled when pushed downhill.

"Wise elder, I would thank you again for your continued hospitality and kindness in housing myself and my army," Kaito said, bowing to the elder.

The grooves between his brows deepened at the mention of the army. Kaito had learned early how much the elder detested any implication of war or conflict and avoided them to keep him happy. The same way he'd hidden Suzume away like a dirty secret.

"We accept your gratitude," he said in a rattling voice and dismissive wave of his hand.

Seeing as they hadn't dragged him out of the room, he pressed forward. "While I appreciate your gratitude, I wish to ask you once more for your aid in the war to reclaim Akatsuki."

The air shifted at last, and Kaito felt the change in the elder's spiritual pressure. The other tengu sensed it as well, and they pulled their wings in tight against their bodies and averted their gazes. An oppressive silence fell over the room and Kaito felt his breaths echoing in his ears.

"You ask for too much after we've sheltered and fed you and your people for months," the tengu elder said, puffing up his chest and looking down his bulbous nose at Kaito.

"Forgive me if I appear ungrateful. Your generosity is boundless. But I feel the lives of my men who died to protect your clan from the yuki-onna are worth more than rations and tents along a frigid mountainside for a single season," Kaito said.

The tengu elder cracked a smile. His dark eyes narrowed. "When I fed you by taking from my kin, was that not enough? Then perhaps I should revoke my blessings now and leave you to your own devices before the thaw."

"That's your decision to make, elder. I cannot go against it. It spits in the face of our long history as allies. I came to your aid when you called upon me, and I would hope you'd repay that with a similar force to protect the many other yokai in Akatsuki who will suffer in the coming war," Kaito said.

"What war? You lost the ruins of a fallen palace to a greedy yokai. There have been no movements since. Why would I send my clan to die for ruins?" He raised a single bushy brow.

Kaito swallowed the angry retort that he almost spat out and replied instead, "This isn't about that. With our combined forces, we would win against her and reunite Akatsuki once more."

"The kingdom you wish to resurrect died when the priestess sealed you," the tengu elder said, his voice rising in anger, slashing across the room and sending an icy shiver down his spine. Kaito realized he was standing on a precipice. Either he backed down and approached the tengu elder in a different, more indirect way, like leaving behind a diplomat, or he put him in his place through a show of force, reminding him Kaito was a leader of equal power and rank.

Fragile as the elder might seem, he didn't rule by accident. He was the oldest and strongest among them, one of the first children, an ancient being of immense power. Mori, whose strength rivaled Kaito's, cowered beside his father, head lowered in subservience to a silent command issued by his father's unfurling spiritual power. If Kaito challenged him, he'd win. The dragon he had been years ago would have, because it was simpler. But it would also humiliate the elder and, by extension, the clan. Either he won the elder's approval, or he waited for him to die, which might not be for centuries, despite the wasting sickness.

"Yes, it was fractured, but it can be repaired," Kaito said as he tamped down his own frustration. "We are entering a new age of Akatsuki. I've received an offer of a marital alliance with the human emperor. We will unite and fight to reunite Hisato."

The tengu elder laughed.

"You're a fool to even consider it. The humans have grown too strong. Even if you could trust their offer, they will only turn on you in the end. The humans have severed us, and you'd help them build armies to finish us."

"It is a new—" Kaito said before the elder cut him off.

"Even you can feel how much weaker you've become. Our age has passed. Turn to your own kind and protect what you can. Don't cling to the past. That is my advice."

He'd been naïve to hope the elder would see reason. But Kaito knew there were tengu among them who saw it his way. Mori and others. If only he could appeal to them, to have them join his cause.

"Just because you've hidden away and let time and sickness dwindle our population doesn't mean we all should. There must be some among you willing to fight. To keep the yokai alive." Kaito stood and addressed the room. But when he looked back at Mori, the tengu bowed his head and folded his wings tight against his back.

They were afraid to speak or act against the elder and none would stand against him. Kaito realized, while Mori might agree with his plans in private, he'd never defy his father.

"No matter how hard you try to insight a riot, the tengu remain united. It's how we've survived while others are fading away," the tengu elder said with a smug tilt to his crooked mouth.

"Perhaps it has served you until now. If not Hisato, then some other power will rise to destroy you. Hiding away will not save you," Kaito snarled, letting his anger shape his words. But he was beyond caring anymore.

"Because of the good deeds you've done for us, I will overlook your transgressions today. Do not speak about war in my presence again."

Kaito ground his teeth until they ached as anger pulsed through him like a drum. Let him bury his head in the sand and ignore the world beyond this mountain peak. If the yokai were fading away, it was Kaito's duty to save them. With or without the elder's help. It was their nature that drove them to tear out each other's throats while the humans spread and overtook them. He could undo what was done. But he knew now trying to convince the elder was a losing battle. He stormed out before his temper took hold, and he flung himself at the elder in a rage.

Once he was outside the elder's audience chamber, the frigid mountain air hit him like a hard slap to the face. Mori followed him, but Kaito refused to acknowledge him. Ice melts refroze as his temper chilled the air around. Spring was imminent, and he'd wasted a season. They'd see their errors too late. Once he united the human and yokai kingdoms with Suzume, then it would be he who must grovel for Kaito's favor.

He balled his hand into a fist, which crusted over with ice as he imagined wrapping it around the elder's neck.

"I told you; you will not win the old man's mind by rushing," Mori said, breaking the tense silence.

"I don't want to hear, 'I told you so'," Kaito snarled.

"Please understand, I'm doing the best I can, given the constraints of my position," Mori said, using that reasonable voice of a mediator that he'd always brought to Kaito's counsel before his kingdom had fallen. But today, it felt like salt in a wound.

"Like how you sat on your hands while the yuki-onna had your brother trapped in ice?" Kaito turned to face his friend.

The verbal punch landed, and Mori flinched back from him, hurt written on his face. Kaito felt awful as soon as the words had left his mouth, and he relaxed his shoulders. "Forgive me, I shouldn't have said that."

"You're right, though. I stood by and did nothing then. And I've done the same to you now."

Kaito reached out and clasped him on the shoulder. "We're not who we used to be. One thing I can admit is the elder was right, times are changing. And maybe it's time the tengu change with it. The question is, will you help enact the change?"

Mori lowered his head and said nothing. Not that Kaito expected him to. Kaito patted his shoulder once more and then stalked away from his old friend. Their time at the tengu compound was ending. But Kaito had hoped that their fledgling alliance with the emperor would prove fruitful, or else all hope was lost.

Six

Suzume was alone again. While Kaito was away, she'd filled her empty time practicing creating fireballs to light her rooms, only to extinguish them with her wind. She was in control of her power now. After she'd absorbed Souta's wind, something clicked in her, and it was all effortless. She didn't need practice, but she needed something to keep sleep and the accompanying nightmares at bay. Normally, her exertions were an adequate distraction, but the wind kept whispering secrets.

"… can't take all of it, you great oaf."

"… I've been telling her…"

Brief snatches of conversation drifted in through the cracks under her door. This happened sometimes, but she'd learned to tune it out. But this night, her nerves were fried, and her senses were on alert for danger, and she couldn't seem to block them out.

"… Carry this…"

"... sorry, boys, looks like..."

The voices were coming closer together, a dozen fragments of conversations from around the compound and the camp surrounding it. She needed an escape. A few minutes in the forest where the wind blew gently, and the whispers couldn't needle her. Suzume's mind was crowded enough without everyone else's voice barging in. Suzume threw open her door and the evening air smelt like spring. Suzume hadn't ever thought of the seasons having smells before. In her old life, she might have noticed flowers blooming in the White Palace garden, or noted her servants trading winter coats for layers of lighter silks. The parties she'd attended might have stopped serving warm soups in favor of dishes perfumed by sakura blossoms. That life felt as distant as the fragments of Souta and Kazue's memories, which swirled in her skull and disturbed her sleep.

She walked without bothering to look and see if Noaki followed. Because she knew he would. If Kaito wasn't with her, he was Suzume's constant shadow. She took the long way around, along the outer walls where a thick knot of pine trees grew, and the wind threaded through the branches. It was her only solace.

As she approached, the wind rustled through her hair like the affectionate caress of an adoring pet. The wind rattled the branches like an excited puppy eager to play, and she couldn't help but smile at its antics. As aggravating as her new power was, she didn't hate it, because it was necessary for her to defeat Hisato. With two pieces of Kazue's soul inside her, she was stronger, but the price was she felt herself fraying at the edges too. Without their chatter, she could focus on her problems: the emperor's offer, and Kazue's riddle.

Did Kazue somehow know that her father would offer an alliance? She never dreamt that the emperor would endorse her union with Kaito. It was all too tidy, which made her worried. Unless Kazue meant Noaki was the beginning. He was the one she'd partnered with to take down the Eight. Noaki told her he didn't know what became of them. Kazue knew but couldn't tell her. Was there a way to unlock Kazue's memories without losing herself?

The simplest answer was to ask Noaki. She already knew Kazue's spell prevented him from speaking his own name, thanks to the binding spell that kept him locked to her. When she mentioned it to him before, he hadn't offered any insight, but perhaps she should ask again?

"Something's troubling you."

Suzume spun around, fire burning in her palms on reflex, but lowered them when she saw Ryuu watching solemnly.

"No, there isn't," she said on reflex, internally cursing herself for lying. Why was it hard for her to admit when she needed help? And why was it even harder to ask for it when she needed it, desperately?

"You know you can ask me anything, Suzume."

"It's nothing," she said, kicking herself mentally for not speaking her mind. If anyone knew what Kazue's cryptic message meant, it was him. But there was also a chance telling him might backfire, and he'd worry that Kazue was taking over her body, as Kaito feared. Which meant being sidelined again. She refused to stand down and watch as everyone else fought for her.

Ryuu rested his hand on her shoulder in a fatherly gesture. "I know you must have your doubts about marrying Kaito. We can find another way if you don't want to..."

Suzume reeled back. "That isn't it. Why would you say that?" she asked, glaring at Ryuu. Then, realization dawned on her. "You don't want me to marry him?"

She knew Ryuu and Kaito had their differences, but she didn't think he'd intervene in their relationship.

"Being with an immortal isn't easy. Mortals age and die quicker than we realize, and it can cause... strife," Ryuu said.

It was as if he'd spoken aloud all her deepest insecurities. It was a topic they'd been dancing around for months. She wasn't ignorant of the fact that the tengu merely tolerated her, and she heard the yokai whispering about how they thought Kaito was a fool for having a human lover.

"Is it that hard being immortal and loving a mortal?" Suzume asked, her tone sharp. "That you'd try to chase me away from the one person who loves me?"

Ryuu sighed. "That's not what I meant."

"Then does it make you feel strange that I'd be your stepmother?"

Ryuu chuckled. "He's hardly a father to me. So I don't think it'll bother me too much. I just have my doubts about the emperor's motives is all."

What was between Kaito and her couldn't be severed by Ryuu or her father. Suzume's life was in her hands whether the emperor's offer was genuine, or Ryuu approved. But while she was taking control, she should also come clean and ask Ryuu for help.

Taking a deep breath, she said, "I'm not worried about my relationship, but I've been having disturbing dreams."

"I wondered when I noticed the deep bags under your eyes."

"You know how to make a girl feel good," Suzume snapped, rubbing said bags. It'd been ages since she'd looked at herself in a mirror, and she feared a stranger would stare back at her.

"Forgive me. I didn't mean to cause offense. I was concerned for your well-being," Ryuu amended.

Suzume crossed her arms over herself and angled away from Ryuu. "Promise you won't overreact?" she asked.

One thing both Kaito and Ryuu shared was their tendency to be overprotective.

"I promise," Ryuu said, pressing his hand to his chest.

"Kazue spoke to me in my dream. She said, 'return to the beginning' and shared a vision of the day she won Noaki. I almost heard his name before it ended."

"Hmm," Ryuu murmured to himself, his gaze sliding over to where she presumed Noaki was hovering in the shadows. Her human eyes couldn't see him in the dark, but Ryuu's could.

"I think she wants me to find Noaki's name. Maybe free him?" she suggested.

"I'm not so sure," Ryuu said.

"Are you saying I shouldn't set Noaki free?" Suzume asked, eyes darting in Noaki's direction.

"That's not what I meant. Noaki deserves to be free, but I worry about you trying to unlock more of Kazue's memories. She might try to take over again, or worse, it could reopen your connection to Hisato."

"I think it would be worth the risk. Noaki doesn't deserve to be tethered to me the way he is."

Ryuu shook his head. "I'm sorry—"

But Suzume cut him off. "There must be a way."

"You're not strong enough to venture into the spirit realm—" This time, he swallowed his own words.

"What is the spirit realm? You've never mentioned it before." She jumped on the dangling fragment of information.

"You're not ready. Perhaps after you've worked on strengthening your spiritual powers..."

Ryuu wouldn't meet her gaze, which only whipped up the fiery storm inside her. How many more people had to die? How many sacrifices before she was enough? The fragments of memories and feelings were buzzing around inside her head, driving her insane. If there was some secret that'd help her discover the answers she needed, to stop this slow erosion of her mind, she couldn't wait to find it.

"I don't have time to wait. I need answers now," she said, grabbing onto his sleeve.

"Later. We'll discuss it another day. I have letters to write." He tried to shake her off, but she held onto his sleeve until it smoldered beneath her burning fingers.

"Suzume, let go of my sleeve before I catch fire."

"Maybe if I light you up, you'd take me seriously. I've done all your lessons, learned to control both fire and wind. What else is there to learn?"

"You're tired. Let's talk again once you're well rested."

"And what if I dream again? As it is, I feel like my grip on reality is slipping. I'm disconnected from my body most of the time. Please. Ryuu. I need this."

"Why didn't you tell me this sooner?" He turned to her with concern painted on his features.

"Because I'm scared," she said in a voice just above a whisper. It was the first time she'd said it aloud, because then it became real.

Ryuu was silent for a beat as his eyes roved over her.

"You've connected with the spirit realm before when you fought Hisato. It's the void from which Hisato's power flows and the gateway to the afterlife. If your connection to your body is not stable enough, trying to enter the spirit world could leave you untethered. And you might wander forever in the void trapped between life and death while your body remains an empty vessel."

"But I could find Kazue's memories there?"

Ryuu nodded. "In theory, because fragments of her soul are inside you, entering the void could allow you to explore those facets of yourself to uncover memories locked away within. But it's still dangerous unprepared."

"Then let's do it. Nothing can be worse than what I've already experienced."

Ryuu wouldn't look at her but was staring at Noaki, who'd inched closer to them.

"What do you think?" Ryuu asked Noaki.

"I think it's too dangerous," Noaki replied. But Suzume saw the hunger in his expression. She felt it burning in her gut as well.

"It's my mind, and my life. Don't I get a say?" She planted her fist on her hip. If she had one thing going for her, it was her own stubborn pride.

Ryuu rubbed his palm over his face. "We could try entering the spirit realm tethered together. If there's a hint of danger, I will bring you back," he warned.

"Yes, yes, of course! Let's do it tonight," Suzume said.

Ryuu shook his head as if he couldn't believe what he was doing, but he didn't argue further. Plans were in motion; there was no stopping it. They headed back to Suzume's room. Kaito still hadn't returned from dinner, and it left them space to set up uninterrupted. Noaki stood guard at the door to bar any visitors or delay Kaito if necessary. Ryuu lit some incense and prepared a place for them to meditate together. Suzume sat down cross-legged on the ground, and with a few muttered words, Ryuu created a barrier around the room that closed off the sounds of the surrounding camp, allowing Suzume silence she hadn't known in months. Oddly enough, she missed hearing the sounds of the wind.

"We'll start out by meditating and I shall resonate some of my energy with yours."

"Understood."

Ryuu sat on the ground across from her, his knees brushing against hers, and Suzume closed her eyes as Ryuu poured some of his energy into her. This they'd done plenty of times in practice. Trying to teach her how to connect with other's energy without consuming it. She'd also meditated plenty in the past year, and getting into that space wasn't as difficult as it once was. She closed her eyes and slowed her breathing, focusing on every in and out breath, letting her sense of self slip away. This was the straightforward part. It was easier to float, to stare at her own body as an outsider would, cold and detached. But if that was all it took to reach the spirit realm, she'd have accidentally done it months ago.

"Keep rising until you feel the ceiling," Ryuu's voice instructed in her mind.

Her spirit rose, as if rising into the sky, until she collided with that ceiling Ryuu mentioned.

"This plane separates the living world from the spirit realm. To reach beyond, you must reach beyond yourself to the realm of the gods."

"What does that even mean?" she asked. Suddenly, everything shifted and warbled. Nausea clawed at her insides.

"You're not ready to pass through yourself. But today, I will guide you. Take my hand."

Ryuu was standing beside her, but his body was transparent, as was hers.

A sensation like walking beneath a waterfall passed through her before she was tumbling through a blur of colors and images. A thousand different things bombarded her all at once before coalescing into one image. She shifted again and arrived on a battlefield. People were screaming, and she was in immense pain. Her belly hurt as if someone had driven something through her. She grasped onto the pole in her gut. Ryuu leaned over her, his face splattered with blood and contorted in anguish.

"I can't lose you, Souta." He held a glowing stone in his hand and pressed it to her gut before everything faded away.

She tumbled, spinning out of control before it solidified around her once more. Then, the room came into focus. And suddenly, she was somewhere else. In an opulent room with a painted screen, she recognized from the emperor's throne room. Where he addressed his counsel. She was standing near the emperor, almost his equal. But it wasn't the emperor she was looking at, but Ryuu. His face was sad, and his clothes were ancient and strange. It was then that she realized she was looking through Souta's memories.

"I never wanted this," Souta said to Ryuu, spitting each word. "You've cursed me with immortality, damn you. I'll never forgive you."

Then she heard it, a slow cackle. Suzume knew that sound anywhere.

"There you are, Suzume. I've been looking for you."

She felt the hands grip around her neck, squeezing the air from her lungs and making it hard to breathe.

"You won't like what you find here in my domain. Best to turn back now. Nothing but darkness and pain lives here. Turn back before it's too late."

A flash of light stopped her, and she awoke to Ryuu staring down at her. Her neck and belly still hurt, but when she checked herself for wounds, she couldn't find any. They were only in her memories. Ryuu knelt over her, his face painted with concern.

"What did you see?" he asked.

Suzume's hands were shaking as she sat up and took the tea Ryuu offered her. "I saw Souta's memories... and Hisato." She took a sip of hot tea and let the warmth run down her throat.

"I was afraid of this. I told you that you're not ready."

"But it worked, didn't it? I saw Souta's memories..." she trailed off as she thought about what she'd seen. Ryuu's anguished face, desperate to save his friend, and Souta's anger at being made immortal. That anger lingered inside her, burning up like a fever. Souta never wanted immortality, but he kept on living for Ryuu's sake, and she wasn't sure how that made her feel. She thought she understood his sacrifice a bit more now. But it didn't lessen her guilt, as she hoped it would.

"Hisato nearly took hold of you. We cannot do this again," Ryuu said.

"We can't give up. There has to be a way."

Ryuu stood and shook his head. "We'll work on your meditation and strengthening your spiritual bond for now. There's time to practice as we arrange the marriage alliance."

His tone left no room for argument, and Suzume watched as he dispelled the barrier before dismissing her.

SEVEN

The temple wasn't what Rin expected. When she'd envisioned a temple taking in refugees, she thought it would be a standard temple, if perhaps a bit over-crowded—this was more fort-like than temple. Barriers of sharpened logs surrounded the exterior, and high wooden walls rose to enclose the grounds. A watch tower stood out above it, giving it the distinct feeling of a battlement, rather than a holy place. At the entrance gates, a pair of priestesses wearing the traditional priestess red and white held weapons and watched them approach, pointing said weapons in their direction.

One priestess, with pink puckered skin from a healed burn covering the right side of her face, pointed her comically large katana at Rin. "Stay back, yokai, or I'll run you through," she said.

Her companion, with a closely shorn head, watched them with an intense hatred, even for a priestess. That glare felt personal, though Rin was certain they'd never met before.

Rin held her hands up in surrender, keeping her distance to not appear as a threat. "We're here to meet High Priestess Tomoe. A letter should have arrived introducing us?"

"What business do you have with her?" the scarred woman asked as she jabbed her sword at them with crude, unpracticed motions.

"We're seeking information about the hybrids. Could you tell her Akane sent us?"

Dangers lurked across Akatsuki, like a lengthening shadow. They were right to fear strangers. But Akane assured them their leader was a compassionate person who trusted yokai, unlike most priests and priestesses.

The scarred priestess nodded to her companion before disappearing beyond the gate, while the scarred priestess held them at unskilled blade point.

"They seemed young to have endured so much violence. I doubt they were even full initiates before the attacks," Hikaru murmured to Rin low enough that the priestess couldn't hear.

On second glance, Rin noticed the roundness of the girl's face that she'd overlooked beneath the dirt smudges and disfiguring scars. If Hikaru's guess was correct, these girls had endured a horrific tragedy at a very young age. It softened Rin to the gate guard, despite the glares and mistrustful stares. The shaved girl returned with another young acolyte who shared such a striking resemblance to Suzume that Rin did a double take.

"My guards said you're friends of Akane?" Her voice was girlish but authoritative.

"We are. My name is Hikaru, and this is my wife, Rin. May I ask your name?" Hikaru asked with a formal bow.

She bowed in return. "I am High Priestess Tomoe. Welcome to our temple. Akane told me we could expect you. Please, come in."

She motioned for them to follow her inside. Rin and Hikaru followed, shadowed by a guard as Tomoe took the lead. Rin and Hikaru looked at one another, speaking without words. Hikaru noticed the high priestess' resemblance to Suzume as well. The uncanny connection made her uneasy. They'd had their share of coincidences before, and often, they were precursors to bad things. She tried to rack her brain and remember if Suzume mentioned having any siblings. But she couldn't recall her mentioning any apart from her younger brother.

"You lived in the palace. Was there another princess?" Rin asked under her breath.

"I'm the only daughter of the empress," Tomoe said, hearing her whisper.

Rin straightened, ashamed to be talking about her behind her back. "Forgive me, you look a lot like a friend of ours."

"You must mean my elder half-sister, Suzume. We don't know one another well. I left the palace at a very young age, but we've met a few times since."

Rin remembered an ancient tradition of sending the emperor's oldest daughter to study and become a priestess. The explanation soothed her a bit, but she remained on guard as they followed the head priestess through the temple grounds. There were many wounded and displaced priestesses within. A few tended the wounded; the rest were refugees. Tomoe stopped to talk to a group of bandaged priestesses drinking tea together. She greeted them all with a bow and a short inquiry after their health. Rin and Hikaru stood back, scanning the surrounding area. They'd heard plenty of second-hand accounts of temples raided over the winter, and of the countless priests and priestesses Hisato and his cohorts stole from their beds. Each time reports came in, Kaito sent someone to investigate, but the leads always ran cold and that's where their interest faded.

Rin hadn't thought of what happened to the displaced priestesses whose temples they destroyed. If they didn't have homes to return to or their homes were reduced to rubble, they were adrift.

"How are you able to accommodate them all?" Rin asked.

"Being a princess has its advantages. We're an affluent temple, with patrons who provide rice and medicine. We need to support the influx of refugees," Tomoe said.

Rin nodded, but Hikaru looked pensive.

"Who is this patron?" Hikaru asked.

Tomoe looked sheepish. "You served at the Sun Temple? I remember seeing you once during a Kagura performance."

"I did," Hikaru said.

"I understand your fears. But our patron is far removed from the politics of the court. He's a retired minister of religion, who believes in our work and asks nothing in return."

The answer seemed to satisfy Hikaru, whose shoulders relaxed. It was reassuring to know Hisato's influence hadn't touched this place. Though Rin wasn't ready to let her guard down.

A trio of young acolytes came rushing out as they walked up the temple steps. One of them had a wooden sword in her hand, swinging it as she chased her friends. Tomoe caught her by the shoulder as she attempted to rush past. The girl's face blanched, and she tried to hide her weapon behind her back as Tomoe knelt in front of her.

"You shouldn't be running with blades. If you fell, you could hurt yourself," Tomoe said, holding out her hand for said weapon.

The girl guiltily handed it over to Tomoe. "Forgive me, High Priestess."

"There is nothing to forgive. Save swordplay for the practice yard," she said as she took the weapon from her.

With a smile and a nod, the girl ran off after her friends, without her play weapon. The girl seemed young to be learning swordsmanship. But on second glance, everyone there, young and old, carried a sword.

"Do all the children learn to fight?" Rin asked.

"If they like. Some are too terrified after their ordeal. But we've found arming many of them empowers them to feel more in control after the trauma they endured," Tomoe said.

They crossed a short veranda before Tomoe escorted them into a simple room. Papers and maps covered a low table. If Rin hadn't known this was a temple, she'd have thought she'd stepped into a war general's room.

"Akane said in her letter you're seeking more information about the hybrids?" Tomoe said, taking a seat behind her desk. Despite her young age, she had the upright and imposing stare of a leader.

"We've been trying all winter to find out where the hybrid army is hiding, but despite our best efforts, we've come up empty.

Akane said you're the leading expert on hybrids and we hoped you have some insight into their whereabouts."

Tomoe smiled faintly. "What a terrible expertise. But I suppose you could say I am."

An acolyte delivered cups of tea. Thin tendrils of steam rose off Rin's cup, and the aroma was fragrant and soothing. She took a long sip, and the heat slid down her throat and warmed her belly.

"I wish I had more to share. But we've also been taking shots in the dark. The temple attacks happen at random. We try to warn the temples, but there's too many of them, and we're stretched thin as it is protecting those here. I wish I knew where they took them. Most of the girls here escaped being kidnapped by hiding during the attacks. I'm one of two who ever escaped."

"You were fortunate to have escaped then," Rin said.

Tomoe nodded. "I'm fortunate that Shin and Akane rescued me. That is true. If only I could save more girls who weren't as lucky. We've saved those that we could, but the raids continue on..." She sucked in a shuddering breath, staring off into the distance. She was too young to be burdened so.

"It's good that you've been gathering the girls all in one place. At least here they're safe," Hikaru said.

"Thank you for saying so. We do what we can."

"You mentioned one other girl. Is she here still?"

"Yes. But I feel I should explain something to you first. This girl and I have something in common that might interest you. You see, the former head priestess raised me as a kamigakari, a human avatar for my kami. The hybrids kidnaped me, locked me up with other girls who fate wasn't as kind to. They turned girls right before my eyes. It was horrific." She stared off into the distance, then shook herself and continued. "I tried going back to rescue those girls. And while I didn't find them, I found someone else. A girl who, like me, raised as a kamigakari... but she became something else..."

An icy chill slithered down Rin's spine. "What?"

"Perhaps it would be best if you met her," Tomoe said.

She stood up and gestured for them to follow her out of the room. Down a long hall, with ofuda papering the walls, stood two armed priestesses wearing grim expressions. As Rin approached, the spiritual barriers tingled against her skin, just as she sensed something evil inside.

"They're here to see the prisoner," Tomoe said.

The guards stepped aside to let them in. The windows were boarded up, and the interior shadowy. The strange crackle of energy made her hair stand on end. Beside her, Rin felt Hikaru tense as he muttered a prayer under his breath. A young girl crouched near the far wall and didn't look up as they entered. Rin felt the wrongness of her, and the longer Rin stared, the more her head swam, and her stomach cramped. What was this child?

Then the girl rose, the curtain of her black hair falling into her face. There were bruises on her wrists where the metal of her cuffs had bitten into her skin. Her back arched as she attempted to pull from the wall, slashing bloody fingers in their direction. Her hair parted, revealing eyes devoid of white and dark veins throbbing in her neck, as she strained to swipe at them and Rin took a step back.

When she realized she couldn't attack them, her dark pupils receded, and her face returned to that of a sweet, innocent young girl.

"Tomoe, thank you for coming to visit. Did you bring me visitors?" she asked in an angelic voice.

If Rin hadn't witnessed her transformation, she never would've believed it. The soulless eyes and black veins were gone. She looked like a ragged little girl, both lost and confused.

"Yes, Hitome. We have friends. Say hello."

She looked at them with wide, guileless eyes. It was difficult to believe she'd been a horrific monster moments before. And Tomoe was right. She wasn't like the hybrids Rin had encountered before. This incarnation was insidious and dangerous. Even when she looked at her with a guileless child's eyes, she seemed to emit a strange black aura. It made her head buzz, and her stomach churn.

"They're coming for the rest," she said in a hollow, echoing voice. "They'll come for me, too, and we shall create a new world together." Then she threw her head back in maniacal laughter that reminded Rin of Hisato. They retreated and then Tomoe sang an incantation, sealing the room before returning to her private office.

"When we found her, we thought she was in shock after what she endured. But on her first night here, she attacked three other children before we realized what lurked beneath her skin."

"How did this happen? I've never seen anything like it," Hikaru said in a shaking tone.

"From what we've observed, she's a type of hybrid. One which inhabits a pure kamigakari body. Something about a pure body creates a passable monster who can shift between two forms, both human and yokai. Hitome has told us they call themselves the 'new gods.' They're taking over the bodies of kamigakari," Tomoe said.

A stone settled in the pit of Rin's stomach. But Hikaru was leaning forward, grabbing a hold of the map on the table. Tomoe had marked places on the map. Attack locations. Many she and Hikaru had reached too late.

"They must be attacking the temples with the kamigakari. If we can seek similar temples, maybe we can stop them before they hurt more people," Hikaru said.

Hikaru was right. It was barely a lead, but better than nothing. They should return to Kaito and the others and create a plan to protect the temples.

"Trying to stop the attacks won't be enough. We have to reverse the effects of the hybrid curse," Tomoe said.

"Do you have any ideas?" Rin asked.

Tomoe chewed on her bottom lip. "One. But I hesitate to mention it. When we realized who they were targeting, I wrote to a living kamigakari to warn her, and she wrote back asking me to come to her temple. I can't leave my people unprotected, not with Hitome here. But maybe you could find the answer. To save girls like Hitome?"

The answer was obvious to Rin, but she still looked to Hikaru for confirmation. He nodded his agreement.

"We will."

Tomoe leaned over the map and pointed to a spot, an isolated island off the western edge of Akatsuki. "You'll need to go east, to an island off the coast. The temple there is ancient, and the kami has been protecting it. But I'll provide you with a seal that should grant you entry."

Everything was prepared, and they were off on another journey, but Rin couldn't shake the gut-churning sensation. If they didn't work fast, more girls like Hitome would die. Whatever Hisato was planning with these "new gods," she didn't like the sound of it. And she feared what was to come.

EIGHT

They left the tengu mountain after months of encampment. It felt good to get on the road again. Kaito's army trailed down the mountainside like a great, winding snake. It took days of marching from the tengu mountain to reach the outskirts of the city. It was an uneventful journey, broken up only by the splitting of their forces when they reached the mountain's base. Shin took control of half their forces to scout out Ai's position and slow her march for the capital, while the rest joined Suzume and Kaito as a show of force and protection.

No human or yokai threatened them as they journeyed to the capital. Though they gave a fright to the farmers and small villages, they passed along the way. They left the army encamped in the forest that bordered the city. Kaito reasoned it would give the wrong impression if they marched a yokai army up to the palace gates. But he wanted them close should something go awry. Suzume tried not to think too hard about that, instead she stuffed her fears down deep.

Even though they'd been invited to the palace, they couldn't head straight there without the emperor's direct summons. It was common protocol, Suzume knew, but the wait made her uneasy. Ryuu suggested they stay at his private residence in the city as they awaited the emperor's official summons. As the days passed, she felt a rising tide of anxiety threatening to swallow her up. She'd grown impatient on the mountaintop, frustrated at the inaction. This felt a thousand times worse, and she couldn't shake the feeling of dread that had come over her. Ryuu, noticing her restlessness, had suggested she practice to calm her nerves.

"Find your center," Ryuu instructed Suzume in a steady voice. "And exhale."

Magic flowed through her, like the wind stoked the fire in her belly into a controlled blaze. She envisioned the wind moving the fire, guiding it around her staff. With another inhale and exhale, the flames burned higher. She felt the heat of it against her face. And then, concentrating on the dummy a few feet away, she twirled, striking its shoulders, then its guts. The dummy burned in the spots where she'd hit it, but even from a distance, she could control the blaze, extinguishing it before it consumed the very flammable straw into ash. Suzume stared at it with pride. At last, her powers were in harmony. If only her mind was as stable.

"You've made excellent progress," Ryuu said, nodding his head at the controlled scorched marks on the dummy.

"Then you realize I'm not too weak to enter the spirit realm again," Suzume said with a hand on her hip. It'd been a constant argument between them since leaving the tengu mountain. She'd spent most of the week's long journey to the palace needling at Ryuu, trying to wear him down enough to allow her to attempt connecting with the spirit realm once more. The answers were there, hidden inside her mind. She just had to grasp hold of them.

Ryuu shook his head. "Out of the question. You saw what happened last time. First, let's focus on our meeting with the emperor, and then we'll revisit this topic at a later date."

Suzume growled in frustration. "It's always later with you. Wait until I'm an empty husk, and then it'll be too late."

"It may not seem this way, but I am trying to protect you."

"You're just making excuses, and we both know it." She punctuated her sentence with a swift jab at Ryuu's chest with her pointer finger.

"Perhaps," Ryuu said. "But the fact stands: you're distracted, nervous."

She narrowed her eyes. "Are you trying to bait me into some sort of heart-to-heart again?"

"I know you're putting on a brave face, but you're terrified of facing your father." Ryuu said it with such ruthlessness that, for a moment, Suzume was too stunned to speak.

Suzume threw her arms up in exasperation. "What is there to worry about? We're meeting him over an arranged marriage. It's all a means to an end."

"Should I be offended that I'm being used so callously?" Kaito said playfully, striding toward her, sliding his hand around her waist, and pulling her in close.

An embarrassed blush burned her cheeks, and she clamped her big mouth shut. Not that she wasn't confident she loved Kaito and wanted to spend the rest of her life with him. She did. She had complicated feelings about tangling marriage and her father's wants in their relationship, plus her father hadn't seemed to be a huge fan of yokai in the past. But Kaito was counting on the emperor's alliance, and his army. So, she kept her feelings to herself.

"You know what I meant," Suzume said, waving away his taunts.

"Do I?" Kaito said, tone serious.

Ryuu watched her beside him, raising a skeptical brow. For a father and son pair who despised each other, they were very much alike.

Suzume sighed and ran a hand through her hair. "It's nothing. I'm just nervous about my father's reaction, is all. I know he agreed to meet with us. But it seems out of character."

"But you want to marry me, don't you?"

"Of course?" Her answer sounded like a question. She'd meant it jokingly, like a playful "what do you think," but the truth had seeped in.

The tension was building between them, and she felt it like a familiar crackle on her skin. She didn't want to fight, not when later that afternoon, they'd be going to face her father and arrange their wedding. Kaito said nothing, which only made the awkwardness between them more pronounced. They hadn't talked about their impending maybe marriage alone. There'd been too much to distract them from a serious conversation. And if she was being honest, she was avoiding the topic.

"I should get ready." She walked away before they could press her. Neither Ryuu nor Kaito followed her, which was for the best. For the sake of Akatsuki, she needed today to go well. And she couldn't be ruining it with her doubts.

Ryuu didn't have any servants, so Suzume dressed herself, which was more difficult than she realized. She floundered in the layers of silk and struggled to find the holes for her arms in the voluminous sleeves. After cobbling together a presentable outfit, she attempted to tame her hair into something that looked like court style if you squinted. When she finished, she shuffled outside, burdened by the layers of her outfit, and found Ryuu, Kaito, and Noaki outfitted for the palace.

By the time she'd dressed, the procession had arrived from the palace. Seeing the banners flapping in the wind, winding their way through the city, and drawing a crowd of curious onlookers made her stomach flip in somersaults. There was no turning back now. She had to face her father once more, and hope he was being honest and wanted peace.

The procession stopped outside the villa gates.

"Wait here," Ryuu said to Suzume.

Kaito came over to her and grabbed her hand, squeezing it. When she met his eyes, he was smiling. No matter what happened with her father today, she'd have Kaito, and that's all that mattered.

Kaito leaned in close to whisper in her ear. "You look beautiful."

A blush burned across her cheeks and neck. How did he still make her stomach swoop? "I'll look mediocre compared to the other women at the palace."

"What other women? You're the only one I'll ever have eyes for."

She swatted at him playfully. It was the confidence boost she needed to power through the rest of the day.

Ryuu spoke with the eunuch who led the procession. He and the accompanying retinue of servants reminded her of the group that had taken her out of the city and deposited her in the mountain temple, where she met Kaito. Suzume swallowed past the lump in her throat. She could get through this. She would get through this.

The door to the palanquin opened, and servants ushered her inside. Kaito and Ryuu, each had their own separate palanquins. She settled in, flattening the layers of silk on her lap, and tried to calm her erratic breathing. But as soon as the door closed her in, she felt her chest grow tight. She could do this. She was a diplomat. Akatsuki and Kaito needed her to do this.

The journey across the city was swift. Servants opened the door to her palanquin and Suzume stood blinking into the light. The palace grounds were practically empty, and those that were left gave her sidelong glances. Almost a year had passed since she'd last stepped inside the palace walls, and not much had changed.

Her stomach was in knots as they passed through the gardens led by a servant to a nearby pagoda. Servants served her cakes and tea as she waited for the emperor. Ryuu sat beside her, while Kaito and Noaki lingered close by. Even knowing they were close, she couldn't help glancing back behind her to make sure they were still there. She twisted her sweaty hands in her lap over and over as they waited.

After what felt like an eternity, her father arrived, accompanied by her mother. Her stomach sank. This wasn't part of the plan.

Should they abort the mission? She looked at Kaito, who shook his head indicating she should stay put. She hadn't considered seeing her mother today. Would she tell Hisato she had seen her and pass on everything they discussed, including their marriage-based alliance? Or was it a trap? She wished she'd brought her staff, but she'd left it behind at Ryuu's villa. If she had to, she could fight without it. But a fight inside the palace was less than ideal.

"My beloved daughter, I am joyed to see you in good health and back home at last," the emperor said, assessing her.

Suzume's stomach clenched as she bowed in greeting.

"Thank you for welcoming me back, father," she said.

Her mother arranged her silk kimono around her and Suzume resisted looking at her.

"It's been a long time since we've all been together," her father said.

They all took their seats: Kaito on one side, Ryuu on the other. Servants poured tea into their glasses from a steaming kettle. Suzume kept staring at her mother, who seemed so serene and regal at the emperor's side. She looked like the empress she'd always aspired to be. Had Hisato's influence elevated her status?

"It has," Suzume lied. She couldn't think of a single time they'd all sat together as a family. This surreal family reunion was making her head spin.

A long silence stretched before her mother said, "We're thankful you've brought our daughter back to us, Ryuu." The way her eyes fell on him felt covetous. Suzume had never seen her mother look at anyone that way.

"It is my duty and my honor," Ryuu said. "But she is not here to stay. As the emperor requested, we're here to formalize an alliance sealed by the marriage of Suzume to the dragon, Kaito, the leader of the yokai." He gestured to Kaito.

It was disorienting seeing him here, looking at both her parents with the same cool, imperial stare they both gave him. She felt insignificant between them. A small pawn in a larger game. She didn't fully comprehend the rules either. It made her head spin.

"I agree. It is time you settled into marriage," Izuki said.

Suzume's eyes sliced over to her mother. "You won't oppose this?"

"Obviously, I'm opposed to you marrying a yokai. That would be beneath you."

Beside her, Kaito growled a bit at the back of his throat but didn't move otherwise. Suzume wished there weren't so many people between them. A horrific feeling was crawling at the back of her throat.

"We've chosen a more suitable husband for you long ago, remember? Come in," Izuki plowed on.

Everything moved in slow motion. Her mother turned as if to greet someone, and as Suzume looked up, her eyes locked onto Hisato, who stepped up onto the pagoda. The smile that spread across his face was sinister.

"General Tsubaki is your fiancé, and it's time we held your marriage ceremony."

Beside her, Ryuu tensed, and Suzume's world seemed to tilt for a moment. Her instincts had told her not to come, and she'd ignored them. Now, she was facing Hisato defenseless. The pull of Hisato was magnetic. It overwhelmed her senses, and then, without meaning to, she stood up. The world faded away around them.

"What is this?" Ryuu asked. His voice sounded as if it were miles away.

Suzume felt as if she were drowning. No one else seemed to notice Hisato. Even Kaito hadn't moved. Her gut burned, as if she'd swallowed hot coals and the wind whipped around her.

"You see, she cannot marry the dragon when she's betrothed already," her mother said.

"But that is not what we agreed," Ryuu continued.

"I thought I could trust you, but then you lied to me and told me my daughter was dead. It seems your treachery runs deep," the emperor said.

"You'll be mine, darling Suzume," Hisato said inside her head.

She wanted to reach for him. She wanted to punch him in the face. Torn between longing and stubborn will, she was pinned in place. If she moved, she'd fall into his arms. Then Hisato approached her. A blink and a breath, and he was behind her, grasping a fistful of her hair, pulling it from her neck, and leaning in to whisper in her ear.

"Did you miss me?" he purred.

"No," she gasped.

"Stop fighting it. Convergence is coming. You cannot stop it. We are bound together forever."

NINE

Kaito felt the change in spiritual pressure a moment too late and within that heartbeat, Hisato was there. Kaito moved, and ice cracked at his fingertips as he leapt to grasp hold of Suzume, but she slipped through his fingers. An arrow zipped past his ear, grazing him. Soldiers swarmed the pagoda, surrounding them on all sides. Kaito felt their spiritual pressure and knew they were warrior priests. They cut off Kaito from Suzume as she fell further under Hisato's spell. He had to get closer to her. As warrior priests rushed him, Kaito shot a blast of icy spikes at them, not seeing if his blows landed or not.

Hisato and Suzume seemed locked in a world all their own, as his black tentacles wrapped around her arms. Kaito roared and grasped a hold of her, only to have her flames rise to scorch him. He pulled hard, yanking her away from Hisato's grip with a sickening pop.

When he spun her around, she stared at him with a blank and expressionless stare. Hisato's tentacles reached out for her once more, wrapping around her arm, pulling her closer. They were oblivious to the chaos. Suzume stared at Hisato with the same desperate longing he'd seen in Hikaru's gaze. The pieces of Kazue's soul were desperate to be reunited.

Hisato closed the distance, pulling her closer to him, leaning forward to whisper in Suzume's ear even as Kaito tried to yank her once more from his grasp. Realizing he couldn't pull her free, Kaito flung icy projectiles at Hisato, but he exploded in a cloud of black mist and reformed behind Suzume, pulling back her hair, and meeting Kaito's gaze.

Kaito couldn't hear what he'd said. Then Suzume's eyes widened, and fire crept over her body and ignited her hair, turning it a bright crimson. Despite the heat emanating from her, Kaito surged toward them. The wind picked up and created a gale that knocked him and several warrior priests backward. The fire, which was covering Suzume's body, was growing stronger, and the errant flames caught onto the wood of the pagoda and spread quickly, turning it into a giant pyre.

The warrior priests were shouting at one another and changed tactics, surrounding the emperor and his consort before ushering them away while Ryuu and Noaki clashed with a few who were attempting to fire more arrows at them.

"Suzume," Kaito roared as he dove into the hailstorm of fire and wind, taking hold of her at last.

Even Hisato seemed to fear her firestorm, and he stepped back from her. Her flames scorched Kaito's skin, and every instinct screamed to let go. With Hisato's retreat, Suzume seemed to return to herself, and she looked up at him in bewilderment, as if waking from a dream, and then the flames around her body extinguished, and she slumped into his arms. Hisato was gone, disappeared into the damned mist whence he came. Whatever he'd done to Suzume, he'd pay for, Kaito would make certain of that.

Embers fell onto his shirt and burned through to the skin. The sharp pain dulled his anger, and he focused his energy on getting out.

"Time to leave!" Kaito shouted to Ryuu and Noaki.

Without a second glance, he scooped Suzume up into his arms and jumped over the railing into the garden beyond. And not a moment too soon. As they leapt out, a beam buckled and collapsed in on itself. A few soldiers were there waiting to head them off, and Kaito opened his mouth, sending a blast of ice that flattened them and cleared a path.

He ran through the gardens and leapt onto the rooftop of a nearby building, as soldiers scrambled to shoot ineffective arrows after them. Ryuu and Noaki caught up, flanking him on each side and helping shield him and Suzume until they were over the palace walls. They sailed over the city, leaping from rooftop to rooftop, not once slowing down. Fearing he'd lead the warrior priests to his army, Kaito went southwest.

When he was certain they weren't being followed, he set Suzume back on her feet. She blinked at their surroundings for a moment before turning to look at him.

"Well, that could have gone better." Suzume attempted a nonchalant shrug, but her hands trembled.

"That's a gross understatement. How are you feeling? Hisato had you under his spell." He searched her face, which was pale, but otherwise unharmed.

"Just the usual taunting to return to him. Nothing to worry about," Suzume said, waving away his questions. "What about you? Did I burn you?" She turned his concern back on him.

But his burn wounds had also already healed over. He wasn't like her—fragile, vulnerable. Judging by the stubborn set of her jaw, she wasn't going to confess her fears. So he let it be.

"This is my fault. I should have known the emperor hadn't changed his ways." Ryuu sighed.

Kaito swiveled to direct his anger at Ryuu. It was true. They'd walked into the palace, into that trap because of him.

"I thought you had spies in the palace. How did you not know the emperor was deceiving us?" Kaito growled. "You might as well have delivered Suzume to Hisato!"

"I delivered the emperor's proposal. It was your decision that brought us here." Ryuu jabbed his finger at Kaito's chest.

Kaito's canines elongated in his mouth, and scales covered his body as he lost control of his temper. He flexed his claws, considering slashing at his brash offspring, who dared to question his authority to his face. If they were among other dragons, they'd have fought out their feelings long ago, but he'd been holding back out of a false semblance of making peace. Kaito raised his clawed hand to strike Ryuu, who was flexing and glaring a silent challenge.

Before Kaito could strike, Suzume inserted herself between them, a palm pressed to each of their chests as she said, "Arguing won't get us anywhere."

"Marriage is out of the question, and we need a new plan."

Kaito spun to face her. "Marriage is not off the table. You'll be my wife."

Suzume gave him a long look that he couldn't interpret. His temper was frayed. Maybe they couldn't leverage their marriage for political gain, but he wasn't compromising on having her as his bride. Unless she was having doubts? If she were, it wasn't the time to discuss it. But they'd be revisiting the topic when they were alone again.

"The point is, we cannot rely on allying with the humans. And without them and without the tengu, we're coming up short on allies," Suzume concluded.

"We'll find allies," Kaito said with the sort of false confidence that in the past had won his wars. But now, it earned him pitying stares.

"Maybe it's time to look into other ways of fighting Hisato. He's got the hybrid army and the human military on his side. Even if we recruited every single yokai in Akatsuki to our side, we're still outnumbered," Ryuu said.

"Or maybe I should head back into the palace, behead the emperor, and declare myself ruler instead," Kaito snarled. "That's worked for me in the past." He leveled Ryuu with a challenging stare. He didn't appreciate him trying to take charge by implying Kaito's incompetence.

"You can't kill my father!" Suzume shouted.

"He just tried to kill you," Kaito snapped back, throwing his arms up into the air.

"It wasn't him who tried to kill me. I nearly killed myself setting the pagoda aflame."

"Either way, he's working with Hisato." Kaito gestured at the palace.

Suzume placed her hands on her hips. "I'm not agreeing to any plan that involves killing my family. I don't care what their flaws are; they don't deserve death."

"Kaito is right, though," Ryuu said.

Kaito stuck a finger in his ear, trying to clear it; he couldn't have heard correctly.

"What? You can't murder my father!" Suzume gasped.

Kaito crossed his arms over his chest as he looked Ryuu up and down. Perhaps he and his son were more alike than he realized if he had the mettle to make hard choices.

"I'm not talking about murder. But we could force him into early retirement in favor of the crown prince. There's plenty of precedent for it, and it could swing the humans in our favor and away from Hisato."

"How exactly?" Kaito asked, arms crossed. "We can't walk in and ask him to step down."

"I've been working for this goal for a long time. Today has set me back. They'll be looking for me, and I can't reach my allies in the White Palace as easily. But it hasn't undone all my progress," he said with an arrogant sniff. "If we enthrone the crown prince, we take control of the palace's army and deprive Izuki and Hisato of their most powerful allies."

Suzume crossed her arms over her chest. "Which means sitting around and waiting as men talk and Hisato creates an even bigger army?"

"He's right," Kaito said.

Suzume rounded on Kaito, eyes wide. "You agree with him? Are you feeling alright?"

Kaito shook his head, refusing to rise to her taunts. "Ryuu can stay here and continue to woo the humans to our side. You and I will find where Hisato is keeping the captured yokai he's turning into hybrids."

Suzume frowned. "Then another wild goose chase? Great. Are we even certain they're still alive? All the monkey yokai had were conjecture and rumors."

"Reuniting the fractured tribes of Akatsuki is critical to our success. Clans like the monkey tribe were how I won the last war. We don't need a massive army, we just need enough hungry yokai willing to fight for us and for Ryuu to bring the humans to our side. Banding together is how we prevent more hybrids and stopping Ai in one fell swoop. Simple."

"Simple..." Suzume said sarcastically.

Ryuu looked less than convinced. His judgmental gaze was bouncing from Suzume to Kaito and back again.

"You disagree?" Kaito asked.

"I think there's a way that doesn't require bloodshed," Ryuu replied.

"What's your big idea, then?"

"I think Suzume needs to strengthen her connection to her power and learn to resonate with Hikaru without consuming him."

"You saw how she reacted today when she was near Hisato. She was in a trance! We don't have time for that. We can't risk another surprise attack. It's better we build up our army now before the two opposing forces collide."

"Taking Suzume into the wilderness to chase your dreams isn't fair to her. She needs more practice."

"I'd appreciate it if you didn't talk about me like I'm not here," Suzume said.

"That's right, it's Suzume's decision. What do you want?" he asked her.

Suzume looked between them and then to Noaki before her gaze settled on Ryuu. "I can't sit around and wait for potential peace. It's not fair to me, Hikaru, Noaki, or anyone else who I endanger with my unchecked power. I think it's time to attempt reaching the spirit realm again and seeking answers from Kazue."

"Kazue? What's about her?" Kaito asked.

Ryuu's brow furrowed, and he looked as if he were going to argue. Then, with a sigh, said, "Give me and Kaito a few minutes alone, would you?"

Suzume narrowed her eyes at the both of them, her gaze bouncing between them. But to his surprise, she didn't argue. Instead, she walked away with Noaki shadowing her.

"I'm willing to get involved in this alliance scheme of yours. But I don't think putting Suzume on the spot and pressuring her to stay with you is fair to her. Or help the situation we're in," Ryuu said with a stony expression.

"So you'd rather decide for her?" Kaito said, baring his teeth at Ryuu.

"I'm trying to protect her," Ryuu snarled back. If he were anyone else, his gall would've impressed Kaito.

"And so am I!" Kaito roared back. Kaito's hackles rose, and it took all his self-control to not swing a punch in Ryuu's direction. "I have lived longer than you, pup, and I know what dangers lurk in the shadows. I also know how the yokai feel about her. I'm creating a world where we can be together."

"I won't see you endanger her for your own blind ambition."

The thread holding back his self-control snapped, and Kaito swung, landing a blow against Ryuu's cheek. He stumbled backward a step before coming back with a punch of his own, which Kaito dodged. They traded a few more blows before Ryuu swung out, kicking Kaito's legs out from under him. Kaito wrapped his legs around Ryuu and brought him to the ground. The pair of them rolled on the ground, fighting for dominance.

Kaito pinned Ryuu to the ground with his legs. Growling, he said, "Is this because you can't forgive me for what happened between myself and your mother?"

"I never knew my mother, and I know little about what happened between you apart from what others have told me," Ryuu said, arching his back to grab hold of Kaito's arm and twisting it.

Kaito contorted, twisted around and grabbed hold of Ryuu, catching him in a chokehold.

"Then why bother meddling?"

"She's been discarded enough times in her life. Something I can relate to deeply. I won't stand by and wait for you to throw her away once you've tired of her. I won't be part of it," Ryuu gasped out.

The anger inside him fizzled out as a wave of cold nausea rushed over him. Kaito let go of Ryuu. This was his son. He'd resented him from the moment they met partly because of his relationship with Suzume, and partly because his conception had driven a wedge between Kazue and him. But neither of those things were Ryuu's fault. What Kaito really hated was that he didn't know how to be a father, or who they were meant to be to one another with all the baggage their relationship entailed. It was easier to keep pushing him away.

"You know nothing about me or my intentions," Kaito said in a low rumble. And he didn't mean with Suzume. He'd accepted the fact he would be a father before Kazue sealed him. He'd never had the chance to love him as a father should. And perhaps now it was too late for them.

"Your history might imply differently."

"Will you rob her of her right to choose?"

Ryuu studied him for a moment, perhaps considering arguing against Kaito and taking charge of Suzume. But after a moment's consideration, he said, "Perhaps we are more alike than I realized. If you are who she wants, I suppose I will have no choice but to respect her decision."

He'd won, but it felt like a hollow victory in the end. Because Ryuu was right, he'd done wrong by Kazue and him both. And he felt certain it was too late to make it up to him.

TEN

Suzume had known the emperor wouldn't agree to their marriage, but she should have seen the obvious trap and refused to go along with the plan. She wasn't like this, blindly compliant, bending to other's whims. But she hadn't felt like herself for months... Hisato's taunts still rang in her ear. What was the convergence, and why did her chest still ache when she thought of Hisato's wicked gaze? Her feet wanted to turn around and run back to him, to succumb to this longing that threatened to destroy her. The longer she spent apart from the pieces of Kazue's soul, the more sad and lonely she felt. They yearned for reunification, and she wasn't sure how long she could resist. Maybe that was why she'd agreed to such a foolish plan.

She'd moved away to give Kaito and Ryuu space to talk, but she could hear the tussle of their fight from where she stood. She attempted to intercede, but Noaki held out his arm to stop her.

"Leave them," Noaki said.

Noaki so rarely intervened that she didn't argue and instead paced around the woods under Noaki's watch as Kaito and Ryuu finished their skirmish. When they were done, Kaito stalked over to her with thunder in his gaze.

"We need to talk," he said.

Suzume didn't have time to argue before Kaito grabbed her by her upper arm and led her away from Noaki. They'd need to travel far to escape yokai hearing range. Once they were a fair distance away, she yanked her arm free and scowled at him.

"Spit it out," she braced herself for his rejection. Now that her usefulness as a political pawn had expired, he'd grown tired of her. They'd enjoyed a few peaceful months, and it was more than she'd ever hoped for. She'd always known he'd discard her in the end, though. Everyone always did.

Kaito stared silently for a few weighted seconds, which only made her squirm more.

"What?" she snapped.

"Do you want to marry me?"

"Do you?"

"Don't avoid the question; I asked you first."

She shrugged. "I suppose."

He took a step closer to her, grasped her chin, and tilted her head up to face him. She stared up into his startling blue eyes. "I want you to be my bride, Suzume. What happened today doesn't change that."

He let the words linger between them, and Suzume inhaled, as the truth of it rolled over her.

"I'm a hindrance to your ambitions to reunite Akatsuki. Don't deny it, I've heard the yokai talking, and they've made their feelings clear," she said.

"And I don't care what they think." He cupped her face, brushing his thumb across her cheek. "I love you, Suzume, and I promise I will never abandon you, no matter what obstacles we face. I belong to you. Do you trust me?"

It was as if he'd struck her, and her knees buckled beneath her. But Kaito was there to catch her. He wrapped his arms around her, bringing her closer to him, and she clung to the front of his tunic. A silent tear rolled down her cheeks. She hadn't known she needed to hear those words until they were spoken aloud.

Kaito brushed her tears away with the pad of his thumb.

She hated showing him her tears. It wasn't in her to show weakness, so instead, she leaned forward, capturing his mouth in a fierce kiss. Her fingers threaded through his hair as his hand swept down to her lower back. They broke apart after a few breathless moments as Kaito rested his forehead against hers.

"I want you to be honest with me. What have you been keeping from me?"

She exhaled raggedly, her entire body trembling with fear. "I think Kazue was trying to tell me something until Hisato intervened. She told me to return to the beginning. She showed me Noaki was bound to her, and I almost heard his name when the dream ended. When I attempted to enter the spirit realm, Hisato was there and scared Ryuu, who forced me to retreat. But when I saw him, he mentioned convergence and how nothing I could do would stop it. I think..." She inhaled and exhaled. "I think I need to enter the spirit realm and talk to Kazue again."

Kaito held her close, and she listened to the rise and fall of his chest. They were both terrified when she'd tried to connect to Kazue before and almost lost herself. But whether she talked to Kazue or not, she was fading away. At least there was hope of salvation, however slim, by hearing her out.

"Let's try one more time," Kaito said.

THEY WAITED FOR TWILIGHT BECAUSE RYUU CLAIMED IT WAS SAFEST, AS it was balanced between night and day. They used Noaki as an anchor and her companion as she traveled into the spirit realm. Her gut was telling her he needed to be there. That the vision Kazue had shown her of trading Kaito for Noaki was important. Kaito and Ryuu would have to wait and protect their bodies. They sat down on the ground across from one another, knees touching, his palms upturned and hers on his.

"You'll need to open the gates of your spiritual power to one another and resonate. Then, once you've resonated, Suzume will reach for the spirit realm as I taught her. If anything happens, I will break the barrier and wake you and bring you back. Understood?" Ryuu asked.

A large lump had formed in Suzume's throat, but she nodded her understanding. Noaki nodded, and then they began. The barrier went up, and silence enveloped them. It amplified the sound of her racing heart and unsteady breaths. Closing her eyes, Suzume tried to match Noaki's even breaths. When her breathing had stabilized, and her heart slowed, she started out imagining the gates of her magic, envisioned each one opening inside her, flowing with wind and fire.

Noaki's golden aura glowed in her inner sight, mixing with the red and white of her wind and fire. They'd never resonated before, and she could sense his apprehension. Which he had for good reason. She'd stolen magic by force in the past and tried to consume magic in order to become stronger. She had better control over her powers now. She let his energy in, and she let her energy flow out and into him, until their magic combined, and it was impossible to see where one of them started and the other one ended.

Their energy intertwined, and Suzume envisioned rising to the sky, floating up over her body. It didn't feel wrong this time around; more like putting on a warm winter coat. It was the warmth of Noaki's magic enveloping her like an embrace. As she floated above her own body among the treetops, she felt Noaki's guiding hand beside her.

A red door appeared in front of her. The paint was peeling, and the wood peeked through. Together, they opened it, tumbling forward through an ocean of memories. As she swam through them, she felt Hisato's dark energy lurking just outside her vision, moments before icy hands grasped onto her ankles, trying to tug her down into the abyss below.

"I knew you couldn't resist the temptation. There's a question you want answered. But when you know the truth, you'll come back to me," he whispered in her ear.

Suzume thrashed against those cold hands in her mind.

"I'll never come to you."

Rather than let the tendrils of darkness creep over her, she focused her energy and combined it with Noaki's to disintegrate the tentacle wrapped around her ankle. The shadows receded, and by kicking her legs, Suzume rose to the surface of a vast ocean, then swam for the shore of a sandy beach where Noaki was waiting.

The island stretched out in all directions, and beyond the horizon of the ocean was pitch-black darkness.

"Where are we?" Suzume asked.

"The spirit realm, or the border between life and death," Noaki said as he walked down the beach, leaving Suzume no choice but to follow.

She'd overcome the first obstacle, getting past Hisato guarding the doorway. Now she just had to find Kazue. They walked along the sandy shore, but their footsteps left no marks on the ground. It was eerily quiet, and as they moved through the shadowy in-between world, she couldn't shake the feeling of being watched. Noaki seemed to know where they were going because he led them straight to an islet along the shore which curved inward and ended at a faded, red pagoda.

As they approached, Suzume realized there was someone sitting inside the pagoda. She rose to greet them before stopping dead in her tracks. It was Kazue. She smiled at Suzume, but it fell when she saw Noaki.

"Noaki," she said.

"Mistress." He inclined his head at her.

"But you're gone!" Suzume blurted.

"Yes and no. I continue to live on in the fragments of my soul."

Suzume placed a hand on her chest as if she could feel Kazue's foreign invasion inside her.

"Are you going to possess me again?" She eyed her with suspicion.

Kazue shook her head. "No, fire consumes and wind guides. We are more balanced together. But we are still an incomplete soul."

"Then where are you trying to guide me to? What is the beginning?"

"There are many things I want. Such as reversing and undoing the wrongs I have committed, but I am limited in my capacity."

Noaki said nothing, and in fact, he was continuing to stare at Kazue, immobile.

"Can you tell me anything, like Noaki's name? That would be a start," Suzume suggested. Her head was already aching from the riddles.

Kazue shook her head. "No, I'm afraid I cannot tell you anything you do not already know yourself. Because I am a part of you. But I can share with you memories that are locked away inside you. Here, take my hand."

Suzume hesitated to grab a hold of her. Last time she trusted Kazue, she'd stolen her body and went on a fiery rampage. But she was willing to take a chance to free Noaki. Suzume grasped ahold of Kazue's hand and felt as if she were being hooked at her belly button and dragged beneath the ocean. She opened her mouth to scream, but no water came to fill in her lungs. Darkness closed in momentarily, blinding her before brightening. She rubbed at her eyes as they struggled to take in her surroundings. The ocean disappeared, and water became walls and burning braziers, casting golden light on a familiar room. When it cleared, she was kneeling in front of the boar.

"He's yours now, priestess. As promised, I give you the guardian for the dragon. Speak his name, and he is yours."

"Give me his name, and I'll hand you the dragon," Kazue said.

"His true name is Nakatomo. Use it and bind him to your will."

"Thank you," Kazue said. "Nakatomo, retrieve the stone for me."

From beside the boar, Noaki drew his twin blades which moved so fast they were like falling stars in the night sky. He slashed at the boar, forcing him to drop the stone, which fell to the ground and rolled over toward Kazue, who scooped it up.

The boar shrieked for guards, but it was too late. Kazue and Noaki were already running through the maze of tunnels that made up the forest guardian's palace. They escaped out into the sunlit forest and beyond before they stopped to catch their breath. Kazue was panting as she laid a flat palm against the small swell of her belly.

"You're alright, little one. Your father is safe."

Suzume felt the echo of an ache in her chest, the phantom pain of Kazue's memories. Noaki, in the memories beside her, looked to Kazue.

"What else would you have me do, mistress?" he asked.

"It is what we'll do together, Noaki. Help me capture the sun emperor." She clutched the stone which had once encased Kaito before hanging it on a chain around her neck and tucking it beneath her haori.

"What will you do with him?" Noaki asked.

"Make myself immortal," she replied.

The memory faded, and Suzume's consciousness floated to the next. A woman with beautiful and pale silver hair cascading down her shoulder sat in a low-lit room, on an ornate divan carved with the phases of the moon. There was something sad about her face.

"To make yourself immortal, you must first capture the Eight, unbind your soul, and stitch it back together. You'll be made new, after you've broken your heart in two. Only then will you be immortal."

"That would mean I must capture you as well," Kazue said.

The woman lifted her shoulder in a slight shrug. "I am already a prisoner here, and I long for oblivion. But if I might ask you one favor. Find Noaki, who serves the forest guardian Akio, and set him free. Promise me that, and I shall be at peace at last."

"When it's done, I'll set you free," Kazue promised.

The beautiful woman laughed. "You cannot make promises, but I appreciate the gesture. And if I might be so bold. Watch over my children; keep them safe until their father can protect them."

"Yes, my lady."

The apparition of Noaki stepped in front of Suzume, reaching out to the woman. Who was she to evoke such an expression on Noaki's stoic face? But Suzume had no time to wonder. Kazue ripped them from the memories and returned them to the sandy shore. She was paler now, growing distant and smaller.

"I am growing weak. There is more you must know, Suzume. Return to the places that will evoke the past and find the pieces you need to repair my soul. It's the only way you can stop the convergence."

"Return where? You can't leave me with nothing but cryptic answers," Suzume said. But even as she reached for her, she felt the water rising to her waist, soaking her through, pulling her down deeper. Her head was underwater, and she was sinking as the dream world faded. She came back to her body, sitting in the middle of the forest.

Kaito was beside her, grasping onto her arm. "Are you alright? You look pale as a ghost," he said.

Suzume shook her head. Her throat felt parched. Her thoughts were all in a jumble. The woman with silver hair, Kazue's cryptic warnings. None of it made sense.

Once she caught her breath, she said, "I'm fine." Then, turning to Noaki, she said, "Nakatomo, I release you from my service."

Noaki sat still for an endless moment, staring at nothing at all. It seemed like he was lost in the spirit realm. Suzume reached out to grab ahold of his shoulder, and he flinched away from her, looking up at her with a strange, haunted expression.

"Thank you," he said in a croak.

Then, without another word, Noaki stood up and walked away from them. She was unsure she'd ever see him again.

Ryuu rubbed his face and then said with a heavy sigh, "I suppose now is when I should say my goodbyes to you as well."

Suzume stood up and swayed for a moment on her feet. "You don't have to go already. Do you?"

"There's nothing left for me to do here, and you've made your decision clear."

"Thank you for protecting me all this time," Suzume said, though the words felt hollow.

Ryuu waved it away. "I wish I could have done better by you. I hope you are safe along your travels."

"You did more than enough."

He gave her a half smile and a slight bow before turning to Kaito.

"Take care of her," he said. "Until we meet again."

"I will," Kaito said, baring his teeth in a predator's smile. "The next I see you, I hope it's with an army at your back."

With that said, Ryuu turned to leave Suzume and Kaito alone again.

"Feels like old times, doesn't it?" Kaito said to Suzume with a knowing smile.

She laughed and leaned against his shoulder. It had been a long time since it'd just been them. Kazue's words rattled around in her head, but she wasn't sure if she could make sense of them. There was one place she could think Kazue was leading her to.

"Before we gather an army, there's one stop we need to make," Suzume said.

"Oh, and where's that?"

"The mountain temple where we met."

ELEVEN

A cold wind tangled in Rin's hair and a pit had settled in her stomach as their ship approached its destination. The small island was swathed in a dense forest, and the only sign of inhabitants was the flash of red peeking out from beneath the branches. The air crackled with spiritual power, as if it hung thick and heavy like overripe fruit. She'd never met a living kamigakari before, but she'd heard rumors of them. They were gods in human flesh, a symbiotic relationship between kami and man. Most lesser kami were bound to a place, a rock, a body of water, or the associated shrines, drawing energy from those humans who worshiped them. A kamigakari was not limited in such a way. They could harness the spiritual power of their human hosts and the divine magic of the kami. It was easy, in retrospect, to see the similarities between them and the hybrids. As they drew ever closer to their destination, a fragile hope had begun to bloom in Rin's chest. If kamigakari knew how to merge their body with their hosts, perhaps they knew how to undo it as well. And maybe they could save the hybrids Hisato had already turned. And if it were possible for hybrids, maybe it was possible for Hikaru to be free of Kazue's soul fragment as well. Right now, Kazue's soul fragment sustained him just as it threatened to consume him.

"Worried?" Hikaru asked. His brow was furrowed as if he suspected her thoughts, but neither dared speak them out loud. The potential for answers, for freedom, seemed to swell between them.

She nodded her head since words were tangled up in her throat. The sailors shouted to one another as they prepared to dock. The ship pushed up against the pier, rocking and grinding as one sailor leapt off and tied them to it. Now that they'd made landfall, she could see the torii and the long ascending staircase which wound up the hillside. Though hidden behind the trees, she could just make out the tips of a shrine building.

The crew lowered the plank, and the other passengers lined up to shuffle off the boat. Hikaru threaded his fingers through Rin's as they got in line to deboard. She'd learned on the short ferry ride here that many pilgrims came to this temple to pray, and a small group joined them on their journey upward. The stairs were deceptively steep, and it wasn't long before the human pilgrims were huffing and puffing. Some stopped beneath the shade of the trees with expressions that seemed to indicate they were debating continuing. Long stairways like this were meant as a test of worshippers' dedication to their god.

For a yokai and half-yokai the steep ascent wasn't much trouble, but Rin felt the weight of the place's spiritual pressure crushing her. Hikaru pointed out the wards along the path, meant to deter any creature with malicious intent from approaching the holy place. While she didn't have any cruel intentions, the climb was more taxing than it would have been otherwise. And by the time they reached the summit, her brow was covered in sweat and Hikaru was struggling to catch his breath as well. Apart from them, a single worshipper had made it to the top. The brim of a straw hat covered their face as they strolled past, beneath the final torii that separated the stairs from the courtyard.

A priest greeted them with a serene smile, directing them to wash their hands and mouths before entering the inner temple ground. He dipped the ladle into the spring water, offering it to Rin and then Hikaru. Once they were cleansed, Rin felt the spiritual pressure lighten as if someone had taken a large weight off her shoulders. They must have passed the temple's test.

The temple was made up of half a dozen or so buildings. At the front was the shrine, where worshipers could offer up prayers and leave offerings. Sticks of incense burned, and curls of white smoke rose into the air. A priest swept the courtyard and kept shooting curious glances in their direction. Perhaps he had seen through their disguises and sensed what they were, or maybe he was simply curious. Either way, Rin decided to approach him.

"Excuse me, we've been sent to speak with the kamigakari on urgent business," Rin told the priest.

"Many do. She will be receiving visitors soon," he said, not bothering to stop his sweeping.

"We're not here as worshippers; we've been sent here by High Priestess Tomoe."

The priest's head shot up, and he glanced around suspiciously. But the closest person was the pilgrim who was kneeling before the temple shrine in prayer.

The priest leaned in close as to not be overheard. "Have you come about the attacks on the temples?"

Rin nodded.

"I hoped you had. I shall inform my mistress at once." Tossing down his broom, the priest ran down a path between two nearby buildings.

He was gone for several long minutes, in which Rin started to feel restless and Hikaru went to pay homage to the island's kami at the shrine. The pilgrim had wandered off, and the temple grounds were eerily quiet. Even though her tail wasn't visible, it twitched back and forth. This place was well protected by the isolation of this island, surrounded by wards and guarded by powerful kami. She mourned for all the temples who weren't as fortunate as this one. She thought of all the empty, ruined buildings, the displaced people, and eventually, her thoughts drifted back to her temple. She and Hikaru had been temple stewards for centuries, and a deep pang of homesickness overcame her.

"Makes me think of home," Hikaru said, seemingly reading her thoughts.

"I hope we can go back soon," she replied.

"We will, I know it."

The priest returned with an older priest wearing a sash that indicated he was temple head.

"My mistress is ready to speak with you," said the head priest.

Hikaru bowed in thanks before following down the path the younger acolyte had taken earlier but at a considerably slower pace.

The priest led them into the inner buildings of the temple, past the sleeping quarters of the priests and priestesses, a kitchen, and an accompanying garden. At the end of the path was another torii, this one plastered in fresh ofuda. When Rin passed beneath them, she felt the same weight on her chest, and it stripped her of all disguises, revealing her ears and tail. Rin startled in shock and the priest guiding them gave her an apologetic smile.

"Forgive us, for the safety of our mistress, all must be revealed."

Rin and Hikaru shared a look. An uneasy feeling was worming its way through her gut, but it was too late to turn back now.

They followed the stone path, through a private garden and beneath a covered veranda, where a beautiful woman of indeterminate age with long, silky, black hair was seated. A priestess stood just behind her, holding up an umbrella to shield her porcelain skin from the sun's rays. As Rin approached her, she could feel the spiritual energy that radiated from her and flowed through this place like veins. This, Rin realized, was the kamigakari and the beating heart of the temple's immense spiritual power. When her gaze fell on her, Rin felt it like the warmth of the sun, and her smile was dazzling to behold. Rin thought she understood what it meant to be a god in a human form, but she didn't truly, not until she looked upon this creature. Yet somehow, she thought the moment she'd look away, even her memory would betray the magnitude of her presence.

Rin and Hikaru bowed low before her.

"Welcome, Rin, Hikaru," she greeted them in a soft, melodic tone.

"How do you know our names?" Hikaru asked, his voice a half-whisper of awe.

"We met long ago in a different body. Before I settled upon this island."

Rin furrowed her brow. "Your Grace, forgive me for not remembering your radiance."

The kamigakari laughed, and the sound was like the tinkling of bells. Then, with a wave of her hand, she dismissed the priestess who held her parasol, taking it into her hand. The priestesses bowed as they exited, filing out one by one without a word until Rin and Hikaru were alone with the kamigakari.

"It must be fate that our paths met once again. When I last met you, I was a man starving, who you took in and sheltered in your temple." She smiled serenely at them.

Rin tried to rack her brain for a memory. There'd been countless poor and injured they'd helped over the centuries, but she regretted not remembering. Nor realizing she was in the presence of a kami.

"Forgive me, I do not remember," Rin said.

She laughed off her apology. "I wouldn't expect you to. My identity was a secret. But that is of no material matter. Let's simply say, I am grateful for an opportunity to aid your quest."

Rin looked at Hikaru for confirmation. It seemed too good to be true. When Hikaru nodded, she addressed the kami, "Tomoe told us you had information about the hybrids."

She tilted her head to the side, resting her fist upon her cheek. "Is that all you came to find out about?"

"Yes?" Rin said hesitatingly.

"Hikaru is different than when I last saw him. There is another soul entwined with his."

Rin swallowed past a lump in her throat. "How did you know that?"

"This vessel's spiritual power is immense, though not nearly as strong as Kazue's was, of course."

"You knew Kazue?"

She nodded her head. "There are few who don't."

Rin wet her lips. The real question was poised on the tip of her tongue: Can you save him? Will you save him? Rin would have given anything to the kami in that moment, even her life, if she asked it of her. Anything to save Hikaru.

"You mentioned a vessel. Do you mean the body you occupy? Are they related to the hybrids?" Rin asked, her voice shaking more than she would have liked.

"Direct to the point then. Yes. Vessels, as you call them, kami-gakari, are bodies with enough spiritual power to house the immense power of a god."

"Can I ask, when you enter a body, what happens to the person?"

"If they are worthy, our consciences merge, and we become one, both god and human. The same fate will befall Hikaru if you cannot stop the convergence."

A cold chill ran down Rin's spine. "What is the convergence?"

"It is what happens when a vessel and a strong spirit combine. Kazue wasn't a god, but she bound her soul with the power of the most powerful kami. When the soul fragments were separated the fragments were weakened. But now that they've awoken, convergence is inevitable. The pieces of her soul will continue to be drawn together until they are reunited."

"Is there any way to stop it?"

"The only certain way is death," she said plainly. "No matter how pure or wicked, the twin souls will wear down on one another until the original is gone forever."

Hikaru grabbed Rin's hand and squeezed. She felt as if the ground was falling out from under her. She couldn't let this be the answer.

"There must be another way to separate the two."

"Perhaps. The first humans were rumored to have the knowledge of how to shift souls between bodies, but they were destroyed in the war between heaven and earth," the kamigakari said thoughtfully. "Tomoe witnessed the death of one of the last of them, which is why I wrote to her. I thought she might be the link to the answer, but it was you they were leading me to all along."

"What is it you know?" Rin asked. She knew she was being crass, but she didn't care.

The kamigakari stared off into the distance, drumming her fingers on her thigh. "The only ones who can help. The keepers. They are some of the oldest yokai in existence. Hidden in the root of the mountains north of here. If you seek them and are found worthy, they will help you gain what it is you seek. That is the message I was tasked with passing along."

It was a start. Though not much.

"And these keepers can save them all? Not just me, but anyone affected by the combining of souls?" Hikaru asked.

Rin looked at her husband, glowing with pride. Even facing his own death, he was concerned with the fate of others as well.

"Yes. I believe they could."

"Thank you for your help." Rin bowed low, nose nearly touching the ground.

"Thank me not. It is you who saved me long ago. But be careful of the cost the keepers extract for their knowledge. To them, nothing comes for free."

Before Rin could ask her to explain her cryptic warning, a crash rocked through the stillness, followed by a panicked scream. They rushed out of the courtyard and into the temple yard beyond. A few worshippers who'd arrived after them were running back down the steps screaming, as three priests surrounded a lone figure chanting a sealing spell. Their target turned to look at them, and a bolt of recognition ran through Rin. The person who'd once been Akira and Tsuki grinned like a mad person. Their face was a contorted amalgamation of the two of them, and when they spotted Rin and Hikaru, they rushed forward, raising a black blade above their head.

On instinct, Rin jumped in front of him, catching a glancing blow of their blade against her shoulder. The animal in her roared as she forced a transformation and lunged for their throat. They moved too quickly for her, however, and she missed them by an inch before they dodged and circled back around to attack Hikaru. He threw out his hand, whipping vines in their direction which they sliced through with their sword, leaving them scattered on the ground uselessly.

"Hikaru, run. It's you they want," she roared before clamping down onto their arm. As she bit into them, a bitter, acrid taste filled her mouth, forcing her to release them.

She spat out the poison but felt the numbing effects on her

tongue and jaw. Black goo oozed from their wound as they spun around to face her.

"Try and bite us again, and you won't make it until sunrise," they taunted in their strange, echoing voice.

"Tsuki, Akira, this isn't you. I know you're still inside there somewhere. You just have to fight."

They laughed mockingly. "Don't try to sway us. They're dead. Now, there's only us. Let us take the priest, and he'll find comfort in unification, as we have."

Rin glanced past them to Hikaru, who was chanting under his breath. The ground beneath her feet was starting to vibrate. Then, the ground beneath Tsuki and Akira's feet split apart, opening a small gap in the ground. They narrowly missed falling, by leaping over Rin's head and bolting for the exit.

"You may have won this time. But this won't be the last of us, you'll see. Hikaru belongs with the other pieces of his soul. He'll be reunited."

The priests and priestesses sealed the exit, and Tsuki and Akira's voice was muffled. The edges of Rin's vision had started to turn black, and she collapsed to the ground.

When she next woke, Hikaru was sitting beside her. He grabbed her hands as she started to stir.

"Are you hurting anywhere?" he asked.

She shook her head. "I'm fine. What about you? Did they hurt you?" she asked.

"No. I'm fine. But I've been thinking about what they said. What if the only way to end this is with my death?"

Rin wrapped her arms around him, holding him tight. "I lost you once already. If I do it again, it'll destroy me. Don't talk like that."

Hikaru exhaled raggedly. "I worry about you. The danger you're putting yourself in for my sake."

"I'd do this and more. We're going to find a way to free you of Kazue's soul. I promise you."

He searched her face before leaning forward and pressing his brow against hers. "We'll find a way. Together."

Twelve

The river snaked alongside the mountain path, and the sun glinting off its surface blinded Suzume. She shielded her eyes. Kaito knelt along the riverbank, surrounded by half a dozen kappa who'd come up to the surface, albeit reluctantly, at his summons. The last time they'd passed this way, Kaito had called the kappa vermin after one had nearly drowned her. But he'd changed; now, he waited patiently as the kappa spoke to him. They threw out their arms excitedly, and their chatter reminded her of a burbling brook. They'd taken a short detour to recruit the kappa to Kaito's cause and unlike the tengu, they were eager to help.

Bored, Suzume wandered along the riverbank until she found the boulder where she'd once sat, massaging her sore feet. She vividly remembered her aching feet. It was surreal to think it had been a year since then. Kaito wasn't the only one who'd changed; she'd changed too. The girl she'd been felt like a stranger, a pampered princess who'd never walked, who thought yokai were stories, who couldn't fathom she had power hidden in her veins.

"Remembering the good old days?" Kaito teased as his palm slid around her waist and brought her closer.

She scowled at him for old time's sake. "Yes, if I recall, it was here you first threatened to destroy me and my family," Suzume said.

"That was at the temple. Here is where I teased you about how silly your name is." He smirked mischievously. Suzume swiped at him, but he dodged her blow and ran up the path ahead of her. She chased after him, laughing all the while.

"You've always been insatiable for me. From the moment we met, you were eyeing my assets." He gestured across his body. Suzume's cheeks flamed as she redoubled her efforts to catch him.

If he wanted, Kaito could easily outrun her, but in a few strides, she'd caught hold of his trailing sleeve and pulled. But he turned the tables on her, spinning around, pulling her into a crushing embrace, and trapping her arms between them so she couldn't so much as squirm.

"I've got you now. What shall I do with you?" he said in a teasing lilt.

"Everyone is watching," she muttered. Suzume felt the stares of the army and the kappa lingering on the riverbank burning into the back of her neck. She knew the yokai tolerated her presence at best and resented her at worst. And because of it, she tried not to flaunt their relationship.

"Let them." He dipped his head down to kiss her neck, his teeth grazing over her sensitive skin. "Did I ever tell you, your blush drives me wild?" He breathed against her skin.

Heat pooled in her stomach and along her face, but now was hardly the time or place. She pulled free of his grip, surprising Kaito, who stared at her for a moment with a hurt expression.

"Did you finish making a deal with the kappa?" The words hung heavy and awkward between them for the obvious change of subject they were.

Kaito's brow furrowed as he regarded her for a moment, as if wrestling internally with the decision to argue or not.

"They'll do almost anything for a cucumber. Good thing Ai didn't think of it first. They'll be our eyes and ears in the rivers from now on." He dragged a hand through his hair and surveyed the army milling about a few yards away. The captains were looking conspicuously anywhere but at them.

"We'll make the rest of the descent alone, and leave the army to camp here," Kaito said.

"The priestesses will appreciate that, I'm sure," Suzume said, wishing she had the right words to smooth over the awkwardness that had settled over them but fearing if she tried, she'd only put her foot in her mouth once again.

"It will be faster, too," Kaito replied. He seemed distracted now as he surveyed his army. Moving as a group was slower, to be certain, and the mountain paths were narrow and winding. Bringing them all along would only waste precious time. It was her request that had led them on this possible wild goose chase anyway. There was no guarantee that the beginning Kazue asked her to return to was this temple. While Kaito notified the captains of their plans, Suzume stood on the sidelines, gazing up at the mountainside. From her vantage point, she couldn't see the temple hidden in the folds of hills and valleys, but she felt in her bones that this was where she was meant to be. Kaito finished up with the captains and returned to her side.

His hand slid around her shoulders easily, as if it were the most natural thing to do. And when they were a few feet away from the camping army, he leaned in to whisper in her ear, "Since you wanted us to be alone so badly, maybe we should have that wedding night we never got in the temple."

Her cheeks and neck were glowing red now, and Suzume slapped Kaito playfully on the arm.

"Is that a no?"

She covered her burning face with her sleeve. "It's a solid maybe." She cleared her throat.

Kaito laughed low in his throat, and it sent a thrill of anticipation through her. It was hard to be intimate since they'd left the tengu mountain. Tent walls were not an adequate damper for the whispers carried in by the wind. Every time they were alone, she heard every grunt and howl of the army amplified, and it drove her to distraction. But knowing they would be truly alone, apart from the temple priestesses, she felt a new surge of excitement. Maybe she couldn't soothe any awkwardness with words, but they'd learned a new type of communication with their bodies. Suzume ran ahead, and Kaito eagerly gave chase.

At first, her footsteps felt light, as if the wind made them lighter. They were laughing and flirting until the wind shifted, and she felt a cold chill run down her spine. But it was more than a chill; it was an ominous feeling that froze the blood in her veins. Kaito must have felt it, too, because he took a step in front of her and held out his hand, signaling she should stay back.

"What is it?" Suzume asked.

"I smell blood."

Then the wind carried with it the echo of a scream, a phantom sound worn around the edges as if it were days old.

"You don't think…" She couldn't finish the thought even with the truth sitting on the tip of her tongue.

Instead, she drew her staff from her back holster and followed Kaito, the mood shifting the closer they got to the temple. They didn't need to go far before they saw the body lying on the ground. She'd been slashed through the middle, and her entrails spilled onto the dusty ground, dark blood pooling around her and her sightless eyes staring skyward. She peered at the woman's face and was relieved and ashamed she didn't recognize her. She'd never bothered to learn the names of the other priestesses during her short stint at the temple. None of them had ever liked her, but she hadn't wished them harm either.

They left the body behind on the path and approached the temple gate. The torii were snapped, and jagged splinters of wood lay on the ground. The top half crushed the body of another priestess. The well where visitors were meant to wash their hands and mouths before entering was polluted with the blood of a dead hybrid which lay slumped over it.

The metallic stench of blood surrounded her and made her fight back the bile that rose up at the back of her throat. They proceeded through the temple, finding more upturned rooms, a few dead priestesses, and fewer dead hybrids.

Kaito looked at Suzume, and she saw her regrets reflected in his gaze. It couldn't be a coincidence that Kazue had told Suzume to return to the beginning, and they'd stumbled onto this attack, which couldn't have been more than a day old. They might have just missed Hisato or his hybrid army. Many temples had been attacked in the last few months, but none this small or remote. This had to be Hisato sending her a message. He knew she was seeking answers, and he might have beat her to them...

"Stop right there," a voice barked.

Suzume whipped around as the second-in-command stumbled out of the temple building, brandishing an ofuda in one hand and her other clutching a bleeding wound on her abdomen. It had soaked through her clothes, creating a dark stain much too large for her to be walking around. She took a few wobbling steps before tipping over and leaning against the column of the veranda.

Suzume held up her hands in a sign of peace. "Priestess, do you remember us?" she said.

The priestess' gaze was fogged over, and sweat glistened on her brow. As she squinted at them, she seemed to put the pieces together.

"My lord, you came back." She collapsed onto her knees, and Suzume rushed over to catch her before her head struck the ground.

She was even paler up close, with a sickly gray pallor to her skin.

"We need to get you treatment," Suzume said, looking to Kaito for guidance, but he returned her plea with a pitying stare and a slow shake of his head.

Suzume didn't have Hikaru's healing ability. But even if she did, she wasn't sure she could have saved her. The wound was fatal.

The old woman grabbed a hold of Suzume's arm with bloody fingers. "They killed us all. I tried to protect the head priestess, but they killed her too."

"Shh, save your strength," Suzume muttered. Though she knew there was nothing she could do, she wanted her to at least go in peace.

"You have to protect it now. You're all that's left." She pulled a slim book from within the folds of her haori and pressed it into Suzume's hands. It was covered in blood and brittle with age. "He'll come back for it when he realizes what he took was a decoy. You must protect it at all costs."

"Protect what? What is this?"

"Her last will."

"Whose last will? The Head Priestess'?"

"The first... high priestess... Fuji...kawa... Kaz—" Her grip slackened, and she slid down Suzume as the strength left her body, slumping her head against Suzume's shoulder.

With a gasp, she slid into death. Suzume lowered her gently to the ground before standing up and taking a few steps back. Her entire body was shaking. She clutched the book she'd been handed tightly against her chest, trying to calm down the erratic beating of her heart. She felt the power that pulsed within it calling out to her quieter than a soul fragment but with as much certainty. Whatever was inside, the entire temple had died to protect it. And this must be what Kazue had sent her to recover. She held it in front of her and noticed a piece of paper tucked behind the front cover. It was bright white and obviously newer. She plucked it out carefully and unfolded it. Suzume was surprised to find it was a letter addressed to her.

"Lady Suzume, I have been protecting this document for my entire life. As has my predecessor before me. I was instructed to hold onto it until the day our mistress' reincarnation returned. Recently, a woman claiming to be Kazue came back for the book. I could sense an evil about her and I fear I have not much longer before she returns for it. I apologize for keeping this from you at first. But I sensed you were not ready. If you are reading this, I am dead, and you must take on this mantle. Inside, you will find the words of High Priestess Kazue accounting of her life and deeds."

The letter cut off after that as if she'd been in the middle of writing when the attack happened. Kaito, who'd been reading over her shoulder, frowned at the words written there. She looked up at him, but his expression was unreadable.

"Do you think it is real?" She offered him the book to inspect, but he pushed it away.

"I don't think it's for me to read," he said stiffly as he turned his back on her.

The temptation to read was strong, but now wasn't the time. Instead, she stashed it into the folds of her haori.

They worked until sundown, searching the temple for survivors, of which there were none. When they determined there was no one left alive, they brought the bodies to be burned in the courtyard. By the time they were finished, Suzume was exhausted, covered in gore, and heart weary. They found some clean water to wash, and then both of them collapsed into the bed, neither of them speaking at all.

In the morning, they both gathered up their things and headed down the mountain to rejoin the army. The breathless anticipation they'd arrived with had soured to something sullen and silent. Suzume felt Kazue's diary burning against her stomach. She hadn't dared open it or look at it for fear of what she might find in its pages. What answers did Kazue leave in those pages, and why was Hisato so desperate to have them?

As they walked away from the temple, Suzume watched the back of Kaito's head. Questions were buzzing in her mind that she was too afraid to ask. She knew that his feelings for Kazue were complicated, and without opening the diary she had an inkling of what was written in the pages. It might give a glimpse into their relationship, which felt like an invasion of her and Kaito's privacy and one of the reasons she'd delayed reading it. Kaito's chilly silence was scaring her, and if there was something upsetting in Kazue's diary, she wanted to hear it from Kaito first.

"I was wondering, why would Kazue hide the diary here where she sealed you away?"

"Perhaps she wanted to taunt me with the truth," Kaito said gruffly.

"Or maybe there's a message she wants to share with you. I've long wondered why she chose this place to seal you of all places. Maybe it was to protect you, so no one would use your stone to enhance their own power."

Kaito turned to look at her, thunder in his expression. "She chose it because it was far from the ocean, high up in the sky, so I would remain weak even if I managed to break the seal," he said simply.

"And yet she could have buried you in stone and left you to rot. Instead, she built a shrine around you," Suzume said, feeling oddly defensive of Kazue's motives. Maybe it was because her memories were closer to the surface than ever. "She didn't have to leave the answers there for you to read."

"If you want to know why she did what she did, you can read about it. You don't need my permission."

Suzume crossed her arms over her chest and ignored his taunts. "I wasn't asking for it."

"Good." He stomped off.

And the words left unspoken between them felt as vast as an ocean. Because a small part of her wanted him to stop her. She wanted him to tell her not to do it. Because what if unlocking more of Kazue's memories caused her to lose even more of herself, or worse, what if she found out what Kazue wanted her to do, and she wasn't strong enough for the task?

THIRTEEN

To enter the domain of the gods, you must first prove your worth. The place where Noaki had been forged, in an age of primordial chaos, from a shard of the Sun Emperor's blade, sat at the top of a mountain whose peak scraped against the clouds. Ten thousand steps led up to the Sun Emperor's palace. And many modern temples attempted to replicate those endless stairs as a lesser test of virtue. Noaki and his brothers, all forged in the same fire, had turned the tide in the war of the Eight, securing the Sun Emperor his victory and capture of his rival, Sayuri, goddess of the moon. And so, his creations and the moon were bound to the Sun Emperor for all time.

After the war, he'd walked those ten thousand steps thousands of times to protect the kingdom he'd helped create. He saw each step taken as an act of devotion and love to his creator. It was on those steps he'd first seen Sayuri. Pale as moonlight and ethereal, like those distant stars she governed. The most beautiful thing he'd ever seen and yet so terribly sad.

She often came to stare out across the cloud-covered mountains at the top of the stairs he patrolled. Over the years, they shared a thousand sly glances, which began to linger longer and longer until a slow, unfurling romance began to grow. Noaki had been conflicted at first. She was his creator's prisoner and wife. His feelings were forbidden and treasonous. But despite his love for the emperor, he also saw how his control of Sayuri diminished her, and slowly, the resentment for his creator grew along with his love for her.

His bitterness made him brittle until he had no choice but to break. Noaki betrayed his creator, in his thoughts and his actions. His physical relationship with Sayuri was brief, and it cost him everything. The Sun Emperor cast him out, gifting him to a lowly forest guardian, Akio, as punishment. Sayuri was sent away. Never to see the light of the stars, her creations, again. Within the confines of his bond, Noaki sought her out, trading everything for even a whisper of her whereabouts. But no matter how much he begged, borrowed, and stole, he couldn't find her.

Then Kazue's vision had given him the last hint he needed, a small glimpse into the last place she'd been. Noaki had assumed the Sun Emperor banished her from his mountain temple. He'd been naïve to think the Sun Emperor would let her out of his reach. He'd kept her close, to watch over her, always within his control. Always in his grip.

So once again, Noaki ascended those ten thousand crumbling stone steps through a shroud of clouds. The sun hadn't risen when he'd started his ascent, and by the time it set again, there were a thousand more to go. The crescent moon was rising in the sky by the time he reached the top. As soon as he was in the clouds among the gods, he felt the eerie stillness of this place. It wasn't a taxing climb, but he couldn't quite shake the sensation of being weighed down. As if invisible restraints remained attached around his ankles and wrists. After centuries bound to others, being free was a strange and disorienting sensation.

At the top of the steps, the magnificent gateway, which once guarded the entrance to the Sun Emperor's palace, was crumbled and in ruins. The Sun Emperor had been sealed away centuries ago, and yet Noaki felt a trace of his power echoing through the grounds. It left him feeling uneasy as he scanned the grounds for signs of life.

He entered the main hallway where the Sun Emperor had once held grand feasts and courted with the powerful yokai and kami. The once-busy halls were silent now, crushed by an oppressive silence that put his teeth on edge. The last time he'd been here, he'd led Kazue inside to help her capture the most powerful of the Eight. As he approached the dais, he noticed the skeletal remains of a body pinned beneath the rubble. A sword pierced the chest of the last guardian and time and exposure to the elements had withered and shrunken his body beyond recognition. But Noaki remembered. He was gone. They were all gone. He had killed them. And now only Noaki remained. A shadow haunting places that were once his home. Noaki took a moment of silent reflection for the body of his fallen brother before moving on.

Moving through the first passageway, he turned a corner and walked down a flight of stairs. Though the place lay mostly in ruin, the layout was just as he remembered it. There were rooms on the interior which had been carved from the mountain. Moon murals along the walls, worn away by time and weather and the floor was covered in translucent tiles which gleamed in the moonlight. This was it, where Sayuri had slept before Kazue found her and stole her energy to split her soul apart and gain immortality. The doors were heavily fortified and lay at the heart of the temple, where no one might enter or leave. It was there he realized the Sun Emperor had imprisoned Sayuri after he'd been banished.

Without torches to light his way, the long corridor was incredibly dark. Each step echoed off the stone walls, sending a ripple of apprehension down his spine. Something powerful had dwelled here, powerful and familiar. He felt traces of her power in these walls, but like the Sun Emperor, they had long ago faded. She likely wasn't here, and yet he couldn't stop his feet from moving down the corridor. His hand brushed against the wall, and he thought of her trapped between dreaming and waking forever.

"Who's there?" Someone shouted from the depths of the room. Noaki drew a single blade and moved closer and deeper into a room filled with ornate furniture and a large, empty bed. A woman with white hair sat crouched in the far corner, folded in on herself. His heart lurched, and he moved toward her. But as she turned to look at him, eyes milky and unseeing, he realized she was one of Sayuri's maids.

"I can smell you, reveal yourself," she said.

She was blind and living like a rat in the darkness. She was no threat to him. He could feel how weak she was.

"I've come seeking the Moon Goddess, Sayuri," Noaki said.

She jerked her head around like a blind snake contemplating striking.

"My mistress escaped centuries ago. You won't find her here." She rocked from side to side, her hands grasping outward, seeking, searching. She brushed a hand over his foot, but he stepped back out of reach.

"Where did she go?" Noaki asked.

She chuckled. It was a dry and humorless laugh. "I do not know. She promised to return for me but never did. Torture me and see if it's true. Better yet, kill me and end my centuries of suffering."

Noaki said nothing.

"She's gone. All that remains is darkness. Seeking her will eat away at you slowly as it has eaten away at me, stolen my youth and beauty. Reduced me to nothing."

As repulsed as he was by this creature, he couldn't help but wonder. "Why did you remain here?" he asked.

She licked her dry lips. "Loyalty? Greed? Ignorance? It is hard to say anymore. I thought I loved her once, but I am not so certain now. The thoughts become twisted with time in the dark."

Noaki passed her by and went deeper into the chamber. He could still feel those faint traces of Sayuri's energy, like perfume lingering after someone had left the room. But mixed into the threads of it were the darker notes. The darkness that lingered was corrupted by the time away from her healing light. Darkness needed the moon's light for balance. If Sayuri really had abandoned her servant to the dark, she might never recover.

The wards on the room were corroded, the varnish on the bed stripped. The ground was wet, and something dripped from the ceiling. In the center of the room, a shaft of the moonlight glowed, illuminating a single stone on a pedestal. It glimmered with a rainbow sheen. This had to be it. The stone Sayuri had been sealed within. Noaki, who was born of the fragments of the Sun Emperor's blade, should not have been worthy enough to enter this place. Let alone dare to take hold of this stone. But no matter what the cost, he would take any measure he had to to save the children and bring Sayuri back.

He reached for it, but as he did, there was a screech behind him. He turned in time to see the shriveled servant lunge for him. Her clawed hand slashed at his head.

"Don't take her from me. You can't have her."

She wailed like an injured animal. He knocked her aside, but she didn't crumble and fall. Instead, she slithered back over to him, clawing at him with her brittle fingers. He struggled against her as she clawed at his face, and then, before things could get out of hand, he drew his blade.

"You cannot have it. You can't."

Her milky eyes were crazed as she attacked him. Knowing there was no other way to end her suffering, he drew his blade across her throat. Her mouth fell slack as blood soaked the front of her tattered clothes, and then she crumpled to the ground. He took no pleasure in killing or drawing his sword, but for that thing, it was more of a mercy to let her die.

He knelt down beside her and closed her eyes. Once he had the stone, he would give her a proper farewell and burn the body with all the necessary rights that she deserved.

Noaki turned back to the stone. He wiped the blood from his hands onto the front of his haori and reached for it. He felt nothing but smooth, cold stone in his hands. Sayuri wasn't inside this stone. It was nothing but a trinket. An empty promise. He crushed it beneath his hands, and it turned to dust. An animalistic howl built in his throat as he tossed around the furniture in the room. When the despair and rage faded, Noaki stood in the middle of the carnage he'd wrought, panting for breath.

Another false lead and nowhere else to go. Where could she be? He was shaking when he turned and saw the woman standing in the doorway behind him.

Kazue. Not the one who'd sealed him in stone, but rather the water of her soul who likened herself to the real thing. A breeze from down the tunnel lifted up her hair as she regarded him. Noaki drew his blade and did not move.

"It would have been cruel of me to seal her here, and leave her in the prison she desperately wanted to escape. Wouldn't it?" Kazue said, strolling toward him.

Noaki watched as she stalked closer to him, hand on the hilt of his blade. This woman had changed his children and stolen their identity. She wore a stranger's face, but her assured stride, and jutted proud chin reminded him of the original Kazue. He waited and watched as she approached him. Her attention was on the servant's corpse at his feet.

"You're very predictable, Noaki. I knew as soon as Suzume freed you, you'd come looking for her. But you'll never find Sayuri."

Noaki stared at her without answer, but his fingers itched to draw his sword in anger to exact the revenge he'd dreamed of for centuries on that mountaintop. He wasn't one to rise to needless taunts. The first Kazue had known all his triggers and twisted them expertly. This woman had either guessed at his sore spots, or she'd been overtaken by the fragment inside her, as Suzume almost was.

"I can give her back to you, just like I promised." Her smile was sinister as she evoked the promise the first Kazue had once made him. There was a touch of Hisato's madness in her expression, and he wondered if there was still a human beneath that skin, or if she were merely Hisato's puppet now.

Still, he remained silent, as answering would only goad her. His hand flexed on the hilt of his sword as he contemplated his next move. Even at a fourth of the original Kazue's power, she was still a dangerous opponent, and there was no reason to be rash.

"Aren't you going to ask me how?" She cocked her head to one side, examining him.

"No," he replied.

She threw her head back in trilling laughter. It sounded unnatural coming from her, because it sounded like Sayuri. This woman must have the power of a mimic, or standing here inside her prison was twisting his perception of reality. Either way, this new version of Kazue didn't hold back, and instead had struck his heart.

"You can search all over Akatsuki for me, my beloved swordsman. But you'll not find me sealed inside a stone, but flesh," she said in Sayuri's voice, using her secret pet name for him. The one she used when they were alone, in the dark. If he closed his eyes, he could picture her whispering it against his skin.

Noaki's blood ran cold, and his stomach heaved. He didn't know how she'd learned it, but she was using it to set him off balance, and it was working.

"You lie. This is an illusion."

"Not an illusion, my love. I'm here, trapped inside this body, along with the piece of Kazue's soul. He has awakened me. But only you can truly set me free. Don't you want to be together with our children, my love?" She reached out to cup his cheek. And despite himself, he leaned into her touch. Like the fool he was, he wanted this to be real. He wanted. Gods, he wanted her back.

Sayuri leaned forward and was about to press her lips against his when he got hold of his senses and drew his blade to press it against her treacherous throat.

That slow, mad smile spread over her face once more, and she looked at him with a wicked glint.

"You don't believe me?" she said, Kazue's voice overlapping with Sayuri's, sounding strange and wicked.

He pressed the tip of his blade against her throat, drawing a drop of blood that ran down it.

"You brought me sundrop flowers and left them on my pillow. When I caught you at it, you claimed they were gifts from the Sun Emperor. But I always knew they were from you. He was too vain and cruel to consider my happiness." She sounded like Sayuri, and worse, she touched his hand, tracing the tops of the knuckles the way Sayuri used to.

A shiver went down his spine as Noaki swayed on his feet. He was torn between wanting to believe her and fearing the truth. Those gifts he'd left, the familiar and affectionate way in which she brushed the tops of his knuckles. No one else could have known. Back then, they had to be careful or risk the Sun Emperor's wrath. Even if Sayuri had conspired with the original Kazue, he couldn't imagine she'd have shared such intimate details with her.

A triumphant smile curled on the new Kazue's face, and it was strangely juxtaposed to Sayuri's voice, and mannerisms. Perhaps Sayuri was inside Kazue, in the way his children were bound to the same body. Multiple souls and consciences trapped together. But unlike them, Sayuri didn't seem to have equal control or any at all. The new Kazue was pulling the strings, using Sayuri to manipulate him.

"The only power that could keep Kazue's soul apart was the souls of the Eight. Inside me are both the Lord of the Sea and the Lady of the Moon. Their harmonious forces fuel my spiritual power, while also keeping this soul contained within this body. But if they were to fully awaken, my soul would be free to rejoin the others. As would your beloved Sayuri be free to join you," Kazue said. Her voice and demeanor were nothing like Sayuri's or the original Kazue's.

She grabbed the blade, and it bit into the flesh of her palm, her blood dripping onto the stone beneath her feet.

"Drive the blade. End my life. Free Sayuri. As I know you want to."

His hand hesitated, but his heart wanted to kill her, to free his beloved. But if it was true for the new Kazue, the same must be true for Suzume and Hikaru, too. The new Kazue worked for Hisato; they wanted her dead to suit their own ends.

He withdrew his blade and rested it on the ground beside him.

"I won't kill you. Even if you beg me," he said.

Anger flashed across her expression before she was flying at him, throwing water in his face and trying to force him to fight her. But as he tried to rebuff her attacks, she kept coming on stronger and stronger. As water filled his eyes and blinded him,

Noaki knew the only way to stop it was to incapacitate her. He rushed forward through the wave of water and came up behind her, grasping hold of her. He pressed onto her neck until she went limp in his arms.

He laid her gently on the ground and fled the temple. He had to find Suzume and the others and warn them of what he'd learned.

FOURTEEN

Kaito studied the map in front of him. Markers were laid out indicating Ai's last known position, along with the flanks of his army marching toward their certain doom. The kappa proved effective and swift spies. From the various waterways, they could report on the movements of both his enemies and his allies. But all the knowledge in the world wouldn't assure him victory. By all reports, they were grossly outnumbered; meeting Ai as they were currently would be complete obliteration. Even if by some miracle they won, they still couldn't defeat Hisato and his growing hybrid army. More and more reports were being delivered, more temples obliterated, more missing priests and priestesses. Kaito rubbed his palm against his face in frustration.

Someone pulled back the flap of his tent, and he glanced up to see Hana and the monkey yokai standing in his doorway. Kaito waved them in, and they shuffled over. Both of them looked battered and exhausted. It'd been weeks without any news from his trusted captain, and he'd started to fear she'd ended up a casualty of this bloody war.

"I hope you have good news," Kaito said.

"We found the temple as the monkey yokai promised," Hana started to say.

"The place is crawling with hybrids. I risked my neck to protect your precious captain," the monkey yokai interjected, puffing out his chest in misplaced pride.

"It's not too late for me to kill you. Let her speak."

The monkey yokai shrank back, chastised, and Hana gave him a grateful smile.

"There's a small force of hybrids guarding the perimeter. Until a few days before we left, the Water of Kazue's Soul and Akira and Tsuki were there as well."

"Do you think they'll come back?" Kaito asked.

"I would say the chances are high they will. She seems to be helping create the hybrids."

"Horrid priestess. My poor kinsman. Now that I have proven my worth, will you help us, great dragon?" The monkey yokai stared at him with a pleading expression.

"Did you see your kinsmen then?"

The monkey yokai shook his head sadly. "No, but we saw a room filled with sealing stones and I could tell they were in there. If we could break them free, I know they'd serve you until the end of their days."

Kaito rubbed at his chin in thought. They were in desperate need of soldiers. The humans had been a bust and try as he might to recruit other yokai along their route to their cause, he was struggling to increase his numbers. Walking into that temple could be dangerous; they might lose valuable fighters and come out with nothing to show for it. But if they succeeded, he'd increase his numbers and potentially strike a blow to Hisato, especially if they could manage to capture Tsuki, Akira, and new Kazue.

The tent flap opened once more, and light spilled in from outside, capturing all their attention. Suzume froze in the doorway, eyes going wide as she looked at the three of them.

"I didn't realize you were in the middle of something, I'll come back later..." She turned to leave.

"Don't!" Kaito reached out for her, hating how desperate and vulnerable he sounded.

Ever since they'd left the mountain temple, he'd felt the distance growing between them. As if Kazue's diary had manifested her in the flesh, and with it, old wounds were reawakened in him. They'd hardly shared more than a few words in the past two days.

Suzume's brow arched at him in silent question.

"We've gotten new information about the hybrids, and I wanted to hear your thoughts on the matter."

She stepped inside and let the tent flap fall closed behind her before strolling over to stand beside Hana and the monkey yokai, who looked at her sidelong.

Kaito picked up a marker and handed it to Hana. "Show her where you found the temple."

Hana did as she was told, and Suzume inched closer to the table, peering down at where the marker had been placed on the map. It wasn't far from their current location. Suzume studied the map, eyes sweeping over it without a word.

"Now that we know where he's taking the priests and priestesses to turn into hybrids, we can attack and cripple his army."

"And will you bring the priests and priestess into the army?" Suzume asked, without looking at him. Her tone was impossible to read.

"That's preposterous. We couldn't fight alongside priests and priestesses. We'd all be worried about a dagger landing in our backs," the monkey yokai scoffed.

"I did not ask your opinion," Kaito said coolly.

The monkey yokai shrank back under his icy stare. Suzume had brought up a good point. He'd been ready to partner with the White Palace, so why not the priests and priestesses whom Hisato had captured? They might be as eager as him for revenge after what Hisato had done to their homes.

"He's right. It might cause a problem." Suzume traced her finger along the map, leading along a river to a destination that felt painfully familiar. She couldn't have known, he told himself. It was probably a coincidence. Unless Suzume had been reading Kazue's diary and knew the location of the place where he'd hidden her before she'd sealed him away.

"Leave us," Kaito growled.

Hana and the monkey yokai scurried out without a second glance, leaving him and Suzume alone again. She still hadn't turned to look at him, and he could just imagine what was running through her head. More and more, she was like this, quiet, despondent. So unlike her usual self. After she'd absorbed Souta's soul fragment, she'd told him she needed time to process. He was willing to give her space and wait. But the introduction of the diary and Kazue's cryptic warnings in her dreams had put him on edge. Because this was how Kazue had acted just before she'd entrapped him in stone for centuries. He pretended not to care about the book in Suzume's possession and told himself that he'd put the past and Kazue behind him. And yet, his mind kept drifting to what might be written on those pages. Would reading her inner thoughts make the pain less? Would knowing more about her justifications erase hundreds of years of suffering? He doubted it, and yet he couldn't let it go.

"Have you read the diary?" Kaito asked, fearing the answer.

She glanced at him. "Not yet."

"Good," he said. Because there was nothing else to say in that moment.

"I want to rescue those priestesses, but I don't know if asking them to join the army is a good idea," Suzume said.

Kaito arched a brow. "Why not? We have a common enemy."

Suzume turned to face him then, crossing her arms over her chest. "You know why. Our kind are always at odds. Even if they agree, do you think the yokai will go along with it quietly?"

Kaito waved away her concerns. "They'll do what I tell them to."

"And you see where that's gotten you so far." Suzume rolled her eyes.

"Do you have any better ideas?" Kaito said, snarling, losing control of his temper.

She simply glared back at him for a long time, neither of them speaking and the tension rising higher and higher between them. Kaito should have reached out to her then, soothed the hurt feelings. But instead, he said, "We're leaving for the temple in the morning. Be ready; we'll need you to break the seals."

She tilted her chin upward. "Yes, Dragon," she snapped before storming out of the tent.

When she was gone, Kaito leaned forward on the map table and growled in frustration.

THE TEMPLE LOOKED MORE LIKE A SET OF RUINS. TORII ARCHES WERE torn from the ground and splintered into a thousand pieces. Monstrous, lumbering hybrids patrolled the exterior. When Kaito gave the signal, his soldiers moved in and removed the guards with ease and little commotion. Kaito, Suzume, and a few of his soldiers crept through the shadows and approached the main grounds.

There were more hybrids lurking around the grounds, which they snuck past to hide in empty, sacked temple rooms. Suzume had gone to bed angry and woke in a similar chilly silence. But now that they were in the thick of it, she was focused and alert, scanning and peeking outside the door into the temple beyond.

"There's a room across the way where they've got priestesses locked up. I'm going to talk to them."

"We haven't gotten sight on Kazue yet or Tsuki and Akira. We need to—" But before he could even finish his sentence, she was across the hall and crouched down in front of the door where they were keeping the priestesses. Kaito signaled to his soldiers to survey the rest of the temple before following Suzume.

"We're not here to hurt you," Suzume assured them.

The group of perhaps fifty priestesses had recoiled from her and were all bunched against a far wall of their makeshift cell. They looked at Kaito in wide-eyed terror, and Suzume glanced over her shoulder at him and scowled. "You're not helping," Suzume said under her breath.

"Who are you?" one woman asked, taking a step forward from the group. There was a steely look in her gaze as she looked Suzume and Kaito over.

"My name is Suzume, and this is Kaito," Suzume said, gesturing to him.

"I'm Amari."

"Nice to meet you, Amari. We're here to free you. But before I do, I need your help. Other than the hybrids, is there anyone else guarding this place?"

"The woman left a week ago, and she hasn't come back. But she put the new kami in charge, and he's much worse."

"The new kami?" Suzume frowned and looked at Kaito. Her fears reflected his own. He didn't know what this new kami was, but he wasn't sure he liked the sound of it.

The girl nodded slowly. "He's a monster. He looks like a man, but he's worse than those abominations they create by forcing the stones on us." She shuddered.

Kaito didn't like the sound of this new kami. But they didn't have time to worry about it. "Where are the stones being kept?" Kaito asked.

"I'm not sure."

"We'll find it on our own," Suzume said as she fumbled with the door lock. She placed her hands on it and heated the wood of the door until it burned and crumbled to ash. Then the door swung open, and Suzume made a gesture for them to come out. But the priestesses seemed reluctant to take the offer of freedom.

"They can leave when they're ready. We should find the stones and break the seals first."

Suzume looked at the priestesses, seemingly torn between staying and following, but in the end, she did. They searched the rest of the temple and found another room, this time filled with priests. As they had done with the priestesses, Suzume opened the door and let them go free. Everything was going surprisingly well until they turned a corner and found a group of hybrids and caught them by surprise. Suzume acted quicker than him, shooting a ball of flame that provided a distraction, allowing them time to run. They looped around the building in an attempt to evade but were blocked by another pair of hybrids who pinned them between the two groups.

Standing back-to-back, they faced the hybrids and waited for them to rush them. When they attacked, Suzume shot fire and blasts of wind to knock them back, and Kaito covered them in ice. Within a few minutes, their opponents had fallen to the ground, and Suzume was panting for breath. Suzume motioned to go and search a nearby building, but he grabbed a hold of her wrist, and she spun around to face him, a question in her gaze.

"Are you hurt anywhere?" he asked.

Her expression softened. "I'm fine, don't worry."

There was more he wanted to say. But he felt a change in spiritual energy that sent a wave of nausea washing over him. It was so strong he had to grasp onto a nearby pillar to stay upright. It felt like Hisato but so much worse. Suzume grabbed his shoulder, murmuring a question that he couldn't quite hear. It felt as if he were underwater and the world around him was spinning.

Suzume grasped onto his face with both hands, and asked, "Is something wrong?"

As her back was turned, a shadow crept along the wall behind her, coming closer and looming over her shoulder. Kaito grabbed a hold of her and spun around, taking the slash to his back. Pain seared through him as if he'd had boiling water poured down his spine. Suzume pulled away from him and shot a flaming ball of fire in the direction of their attacker.

Kaito turned and drew his own sword to face the thing, but it wasn't what he had expected. It was a young man wearing a black kimono.

"I heard about you, and the part of me that is a monster remembers," it said in a strange echoing voice, as if multiple people were speaking at once.

"What are you?" he spat.

But it didn't waste time giving an answer. Instead, it shot out black, translucent tentacles that grasped around his neck, cutting off his airway.

"We always knew you'd come looking," it crooned as the edges of Kaito's vision grew dark.

With a primal scream, Suzume launched at the creature, jabbing her flaming staff into the thing's stomach. The tentacles around his throat slackened. He wriggled his arm free to slash at a tentacle, and thick, black blood poured from it and coated him in its ichor.

It screeched and tried to escape, but Suzume's fire was consuming its entire body. The flames were growing hotter and stronger until they rose up into the sky. He collapsed onto the ground in a burning mess of foul-smelling rot.

Kaito stood over the burning corpse, panting for breath. The wound it'd inflicted was healing but slowly.

"What was that?" Suzume asked, staring in horror at the thing she'd just burned to a crisp.

"My guess is it's the new kami Amari mentioned. Though I've never seen anything like it before. It felt wrong."

"It felt like a hybrid. But not. It was stronger, and more human at first glance," Suzume said, and then she shivered. Kaito grabbed her hand, and she tensed at first before relaxing her grip against him. "You don't think the hybrids are getting stronger, do you?" she asked him.

That was exactly what he feared. If Hisato had an entire army of things like that, they'd obliterate his yokai army with ease. Their ability to wound and slow the fast-healing capabilities of yokai could be devastating. His injury didn't feel like wounds inflicted by priests, which wouldn't heal at all, but it also wasn't like a normal cut from a yokai's claws. These hybrids were dangerous.

"We need to find where they're keeping the sealed yokai and free them," Kaito said. It was easier to focus on the task at hand rather than focus on the what-ifs.

Suzume nodded and they went searching around the temple. In a vault-like room, they found hundreds of sealing stones. As soon as he entered, the cumulative power tingled over Kaito's skin. This was what they'd come for, the army that would win against Ai.

"Do you mind?" Kaito asked, gesturing at the seals.

"With pleasure," Suzume said.

She inhaled, exhaled, and then she started to sing. The notes tingled over his skin and flowed around the room. Her power had grown immensely in the past few months. It was hard to look at her as she worked and try and compare her to the girl she'd been when they first met. She had completely transformed. All around them, the sealing stones started to shake and warble, and then, one by one, they burst open with puffs of smoke. It got so thick that Kaito couldn't even see past it all. There was a large cacophony of sound and then a great burst of light. The room couldn't contain all the yokai, and the walls broke down around them.

They were standing outside, blinking into the sunlight as a whole host of yokai looked at Kaito and then at Suzume.

"How did we get here?" one of them asked.

"You were captured, and we've come to free you. There's a war rising against humans and yokai. Will you join us?" Kaito asked.

Some were quick to join, while others took more convincing, but in the end, almost all of them joined him. While Kaito convinced the yokai to fight for his cause, Suzume went and talked with the newly freed priestesses and priests. By the time Kaito had brought his new recruits to camp, Suzume was walking up with a single priestess. Seeing one recruit made his stomach sink.

"They want to join but they have conditions," Suzume said and looked at Amari, the priestess who'd come with her.

Kaito leveled a stare at the young priestess.

"What is it you want?" he asked.

"Assurance of our safety from your people." Her gaze slid past him to the yokai army gathered behind him. "And when the time comes, a chance to claim vengeance for our fallen brothers and sisters."

"Done."

FIFTEEN

The full moon illuminated the garden as Ryuu silently leapt over the wall. A guard drowsing near the entrance didn't stir as he landed lightly on the stone path. Silence hung in the air, and the house was dark, but for a single candle flickering in a nearby window. As he'd suspected, the former minister of religion was awake well past the rest of his household. It was good to know the minister's habits hadn't changed with retirement. If this meeting went awry, the fewer people that saw Ryuu, the better. His lack of access to the White Palace put him at a disadvantage to Izuki. And he couldn't risk his movements getting back to Izuki.

When he reached the porch outside the window, he stepped gingerly over the wooden floorboards and used the long shadows to conceal him until he could slide open the doors to the former governor's room and slip inside undetected. Not that it mattered; he was too absorbed in writing to notice anything else around him. Ryuu watched him for a long moment. The former governor had retired nearly a decade ago, and it'd been nearly as long since Ryuu saw him last. The transformation in that time was stark. Deep lines bracketed his mouth, wrinkles furrowed his brow, and his once-black hair was entirely silver now. Time ravaged all humans; Ryuu had grown accustomed to that. What struck him was his resemblance to Souta and the unexpected wave of guilt and grief that washed over him. The minister was Souta's descendant, his many times over grandson.

Souta never wanted immortality, but Ryuu had thrust it upon him in his greedy youth. Ryuu had lost so much before he was ever born, and feared losing his first and dearest friend. Their friendship had been strained for centuries, which was why he tried to rationalize his choice to pass the fragment onto Suzume. To accept his decision with dignity and grace. But the pain of losing him felt like a fresh wound reopened, and it took Ryuu a few moments to recompose himself and focus on the task at hand.

"Are you going to linger about in the dark all night watching an old man, or are you going to say a proper greeting," the minister said briskly, without raising his head from the documents he'd been poring over.

"I see old age hasn't dulled your perception," Ryuu said, stepping into the light. "Greetings, elder. I hope you've been well." Ryuu bowed in a respectful greeting.

The former governor glanced over at him, and a flicker of surprise passed through his canny eyes. "You haven't changed at all, and yet I have grown very old in the last ten years," he said with feigned disinterest. Then he gestured for Ryuu to take a seat across from him.

Ryuu knelt, placing his palms flat against his thighs, and didn't respond to his statement. Trusting people with the secret of his near-eternal life wasn't something he often did. But Souta's lineage was different, they had a spark few human families had. An uncanny ability of knowing. Even when he tried to hide the truth from them, generations after Souta's first death, they saw through the lies he cloaked himself in. It was why so many of them went on to become religious ministers. And it was why he continued to support them and raise them up into positions of power at court. Just as Souta, who reluctantly took on provincial roles of power, used his centuries of accumulated wealth to raise up his family in subtle, unseen ways. He'd carefully nudged them toward profitable ventures and fortuitous marriages. After a century or so, they'd given up on pretense and began sharing the truth with the heads of their house, buying their silence with their continued support.

"You might have a guess as to why I am here."

"The Governor of Osaka died months ago without a son and my cousin mysteriously was granted his position and land... I was sorry to hear of his passing; he was a good man."

Ryuu made no comment. The pain felt too raw. He hadn't come here to reminisce about Souta anyway.

"That's not why I came."

"I know your life is long, old friend, and such things must seem trivial, but your favoritism hasn't gone totally unnoticed. Claiming we are charmed or favored by the Eight can only carry us so far. Not when the court is buzzing with treasonous plots. You put a target on my family's back at a time when I have sworn to remove myself from court politics for my health. I am daily bombarded with letters asking for me to intercede from both sides."

"Perhaps I should stop meddling in your family's affairs if it causes you such hardships," Ryuu said.

"Is that a threat, or a promise? Because I must admit, I am weary."

"And yet you continue to work despite your poor health for the betterment of the country. I know you've been sending aid to the refugee temple." Ryuu took a quick glance at the documents on his desk. It looked much like Ryuu's desk of late, filled with correspondence from this governors and ministers begging him to intercede as the court continued to spiral out of control.

"My family has followed your instruction for years, thanks to the blessings you bestow upon us. But I'm not sure I have the stamina to wait out a war against a tyrant the way my grandfather did. That took years, and he was killed not long after the war was won. My father often lamented that fact, while simultaneously praising your generosity."

Ryuu hadn't forgotten the tyrant king. The current emperor's great uncle. Ryuu hadn't been involved in the running of the country then; he thought he could trust the then emperor. But it turned out he was more power-mad than he realized. Ryuu had organized the uprising to remove him from power, a war that stretched out for years. After the tyrant king, he thought he was done with politics. But he'd underestimated his own jealousy and greed. When Izuki became candidate for future empress, he'd meddled to keep her to himself. But her ambitions were too great, and he remained at court to protect her. The same cycle had played out unending and exhausting, and each time, he told himself it would be the last. And yet here he was again, planning a coup.

"The emperor has allied himself with a creature that will not only destroy our kingdom but everything we know," Ryuu said, getting back to the topic at hand.

"And there it is. You wish to thrust my family into another bloody struggle. What other allies do you have beside me? I already know Izuki outsmarted you and had you banished from court," he said.

"Too few," Ryuu said bluntly. "But those who refuse to ally with me do not know my true nature."

"Even a creature of such power as yourself cannot overturn an entire court by sheer will."

"I've done it before with more bloodshed than you can imagine. You may not believe it, but I am trying to spare lives if possible."

The old man stroked his long, silver beard and stared off into the distance for a few long moments.

He wouldn't deny him. Despite his many complaints, he wanted what was best for Akatsuki. That was why Ryuu had come here instead of the few other powerful warlords and governors who had stronger armies and more dubious loyalties. And Ryuu meant what he said, he didn't want to start a war. He wanted to remove a tyrant before he became too powerful. And take away all of Izuki's power in one fell swoop.

Finally, the old man leaned back in his seat and folded his hands on the desk in front of him.

"I've often wondered why you meddle with politics from the shadows rather than take on the role of emperor yourself."

"The people tend to distrust what they cannot understand. And an immortal emperor who does not age might instill fear and more unrest. Better to be the guiding hand that leads from the shadows."

"Is that the role you hope to take? To make the crown prince your new puppet king?"

Ryuu had considered the risks in backing the crown prince in place of his father. There were other distant relatives of the emperor who were older and might even muster a following. But he found for the most bloodless transition, placing the intended heir was best. But the crown prince was barely a man, newly married and as of yet without an heir of his own. Until his young wife had a son, they would be vulnerable to further instability. And even worse were the ministers and advisors who would take advantage of his youth and inexperience to try and take control of the capital for themselves.

"Do you wish to put forward a member of your family as the future emperor instead?" Ryuu replied.

The old man scoffed. "Our family has consolidated enough power. I fear they'd only use the power of the throne for ill."

"What do you want then?"

"I've heard rumors from the mainland of a new style of government. One where the people choose who rules. Rather than gamble with each generation or let the most cunning influence the gullible. Each minister gets a voice and bigger influence in the governance of the island."

"It sounds like a dream. But I've seen the reality of men. They'll never be able to share the power. One will try to dominate the others, and we'll be left with another dynasty of cruel tyrants."

The old man shrugged. "From where I sit, I see it as a chance to start fresh. But if you do not agree, it matters little to me. I suppose my time is winding to a close on this plane, and whether or not the emperor starts a war affects me little."

"You've spent too long with your books and have grown too sentimental if you think changing a government is as simple as making a wish."

"You would know, wouldn't you? What was it like in those early days? What made you give it all up?"

Ryuu crossed his arms over his chest. He didn't like this line of questioning. There'd been others who'd suggested he reclaim his title over the years. But he dismissed them all; power was poison. It'd destroyed his friendships and loved ones and him. He wouldn't go back to who he'd been when he'd united the clans.

"Then you will turn your back on the empire and watch it burn around you?" Ryuu asked him.

"I could ask you the same." The old man looked down his nose at Ryuu.

They were at an impasse and unless Ryuu was willing to make some concessions, they weren't going to move forward.

With a heavy sigh, he said, "I will consider supporting the crown prince in serious government reform. But it will take time, perhaps decades, to convince the ministers and royals to let go of their control."

He stroked his beard again. "The best things are worth working for. I'm glad you agree. Now that you have my support, the most important thing remains. Do you have the crown prince in hand?"

"Not yet, but I am seeking him and the empress as we speak," Ryuu admitted. He'd sent the neko out to search for him, and he felt confident if anyone could find them, it was him.

"Bring him to the palace and I shall reach out to the refugee temple and see if they will provide aid as well."

"I thank you for your help and wisdom," Ryuu said, bowing his head before exiting the way he came, hardly making a sound, moving as a shadow would.

Ryuu traveled through the rest of the night, back to the place where he and the neko had agreed to meet. When he arrived, the safe house was empty. Exhausted from the night's negotiations and haunted by his past, Ryuu flopped onto his futon. He rarely let himself rest. He'd lived his entire life looking over his shoulder, whether it was because he was hanyou, despised by both humans and yokai alike, or because he was a man in power with enemies. But tonight, he wanted the dark to swallow him whole, and for a little while to forget.

He must have been exhausted because after staring at the ceiling for a while, he drifted into a dreamless sleep. When he woke, the neko was standing over him with a sardonic twist of his mouth.

"Master, are you sleeping? What a rare sight," he commented.

"Contemplating slitting my throat as I sleep again?" Ryuu asked, while fighting the instinct to stand up and loom over his neko servant. But any sudden movements would be an admission of fear, and letting the neko know he feared him, even a little, would be his demise.

"I would never," the neko said with fake indignation, pressing a clawed hand against his chest.

"Have you found where the crown prince is being held?" he asked.

The neko nodded. "Indeed, I have. He's at a home, not too far from here, actually. But under heavy guard. His mother's family faction is trying to keep him, and his younger brother protected. Getting in and convincing them to return to the palace won't be easy.

"A coup rarely is. Let us prepare for the journey and to move him to the palace. We cannot delay on our plans."

Everything was in motion. And yet he felt doubts linger in his mind. The past seemed to cling to him like cobwebs, impossible to shake off. All he knew was the emperor and, by extension, Izuki, couldn't remain in power. While he made promises to get the former minister's help, he doubted his idyllic government's validity. Could such a future be possible? Was there a way to free himself of this endless cycle at last?

Sixteen

The army had swelled as they traveled and Kaito was busy, leaving Suzume to her own devices more often than not. After they'd freed the yokai and priestesses from the hybrid temple, adding to their numbers was easier. Lesser yokai seemed eager to join them, as if they could scent the blood thirst in the air. They were careening toward a confrontation with Ai's army. Runners from the other branches of Kaito's army were in and out with messages all hours of the day and night. There was a crackle of expectant energy in the air.

Suzume felt that same buzzing building in her, but for different reasons. Despite her gnawing curiosity, she hadn't read Kazue's diary. The thought of reading the truth terrified her. Finding out what the true beginning was felt like standing on the edge of a cliff. Dive in, and there was no turning back. To try and calm her rattled nerves, she'd been working on trying to meditate, as Ryuu so often urged her to do. She lit candles and sat in the center of her tent, concentrated on her breathing, and tried to find her center.

Outside yokai grunted and shouted orders to one another. The priestesses and priests were chanting prayers. Suzume tried to block out the sounds, but no matter how much she counted her breaths, the outside kept clawing in, burrowing into her brain until she was growling and throwing her hands up in frustration.

Standing up, she paced the perimeter of her tent. Inhale in. Exhale out. She could do this. She could force calm even if curiosity was digging fingers into her skull, begging, pleading with her to read the damn diary. She inhaled and exhaled again. Slowed her racing heart and sat back down to try again. With concentrated effort, she was able to let her mind drift. For a moment, she felt as if she were lying on a cloud, floating in space. She concentrated on that feeling and let everything else go, including the journal. She saw it in her mind's eye, buried at the bottom of her pack. It was a feeble attempt to hide it, as if being out of sight would stop her thoughts from returning to it over and over.

She tried to push the thought from her mind. Tried to think about the fluffy clouds, floating and drifting without a care. But Kazue had brought her to the journal for a reason. Hisato wanted it. Had killed for it. She shook her head. She didn't need to know about Kaito and Kazue's past. She didn't care. For all she knew, the diary was all part of some convoluted plot of Hisato's.

But even when she tried to lie to herself, she knew that wasn't the reason she was avoiding reading the journal. Because once she did, there was no turning back. Whatever destiny Kazue had planned for her, Suzume couldn't turn her back on it. And selfishly she'd been running away. Even as more and more of her soul chipped away each day. As her greed cost Hikaru a little more of his soul. As she spat in the face of Souta's sacrifice. There'd never been a chance to turn back, and she knew that from the start.

Suzume opened her eyes and scrambled across her tent, tearing apart her pack to retrieve the journal. She'd put it off for long enough. Hands shaking, she flipped open the cover and read the first line.

"My name is Fujikawa Kazue, and I sealed the Great Dragon."

Before she could read more, the tent flap flew open, and afternoon light spilled into the tent. Suzume buried the diary under her pillow before spinning around to face the yokai filling the doorway to her tent.

"What do you want?' Suzume snapped, annoyed at being interrupted as soon as she was about to read.

"Where is the Lord Dragon?" he asked slowly as if she were stupid.

"I don't know. Not here. Try the training grounds." Kaito was spending an unusual amount of time drilling the soldiers. He said he wanted them to be ready for the fight ahead, but she suspected he was avoiding her.

"Maybe you can help; you're human after all," the yokai said, ignoring her direction and apparently oblivious.

"I can't help. I'm busy," Suzume said, shooing him away with a wave of her hand.

"The humans won't listen to us. But they'll probably listen to you." He reached out to grab her by the wrist, physically dragging her out of the tent before she could protest.

She shook free of his grasp as soon as they were outside and should have singed him for the impertinence. But since he mentioned the humans, she felt obligated to investigate. She was the one who convinced them to join Kaito's army. If there was a problem, she should try and solve it. With her thoughts lingering on Kazue's diary back in the tent, she followed the yokai to the human portion of their camp. He led her through the rows of tents to the edge of the encampment, where a priest faced a boar yokai whose looming shadow engulfed him. Several more priests and priestesses stood behind him, simmering with rage. Suzume could feel the crackle of their spiritual energy as she approached.

"What's going on here?" she asked, and all eyes swiveled in her direction.

"These monsters have been sneaking into our side of the camp," the priest said, pointing an accusatory finger in their direction.

"We were told to patrol the entire camp and to keep the humans safe. Do you think I'd risk my hide going near them otherwise?" the boar yokai said with a derisive snort.

"A likely story. Yokai would never protect us. They don't even give us enough food to feed our people." The priest gestured to the people behind him.

"They're hoarding food. We've seen it," said another yokai who'd wandered over. He pointed to a tent behind the priest, and a couple of priests shuffled in front as if to block it from view.

"We're fending for ourselves. We agreed to help in this battle, but we can't live off the scraps you give us, or keep marching at this bruising pace," Amari protested, coming to the foreground.

"There isn't enough to go around as it is, and yokai need much more food than humans. You should be contributing to the group, not keeping it all for yourselves," the boar yokai roared, and took one single step.

Amari withdrew an ofuda from her sleeve and flung it at the boar yokai. Suzume lunged between them, slashing her staff through the ofuda, severing it in half. The magic in it fizzled as the pieces fell to the ground.

Both sides stared at her and the fallen charm with slack-jawed stares.

"That's enough," Suzume said in a commanding voice.

"Are you really siding with them?" Amari said, accusation in her gaze.

"I'm trying to keep you alive so you can get your revenge," Suzume said, glaring at her. "Picking a fight with these yokai won't end in your favor, trust me."

Amari glared at her, hands balled into fists at her side. Suzume hadn't noticed before just how young the priestess was. She'd seemed so poised and in control when they first met, but on closer inspection, she wasn't much older than Suzume. A young woman in way over her head. Suzume could relate.

"How can we work with them when we fear for our lives?" Amari asked.

Suzume sighed and rubbed her temple with her forefinger. She'd been just like her before. But how could she assuage her fears when it'd taken months and multiple close calls before she trusted even a few yokai? They didn't have the time, nor the patience, to keep breaking apart these fights. Maybe she couldn't convince them to fully trust yokai. But they had come to fight a common enemy.

"Do you trust me?" she asked.

Amari jutted out her chin again and said begrudgingly, "I suppose."

"Then trust me when I say, if anyone lays a hand on a single one of you, they'll face my wrath." She held up a ball of fire to punctuate her point. A small crowd of yokai had gathered around, and she met each of their eyes as she said it. They'd heard rumors of her power before or seen it in action. Putting it on display now would send the right message, and force the yokai to back off the humans or else.

"That's all well and good, but we should have equal representation in these war plans. I heard a rumor we're marching into a fight with some other yokai warlord?" the priest said.

"We are." Suzume nodded in confirmation.

"That's not what we agreed to," Amari said, narrowing her eyes in suspicion once again.

"It's necessary. Ai is an ally of Hisato's, and we need to eliminate her, or Hisato and his hybrid army will be too powerful."

The priests and priestesses shared a few loaded looks amongst themselves.

"If we're going to fight, then we want a representative at the dragon's war meetings. We've seen him consulting the yokai leaders. We should be involved as well if our lives are on the line."

"I'll tell the dragon." Suzume sighed. "Anything else?"

"And we want to patrol and protect ourselves. No more yokai skulking about."

She looked to the boar yokai, who was scowling and seemed ready to interject, but she cut him off before he could. "Understood," she said. "Who would you elect as your representative then?" she asked as her gaze roamed over the assembled humans. They wouldn't meet her gaze as they scuffed the ground with their shoes.

Suzume planted her hands on her hips. "You can't have a voice if you're too afraid to face the dragon," Suzume said.

"Who's too afraid to face me?"

Suzume looked over her shoulder and found Kaito standing behind her, glowering at the crowd that'd gathered. The priests and priestesses reeled back at the sight of him.

"The priests and priestesses have some concerns about the yokai stalking around their side of the camp. And they want a voice in your counsels if they're going to fight for you."

Kaito looked them over and nodded. "Then you'll be their voice."

Suzume flapped her arms. "Why me?"

"Because my counsel already knows you and respects you, and you're actively working as their intermediary as we speak."

A flush burned across her face. That was far from the truth. The council didn't respect her. They tolerated her. But she wasn't going to correct him in front of this crowd of onlookers.

"Then, if all that is settled." He pressed his palm to the flat of her back and guided her away.

The matter was far from resolved, she was sure. But it was enough to keep tensions simmering rather than boiling over for now. She didn't want to threaten his authority with a crowd looking on and waited until they were alone in the tent to confront him.

"This isn't going to work the way you think it will," she said to Kaito once they were alone.

He crossed his arms over his chest as he said, "We've dealt with some growing pains, but nothing we can't deal with, surely."

"Yokai and humans naturally don't trust one another; how are they supposed to fight together?"

"We have a common enemy. I've brought warring clans together on the battlefield to great success. You don't need to worry about it."

He reached out to brush a hair behind her ear, but she recoiled. He wasn't listening. The same fears she'd had since she first committed to loving him were resurfacing and she worried it would always remain as a thorn between them. Why else would he have been so distant lately?

Kaito crossed his arms over his chest. "What?"

"You can't simply brush this all under the rug. The distrust will only fester and get worse."

"Are we still talking about the humans and the yokai, or are we talking about us? Have you been reading Kazue's diary and decided I'm scum after all?" he asked.

It felt as if he'd punched her in the gut. She hadn't read the diary, but she'd been thinking about it. A lot.

"For your information. I haven't read it yet. What are you afraid I'm going to find out? Is that why you're avoiding me?"

Ice frosted over his gaze. "What do you hope you will find out? Do you think she had the answers? She was a scared woman who feared death and defied the gods, and betrayed me to gain immortality. You don't need to read her diary to find that out. I know exactly what sort of person she was."

"But she told me to return to the beginning. There must be an answer to defeat Hisato in her diary."

"And if the answer is sealing me back up? What will you do?" he asked, his eyes blazing.

Suzume clenched her hands into fists and felt the spark of flame arch against her palm. She wanted to slap him for insinuating she'd ever hurt him to stop Hisato. Especially when it was obvious he'd be the one to abandon her first if it suited his ambitions. The same way he'd hidden away Kazue to avoid a scandal.

"I thought you knew me better than this," she said.

Before Kaito could respond, the flap to their tent opened, and Shin, Kaito's general, poked his head in. His branch of the army must have arrived.

"Sorry, was I interrupting?" he asked.

Kaito turned his back on Suzume and walked toward him.

"Not at all. Do you have something to report?"

"We've gotten word on Ai's location. The oni are a day away, and if we can organize the two flanks of our arm, we can surround her and claim a victory."

"Summon the generals. We need to make plans." Kaito stormed out without a backward glance at her.

She watched him go, her stomach churning with frustration and nowhere to direct it. She clenched her fists so hard they ached, fighting the urge to pick things up and throw them at the tent door. Not that it would make much difference. She turned around to her bed and where the diary was hidden under her pillow, as if taunting her. She sank down onto the futon and picked up the diary once more.

It was nothing but bits of paper and ink, yet she felt a pulsing energy emanate from it. Whatever Kaito feared she might read, no matter how it might change them, she had to know.

As Suzume read, she heard Kazue's voice echo in her mind.

"I sealed Kaito, and I don't regret it. In this world, there must always be balance. Great ambition takes sacrifice. To obtain what I desired, I had to give up the person I loved most." Suzume lowered the book into her lap and stared at the door Kaito had just stormed through then kept on reading.

"In case my plan fails, I've put in safeguards. This diary is one of them. I've documented every place and person I crossed along my journey to immortality. For a human to gain immortality spits in the very face of the gods. And yet I would move heaven and earth to protect our child and maybe one day get Kaito back. If he can ever forgive me."

Suzume closed the book, the weight of the emotions written in those pages for a moment overwhelmed her. She felt a deep aching in her chest, a phantom pain belonging to Kazue. If she read more of this diary, would it awaken Kazue within her again? Would she lose herself to the force inside her?

She'd already gone this far; there was no turning back now. Suzume reopened the diary and flipped to the next page. There were detailed drawings of spider lilies around what seemed to be a map. She squinted at the details.

"This is where I betrayed him. This is where it began," the inscription read.

She flipped through the rest of the pages, devouring the written accounting of Kazue's life on her journey to immortality. She mentioned the gods she met, the deals she made, and the betrayals she inflicted on those closest to her. But her mind kept going back to that first page. The map of the place where it all began.

If it ended at the temple where Kazue had left Kaito, then the next clue must mean returning to the place she betrayed Kaito.

SEVENTEEN

Their destination was a pile of old stones, remnants of a long-ago decayed structure. When Rin first spotted the crumbled remains, her heart dropped into her stomach as she checked and rechecked her map. This was the place that they were supposed to go. But it looked as if no one had been there in centuries. The kamigakari must have been wrong; the keepers must be long gone, and with them, the answers she desperately sought.

"I think we've reached a dead end," Rin said. "Maybe we should return to Kaito and the others. Look for another way..."

But Hikaru didn't seem to hear her; he was wandering through the runes, turning over rocks and picking up pieces of rotted wood while turning them over in his hands as if they held some answer. Fear gripped her like an icy hand at the back of her neck.

"Hikaru?" she asked, her throat tight with fear.

He didn't respond to her call, and she took a step toward him as he wandered through the long grass that grew through the rubble. She was struck by the sudden realization that she might be losing him. Despite separating him from Suzume, he was still fading. The nightmares hadn't gotten better, and at times, he seemed more and more distant. His gaze was often lost on some far-off point only he could see. He stopped at a jutting column of stone, thrust upward as if defying nature and the decay of time. He pressed his hand against the weathered stone.

"Hikaru!" Rin ran, closing the distance between them, and grasped hold of his upper arm.

He startled and turned to her, eyes clear and alert. "I think I've been here before," he said.

"That's impossible," Rin replied.

He knelt down on the ground, pressing his ear to the earth at the base of the broken column.

"What are you doing?" she asked in bewilderment, kneeling down beside him. Torn between pulling him away and indulging this strange certainty that had overcome him.

"The earth here is hollow, and I can feel a faint trace of power down deep," he said as he pressed his palm against the ground as he studied the earth.

When Rin concentrated she too felt a faint echo of power. But it could very well be the last remnants of some ancient creature who'd died long ago.

"What did you mean when you said you've been here before?" she asked.

He blinked at her, his gaze unfocused before he shook his head. "It wasn't me who has been here before. But Kazue."

Her name hung in the air between them. But a new hope also surged in her chest. Hikaru placed his hands on the ground, and it rumbled under her feet, then groaned. A hole in the ground opened up, and he leapt backward to avoid it. A dust cloud choked the air, and when it cleared, they saw a stone stairway descending downward into darkness.

"See, I remembered these stairs. The keepers are at the bottom, I bet," Hikaru said with a boyish grin.

Before he could scurry down the steps, she grasped hold of his arm once more. "Do you remember anything else? What the keepers are like?"

The smile faded, and he shook his head slowly. "I don't." He scooped Rin's hands in his. "If you don't want to, we don't have to go down there. We can return to Suzume and the others like you suggested. Forget this quest..."

Rin squeezed his hands and bit back the accusations. Is that what he wanted? To be closer to Suzume? She knew the bonds between them were pulling tight like threads. They were already living on borrowed time. They'd always been on borrowed time. She was immortal, and he wasn't. But she wasn't willing to give him up. Not now, possibly not ever.

"Let's go."

Hands threaded together, they walked down the steps. The light slowly faded as they made their descent. And as the moss-covered stone walls closed in around, Rin lit a ball of fox fire and held it out to guide them.

A thick layer of dust covered the steps. Each step they took disturbed it and sent thick clouds into the air that clogged her throat and made her cough. And still, they descended, down and down, as if they were reaching into the very bottom of the world. The deeper she went, the more the spiritual pressure she'd mistaken for a trace of ancient magic revealed itself—not faded but buried down deep. Something ancient and powerful lived at the bottom of this chasm. She hoped it was friendly.

It could have been hours they walked. Rin lost track of time in the dark. The end of stairs and the glowing orange light of a doorway came as a shock. They stepped through it and into a cavernous, empty room but for two braziers flanking, and a door hewn into the stone itself. The power she sensed before was all around her, as if they'd stepped into the innards of a great and powerful beast.

The door had no knobs or hinges, but a seam in the stone. It was worn smooth, as if touched by thousands beforehand. They approached it, staring at it for several long minutes, puzzling how to get through. Then Hikaru pressed his palms flat against it, and the door shuddered before slowly opening. It scraped across the stone floor, as if it hadn't moved in a very long time and had warped since. It revealed a second, larger room, this one filled floor to ceiling with shelves of books. The scent of paper and ink was almost overwhelming to her senses, as was the pulsating power which centered in the room.

It was deadly silent, and their footsteps echoed loudly as they walked between shelves toward a glowing light from which the power seemed to emanate. A hunched-over creature sat at a desk and did not look up even when they were standing over it.

"What are you doing here?" snapped the yokai, without glancing from the parchment he was scribbling on.

"Are you the keeper?" Rin asked.

"That's a stupid question to ask," the yokai said, stabbing his brush against his paper before finally looking up at her for the first time. His eyes were bulbous, taking up most of his face, and were milky white. His skin was pale, as if he'd never seen the sunlight before.

"We've come here seeking information; perhaps you could help us?" she said.

"When the earth was nothing, but the Eight's immortal playground, and the first children were freshly born, they created us to record the history of the world. Everything that has ever happened or ever will happen is seen through our eyes."

Rin looked at Hikaru, not sure how to respond. "Is that a yes?"

The keeper sighed and resumed scribbling on the paper in front of him.

"Is there someone else here that we could talk to?" Hikaru asked.

"Another stupid question," he replied. "Isn't it obvious there's no one else left but me?"

"You live here all alone? For how long?"

"Don't waste your pity on me. It is my duty to record the history of yokai. Though time has scattered my kind, our work does not cease. So many yokai, so many stories left to record..."

"I see you are busy, so if you would merely let us search through your records for what we're looking for..."

He stopped again and narrowed large, bulbous eyes at her. "One could spend a lifetime searching these halls and find nothing. If that is what you wish to pursue, I cannot fault you seeking knowledge." He waved them away, and it was as much permission as they were ever going to get.

They each took a side and started searching through the stacks. But it didn't take long before Rin realized that the keeper hadn't exaggerated when he said sifting through these stacks could take a lifetime. The first couple of rows dated all the way back to the time when the Eight first established Akatsuki. Finding records a thousand years after that took her hours, so trying to find the age Kazue lived might take years. But she was determined to find the answers. She read book after book until her eyes were blurry, and she lost all sense of time and space. It might have been hours or days she searched, but she read endless accountings of yokai movements over the centuries without seeing any hint of hybrids or anything useful.

Properly defeated, she went in search of Hikaru, hoping he had found something. He was leaning against the stacks of books, his head slumping forward onto his chest. She shook him lightly, and he roused, turning to look in all directions.

"I think we need the keeper's help if we're going to find out any information," she said.

Hikaru yawned. "I think you're right."

They returned to the keeper, who hadn't moved from the spot where they left him. If he heard them approach a second time he didn't give any indication. He was absorbed in writing on the paper in front of him, and he wouldn't tear his eyes away from it.

"If we might beg of you a favor," Rin said, trying to catch his attention.

"You may not," he replied.

"It is rather urgent; lives are at stake."

"It isn't my job to save lives. My job is to merely record them. I've recorded the memories of a thousand yokai from all ages since the dawn of time in these halls. But you think that your petty matters are urgent?" he said with a curling lip of disdain.

"This is about the destruction of Akatsuki," Rin said, her voice rising with her growing frustration. It echoed through the massive room and returned her own voice, mocking her desperation.

The keeper shook his head. "Many things have threatened Akatsuki, but nothing has destroyed it. Ever. Even with the Eight gone, we remain."

"But you're all that's left; what happened to the others?" she asked.

He stopped again and looked at her. "Some left. Others got sick. We closed the doors and locked them out, but nothing stopped it. Until only I remained."

"When was that?

"Five hundred years ago."

Rin felt a fluttering in her chest. It couldn't be a coincidence. When Kazue bound the Eight, the yokai had started to disappear. She'd heard rumors of instability. Yokai destroying yokai. She'd always assumed outside the protection of the temple she and Hikaru had served at that the world was dangerous and cruel. But what if it had been something else? What if Kazue had set into motion the events that had changed the world for the worse?

"Is there a way to bring the kami back?" Rin asked.

She seemed to have his full attention now. He studied her with curiosity. "The one who sealed them has to break their seal."

"Which means the pieces of Kazue's soul," Rin said hopefully.

"No. Not pieces. The Whole."

Rin felt her chest swell. They were on the right track. "And is there a way to remove the pieces of a soul bound with another?"

The memory keeper narrowed his eyes at them. "Nothing comes without a price. You want answers you'll have to pay something."

Rin bristled. "What do you want exactly?"

He gestured around the room. "Something to complete my collection. Memories, history..."

"You can have my memories," Rin said without hesitation.

He scoffed. "I have kitsune memories in excess. But what I have yet to include is a hanyou." He looked at Hikaru with a greedy gleam in his eye.

She felt suddenly defensive and put herself in front of Hikaru. "What do you want with him?" she asked.

He flapped his hand. "I won't hurt him, don't worry. Just a quick skim off the top."

Rin and Hikaru shared a look. He nodded and put a reassuring hand on her shoulder. "Don't worry. It's a small price to pay."

She heaved a sigh. What could she do if he was willing?

"Alright." He stepped aside. The creature came around and pressed his long, skeletal thumb and forefinger against Hikaru's forehead, while humming something under his breath.

A thin, silver strand of energy coiled out as his hand moved away. Rin and Hikaru stared at it wide-eyed as it fell out of him.

"There we are," said the yokai.

He put the thread in a jar, which he tucked into his sleeve. "As to your question. The one who would best answer it is also like me, the last of her kind. She has the skill and knowledge of such things that even my records cannot answer."

"Who is she?" Rin asked.

"The woman who created the weapon which captured the kami. Only she knows how to undo what's been done."

"Then you took payment for nothing?" Rin groused.

"No. No. Only I can tell you where to find her. Because she has been sealed away from the eyes of man and yokai alike. Like the rest of her kin. And only one other has come looking for these answers. The woman whose soul is lodged in yours." He looked long at Hikaru again, as if he was seeing through him.

"Then tell us, where is she?" Rin snarled.

He hurried down the hallway and was gone for several long minutes before he brought back a yellowing scroll. "Yes, here it is." He rolled it out between Rin and Hikaru, then ran his hand along it. "Here. The maiden in the mountain. Go to her and find the answers you seek."

It was a half-answer at best, but it was better than nothing, she supposed. Rin bowed her thanks to the keeper, and they left.

"Anything hurt?" she asked Hikaru as they made their ascent.

He shook his head. "I'm fine. I don't even know what he took."

"Good." Rin stared up at the long climb ahead of them. She hoped they weren't on some wild goose chase and that their next destination would yield answers. But what choice did they have but to keep pushing forward? She wouldn't stop until she knew Hikaru was safe.

Eighteen

Her dreams were filled with fields of spider lilies, their delicate red petals swaying in the wind. And when Suzume woke in the morning, it felt like a weight was resting on her chest. Kaito wasn't in bed when she got up, just as he hadn't been there when she'd fallen asleep. Kaito had stopped even going through the motions of seeing her. They were both so absorbed in their individual tasks: him with the confrontation with Ai just days away, and her acting as liaison to the humans. She'd been running back and forth, passing messages between the priests and priestesses they'd freed and the yokai counsel that consulted Kaito on battle plans. She needed to tell him about what she'd read in the diary, but they were never alone long enough for her to bring it up, and she feared that was by design.

The charged energy that had been prickling over her skin for days began to feel more like a pot boiling over. The pieces were set up on the board, and Suzume knew she was a key player in Kaito's plans in the upcoming battle. But though her powers had grown, her mind continued to drift even during practice.

She couldn't shake the feeling that she shouldn't be here. In this tent, in this field. If all it took was an army to defeat Hisato, then Kazue would have told her as much; there wouldn't be a need for this cryptic search for clues. There was something deeper, some hidden tool Kazue had left her.

Her hand drifted to Kazue's diary and flipped it open to the page with the spider lilies. She'd read it back to front, hoping to find an alternative solution, some hidden message that would reveal how to defeat Hisato. But the diary wasn't that different than any other. Pages were filled with the thoughts, regrets, and daily life of Kazue. It chronicled her meeting with Noaki, Tsuki, and Akira. She wrote several entries on her fears and misgivings about becoming a mother, and then the birth of her son, how she left him in Rin and Hikaru's care before making final preparations to tear her soul apart. These things Suzume already knew, and reading them from her perspective felt more like an invasion of her privacy than some great insight or guide as to how to defeat Hisato.

Over and over, Suzume kept returning to the first page, the one with the spider lilies. No other page in the diary had such detailed illustrations. This had to be the beginning Kazue referred to. And now she simply had to convince Kaito to take her there. Because while the page had detailed illustrations, there was no indication of where it was located. She told herself that she would wait until after the battle with Ai. But with each passing day, finding the truth felt more urgent. More necessary, as if some calamity might befall them if she didn't follow this instinct. Suzume slammed the diary shut once more and stood up. She had to tell Kaito now, before she had more second thoughts.

She exited her tent and went in search of Kaito in the training yard and found him watching over soldiers' drills. His back was to her, but when she took a step toward him, he swiveled to face her as if they were tethered by an invisible thread. He smiled at her, but there was a wariness to that smile. And as his gaze swept across the gathered yokai, he seemed to measure his next move. Suzume held her breath, wondering if he'd turn away from her to busy himself with some task or another. Then he strode over to her, and the knot in her chest untangled just a little.

Kaito pulled her into a tight embrace, strong arms enveloping her. "I came in late, and you were already sleeping, and then I was needed..." he murmured an excuse against her hair.

"That's alright. I've missed you," she said against his chest. And it was true. Ever since she'd found Kazue's diary, he'd been distant and cold. Or maybe it was even before that on the tengu mountain. It felt like ever since they'd gone on this warpath, they'd been orbiting around one another, just out of reach. Perhaps they'd always been destined to be this way, hopelessly entangled, unable to escape, but also unable to come together. Just like him and Kazue. The thought sat like a stone in her stomach.

"It'll be over soon," Kaito said.

"Mmm," she replied. The words she needed to say were tangled in her throat.

"I hope the humans aren't giving you too much trouble?" he asked.

She tensed at his words but tried to bite back any irritation at his insinuation that humans were the problem driving a wedge between them.

"They're fine," she replied.

"But there's something on your mind?"

"I read Kazue's diary," she blurted. And gods it felt good to let it out finally. She didn't realize how much that secret had been festering in her chest until she did.

His entire body stiffened, and he pulled away from her.

"Oh?"

"I read it and realized what she meant by go 'back to the beginning.' She wanted us to go to the place she sealed you. That's where everything started…" Suzume trailed off upon seeing the thunderous look on his face.

"She said that in her diary?" Kaito asked, raising one skeptical eyebrow.

"No, but she referred to that place as the beginning in her diary, and there were drawings of spider lilies, and now all my dreams are filled with them. You could take me there? I think she left a message for me. Like the diary from the temple." The words poured out of her in a rush.

"We don't have time for a detour right now. We located Ai and we need to focus on our energy on that," he said, and the words hung in the air between them.

"Then let's go after," Suzume said, offering an olive branch of compromise. Though in her gut, she knew it wasn't right. It had to be before. Not after.

Kaito simply shook his head. "It's best to forget about the diary and focus on what we can control: growing an army and marching for the palace."

"If all we needed was an army, don't you think Kazue would have done that? Hisato cannot be defeated by anything except her magic. We need whatever tool she's offering us."

"I've entertained this foolishness enough!" Kaito roared.

Suzume's mouth slammed shut. He'd threatened and shouted before. They'd argued and postured, but he'd never made her feel as small and insignificant as he did in that moment.

Kaito must have realized his mistake because he reached out for her, trying to bridge the gap that was growing ever larger between them. But Suzume shrugged off his touch.

"You're right. Forget I said anything," Suzume said.

And while she could argue and rage, try to cajole him into seeing it her way, she just felt tired. Kaito was absorbed in his battle plans and couldn't see beyond that. Hisato was just another item on his way back to ruling over Akatsuki as he once did. Finding out the answers to Kazue's cryptic riddles didn't matter to him like it did to her. And that was when Suzume realized that asking him was the wrong approach. It'd always been her task and hers alone. She had to find the truth alone.

He stared at her with a conflicted expression, his hand flexing by his side. Then he said, "Go rest. We're leaving in the morning."

She nodded and strode away from him, making a show of heading back to their tent. Then when she was certain his attention was elsewhere, she made a detour to the larger tent they reserved for meetings amongst the generals. She'd prepared excuses if she happened to find anyone inside but was lucky to arrive when it was empty.

The map was spread out across the table. Figures were placed in strategic locations across it. Kaito's battle plans. She didn't have any concrete plans; she never did. She trusted her gut and it was telling her she'd know the place if she saw it on the map. Maybe Kazue would guide her through the soul fragment inside her. She looked over the map for a few moments, but the lines of topography, roads, rivers, and villages looked like nothing but lines. Suzume stared at it until her vision started to blur, and it began to resemble a field of spider lilies.

It couldn't be, could it? Doing a double take, she pulled out Kazue's diary that she now kept with her at all times. She compared Kazue's sketch to the map on the table and found one place where the drawing overlapped with the lines on the map. What she'd mistaken for crossed stems and petals were lines on a map, and at their center, two rivers intersected, surrounding a circled location. Her heart fluttered in her chest. It couldn't be a coincidence. That must be the place where Kaito had hidden Kazue, and she'd sealed him. That was where she had to go.

It wasn't far away either, just over the hill and a short walk from her current location. The painful tug yanking at her chest must have been Kazue trying to lead her to the next destination along her quest. She'd felt this longing growing stronger with each passing day. She'd tried to ignore it but seeing it written in front of her in black and white, she could no longer deny the truth. Either fate or sheer dumb luck had brought her here, and she had to seize this opportunity.

The tent flap opened, and with it, a bright beam of light. Suzume spun around, expecting to see Kaito filling the doorway. Instead, she found Shin, his general, watching her with an odd expression.

"I came to deliver a message from Amari," Suzume said.

"Oh?" He didn't pry further, and Suzume seized her opportunity to push past him.

"What about the note?" he asked before she could escape out the door.

"Uh-I forgot, I already delivered it to Kaito. My mistake." She ran out the door before he could question her further.

She fast-walked back to her tent, where she gathered a few things for her journey. Her staff, some candles, incense, and water. The longing inside her was only growing stronger as she made preparations. She stood and slung her staff and pack over her shoulder and then lingered a moment. If she were lucky, Kaito wouldn't notice her missing before she returned, but just in case, she wrote him a note letting him know where she'd gone and begged him not to send a search party after her.

Note written, she headed out the door and through the camp. She moved with purpose to the human end of the camp, where no one would suspect her reason for being there. But as she got closer, she walked between tents and out into the forest which surrounded their camp. She needed to go in the opposite direction, so she had to double back and walk past the camp's perimeter. She kept her pace quick and determined, fighting the urge to look over her shoulder and see if she'd been spotted leaving. With any luck, anyone who saw her would think she was on important business and not think anything of it.

At the top of the rise, the sun fell down on her skin, and she felt it warm her inside, reinvigorating her and urging her forward on her task. The walk was long but not too difficult. By the time she reached her destination, the sun was low on the horizon but not quite dusk. The call of Kazue's power was drawing her to the place, and she didn't need to reference a map to know she was getting closer.

Around a bend, she spotted the small, crumbling building. It stood in the middle of an empty field of leafy green plants she recognized as spider lilies yet to bloom. Even if she hadn't recognized it from the map, the feeling of the place was right. As if she'd paced this way a million times before. Realizing it was Kazue's memories once more bubbling to the surface, a deep ache settled in Suzume's chest.

The door was stuck open and inside was dust and debris. Suzume slipped through the crack left by the broken door and stood in the center of the room. Any furniture or personal items that might once had been there were long deteriorated. But she could see it all in her mind's eye. The hearth where Kazue cooked. The place where she'd rolled out her futon that she sometimes shared with Kaito. This had been Kazue's home, but it had also been her prison. Suzume sifted through the rubble, hoping to find some clue or relic that Kazue had led her here on purpose. But as the darkness closed in and nothing revealed itself, Suzume started to suspect that she'd impulsively left without reason. Maybe Kaito was right. Maybe Kazue was leading her on a wild goose chase or, worse, trying to force her into a deeper connection to steal her life once again.

She plopped down onto the ground in defeat. It would be wise to head back, before sunset and before Kaito noticed her missing, but she'd been so sure this was the answer that giving up now felt like a waste.

"What is it you wanted me to learn from this?" Suzume asked the wind. "What is the point of all of this?"

There was no answer, of course. Then, a thought struck her. One that should have been obvious from the start. Kazue didn't exist in this plane of existence. She was somewhere outside Suzume's reach. But she was there inside her, and she merely had to reach her.

Ryuu had warned her against going into the spirit realm unguided and she knew the risks she faced in doing so. But she knew deep in her gut that was what she was meant to do.

She had to enter the spirit realm to find the answers from Kazue herself.

NINETEEN

Kaito had been poring over maps and making plans for so long his eyes ached in their sockets, and the words coming out of Shin's mouth were garbled as if being spoken under water. His mind kept drifting back to Suzume as he delivered the latest report. He regretted how he'd spoken to her and wished he could take the words back. The diary made him feel as if she'd sliced open an old wound, and every mention of it felt as if she were rubbing salt into it. He should have listened, considered her plan. Maybe when the battle was done they could go together. Perhaps it would be healing for him to return to that place and look into the face of the past he'd been running from since the seal broke.

"Have you been listening to a word I said?" Shin asked.

"Repeat that last part?" Kaito said, rubbing his tired eyes.

"I was saying everything is in place. But are you? You've been distracted..."

If Shin noticed, the soldiers might have sensed it and taken it for uncertainty. Bringing the humans into the fold of his army had been a gamble, one he hoped paid off. But as it were, he felt like he was trying to contain a storm in a bottle, and cracks were starting to form. He only needed to keep them together a little while longer, just until the threat of Ai and her army were eliminated. He hoped his make-shift army would stand up to the test. At dawn the day after tomorrow, they'd find out.

"I'm fine. Tired is all. Let the men rest; they'll need it for the battle ahead."

Shin placed a hand on Kaito's shoulder and squeezed. "Go and talk to her. I saw her come by looking for you just before our meeting. I think she wants to smooth things over as much as you do."

Kaito nodded and excused himself to go and seek out Suzume. The light of the dying day was falling behind the tents, the day's preparations had gotten away from him, and he realized he should have gone and apologized sooner. Yokai were gathered around cook fires, murmuring to one another. As he went, Kaito stopped by and gave encouraging words to the soldiers to try and boost spirits. He felt the apprehension and excitement simmering in the camp. Some had fought with him in the last war, but most were too young to remember. He needed their love and trust to make it through the battle ahead. And maybe he was stalling just a bit. Apologizing wasn't easy for him, but he wanted to be better. For her. For them.

Realizing he'd dallied long enough, he returned to their tent. His hand was on the tent flap when Shin came jogging up him. Concern painted his face.

"What is it?" Kaito asked.

"Bad news. Ai's army is marching toward us right now."

Apologies would have to wait. Kaito swore and dropped the tent flap, turning to join Shin. The element of surprise was their trump card, and if Ai caught them unawares, it might turn the tide of battle against them.

"Ring the alarm, get everyone to arms at once," Kaito said.

Shin ran off to do his bidding as Kaito went to tell Suzume about the change of plans. He threw back the tent flap, expecting her to be up and ready to fight, but it was unnaturally quiet within. There was a lump of blankets balled up on their futon, and he approached it, hoping she was sleeping heavily or was still mad and giving him the cold shoulder. He reached out to nudge the pile, but his hand flattened them down. Suzume wasn't there.

He tried to convince himself she must be with the humans, but despite those rational reassurances, he ran outside, a knot of panic tightening in his throat. The camp was in chaos, yokai rushed to put on armor and grab weapons. Running past them, and ignoring questions flung his way, he stormed up to the priests and priestesses who were gathered together, their leader Amari passing out ofuda by the stack.

"Where is Suzume?" he roared, drawing the attention of the priestesses and priests who circled around him, their spiritual charged ofuda crackling with power.

"I was about to ask you the same thing. We heard we're under attack, but she hasn't come to lead us as she promised she would." Amari glared at him. "Did you trick us?"

The priests and priestesses were closing in around him. He felt their power licking over him like fire, and it took all his self-control to not lash out at them. If she wasn't there, where was she?

"She's preparing for the battle ahead," Akane said, stepping up with her hands in the air to show she wasn't a danger to the priestesses.

Amari didn't look convinced. "And who are you?"

"My name is Akane. I was once a temple guardian. I've come to lead you in the battle."

The rest of their conversation turned to a buzzing in his ears. His thoughts were roaring with concern for Suzume. Kaito left Akane to deal with the humans and continued his hunt for her. He spread out his senses, searching for her as he should have done from the start. But beneath all the chaos, he could not feel her anywhere. It was as if she'd simply disappeared in a puff of smoke. Had Ai gotten hold of her? Would he soon be receiving a ransom note?

Metal clanged, and the shouts of the two armies colliding rocked through the forest. Kaito roared in answer, flexing dragon claws and letting his body stretch as his dragon form threatened to take over. He was about to launch into the air and search for her when Shin ran over to him.

"This wasn't the plan. Your army needs you," he said. "You can't go rushing into danger to find her. We do it how we planned."

Kaito saw red, frustration coiling around him, making him desperate and impulsive. But if Ai had taken Suzume as he suspected, that was exactly what she wanted from him, to make stupid mistakes. Kaito nodded and then flew into the air, leading his army with a roaring battle cry. The army began swarming up the hill and out of the forest where they clashed with Ai's army sneaking up the hill from the other side.

Shin and his mate Akane had transformed into their wolf forms and were tearing apart a group of yokai under Ai's control, cutting a path through which the other the priestesses and priests could follow. Their ofuda flew through the air as the song of their holy spells burned on the breeze, freezing yokai in place or setting them ablaze. Kaito watched it all from a distance. His eyes scanned the horizon for Suzume, hoping beyond reason he'd see her in the fray, but saw no sign of her anywhere.

He was holding back from unleashing an icy blast onto Ai's side for fear of inadvertently hurting her. But as he flew overhead, flinging ice and shouting orders, the battle was turning bloody. They were losing more people on his side, and Ai's army was advancing. If he held back much longer, they'd be forced to retreat. Unable to sense Suzume nearby, he gave himself permission to unleash his full power and rained down icy shards upon his enemies. Archers shot arrows at him, which he dodged and weaved through the clouds to avoid. The priests and priestesses were coming up from the back, hurling their magic, which exploded in the midst of the enemy, filling the air with the stench of burnt hair and leaving a tingle of spiritual power against his skin.

Then he saw Ai, tentacles wrapped around one of his yokai soldiers, tossing them through the air as if they were a child's toy. She was surrounded by a mixed group of both sides, and if he shot ice toward her, they'd take casualties, and it would give her a chance to escape. So he swooped down low, taking up the sword slashing and hacking at his enemies in his path to her. A thousand small skirmishes surrounded him as Kaito swung, cutting his way toward the center where he sensed Ai and her power coiled like a giant serpent. She was a massive, black shadow over the battlefield, wielding her tentacles to sweep away any who would come near her, while also slowly suffocating those who dared get close.

Kaito searched those tentacles for Suzume but found no sign of her, which was both a relief and a source of anxiety. If the last words he ever said to her were angry, he'd never forgive himself. Kaito ran through a nearby soldier and left him bleeding out on the field of battle, clearing the final path to Ai.

"It's time we ended this, Ai!" Kaito shouted up toward her.

The dark, undulating mass that was her true form turned toward him. It squeezed his soldiers in front of him until they popped and sprayed him with gore. Kaito didn't flinch nor look away.

"You will learn your place at last, Kai." Ai roared and rushed toward him.

Kaito once more transformed into his true dragon-self and took to the air, but her large tentacles wrapped around his body, pulling him back toward the ground. He twisted in her grasp, biting into her flesh and thrashing about as she wrestled with him. Her tentacles coiled tighter and tighter, attempting to squeeze the life out of him, little by little.

Darkness danced around the edge of his vision. He unleashed a burning cold that came from the deepest core of his power, expending more of his magic than he normally would. It frosted over her tentacles, and she screamed as the burning cold fused her to his skin, preventing her from removing herself from him. As she thrashed, Kaito lurched forward in her grasp, biting at her face and tearing at her torso with his claws. Thick, black blood oozed from the wounds and slowed her down. Ai thrust her tentacle, reshaped like a blade into his shoulder.

She yanked her tentacle back for another strike, and blood poured from his wound. His left arm hung useless at his side. Kaito stumbled forward and swung again at her. She landed another strike, this time grazing against his stomach. The loss of blood pulled on the deep reserves of his power, making him weak and his healing slow. He was starting to feel woozy, and the edges of his vision were dancing with stars.

"You were a fool to challenge my authority; your time has come to an end," Ai crowed.

Kaito saw the triumph in her face and knew she was going to try and kill him. All this struggle, all the centuries of waiting to reclaim what he lost, all of it to end like this. As she gloated, she exposed her underbelly. Kaito saw his opening and thrust upward, striking her in her heart. Her eyes widened as the strike landed, and she looked at him in shock and horror. Black ichor foamed on her lips before she slumped against him. Ice crusted over her as her life bled from her body. Then Kaito shook her off and stared down at the remnants of what once had been his mistress and friend. All around him, the battle was coming to an end. His army had won and those that continued to fight would run or be put to oath to serve him.

Now that the battle was won, nothing else mattered to Kaito but finding Suzume. He was leaking blood from his many wounds that had yet to heal, but even as he stumbled around, spreading out his senses searching for her, he couldn't sense her. Panic had him in a vice grip, and he feared the worst: that she'd died before the battle had begun. Surely, he would have felt it or heard her scream. Suzume wouldn't go down without a fight. There would be a body.

He stumbled off the field of battle, knowing his generals would take charge of capturing prisoners and seeing to their wounded and dead. So, he searched, turning over the bodies of humans and yokai alike, searching for her on the battlefield. Shin came up to him once more.

"The army wants to hear from you now that the battle is won."

"I cannot find Suzume," Kaito said, looking at his friend, who watched him with a wary expression.

"I've been asking around, and someone saw her leaving just before the battle, traveling through the forest."

Kaito felt a sweep of relief quickly followed by anger. She'd gone looking for the place Kazue had sealed him, without him. How she had found the place, he didn't know. But he'd know they were uncomfortably close. Maybe Ai had chosen this place for their battle on purpose to rattle him. Either way, he knew where to find Suzume.

"Take the lead, I'll be back soon." Kaito transformed once more. Flying would be faster. But the transformation was slower and painful. His wounds stretched taught and bled more.

"You need to heal before you fly—" Shin shouted, but Kaito was already rising into the sky.

As he left the battlefield behind, his senses cleared, and he noticed a bright flash of pure energy in the place he'd been sealed. But it wasn't Suzume's energy he felt, but Kazue's. He flew faster, heedless of his injuries, praying he didn't arrive too late to save her.

The flow of the spiritual river threatened to sweep her away as soon as she entered. Kicking wildly, she swam upward to the faint light of the surface, but like the last time she'd attempted to enter the spirit realm, tendrils of dark shadows grasped at her wrists and ankles, pulling her down, down into darkness. Panic strangled her as she struggled against them, writhing in the river, unable to reach the surface. Though there was no actual water, her mind was desperately gasping for air. What if she was wrong? What if coming to the spirit realm had been Hisato's trick? Last time there was Noaki to pull her out or Ryuu to guide her through. This trial she must complete on her own. She grasped ahold of the tendrils with both hands and focused her spiritual energy into them. Hisato's mocking laughter filled her ears.

She lost sense of what was up and what was down as the darkness tangled around her, blocking out all light, wrapping around her throat, and attempting to squeeze the last breaths from her lungs. She couldn't let the darkness win. Couldn't let Hisato win. She pulled from the ember of her fire burning in her gut and grasped it, letting the fire consume her. Bright red light burst out of her, evaporating the tentacles into small particles. As the darkness retreated, fearful of her fire, Suzume swam to the surface. When she broke through, she gasped, bobbing along the gentle current of the immaterial river. After taking a moment to find her bearings, she swam for the sandy shore, where she collapsed, taking a moment to regain her strength. Banishing the darkness had drained her body and soul, and whatever form of her entered this plane trembled.

Water lapped at her as she stared up at the watercolor sky, the color of a bruise fading into the pink of a cherry blossom. The golden sand clung to her skin as she pushed herself up into a standing position and looked around her surroundings. It was different from when she'd entered with Noaki. This time, she was standing outside a homey cottage with smoke rising from the chimney. It was the place where Kazue had lived, where Kaito had kept her like a bird in a cage. Where they'd cobbled together a shadow of a life together. Kazue's memories of warm days filled with laughter drifted through Suzume's mind, followed by the feeling of bitter anger when she was left alone for weeks on end. She shook off the phantoms of false memories and walked over to the cottage, pulling back the hanging partition in the doorway. Kazue knelt beside a low table with two cups of tea set out.

"I was right; the beginning was when you betrayed Kaito?" Suzume asked her.

"Sit," Kazue said.

The rebellious part of her wanted to stand out of defiance, but it was petty and a waste of time. She'd followed her instructions this far; she may as well do as she told her. Suzume sat across from Kazue and reached for the steaming cup on the table.

Warmth radiated into her fingers, and the floral aroma of tea filled her senses. How a place as incorporeal as the spirit realm could have warmth and smells, she couldn't say. Nor was she certain she wanted to know.

"I've followed your clues, now will you tell me how to defeat Hisato?" Suzume asked.

Because surely the trials she'd endured were enough. Hisato wanted the journal presumably to lead him to this place, to this version of Kazue hidden in the spirit realm at the place where she and Kaito had built a life together.

"We leave a part of ourselves everywhere we go. Sometimes, it lingers; other times, it fades, with time, with death. Strong emotions tie us to a place in a way we can never escape," Kazue said, her gaze drifting across the cottage, a deep sadness settling over her features.

"Is that what you are? Another fragment of your soul?"

She shook her head slowly. "I'm nothing more than a memory now."

"Why did you bring me here?" Suzume prickled with unease. What if Kaito was right and this had been a trick all along…

"You don't trust me." It wasn't a question but a statement, as if she read her heart as easily as reading a book.

"There haven't been many reasons to."

"He tried his best to make me happy. It was me who'd never be satisfied."

She saw Kazue's memories play out in her mind's eye, as if they were her own. The painful longing during the times they were apart. Moving from place to place constantly, fearing his enemies would discover her. Followed by a growing desperation for something more. To be powerful. To become his equal.

Suzume shook her head, trying to shake free the memories. "I don't care what your motives were. Tell me how to fix it."

There was a sad smile on her face. It was the same one she had seen when they'd first met in the cave. That time felt like a lifetime ago. She said, "Will you trust me?"

"You've tried to trick me before."

"The fire inside burned with the desires of my heart. But as I've said, the wind balances. Souta's life balanced me and has given me clarity and direction for now..."

"Are you saying you'll try again?"

"I'm saying the fragments are being drawn tighter together. Surely you feel it."

They were talking in circles, and Suzume had to take a long breath to stop herself from screaming out of frustration. Suzume inhaled sharply, biting back her anger and as she exhaled. She felt the other pieces of Kazue sharp as a knife to her chest. They felt closer here in the spirit realm, but also miles away. Two bright lights and one dark consuming void in the distance, which all of them were gravitating toward. She couldn't deny the pull she felt, the magnetic draw to Hisato.

"Time is running out," Kazue said in a sing-songy voice that echoed slightly like Hisato's.

It sent a chill down her spine. Was even this last fragment of Kazue unable to escape him?

"Then tell me how to stop him!" Suzume slammed her hands down on the table.

Kazue snapped her gaze to Suzume, the trance-like state she'd fallen into falling away, and a clear and clever woman stared at her. This was the real Kazue. The woman who'd defied the Eight and won. Who'd torn her soul apart to gain immortality.

"You can't. Convergence has always been inevitable."

"Then what was the point of all this? Why lure me back here? Are you hoping to steal my body so you can be immortal when we do?" Suzume stood and reached for her staff, but her fingers grasped nothing. Instead, Kazue stood across from her, the staff held loosely at her side, looking at her placidly.

"Because this between is the only way you can speak to us." Then suddenly, Kazue shifted. She was no longer herself but Souta smiling at her.

Suzume's stomach lurched as she recoiled from him. Apologies tangled up in her throat, but before she could voice a single one, he shifted again. This time, a stranger stood before her, a beautiful woman with bold red eyes and hair that flickered with flames.

"You know the answer," she said, her voice crackling like popping embers.

"You told me to go back to the beginning, and I did."

"I was the first among the Eight. Am I the beginning?" asked a man with brilliant golden bracers and a gold sun emblazed on his chest so bright she couldn't look him in the face. She held up her arm to block out his light.

"Who—" she couldn't finish the question.

They'd changed again in quick succession. Now a woman made up of blowing leaves stood before her, who seemed to disappear when Suzume tried to get a better look at her. Then, a man with horns and a wicked gleam in his eye.

"We are all here inside you, Suzume. Think." They all spoke to her and their voices rattled around in her skull so loud she involuntarily pressed her hands to her ears to block it out. But she couldn't, no matter how hard she tried.

"What is the beginning?" Suzume asked. "If not, when you sealed Kaito, then when?"

"You know it. Think, Suzume."

She growled and stood up to pace around the room between them. There wasn't an obvious answer. Kazue was tricking her as usual, trying to make her play her games. Maybe even now, she was using her body to wreak havoc on the mortal plane.

"You know what must be done," they said.

"I don't," she cried out.

"You do." And suddenly, they were looming over her.

She turned to flee, but she didn't get a few feet beyond the cabin before she was sinking into the sand; it rose to her thighs. The shifting faces of the creatures moved in front of her: Kazue, the flame, the sun, the wind, the animal.

"Set us free," they said, grasping onto her shoulders.

Their voices were echoing in her ears. The truth of it was caught in her throat. A fate she didn't want to face but one that had been lingering in the back of her mind since Souta had sacrificed himself for her.

"Souta began it," Suzume said haltingly.

Kazue's face returned, let go of her shoulders, and took a step back. She looked at her with kindness and compassion in her gaze, urging Suzume without words to continue.

"And I have to finish uniting the pieces of the soul. In one body."

"Yes," Kazue said.

"And then what happens? Who will I become?" Suzume asked, her voice barely above a whisper.

"You and I will be one. But the work is not done. Hisato will seek to break free. Now that he's gained a form, he does not want to return to the void from whence he came. He will fight. To stop him, you must bring him here and walk through the final gateway."

The cottage they'd been sitting in faded away, and Kazue pointed to a torii. It shimmered with a strange light, and she felt a sudden longing to pass through. A whisper seemed to be picked up by the wind, promising her eternal rest.

"And what happens to me?" she repeated, though she already knew the answer.

Kazue lowered her head. "You will die."

Suzume stumbled back, recoiling in horror at the news. Kazue approached her, holding out her hands as if she would forcefully pull her into an embrace.

"We can do it together, Suzume. Help me right the wrongs and save Akatsuki."

Suzume kept struggling against the sand as the torii seemed to grow bigger, looming above her. "I don't want to die." Her voice trembled.

"We all die someday." Kazue grabbed her arms, trying to drag Suzume away.

"No." Suzume threw up her hands. Flames burst from them and broke Kazue's grip. Without her grasping onto her, Suzume was able to pull free of the sand, and she ran for the water.

She dove in before she could second-guess herself and fell into a deep, endless pool. She swam through the darkness, pumping her arms and legs as she fought to return to her body and the mortal realm. Her lungs burned. She was dying; she was sure of it. She had to get out. She had to get away.

"Suzume. Suzume!" Someone was shouting her name. It was Kaito. She swam toward the sound of his voice as a light illuminated the distance.

She slammed back into her body, and she realized she was drenched. Not with water but sweat. Kaito held her in his arms, his body glowing in the dying light of day.

"What happened? Are you hurt?" he asked. His blue eyes searched her for answers.

Her hands were shaking. She didn't want to repeat what she had been told. A knot tightened her stomach. She didn't want it to be real. She'd never asked for this destiny. And now it seemed the only way to save everyone she cared about was to die? She refused. She wouldn't do it. There must be another way. She had to find another way.

"Nothing. I'm fine. I tried to reach Kazue again. But I failed," she lied. She tried to get up, but the room was spinning, and she stumbled back into Kaito's arms.

"Be careful; you've expended too much energy already," Kaito said. And that's when she smelled the blood on him and saw how his arm hung at his side.

"You're hurt," she said, searching his body.

"I'm fine. The battle is won. Ai is defeated."

Suzume nodded. "Good. I'm sorry, I should have been there."

"Don't worry," he said, holding her close to him and stroking her head. "I don't care as long as you're safe. That's all that matters to me."

Suzume pulled back from him, guilt coiling around her. If she couldn't find another way to stop Hisato, if the only way to defeat him was her death, then Kaito would lose her. Lose another person he loved. She couldn't make him go through that again. It would be better to end things now. Because either she ran away and hoped Hisato never found her, or Hisato won. The ultimate outcome was her death; it was simply a matter of when.

"Don't," she said, hands falling to her side.

Kaito frowned as he looked at her, concern furrowing his brow as he reached for her again. Suzume backed away.

"I think it's best we end this here," she said.

Twenty-One

"What?" Kaito gasped as Suzume's words hit him like a blow to the chest, knocking the breath out of him.

In this place, he tried to forget; the past and present overlapped. He'd tried running from it, but it seemed their entangled fates were always going to bring him back to where Kazue had betrayed him. The start of his ruin.

Suzume and Kazue weren't the same person; that was her constant refrain. And yet she'd cut him deeply with just a few words. Maybe love was pain. Because the thought of losing her hurt more than the oozing wound on his shoulder. He thought he knew Suzume, that she wouldn't hurt him as Kazue had. But she stared at him, arms crossed, chin jutted defiantly, much the way she'd greeted him moments after freeing him from his stone prison. But her eyes gave away her true feelings. They were darting around him, focusing on anything other than his face.

"We can't keep doing this. Humans and yokai are not meant to be together. I'm sorry." Suzume turned away from him.

In the past, he'd let her walk away. Let his own fears and inefficiencies keep him from holding onto those he'd cared for. He'd locked Kazue away, even though it diminished her. He'd taken her for granted, and she'd turned on him. Suzume had asked him to come here but he'd put it off until she'd risked her life to come here on her own. Humans were complicated and confusing to him. But one thorough line remained: he wasn't listening to what she needed. Her words said she was done, but the look in her eyes told him there was more she wasn't saying. He was so caught up in what he wanted, he wasn't paying attention to what she needed.

Kaito caught hold of her arm before she could slip out of reach, and spun her around, pressing her against his chest. Her body tensed, and the wind and flames of her dual spiritual powers flickered against him. They hadn't come this far, gone through hell and back, just for her to call it quits now. He'd fight for her, tooth and nail, if he had to. The yokai could raise an army to try and part them, and he'd reduce them to rubble before he let her go. As long as she loved him, he would stay by her side. Suzume trembled, not out of fear. Suzume was rarely afraid. She didn't struggle, but held still as if she were fighting the urge to lean in. Kaito laid one palm flat against her back to keep her close and used his other hand to cup her chin and tilt her head up. Tears brimmed in her eyes, and a wave of protectiveness washed over him. Those specters of his past wrapped icy fingers around his neck. Kazue, crying in his arms and terrified to fall asleep, afraid of another assassin's knife. Suzume hardly cried, and yet one single tear was rolling down her cheek. Kaito wiped it away with the pad of his thumb.

"Look me in the eye and tell me you're doing this because you don't love me, and I'll let you go." His voice caught, but he held her gaze steadily.

Suzume's bottom lip quivered, and her eyes flicked away from him.

"I'm doing this so you don't get hurt." Her voice wobbled, on the verge of crumbling under an invisible strain.

"You don't get to choose that for me." He cupped her cheek.

"Let me go," she said, but it didn't sound like a demand. It sounded like exhausted defeat.

Out of respect for her wishes, he took a step back. Though every fiber of his being was rebelling against it.

"What's changed?" he asked, voice rasping.

"I came here to meet Kazue in the spirit realm and learn how to defeat Hisato."

"And did you?"

"Yes."

A cold dread crept up over Kaito's skin. Kazue did nothing by halves. She'd split her soul into pieces to gain immortality. What terrible price had she asked of Suzume to stop the darkness of her soul?

"It's my burden to bear. I'll do my duty, and you do yours," Suzume said, still refusing to meet his gaze.

"You don't have to do this alone. Whatever it is, we'll do it together." Kaito reached a hand out to her, offering her a bridge to cross back to him.

She stared at his hand, longing in her gaze. "You can't help me with this."

"What is it? Why can't you just tell me?" Kaito approached her, but she put out her burning hands in front of her to stop him.

That same disorienting feeling overcame him. As if he were reliving a moment in time all over again. The rotten walls of the hut were closing in around him, suffocating him as the stone once did. Kaito grasped a hold of his chest, felt the thump, thump, thump of his heartbeat, and took a few steadying breaths. She wasn't Kazue. She wasn't going to betray him. The only thing that was the same about this scene was him. And if he were to go back, what would he do differently? What would he change?

"Forget it," Suzume said with a tone of finality before turning to walk away.

If she passed through that door, he knew that something irrevocable would change between them. He felt as if he were sinking into mud, and the more he struggled, the harder it was to pull himself out of the mire. But despite his better judgment, he kept fighting even as it rose up around him, the pain threatening to suffocate him.

"You can't run from me. I'll follow you to the ends of the world if I must."

"Where I'm going, you can't follow," Suzume said, pausing at the threshold. And he knew then the truth that she'd been holding back. The horrible certainty. The cruel twist of the knife that would be the end of everything.

"Suzume!" He shouted her name. As if it could bind her to him, save them from this inevitable end.

"Kaito." She sounded exhausted. Worn out. Drawn thin in a way he'd never seen her before. As if she were going transparent around the edges. How had he not noticed? The way she seemed to be fading day by day. A little less flame and more charred embers.

"Tell me it's not that." He reached for her, hand hanging in the air with nothing to grasp hold of. She stood just outside his reach. Impossible to touch, cold and removed as Kazue had been moments before she sealed him in stone. Somehow, this hurt worse.

"To defeat Hisato, I have to die!" Her voice shook.

Even though he suspected it, it still felt like a blow to his chest hearing her say it. He'd known loving a mortal meant their time would be finite. But in his naivety, he'd assumed they'd have years to go. They were meant to defeat Hisato and live in bliss for years after. Not race to a hasty ending.

"There has to be another way," he said in a futile attempt to deny the truth, even as it stared him in the face.

Tears rolled down her cheeks unfettered as she shook her head. "The fragments must be reunited. It is inevitable. And the vessel with all the pieces must take them beyond that final veil, or Hisato will rise up again."

"Then give your fragment to Hikaru; let him be the hero," Kaito snarled, as if shouting about it could make it real.

"Even if that were possible, you wouldn't do that to the husband of one of your oldest friends. Would you?"

He hated that she was right. Even as much as he loved Suzume, he couldn't inflict more pain on Rin. She'd lost Hikaru once, and he couldn't do that to her again.

"Do you see why I have to let you go? I can't make you suffer another loss," she said, her shoulders slumping in defeat.

"I refuse," Kaito said.

She looked at him with a watery gaze. "You can't deny fate."

"I know you, Suzume. You haven't given up yet, and neither will I."

She squared her shoulders and stared at him without speaking. For once, he'd rendered her speechless. But within her glare, he saw the faintest glimmer of a familiar spark in her eyes. That was the Suzume he knew; she was never quite defeated. She kept on fighting no matter what. Kaito took her hand in his.

"I understand why you'd try to protect me by letting me go. But giving you up now, without a fight, would hurt more than trying and failing to save you. Until your last breath, I will love you. Whether that is tomorrow or decades from now."

"What if I can't face you knowing that you'll be left behind to pick up all the pieces?"

"Would it soothe you to hold me at arm's length? To go back to doing it all alone?"

She stood very still, as if suspended between despair and hope. He would be that for her, a beacon of hope.

"I thought you died today. When I couldn't find you on the battlefield. I was certain you'd been killed. I know your life is short. But I would do anything to keep you by my side as long as possible. If you'll have me."

He should have known from the start what was weighing on her. The burden she carried, that he didn't fully comprehend. She leaned in ever so slightly, and Kaito opened his arms, giving her the choice to come to him if she wished. And when her feet finally moved, she crashed into him, grasping fistfuls of his haori. She buried her face against his chest and lightly struck him over and over.

"I'm really afraid." She said this part barely above a whisper.

"I'll keep you safe, until the end. Whenever that may be," he murmured against her hair.

"Don't," she mumbled against his chest. "It just makes it harder."

"Believe me, I don't want to live a moment without you, Suzume. But I'll savor each second we have together."

She sniffled. "I wish it wasn't this way."

They were both silent for a beat. He felt her heart fluttering against his chest, fragile and temporary. Trapped within her were two fragments, and three more were out there pulling her closer together. He'd seen how she was when she was near Hisato. Maybe it was inevitable, but it didn't have to be Suzume who passed Hisato beyond the veil. Hikaru was out of the question, but what about the other Kazue? The water of her soul?

"Maybe there is another way," Kaito said, pulling back slightly to look at her.

Suzume blinked up at him and rubbed the tears from her eyes aggressively. Her stubborn, fearless mask slipped back into place.

"Don't try and give me false hope."

"But you said it yourself. We can't ask Hikaru to make this sacrifice, but he's not the only one with a soul fragment. Nor the only one who was born with it in them."

"Kazue…" Suzume said, her expression lightening. "We could never convince her to come to our side. She's made her position clear."

"We don't need to convince her of anything. We need to capture her."

"And lure Hisato to us," Suzume said, rolling the words around as she considered what he was suggesting.

But he could see the fire of the idea building in her mind. They'd been building this army, and laying all these plots when the answer was right there in front of them. If the fragments of Kazue's soul could not resist one another, they were bound to be pulled together. Capture Kazue and hold her hostage with Hikaru and Suzume nearby. They'd simply destroy Hisato's form, or weaken it long enough to bring the fragments together in Kazue. Between Suzume, Ryuu, and Hikaru, they could bind her powers long enough to kill her and banish her through the veil.

All this was simpler said than done, but it was the slim hope they both needed to keep pressing onward. Kaito had to believe it would work. For both their sakes.

TWENTY-TWO

Ryuu found the empress and the crown prince tucked away in a countryside villa. He'd walked up to the villa gate, announced himself, and been promptly escorted to a private room from which he was not allowed to leave. Meals were delivered three times a day by a pretty maid who brushed his hands with alarming frequency while trying to serve him tea or his soup. And when she laid out his futon at night, she lingered too long, sending him intense glances that he pretended not to notice. Despite being treated as a guest, Ryuu knew he was a prisoner. His polite requests to speak with the empress were all deflected with a giggle and a sly look from his maid. The empress was a powerful woman, daughter of a respected clan, but she had Izuki's style and cunning when it came to subterfuge. The maid was obvious bait. She hadn't killed him outright because she was curious and even more likely needed his help.

If he wanted to, Ryuu could leave this room, disarm his guards, and pass through the shadows until he found the crown prince and then whisk him away. He'd considered that plot; it would be simpler, but the risks were great. It wasn't placing someone on a throne that was difficult. It was keeping them there. Ryuu needed the support of the empress and her family if this plan was going to work. So for three days, he waited, playing oblivious to the simpering maid and sent his neko hunting the shadows in his place. He'd been coming in at night after the maid left and the house had fallen asleep, feeding him what information he'd gleaned that day.

The hour was late, and the braziers had all been dimmed down to embers, except for the one in his room. To fill the empty hours, he'd taken to reading. The soft, steady footsteps of a guard passed by. Twice a day, they changed guards, and he heard their low murmured exchanges. In the gap between those moments, the air of his room shifted, the pressure changed, and his brazier light flickered. Familiar with his yokai energy, Ryuu didn't bother lifting his head when the neko stood before him.

"Any news?" Ryuu asked.

"Growing impatient?" the neko asked.

"Either report or leave me," Ryuu said, a bit too snappish, and he instantly regretted his impatience. Though he didn't technically have to wait in this room, he'd been trying to keep up a human appearance. The empress didn't know him as anything other than a priest and he preferred it stayed that way. But the longer she left him waiting in this tiny room, the more restless he felt.

"Hard being locked in a box, isn't it?" the neko teased, his twin tails whipping behind him and a delighted grin on his face.

"Are you done?"

"It's not often I see you this agitated. What a delight," the neko said.

"You must be enjoying your time."

"It lacks wards, and the kitchens are generous with their offerings to a stray cat." He patted his belly.

"Maybe I should send you off on some other errand if you're not going to serve my ends here."

The neko narrowed his eyes at Ryuu. "Spoilsport." Then, with a great huff, he said, "The empress receives many letters but no visitors. I snuck into her chambers today while she was out and saw signatures from three different governors. One said that the White Palace has become chaotic and uncivilized. The emperor rambles about yokai with alarming frequency, and some blame Izuki's poisonous influence for his decline."

Ryuu resisted the urge to ball his hands into fists. Izuki's schemes were a noose around her neck, and it wasn't his responsibility to rescue her. She'd betrayed him, yet again, but he couldn't resist the urge to go rushing back to her side. Her mistakes were to his advantage; he needed to remember that. And yet, when he tried to harden his heart against Izuki, her face swam up in his memories, and he remembered the hint of desperation in her voice when she'd begged him to protect Suzume. Was that another trick to soften him to her? Or was there some hint she was trying to give him? He couldn't know and wouldn't risk all his plans for her. Not again.

Ryuu shook himself of the past; there was only going forward now. "That explains why they didn't kill me as soon as I arrived."

"I think so," the neko said.

"Send word to the dragon. Let him know we'll be heading for the palace, and he should meet me there."

The corners of the neko's mouth downturned. "That's bold, when you're still locked in this room."

Ryuu slashed his hand through the air to silence the neko. The empress was desperate, and she'd be coming for him very soon. He could feel it. Tonight, while the servant brought his dinner, he made a casual mention of wanting to see change in the White Palace. The maid should have delivered that small morsel to her mistress by now. She'd know they were aligned, or she'd attempt to kill him. Either way, this was the final night he'd wait in this room. As if on cue, the servant returned.

"My lord, the empress wishes to speak with you," she said.

The neko looked at him and, with a swish of his forked tail, disappeared in a cloud of smoke. The door slid open and revealed the servant girl holding a lantern to light his path to the empress' chamber.

The guards fell into step behind him, a silent reminder that he wasn't merely a guest. They walked down a long hall that led to one of the only illuminated rooms. The servant girl opened the door, and Ryuu stepped inside. The empress sat sipping tea, flanked by four of her ladies. She did not look up to acknowledge him but dismissed her ladies with a glance. They rose before shuffling backward out of the room on slippered feet, and cast curious glances at him as they passed by him. The door closed, leaving them alone. It was a silent sort of truce. An uneasy trust which was beginning to unfurl between them.

She drank her tea as if he weren't there for several more minutes. And Ryuu, knowing it for the power play it was, let her. He knew the empress perhaps better than she knew him because he'd chosen her in an attempt to thwart Izuki's early designs for the throne. While she was beautiful, cunning, and had a wealthy family at her back, those were not the qualities that made him choose her. She was made of steel. It balanced the emperor's sometimes emotional and impulsive nature. He hoped her son had similar mettle. There had been many crown princes during the empire's lifetime. Few became emperors, whether through sickness or human machinations. In the past few decades, he'd stopped paying attention to them. Not until they were enthroned. But he needed to pay attention now.

"My father is convinced you're that woman's assassin," she said, setting down her teacup and lifting her gaze to meet his eye at last.

"Why bother with you, when your sons are the threat to her plans?" Ryuu said.

She smiled, as if talk of murdering her sons was the same as discussing the weather.

"Did the emperor send you, or are you plotting your own schemes, Ryuu?" she asked. Her eyes were cold and calculating.

"Who's asking, you or your father?"

Her eyes glinted for a moment, and Ryuu knew he'd struck a nerve. A woman in her position was limited by the influence of the men around her. He knew that she would resent the statement. It was also why he'd come seeking her and not her father. Her son was young enough that his mother's influence could impact his reign. And he'd rather have her on his side over her father, who'd try to rule through his grandson. He'd seen it enough times before.

"Perhaps I should heed my father's warnings, and have you executed," she replied coolly. The cold tone hid the anger in her words.

"You wouldn't be able to," Ryuu replied, subtly revealing his true nature, and then he waited. If she even flexed a finger, he would have to strike. She'd be dead before the guards realized anything had happened. And he'd have the prince and be on his way before her body cooled.

Her eyes widened slightly, and a subtle smile tugged at the corner of her lips, as if he'd confirmed her own long-held suspicions.

She stood and strode closer to him.

"Then have you come to make my son emperor?" she asked.

"I have."

"That woman will be furious to see you standing by my side." Her lips curled with malicious delight. "Why cross her now?

"It's because I love Akatsuki more."

"Do you?" she replied with a hint of skepticism. She paced around him as if she were a spider, and she had wound him up in her web. "I sent that girl to tempt you, but you didn't once falter. I must wonder if you remain devoted to Izuki, even now."

"I saw your ploy for what it was. I'm much too old to be lured in by pillow talk."

She stopped in front of him, her icy stare moving up and down his body. "Then will you swear yourself to me?" she asked, arching a brow.

"I swear myself only to the emperor."

"The new or the old?" she asked.

"I will help the crown prince ascend to the throne, as is his right. And it is my sworn duty to protect the line of succession to the Golden Throne."

Something flashed in her eyes as she studied him. "I see. Either you do not know, or you are a more skilled liar than I realized."

"What do I not realize?" he asked.

"The crown prince is dead." The words were delivered flatly, but for a tiny catch at the end. She turned away from him, and he suspected it was to hide her tears.

The realization had set him off balance, as if he'd taken a blow to the head. How had the neko not known? Or had he not reported it to spite him? He'd grown more audacious as of late, testing Ryuu's patience, bending the parameters of their bond. It was possible he'd kept this crucial information from him. If that were true, he needed to watch his back. If not, the empress was a terrible liar.

"You lie," he said.

"Do you think I would lie about the death of my son?" Her voice rose, and she couldn't hide the emotion which thickened her words.

She collapsed onto the ground, head in her hands. The empress was a skilled manipulator in the way Izuki was, but he knew this wasn't a performance. Ryuu knelt beside her, as it felt wrong to loom over a grieving mother. Her mask had slipped, and he saw her pain and grief written in each line of her face. The crown prince was dead. Then the mask was back, and she was looking at him with that hawkish gaze.

"She poisoned the crown prince, and he died in my arms. I fled to protect my younger son and hid the crown prince's death as an illness. Then she twisted the truth into an exile."

"The prince is practically a child."

"Older than her brat," she spat the words.

Ryuu's temples throbbed. The younger prince was 17. Not the ideal age to be thrust onto the throne. In fact, he would be even more ripe for exploitation than his elder brother. But the alternative was Izuki's son or some other concubine or consort's child. There was no other choice. Ryuu rubbed his throbbing skull as he tried to think.

"Now we've both shared a secret. What will you do?" she asked.

The choice was obvious. With the neko's loyalties in question, and Kaito and Suzume counting on him to provide the White Palace to them, he had to ally with the empress and the boy emperor.

"I will help you place your son upon the throne. But remember, I am also removing an emperor from power as well. It won't be the first time and likely won't be the last."

She inhaled through her nostrils before nodding. "You make such pretty threats, but I have no choice but to join hands with you. I don't like bloodshed, but I will do what is necessary to put my son on the throne."

"Then we are in agreement?"

"We are in agreement. But I have a stipulation as well: Izuki will die to pay for my son's life."

Ryuu clenched his jaw hard enough that his teeth ached. It was the price Izuki had to pay, and he knew it. But his mouth couldn't seem to make the words. Though he knew that this would be the price, she extracted from him from the start.

"Having second thoughts?" the empress asked with a wicked, triumphant smile.

He worked his jaw and said, "Understood. But we move now, as fast as your father can raise an army. There's no time for waiting while the yokai the emperor has partnered with grow stronger."

Her smile faded, and he stood up to excuse himself, not wanting to let his feelings show. He'd made sacrifices for Akatsuki before. And he'd do it again.

TWENTY-THREE

Knowledge burned inside Noaki's chest. He had to tell Suzume about what he'd learned atop that accursed mountain, but the journey back felt longer than the one up. His steps were dragging, as if invisible threads were tugging at him, trying to pull him back to Sayuri. This false skin she wore wasn't her. He had to remind himself leaving her behind for now was the best thing he could do to save her. But after centuries of searching, it was difficult to walk away. No matter what the water of Kazue's soul said, no matter how she played her part. It wasn't real. If anything, Sayuri was nothing but a tiny fragment within her from which she extracted her thoughts, mannerisms, and memories. He couldn't trust this fake Sayuri. He knew that Hisato had his hooks into her. Despite knowing all this, he still fought each step.

By the time he reached the bottom of the mountain, some of the fog around his mind had cleared. It felt as if he'd had a fever that had been burned out of his skin, though that invisible thread tethering him to Sayuri remained. But his resolve was reaffirmed. The entire stretch of Akatsuki lay between him and

Suzume, and there was no way of knowing for certain where she was. If he had the power of flight, he would have flown to her, or if he had the ability to fold the world around him and move from one place to another as if taking a step, he would. But all he had was a sense of her direction and two legs.

His journey was long and arduous, traversing hills and valleys. All the while, he felt the lingering sense of being followed. Noaki was attuned to the spiritual energy around him, and even more so to the water of Kazue's soul's resonance. Though he felt eyes on him, he couldn't sense a body attached to it. After days of this, he was convinced he was imagining things. And he spent too long searching for Sayuri in the dappled shadow of trees or in the faces of the farmers he passed toiling in their fields. But she wasn't there. Perhaps he'd mortally wounded her and left her to die on that mountain, and his guilt was playing tricks on his mind. Once or twice, he thought he caught the barest edge of a powerful figure, but as he tried to focus on them, they slipped out of sight and beyond his senses. Trying to find his stalker was like trying to catch mist between his fingers. It could have been the water of Kazue's soul posing as Sayuri. His traitorous heart hoped she'd survived and followed after him. But as he continued his journey uninterrupted, he started to doubt.

Whoever was following him would either slink away or confront him. He simply had to await their choice. And so, he continued onward, slipping in and out of shadows in an effort to escape his follower. A couple times, he thought he'd escaped them, only for them to reveal themselves at the edges of his awareness like a taunt. He started to doubt he'd ever lost them at all, but he was a dog on their leash, and they were letting out enough rope for him to get tangled up in. When he realized that, he changed strategy and moved to more crowded areas hoping he could hide amongst the press of bodies. If his pursuer was working for Hisato, he couldn't lead them to Suzume or risk endangering her. And so, he delayed and delayed and delayed.

Days turned into a week or more, and he rested at a roadside inn frequented by yokai who'd adapted to living alongside humans, oftentimes taking on the appearance of humans in order to move among them. It was the third such establishment he'd stayed at in as many days. He'd been alternating between human and yokai establishments, each time in an attempt to throw off his follower. Noaki sat at a table in the farthest, darkest corner, surveying his surroundings from beneath the brim of his straw hat. The sizzle of the grilling meat and its scent filled the air, and his stomach rumbled. He normally didn't need to eat much but he'd been pushing his spiritual powers to their limits over the past few days trying to catch a glimpse of his stalker.

The inn's purveyor, a pleasantly round tanuki woman, walked over and deposited an earthenware cup of steaming tea and a skewer of barbeque meat slathered in a thick sauce in front of him.

Noaki nodded his thanks, and she smiled before hustling over to another table, which had summoned her with a wave. As far as he could tell, all the tables' patrons were regular yokai. Merchants and travelers like himself. The flap at the door opened, and a dust-covered kitsune walked in. She gazed across the room, and her eyes snagged on him for a moment. Noaki grasped the hilt of his blade. Then, the table beside him waved her over, and she took her seat as her companions poured her a cup of tea. Noaki relaxed by a small measure and took a large bite of his food.

His stalker had him on edge. And maybe that was their intent, to keep him distracted.

"I just came from the west," the kitsune said, removing her bag and setting it down beside her.

"Any news on the war?" asked the tanuki.

"I'd hardly call it a war at this point. More a slaughter. The armies met, and the dragon was victorious," the kitsune said.

Noaki tilted his head ever so slightly in their direction. He'd heard rumors of the marching yokai army mixed with priestesses and priests at other roadside inns. But this was the first he heard of the outcome of their battle.

"Then the rumors are true? The great dragon has returned?"

"Pff. I'm sure it won't last," replied a neko, who among the group seemed less than enthused at the news of the dragon's victory.

"What makes you say that?" asked the kitsune, clearly put out that the neko was taking the wind out of the sails of her tale.

"He's got humans with him. And rumor has it another priestess has him under his thrall." The neko shrugged, as if such foolishness was to be expected of the dragon.

"He doesn't seem to be under anyone's spell. I traded with a tanuki who saw the battle and I hear he's got a glorious plan for the future."

"Such as?" the neko asked skeptically.

The kitsune delayed her response by taking a long sip of her tea. The others were watching her with bated breath, desperate for any scrap of information. Noaki, too, found himself waiting with bated breath for her answer. He hadn't thought he'd miss Suzume and Kaito. Gaining his freedom and finding Sayuri had been his obsession for so long. But as he spent many weary days on the road, he realized how much comfort their squabbling had brought him. He'd spent many long centuries trapped on the mountain. When Suzume freed him and reunited him with his children, it had awoken a flame of hope he thought long smothered.

When the kitsune had sufficiently drawn out the information, she said, "He's marching for the palace as we speak. And plans to retake Akatsuki for yokai from the humans."

"If that's true, what a happy day it will be," the tanuki cheered.

"I'll drink to that." They clinked glasses together.

Then, they were on their way back to the White Palace. They'd progressed faster than Noaki thought they would. Now, if he could just shake his tail, he could return to Suzume and deliver the news that might change the trajectory of the war.

As he contemplated this, he felt a brush of his follower's spiritual power. But instead of retreating as it had before, it grew stronger and sent a jolt down Noaki's spine. He sat straighter and glanced across the inn. While he'd been preoccupied with eavesdropping, another figure had entered. The newcomer's eyes were covered by a straw hat pulled down low. Despite that, he felt their gaze still trained on him.

So the stalker had decided to show themselves at last. Noaki set down a few coins on the table and stood to leave. As he suspected, as soon as he stepped outside, his stalker followed. They didn't bother to disguise themselves any longer and dropped their barriers, revealing the chaotic clash of two souls whose minds overlapped like a feral scream. Tsuki and Akira had found him.

Noaki's entire body tensed, but he kept walking as if nothing were wrong. He couldn't guarantee the monster his children had become wouldn't attack casual bystanders. The further he got them away from crowds, the better. And the further from the inn they got the more he felt their power crawling over his skin and setting his teeth on edge. Beneath that undercurrent of the dissonance was the cool serenity of Kazue's water. She'd been following him all along. He should have known, but their combined power was enough to overwhelm him and distort his senses.

A blade swung for his back, and he spun, drawing his sword and blocking their strike before bringing up his second sword and to lock their blade between his. Their features were a mangled mash of his children, both familiar and unsettlingly strange. They glared at him with a menacing, disjointed smile reminiscent of Hisato.

"You've been leading us in circles for quite a while, but we've grown bored of this game," they said in their strange, echoing voice. If he concentrated, he could pick out the individual threads of his children's voices.

He pushed them backward and onto their back foot before slashing at their undefended middle. They stumbled and nearly fell. If Noaki pressed his advantage, he could have pinned them or driven his blade through their heart. But even though they were a twisted shadow of what they'd once been, he wouldn't harm them. It was his failings which subjected them to this fate, and he was determined to find a way to save them from it.

They tilted their head. "You should have taken that opening, killed us, and ended our suffering." He might have imagined it, but he thought he heard a note of pleading in their tone.

Noaki said nothing in response. It was the same request Kazue had made of him. Why were they both determined to place their blood on his hands? Was this some twisted trick of Hisato's? To twist his guilt like a knife in his gut? To torture him until he relented and ended them all to spare himself? Noaki wasn't a stranger to suffering. To watching as the things he loved were ripped from his hands. He'd rather take his own life before letting any harm befall those he loved again.

He felt, but didn't see, Kazue lingering on the edges of their battlefield. It felt as if she were watching and waiting. For what, he couldn't be certain. But Noaki had a feeling this was a test.

His children lunged at him again, and their blades clashed, ringing out as they circled one another in a deadly dance. They slashed at him when his guard dropped and sliced a cut deep into his side. Noaki ignored the pain. He'd been cut a thousand times before, and he'd always endured. They continued circling one another, seemingly giving and taking ground back and forth. A dance that seemed to have no end. While they exhausted themselves against his might, Noaki was trying and failing to see a way to subdue them without harming them. It was bad enough he'd struck at Kazue, knowing she contained some piece of Sayuri. He didn't want to taint his soul by doing it to them, too.

"You cannot block our attacks forever," they sneered.

Noaki countered without speaking. Internally he'd sworn not to give up, even if they must battle until the end of time. He wouldn't cut them down.

They were growing frustrated at his lack of communication, or they were more tired than they let on. Their arm drooped to their side, and their swings became slower, leaving him more openings to attack. Noaki pressed his advantage, pushing them back and back until finally they stumbled and fell onto the ground. He stepped on their chest and pointed his blade to their throat. If he had the power like Suzume, he might have sealed them in stone until he found a way to reverse what Kazue had done to them, but he did not. They looked up at him, and for a moment, the facade broke, and for the briefest moment, he saw his children.

"End it. Please," they begged. "There's no bringing us back. We'll only be free in death."

Noaki's hand clenched, as he considered their plea. If it were true, if there was no reversing what was done, wouldn't it be kinder to end their suffering?

"But I do relish this," a voice whispered in his ear.

It'd been a trap all along. A distraction from Kazue, who'd crept in while he was focused on Akira and Tsuki. He felt her spell envelope him a moment too late. The first notes of her song rang through the air. He was too slow to react, and the last thing he saw was Sayuri smiling at him as if to reassure him everything would be well.

Twenty-Four

The old woman lived at the top of a volcano. Heat bubbled in pools of molten lava and leaked out in thin rivulets down the slope. The pathway up was close enough to these rivers and pools that one misstep would singe her fur. Hikaru, who was heartier than most humans, was dripping in sweat and struggling for each breath as they made their ascent. They weren't even a quarter of the way up before the heat became too much for him, and he had to rest. There wasn't much in the way of cover on the barren slope, and they sat down on a cragged boulder. Rin offered the water flask, and Hikaru drank deeply from it. Beads of sweat gathered on his brow, and he wiped it away. Even at rest, his breaths were labored, and the smell of sulfur choked the air. The heat and fumes were only going to get worse the higher they climbed.

"I'll go on ahead. You return to the foot of the mountain and wait for me," she said.

"Are you certain?" Hikaru asked. His gaze turned to the distance away from the mountain, and in the direction of the other soul fragments; Rin was certain of it. Leaving him behind meant leaving him vulnerable to attack from Tsuki and Akira, or worse, him leaving her behind to reunite with the other pieces of Kazue's soul. The thought squeezed at her insides. Rin looked between Hikaru and the mountainside before her. Hikaru couldn't make this hot, steep climb. And they needed the answers she hoped the old woman held. If a solution for their problem lay at the top of the mountain, she'd risk it.

"I'm sure."

"I'll wait for you at the foot of the mountain. Good luck." He gathered her hands in his, meeting her gaze with a meaningful stare. As if saying with a glance that he wouldn't leave her behind, no matter how the call of the other fragments tugged at him.

She trusted Hikaru. She had to. After one last lingering kiss, she resumed her climb. Hikaru didn't immediately head down the mountain, but watched as she climbed. She kept looking back over her shoulder at him until he was just a smudge against the barren, volcanic landscape. When she couldn't see him any longer, she turned her attention to the climb ahead. The terrain grew more difficult the higher she went. The path she'd been following was swallowed up by lava flows. Pools of lava and steam vents hissing and popping forced her to double back and rethink her course more than once. Eventually, the only passable way was over sheer ledges of sharp, volcanic rocks that sliced her hands open and covered her palms in blood. Hands wet and sticky with blood made climbing that much harder, but she persevered until she reached the summit covered in dried blood from her various and healed over wounds.

At first glance, the mountaintop appeared to be nothing but the thick, black crust of cooled lava sheet. The heat was even more intense, and sweat ran in rivulets down her spine and legs. She circled the perimeter, seeking a hut or any structure where the old woman of the mountain might reside. The sun was starting to sink down below the mountain's peak, and long shadows drew across the mountaintop. Rin began to fear the archivist had been wrong. Maybe the old woman was long gone, nothing but myth and another dead end. Just as she was about to succumb to despair, she spied a door placed into the rock itself. Its black paint had blended it in with its surroundings, except for where the paint had peeled and bubbled, revealing weathered wood beneath. As she got closer, Rin heard the clang of metal and smoke rising from what she'd previously taken as another vent but was actually a large chimney.

The clanging stopped and was followed by the hiss of heated metal hitting water. Rin walked up to the door and wrapped upon it, holding her breath as she waited for the door to open. Several long minutes dragged out, and there was no response but the clanging of metal that resumed once more. Rin knocked louder this time. As she did, it seemed the hammering only got louder, as if to drown her out.

Not easily deterred, Rin called out, "Hello, is anyone inside?"

The hammering stopped, and a woman muttered under her breath. She could hear footsteps shuffling before she flung the door open. Rin wasn't sure what she expected but it wasn't the woman standing in front of her. She was average, with broad, muscled shoulders presumably from working a forge. She had a ruddy face and shrewd black eyes that scanned Rin up and down.

"I'm not selling my swords to yokai; you've come here without reason; now please leave," she said and attempted to slam the door in Rin's face, but the kitsune got her foot in the threshold before she could.

She was rather strong, and as the door slammed into her foot, it sent a ripple of pain up her leg. The old woman looked where her door had connected with Rin's flesh and then back at Rin.

"Excuse me," Rin said through gritted teeth.

"You're not excused. Get your foot out of my door before I stab you with a hot poker." She gestured back to her work area.

Long strips of molten metal lay on an iron and the red-hot poker in question was stabbed into a pool of lava used as a hearth. When Rin didn't move out of the door, the woman moved as if she would make good on her threat, and Rin took a step back.

"I'm not here for a sword," Rin said before she could slam the door in her face again.

The woman sniffed skeptically.

"No one comes without reason. And the only reason to visit this mountain is a yokai blade. If you think your kitsune wiles will deceive me into giving you one, you're a fool. Leave before I dump lava on your head." She slammed the door in her face.

Rin raised her fist to knock on the door again. But the old woman's voice cut her off, "Knock again, and I'll use your bones for my next yokai blade."

Rin let her hand fall to her side. The old woman was impossibly stubborn but so was Rin. She hadn't said anything about speaking. She pitched her voice loud enough to be heard through the door and over the clang of her hammering metal.

"I've not come for a blade but information. I heard you created an enchanted staff for Kazue."

The clanging stopped. "Don't waste your time here. I've nothing to tell you!" she shouted back before resuming her hammering.

"You might have forgotten. It was a long time ago."

The hammering stopped, and the door swung open once again. This time, she was brandishing the poker at Rin's face. She barely escaped the hot brand by inches. Rin stumbled backward as the old woman swung it at her.

"You get off my mountain. Now."

Rin moved out of reach of her swinging arms, but did not fully retreat. The old woman was holding back secrets. And she hadn't gone to the depths of the earth and scaled this mountain to leave without information. She also knew that if she pushed the old woman too hard, she'd lose her chance to learn. And a strategic retreat was necessary.

"I'll come back again tomorrow."

"Feh," the old woman said as she slammed the door.

Rin descended the mountain and went in search of Hikaru who was waiting for her as he promised at the base. He greeted her with a smile, which fell a bit at her expression.

"Did you find her?" he asked.

"I found her, but she refused to speak with me," Rin said. "She knows something, though; you should have seen how she changed when I asked her about Kazue." Rin bit her lip.

"Will you try again?"

Rin nodded. There was no choice but to try again.

The next day, Rin scaled the mountain once more and sought out the old woman at her forge. And just as she had the day before, she asked her about Kazue. The old woman pretended not to know her and banished her from the mountain when she asked. So, Rin left and promised to come back again the next day. When she returned to Hikaru the second time, he seemed distracted. She tried asking him about it, but he shrugged off her questions. When she returned on the third day, the old woman lobbed molten metal in her direction as soon as she came into view. Rin dodged the projectile by a hair. The woman wouldn't even hear her questions, and she was forced to retreat back to Hikaru, who looked paler and more drawn than he had that morning.

"Something wrong?" she asked him.

"Suzume. She did something. I can't tell what. But I can feel it." He rubbed at his chest as he said it.

By the fourth day, Rin was more determined than ever to get answers. The old woman seemed to be anticipating her. She was working on wrapping the hilt of a sword in leathers, seated outside her door. At least this time, she wasn't flinging molten metal at her.

"You don't know how to listen, do you?" the old woman said when Rin approached. Her tone was almost affable.

Rin knelt down on the ground. Even just the touch of it was enough to blister her skin. She didn't care. She'd endure worse to find the answers she sought.

"I'll keep coming back until you answer my questions," Rin replied.

"Suit yourself. Die here if you must. I have nothing to tell you or say," she muttered before going back to her work. "Never met a kitsune quite as troublesome as you." The old woman's gaze slid in her direction.

"Have you known many?" Rin asked.

"I have. And other yokai over the years. All of them rotten." She spat onto the ground, and it sizzled, evaporating immediately.

Rin stayed kneeling until the sunset and her knees were aching from the blisters that hadn't quite healed. The old woman only shook her head as Rin hobbled down the hill. When she reached Hikaru, he tended to her blisters and offered her a chance to give up, but she endured.

On the fifth day, when Rin reached the mountaintop, she knelt and waited for the old woman to come out before sunrise. But once she emerged, she refused to even look her way. Rin sat until the sun set and her knees were aching from the blisters and burns that had formed from sitting on the hot ground. Rin repeated the same healing and kneeling ritual for three more days. Neither she nor Hikaru spoke much during those days. But giving up wasn't an option.

Rin would have endured twice as much torture, but on the eighth day, the old woman came to loom over her where she kneeled.

"You'll kill yourself at this rate. And for what?" the old woman asked.

"I can do more than this for the man I love," Rin replied.

The old woman studied her for a moment. "Kazue said something like that too."

Rin tried not to let her excitement show on her face. She didn't press, though the questions were on the tip of her tongue.

The old woman realized her mistake, cleared her throat, and went back to work. But this time, she didn't do it in silence.

"There used to be more of us, at the beginning of the world. I had sisters whose magic was like mine. Before the first kami wars killed them."

Rin said nothing, fearing an interruption would silence her.

"For a long time, my sister and I were all that remained. But she was hungry for vengeance against the gods, against the yokai, and the humans who'd forgotten what they'd been. Once she shed her first skin, there was no going back. She craved more. She took bodies as the kami do and trained up the ideal vessels. Then one of her protégés learned of her plots, and that girl came to me, looking to do the same. Wanted to shed her skin and become a kami herself. If you can believe it."

Rin could, but she wasn't going to say as much. She'd frozen in place, waiting for her to continue.

"I thought my sister's mad quest was foolhardy, but I craved vengeance too. So, I made her student a weapon in one of my weak moments. That staff was powered by the scale of the one who'd faced the Eight and won. The Great Dragon. I thought once she'd conquered the Eight, I'd feel at peace. I was wrong. Its making took a good deal of my power. More than I had to give, if I'm being honest. But I thought that's what I wanted. Vengeance for my lost sisters. But I was wrong, and I suppose so was she."

She turned to look at Rin now. "The thing she sought was right in front of her the whole time. A soul shed from its body can only consume. Seeking more and more. But a soul shared. Well, that could sustain someone for an eternity."

"Is that possible? I thought those were all just legends."

"Legends start somewhere. Come here. Let me give you something." She walked inside, and Rin followed her.

Despite being hewn out of volcanic rock, it was rather domestic and lacked what Rin realized was any sort of spiritual energy. She'd assumed because she'd lived in a volcano, the old woman was yokai, but that wasn't right. There was something off about her.

"Are you... human?' Rin asked.

"Took you this long to realize?"

"But how is that possible?"

The woman sat in her chair and groaned. "There was a time humans were immortal as well."

She had always thought that was a myth.

"I'm the last, and you can't really call us human anymore, I suppose." She huffed as she shuffled through her small home. Her steps were slower and more labored than when Rin had first arrived. And she had to lean over the table where a sword lay. It was the same one she'd seen her working on these past few days.

"You said a soul could be shared. Does that mean there is another way for a human to gain immortality?"

"Just one," she said and gestured to the sword.

"What is that?"

"A way for you to save your man, I suspect. A way to sever souls as easily as that staff binds them."

"Could I cut a piece of something that's been attached to a soul?"

Rin's hands shook as she hovered over the weapon on the table. It seemed too good to be true. The answer to all her prayers. Before she grasped a hold of it, the old woman grabbed her wrist with her calloused hand. She could use this to sever the piece of Kazue's soul from Hikaru's. But would he survive the cut?

"Yes. But not without consequences. Simply cutting a soul free won't work. Or else it will attach to anything it wants. Which can have terrible consequences." A dark shadow passed over her face. "You must tie the severed soul to something else. But tie the wrong knots and both parties will die tangled together. This doesn't grant immortality like the staff. It binds lives and their life spans together. Never to be parted." She let go of Rin.

There was no doubt in her mind that this was exactly what she needed.

"And what happens to the one who was cut?" Rin asked.

"Like any wound, they bleed. Unless something can sustain that life, they'll die."

Rin felt certainty sweep over her. She knew what she must do. She grasped hold of the blade and felt the weight of it in her hand. If it could cut and bind, she'd use her own life to protect

Hikaru's if she must. She was about to turn and thank the old woman for her help when she collapsed onto the ground. Rin caught her before her head cracked open, but she felt lighter in her arms, as if she were fading away.

"Use this gift wisely. My last sword." She smiled faintly as her breathing faded, and then she died in Rin's arms.

TWENTY-FIVE

Fire and wind thrummed through Suzume's aching chest as she stared into the distance. Kaito requested she open her senses and search for Kazue. She'd been distantly aware of the other pieces of Kazue's soul for a while now, but she'd been ignoring that tug. Since she'd gone into the spirit realm, the tethers that connected them felt even stronger. For the first time, Suzume embraced the tug on her soul and used it to guide them to the water of Kazue's soul. It shouldn't have surprised her that she was hiding in the White Palace alongside Hisato. She felt both of their fragments like two glass shards stabbed into her chest. Further away, but moving closer, she felt Hikaru. As she marched for the palace, she felt Hisato and the water of Kazue's soul drawing closer to her. They were frequently in her dreams, and she wondered if they dreamed of her as well. Hikaru was getting closer also, though he was farther away than the other two. The threads that bound them all were pulling tighter by the day. And with each step, she felt the coil of Kazue's power tightening around her heart. As the distance shrunk between them, the more her soul cried out for reunification.

She hoped Hikaru stayed away, or else she might not be able to resist that pull for much longer. If their plan went awry, it'd be up to him to stop Hisato alone. She clutched her staff in her hand. Knowing Kazue was within the walls of the White Palace, they figured finding her in the chaos of the impending coup would be the easiest way to get her out of the palace without Hisato noticing. They'd need to keep her somewhere safe until Suzume fused Hisato's soul and hers. Then she'd bind Kazue before killing her, and following her into the spirit realm, force her beyond the veil. It all made sense in her head, but she feared what that would look like in reality. Now, they waited for Ryuu and his promised army to come and put their plan in motion. His neko had delivered a message days ago letting them know he'd been successful in winning over the empress to their side.

Kaito came up from behind her and placed a hand on her shoulder, and she leaned against him for support. She wasn't sure she'd be able to do this without him. Columns of soldiers marched toward them, carrying banners she recognized belonging to the empress' clan. As the group drew closer, she spotted Ryuu riding at the front. He looked at ease in the saddle, with a confident swagger she'd never noticed from him before.

It was strange seeing him as a warlord general. She knew he'd united the human clans to form the empire of Akatsuki, but it was still disorienting. Kaito and Suzume had been busy plotting out how they'd capture Kazue, so she hadn't considered the coup Ryuu was planning. But seeing him riding with an army at his back, she felt a surge of confidence in their plans that she'd been lacking for far too long.

They waited for Ryuu and his army to greet them. The wind picked up and sent an ominous chill down her spine. She recognized the various clan banners among their numbers. Countless families who'd be tried as traitors should this attempt fail. There was no love lost between her mother and the empress, but it felt strange to be partnering with the empress' clan and her allies, nonetheless.

Ryuu dismounted and bowed to both Kaito and Suzume.

"Greetings," he said.

"You've made good on your promises," Kaito remarked with a grudging sort of acknowledgment.

"Indeed, I have," Ryuu replied.

"Where is my brother? I'd like to greet him," Suzume asked. She was searching the soldiers for a man on a horse. Her eldest brother was a few years older than her, a strong swordsman and scholar. They'd never been close, given the animosity between their mothers, but he'd never been unkind to her. And if he were willing to risk a traitor's death, she ought to see him at least.

"I am here, sister," said a young voice.

Suzume's gaze swept the crowd.

There was a slight shuffling and then four soldiers surrounding a mounted teenage boy rode to the front of the line. Suzume's stomach dropped seeing her younger half-brother. He was a young man, little more than a child, with the faint ghost of a mustache on his upper lip. This wasn't the crown prince, but his younger brother.

Suzume looked at Ryuu. "Where is the crown prince?" she asked. A horrifying realization crawled over her.

"I am the crown prince," the second prince said, with a stubborn tilt of his head and a scathing look at Suzume that reminded her very much of his mother.

Suzume scowled right back at him. "You are a child playing at a man."

"And you are what, a witch?" he asked.

Ryuu shot him a look, and the prince wilted beneath it. Then Ryuu turned to Suzume. "I think we should speak in private."

Kaito was glancing at the army gathered and then at Ryuu. "Perhaps we should."

They retreated, leaving the army to set up their encampment, and retired to Kaito's private tent.

When they were alone, Suzume launched at Ryuu with questions. "You were going to find allies. Not recruit my younger brother into this mess."

Ryuu looked tired and pale; dark circles shadowed his eyes.

"The crown prince is dead," Ryuu said.

The words fell like a stone into a still pool. Suzume stood frozen a moment as the reality rippled over her. A normal sister would have grieved. Would have cried. But she felt hollow and lacking, especially for her first thought being: What now? It was one thing to ask an adult to stage a coup; it was quite another to thrust a boy-king onto the throne. This was too big a burden to request of that child. Who was to say some other adult wouldn't use him like a puppet to do their bidding? What fate was she dooming her kingdom to by making her younger brother emperor? Was she any better than her mother and her ambitions for her son?

"And you'd put that child on the throne instead?" Kaito asked. His tone was indifferent, but Suzume heard the note of disgust in it.

She pressed the heels of her palms to her burning eyes. She hadn't been sleeping, and the exhaustion felt as if it would overwhelm her in that moment. Kaito caught her by her elbow as she swayed on her feet. They were going to insight a coup and put a literal child in place of her father. Was this wise? Would it be better for her to go alone? Could she face Hisato and drag him beyond the veil with her own two hands, even if it meant her death? That must be better than this mess she'd found herself in, surely. Suddenly, she felt as if she couldn't breathe. The air was being forced out of her lungs like a snake wrapped around her torso, squeezing the life out of her.

"Suzume?" Kaito grabbed onto her shoulders, and she looked up into his eyes as she wheezed in and out. "What's wrong with her?" Kaito asked Ryuu.

Ryuu came over and touched her brow. She felt a jolt go through her. A sudden calming energy washed through her, and she felt her chest loosen and her breaths come easier. She leaned forward, head between her legs, trying to reclaim her center. When she was calm, she looked up at Kaito and Ryuu.

"I'm fine now," she said, even though they all knew that was a lie.

She felt as if she were becoming as brittle as sun-bleached bones, and with each new day, more and more of her was being chipped away. Whenever she closed her eyes out of sheer exhaustion, Souta and Kazue's memories flooded through her mind. There was no escaping them. Entering into the spirit realm a third time had broken the dam, and the lines between her and Kazue seemed thinner than ever. She was running out of time. Even if her brother was young, they didn't have another plan. It was this or death.

"Any other surprises?" Kaito asked. Thankfully taking the pressure of attention off her.

"I know it's less than ideal. It was the only way I could secure the empress' clans' support," Ryuu replied.

Kaito grunted a non-answer. And for a moment, she feared they would be at one another's throats again. But there was a strange sort of respect that seemed to pass between the two of them, as if they'd come to an unspoken understanding.

"Is there something I should know?" Ryuu looked at Suzume pointedly.

"We've recruited priestesses and priests to our cause."

"Oh? And how has that worked out?"

"Rocky. But we're finding our equilibrium." Kaito said it with such easy confidence that Suzume almost believed him.

"What happens next?" Suzume asked, growing sick of the small talk. She needed a solid plan. Something to cling to and give her purpose and a way forward.

"We'll need to move quickly, before the palace can build up their defenses. They would have received word of the army marching their way them by now," Ryuu said.

"Let the humans focus on making the boy emperor. I need you for an important task," Kaito said.

"What's that?" Ryuu arched a brow.

"Helping me capture Kazue and trapping her."

Ryuu's brows rose higher and higher as Kaito explained everything they'd learned from Suzume's trip into the spirit realm and their plan to capture Kazue.

Ryuu was rubbing his face as he took in all the information.

"To bring her beyond the veil, we'll need to first bind Hisato to her. And there's no guarantees I can hold him for very long. We'd have one shot."

"Can you do it?" Suzume asked. They both looked at her.

The weight of their stares felt like they might suffocate her. She'd been secretly hoping Ryuu could help. That he'd have the answers to her problem.

"I'll do what I can," Ryuu assured her, but she thought she saw a shadow of doubt lingering in his gaze.

There was more to plan but Suzume felt the walls closing in around her as Kaito and Ryuu discussed the details of their coup and palace invasion. She got up and declared, "I want to head out for some air."

"I'll go with you," they both said in unison before turning to look at one another.

"I'd rather be alone."

Suzume waved off their offer and headed out. The camp was in chaos. With the introduction of more humans, the yokai were restless and grumbling. The new humans were looking at the yokai with sideways glances. Amari and the priests and priestesses were doing their best to bridge the gap between them all. She elbowed her way through a group of humans, who looked over her without a second glance, which was both comforting and disconcerting. She'd become almost accustomed to their stares that anonymity felt foreign. She was near the edge of the encampment when someone crashed into her. Suzume reached for her staff on impulse and turned to see a soldier bowing to her profusely.

"Forgive me. My mistake, Princess," he said.

As he bowed, a piece of paper fluttered out of his haori.

It all happened so fast she didn't have time to process that he'd called her princess until he'd disappeared into the crowd, leaving the paper on the ground. She stooped down to pick it up and was going to shout after him when her name written at the top of the page caught her off guard.

Suzume,

He knows what you're planning. And I know that you think dying is the only way to stop him. But if you want to live, meet me at dusk and come alone. I can save you.

There was a location noted on the map, near where she was. Not only had her mother slipped a spy into their camp, she knew where they were, and had a meeting place. Suzume's breath hitched as she crumpled the paper, determined to toss it away. But she clung to it despite her better judgment.

"What's that?" Ryuu asked.

Kaito was standing next to him, looking concerned. "Did they hurt you?" he asked. "I'll find them and make them pay." He turned to follow them before she could stop him.

They'd followed her out, despite her assurances otherwise. She held the letter in her hand and, before she could think it through, handed it over to Ryuu.

"It's another trap," she said, certain that he would concur, and she could push the desire to go to her summons from her mind.

Ryuu's eyes roved over the paper as if he were a man starved. His lips parted, and then he shook his head. "Right before we tried to enter the palace, she attempted to warn me against bringing you there. I thought it was in serving her own interests. But one thing stood out. She begged me to remember my promise to protect you."

"Are you defending her?"

Ryuu shook his head. "It's your choice whether you meet her or not. But I do think in her own way she is trying to protect you."

Suzume curled her hand into a fist. Anger and fear ricocheted around inside her chest. She hated her mother, but even as much as she resented her, she loved her, too. What if she did know something that could be useful? What if she could help them on their quest?

"I want to go see her," Suzume declared.

Twenty-Six

Noaki was suspended somewhere between waking and dreaming, and in his dreams, he was back on the mountain serving the Sun Emperor and watching as Sayuri slowly faded. This time, he reached out to her, but his fingers slipped through her, as if she'd been made of moonlight. Sayuri turned to him, saying something that he couldn't hear. Then she was standing at the end of a long hallway and no matter how fast or hard he ran he couldn't reach her. Noaki stumbled and fell before waking with a gasp. The dreams lingered in the waking world, and he smelt her perfume hanging in the room. Blinking in the too-bright light, he gazed around the unfamiliar room he'd been tied up in. Chains imbued with spiritual power wrapped around his torso and pinned his arms to his side, weakening him so any attempt to free himself would be futile. His swords were propped up against a painted screen depicting a mountain scene with a tree in the foreground. He recognized the mountain as the Sun Emperor's, as if his dreams had been transposed onto canvas.

The doors slid open, and Noaki rolled his head to the side. The new Kazue, the water of her soul, strode into the room. She was dressed as a noble, with layers of silk and her long hair cascading down her shoulders. It was another echo, another attempt to confuse him between past and present. She knelt before him with the ghost of a smile on her lips, a pale parody of Sayuri's secret smile.

"Forgive me. This isn't how I wanted our reunion to play out."

Noaki didn't dignify her words with a response. But he couldn't stop himself from scrutinizing her expression and seeking some proof that she wasn't Sayuri and Kazue combined, that she wasn't toying with his heart to her own malicious ends.

"Are you going to say anything, or are you going to keep staring at me?" she asked.

Noaki didn't trust himself to speak and instead remained silent.

She sighed and pushed her hair behind her ear, a nervous habit of the previous Kazue's. Noaki had seen her do it thousands of times on the road together. Seeing those mannerisms on a stranger's face mixed with those bright reflections of Sayuri felt as if he were looking into a broken mirror.

"I'll have you know; I had no choice but to bring you here," she said. He recognized Kazue's exasperated tone leaking through.

She searched his face, waiting for him to reply, but if she were really Kazue or Sayuri, she would know none would be forthcoming.

She stood up and paced the room around her, wringing her hands together. "He wants to use you as a vessel. Another step in his glorious plan for reunification. I just barely managed to convince him the priest's sacrifice wasn't worthy of your power.

But I think he knows I'm starting to unravel. There's too many voices shouting in my head now." She wrapped her arms around her torso as if she were trying and failing to keep herself together. In reality, she was falling apart like broken pieces of porcelain.

Though he wanted to hate her, he also pitied her. The girl, the host, whatever she might be called. They'd stolen her life, her soul, to bring back Kazue to be used as Hisato's pawn in a power gambit that would only destroy her.

"Do you want to break free?" Noaki asked, despite his better sense that said to keep his mouth shut.

She spun around, her lips parted as if she were surprised he spoke or perhaps afraid to move and scare him away again.

"I don't know anymore," she whispered. "I'm not even sure if these thoughts are mine any longer..."

Noaki didn't reply again. This could be a trick, but he waited for her to unspool more of her tale for him. Kazue used to talk about her plans out loud with him, or maybe she was talking to herself, and he was there to hear it. Either way, she shared too much of her inner thoughts with him, and if he was right maybe this version of her would too.

"I thought I was sacred. A vessel. That's what they called me at the temple where I was raised. I was to be the next coming of High Priestess Kazue. My entire identity belonged to her. Who I was outside of that I never considered. I thought becoming her was all I wanted. But I've been seeing her life—Sayuri. The woman you loved. More and more since the mountaintop. As if she's trying desperately to break free to the surface. Her love for you and her children...it's burning in my chest." She trailed off.

She looked at him with an imploring gaze, as if begging him to see Sayuri trapped beneath her skin. And though he knew he shouldn't, Noaki believed her. The same thing was happening to Suzume. He'd seen the effects on her. Human flesh wasn't meant to contain this much dissonance and divinity.

Something in her gaze changed. And he saw it settle over her as if she'd put on a mask, one that seemed achingly familiar to him even though he tried to deny it. She stood incredibly still and there was a glow from within her that wasn't there before. He felt her presence, and even though nothing physically changed, her spiritual pressure did.

"I wondered if you would forgive me for what I did. Even though you are loyal to a fault, you must have your limits. But you know by now, I did what I had to do to create a better world. One that wasn't ruled by him," Sayuri said through Kazue.

Gods above, it hurt to hear her, to see her look at him through a stranger's eyes, and not be able to reach out and touch her.

"I could never stay angry at you," he said, the words stolen from him as if in a whisper.

She moved closer to him, so close the breath caught in his lungs, and he could do nothing but stare into her eyes.

"I never thought these tangled roads would lead us back here. I'm a captive once more, but the cage is filled with barbs, and a knife is being held to my heart."

The eyes that bore into him in that moment were aching in their familiarity. He wanted so desperately to believe her. To accept that deep down beneath this stranger's face was the woman he loved. But the reasonable part of his brain knew it couldn't be true. Sayuri would never have partnered with someone as vile as Hisato. This must be a trick. Some way to sway him as she had done to his children before turning them into a monster.

He turned away from her and refused to speak.

She stood once more and glanced down at him, taking on a regal and poised pose that Sayuri often took when she was upset. It was another mask, a defense, he realized, to hide her real emotions. And it made the deception all the more effective. Because this was the Sayuri he knew. Not some caricature of her, but the woman he'd glimpsed trapped in the Sun Emperor's lonely palace.

"He's going to come for you soon, and I cannot protect you. Not unless you're willing to free me from this prison. From this flesh trap. Will you or won't you?"

"And play into what Hisato wants?" he asked.

She stared at him for a long moment without speaking, as if she'd let the weight of her silence do all the talking for him.

"Either way, this vessel is going to die," she said. "Better it at your gentle hands than his."

He didn't respond but he didn't think she expected one because she strode out of the room without another word.

Days passed, and the passage of time was marked by the shadows moving across the floor of his prison, extending and receding like the tide. She didn't come back to him. He saw not even a whisper of her for days and he feared she had abandoned him at last. That all his seeking had led to nothing at all.

The door opened, and the light spilling in was enough to blind him. Noaki flinched as the person entered; the twisted creature who'd once been his children leered at him. Kazue wasn't in sight. They grabbed ahold of him, dragging him from his prison and out to his execution.

A menagerie of hybrids lingered around the courtyard, roaring, snorting, and stamping their feet at his approach. They brought him before Hisato, who stood on the steps of the temple building as if he were both priest and emperor. He was swathed in silk and looked at Noaki with a malevolent gleam in his eye. Kazue was standing at his side. She wouldn't look at him as she approached, and neither of them acknowledged the young woman who was tied in front of them. The girl was whimpering softly, wearing a bag over her head. Hisato strode forward.

Noaki's transformed children forced him to his knees, and he collapsed, weak as a newborn kitten. They'd bound his power, so he had no choice.

"I have found the perfect vessel for you," Hisato said. "A pure priestess of exceptional power. All that remains is the choice you must make, Noaki. Will you join us by choice or by force?"

"You know my answer. Don't pretend you don't," he said.

Hisato's mouth curved in a cruel smile.

"And so I do."

He removed the bag from the girl's head, and Noaki could see how young she was. Tears were flowing down her cheeks. Noaki wasn't afraid of death. He'd lived a thousand lives and taken as many. But he hoped whatever found him on the other side would allow him to be reborn so he could be with Sayuri in the next.

Kazue stepped forward and started to sing. He felt the pull of it on his body. Felt the parts of him being ripped apart, and then suddenly it stopped. As he sat on the edge of oblivion, he felt suddenly at peace. Easier to slip below those dark waters at last rather than continue fighting and struggling. Just as he was giving way to the darkness, he rose out of it. Noaki came back to his senses as his magic returned in a rush, and the chains which had bound it clattered onto the ground. Soft hands pressed a blade into his hands. Kazue was staring up at him, the tip of the it pressed against her abdomen.

"Do it," she begged. She wanted him to kill her to free her from the mortal prison. But he knew even as his hands shook, it wasn't possible.

Instead, he shoved her to the ground and rose, swinging his sword and fighting his children who rushed him the moment he'd broken free. They slashed at one another, exchanging blows in a slow and steady dance. Hisato watched it all happen with an amused expression on his face. Noaki knew that fighting his children and refusing to draw their blood or kill them was pointless. He had to kill Hisato. He knocked through his children's defense and then lunged for Hisato, sword held high, ready for a killing blow. But as he made to swing down, his hands froze in the air.

Hisato walked forward, clapping his hands as he approached the frozen Noaki. No matter how his mind protested, he couldn't make his body move.

"You've played all these games too well. She wanted you to kill her to avoid the reunification. But there's no escaping it. Seeing as you have the will to live. I think I can find greater use for you after all. We will all return together, and you will be what brings Suzume to me because, in the end, that's what fate demands."

Hisato grasped a hold of his face and looked him in the eye.

"Suzume might have released you, but she is not the only one who holds the memory of your true name."

Hearing it sent a spike of fear through him, and Noaki stood frozen in horror as Hisato formed the words.

"You will best serve us by going back to Suzume and bringing her to me. Lead them and their army into my bosom, and when the moment comes, you will turn her over to me."

The compulsion rippled through him. He couldn't fight it.

"You will speak of this to no one," were Hisato's final words before he was shoved out the gate and sent on his way back to Suzume, prepared to betray her.

TWENTY-SEVEN

Suzume's palms were slick with sweat. After a long debate between Kaito, Ryuu, and herself, they decided it would be best if she didn't met her mother alone, though she'd appear as if she were. Kaito & Ryuu hid in the shadows. Knowing they had her back made this meeting just a little bit easier. Their meeting place was an abandoned shrine building. And as she passed through the decayed torii arches, a prickle of unease wormed its way up her spine. They intended to capture Izuki and use her for information. If Izuki could divulge more of Hisato's plans and tell her how to find the water of Kazue's soul inside the palace, it would make Suzume's job that much easier. It was a rather straightforward plan, but nothing was ever that simple when it came to her mother.

The temple was empty, so either her mother wasn't there yet, or she was planning on making a dramatic entrance. Which would be just like her. Suzume risked looking back to where Kaito was hiding. Though he was mostly invisible, he gave her a reassuring thumbs-up, and she took a deep breath as she approached the crumbling shrine.

The night air moved across her skin like a gentle caress, assuring her that everything was going to be alright. The knot of tension in her chest untangled, if only a little. Then her mother stepped out of the building, and Suzume tensed. Until this moment, a small part of her assumed she wasn't going to show. As if the note and this meeting would be just another time her mother abandoned her when she promised she would. Izuki was poised and beautiful as usual, wearing a simple kimono that lacked the many layers and flourishes of court style. She was also alone, which Suzume found even more surprising. She half-expected to see Hisato leering at her over her mother's shoulder.

"I wasn't sure you'd come," Izuki said. Suzume might have imagined it, but she thought she saw a hint of relief on her mother's face.

Suzume tightened her hand in a fist and took a deep breath to try and keep her temper in control. The audacity of this woman for betraying her and then summoning her here as if nothing had passed between them.

She exhaled and said, "Why did you summon me here? To make more threats? How did you get a note into the heart of the empress' army?"

"I've been worried about you," her mother said, as if that answered any of her questions. She was a fool to expect her to be honest with her. It wasn't her style.

Suzume felt as if there was a hand squeezing around her heart, threatening to burst it in her chest. She kept her expression cold. Neutral. She didn't want to give her the satisfaction.

"Is that why you betrayed me to Hisato?"

"It's not what you think." She took a step forward, her expression almost earnest. But Suzume had seen the way she used her charms on governors and petty noblemen, bending them to her will.

Suzume held up her hand to halt her. "I don't want your excuses. Tell me what you came to say."

Izuki's eyes were welling with unshed tears, but it was another trick; Suzume was sure of it. She hoped that Kaito or Ryuu would make a move and capture her soon so she wouldn't have to endure more of her false tears. "I came to tell you to leave Akatsuki. Travel as far and as fast as you can. He's planning on absorbing you. He thinks you can create a new world together..."

"Isn't it a little late for you to care? You did this," Suzume said.

She'd heard enough. She should have known she'd get nothing but excuses from her. Suzume moved to give the signal for Ryuu and Kaito to move in, but as she did, another figure stepped out of the shadows. Suzume drew her staff and illuminated it with fire as the water of Kazue's soul stepped out of the shadows. But instead of attacking Suzume, she drew a dagger and held it to Izuki's throat. She'd snuck up so suddenly, or perhaps she'd been so consumed by anger at her mother that she hadn't felt the tethers tying her to the other Kazue pulling taut.

"I was wondering where you slunk off to," Kazue said, scoring a bright red line against her mother's throat.

Despite the weapon held against her neck, Izuki held her head high and regal and proud as always. Suzume hesitated as she looked between them. What sort of trick was this? Why threaten her mother? Suzume felt the flames coursing through her, the wind whipping around her hair. Kazue's eyes flicked in her direction as if she were an afterthought, though they both knew that wasn't the case. Despite the dangerous position they were in, Suzume felt her soul cry out to this imposter Kazue, and it took all her willpower to not approach her.

"Let her go; she has nothing to do with us," Suzume ground out.

Kazue smiled. "She has everything to do with it. She's threatening to ruin all my plans."

She backed up, dragging her mother along and Suzume could do nothing but stand still and watch. This was her moment; she needed to capture Kazue. But her feet were too afraid to move. She might hate her mother, but she didn't want her dead.

"And what plans do you have?" Suzume asked, swallowing past the lump in her throat.

Ryuu and Kaito were closing in; she was sure of it. They'd intervene and somehow save them both.

"You've been in my dreams for months. Did you think I wouldn't figure out your plan? The closer we are together, the stronger the resonance. Where I stop, and you start blurs more each day. You're greedy and a fool to think I would stand aside and let you make me the sacrifice. If I take on the fragments, there's no chance of reincarnation for me. I would be the one to pay for Kazue's sins, trapped beyond the veil, neither alive nor dead." She pressed the dagger closer to her mother's throat as if to accentuate her point.

Suzume felt the truth of it ripple through her. In her gut, she knew she was telling the truth. And as much as she wanted revenge, the thought of condemning her to eternal purgatory seemed too cruel a punishment.

"I don't know what you're talking about," Suzume said, inching closer to them. But Kazue only tightened her grip, and her mother gasped.

"Don't lie, Suzume. We both know you're not a hero. It's not in you. The only way to stop Hisato is to kill him. But you can't kill a thing that doesn't have a body, can you? Someone needs to be the vessel, and it won't be me. What do you think happens to a soul this damaged in the afterlife? Do you think he'll be able to reincarnate?" Kazue glared at her, but Suzume noticed her hands shaking.

"We can help one another. We can work together to find another way," Suzume said, holding up her hands in surrender. But Kazue only shook her head. Where were Kaito and Ryuu? Why hadn't they intervened yet? Suzume didn't dare tear her eyes away from Kazue and her mother.

"From the moment we were created, we could never be friends."

Kazue's muscles tensed, and Suzume watched in slow motion as the blade slid across her mother's throat. Saw the spill of her blood. And heard the soft cry as she crumpled in Kazue's arms. Distantly, she heard Ryuu's anguished cry, but everything had slowed to a single point in time.

Kazue met Suzume's gaze, a challenge in her dark eyes. Her face was splattered with her mother's blood. Suzume lunged for her, but before she could reach her, a barrier slammed in place, blocking her out and giving Kazue time to escape. Even knowing she couldn't get past it, she flung her fire at it, watching it spark and burst into useless embers. Suzume collapsed onto her knees.

Ryuu had rushed forward to hold Izuki, rocking her back and forth, while Kaito came over and squeezed her shoulder. They both felt miles away.

"She put up a barrier before we could intervene. We tried to break it, but it was too strong."

Suzume shook her head; there was no reason for him to apologize. She should have saved her. She got up, her legs shaking as she stumbled toward her mother and Ryuu. Izuki was dying. Coughing, choking on her own blood. Suzume knelt down, hands hovering. There was so much blood. She looked to Ryuu for guidance, and the anguish in his face was enough to undo her. Her mother reached for her, pressing her hand against Suzume's face. Whether an apology or one last touch of a mother's affection, she would never know because Izuki sputtered out her last breath and died.

R YUU CARRIED IZUKI'S LIFELESS BODY INTO THE TEMPLE. THERE WERE A thousand things he should be doing. Chasing down Kazue and exacting his revenge, comforting Suzume in her grief. But Kaito had her. He was holding her in his arms as she stared numbly out at nothing. Ryuu laid Izuki's body down in the temple, folding her arms over her chest. If it weren't for the crimson blood stained down her front, she'd look like she was sleeping.

Izuki had always been so poised and perfect. Always in control of her emotions, her appearance. It would infuriate her to see herself now. Small, fragile. Helpless. Dead.

Ryuu had lost many people over his long life. Death had become as familiar as an old friend by now. There'd been countless women, countless loves, but Izuki's death cut like a knife to the bone. A knife she'd driven into him that he couldn't quite pull out, no matter how much it hurt. Just when he thought he was done with her, she dragged him back in. What was it about her that he just couldn't forget? Why did she continue to bewitch him this way?

Ryuu found a cloth in the abandoned temple that he used to wash Izuki's body. He removed the blood from her pale skin and the palms of her hands. He smoothed out her hair as best as he could. She would have wanted that. To face death with dignity. They would need to erect a funeral pyre to burn her body.

He busied his hands by gathering the wood and kindling. Suzume was in shock and remained seated, staring into the distance, but Kaito joined him in gathering up bundles of wood. They worked together in silence, needing few words to express their needs. It felt strangely comfortable in a way he never thought they'd get along. But since their brawl, something had eased between them. They were far away from being a loving family, but it was getting easier.

"Thank you," Ryuu said.

"I'm not doing it for you. It's for her." He nodded to where Suzume sat, but Ryuu caught the faint smile curling his lips.

They built up the pyre and with each stick placed, the howling grief which was rising up inside him only seemed to grow. No amount of busy work or preparation was going to sever him from the emptiness her death left. But he kept moving forward anyway.

He thought he'd be ready by the time preparations were made, but even as they doused her in oil they found stashed in the temple, he knew he couldn't let go, not yet. The spirit lingered right after death. Without the proper funeral rights, it might wander for an eternity. And though it was a risk to attempt it, he knew he couldn't let her go without one more goodbye.

"Give me one more minute with her," he said to Kaito and Suzume.

Kaito nodded, and he led Suzume away. Ryuu knelt down beside her body and grabbed her oil-slicked hands. Slipping beyond the veil was easy when the doorway to death was so close. He merely breathed in and then out again, opening his eyes to the realm between.

She was waiting for him. There was a small part of him that had known she would be, despite the call of the beyond surely tugging at her. But Izuki was stubborn in that way. Had he not stepped through, she might have waited an eternity for him. She would never go quietly into the night. Not without her last say. And so, he'd come to hear her final words.

"You came," she said. A ghost of her usual mischievous smile pulled at her lips.

He considered what to say in this moment. That, of course, he had. That he'd try and save her again, given the chance, but there wasn't any way to bring her back this time. She'd used up her second chance when he'd used the flame of Kazue's soul, and she'd borne Suzume.

"Yes, I did," he croaked. His words felt thick in his throat.

"Suzume?" she asked.

"Safe." He left it at that. There was no need to worry her spirit, or she might linger and lose her chance to pass on. It was dangerous to even indulge her this much.

She nodded her head. "Good."

"Why did you do it?" he asked.

She tilted her head to look at him, as if confused why he hadn't figured it out. "I came to try and protect her. The only way to save her was to keep her away. But she's too like me. Too stubborn for her own good."

"You know she won't run away, but you can tell me what you know of his plan."

She shook her head. "I would if I could. All he would assure me was that she would be safe, and loved in his embrace. And then..." She trailed off.

"What else are you not telling me?" he asked.

"Just get her away from here, Ryuu. When they meet, she will die." Izuki looked desperate now.

"You lured her to him twice, and now you want me to keep her away. How can I trust anything you have to say?"

A sad smile flickered across her face.

"It was selfish of me to ask you to watch over her that way. I know she's too much like me."

Ryuu heaved a sigh and ran a hand through his hair. "It's impossible not to care about her. About either of you..."

It all felt too natural. As if they were back at the palace, or even before that, back when she'd merely been a lord's daughter and him the captain of her guard. She was twisting her words, speaking sideways to keep the truth from him again. He couldn't let this last moment slip away without knowing what was necessary to protect Suzume.

"For my children, I will do anything...But, Ryuu, he's taken my son hostage. He's safe as long as he's useful to him. At first, I trusted Hisato and thought he would protect her, it's why I tried to arrange their union. Then I learned the truth, that he wants to consume her."

The prince she would have put on the throne above the emperor's older sons. That was how Hisato was using her, holding her son ransom while trying to destroy her daughter.

"I can't choose between them. I can't let either of them die, but I can't just sit back and let him keep doing this." She grasped at him with ghostly appendages that merely passed through him.

He had to remind himself that she was gone. She wasn't coming back, and the longer he kept her here, the harder it would be for her to pass on.

"You should go," Ryuu said.

"I'm telling you this because I need your help. Save my son, please."

Either her standing up to Kazue was a calculated risk that had backfired, or she was desperate.

"Damn you," Ryuu growled.

"You'll do it then?"

"As if there was ever a choice."

She threw her arms around his neck, but they just passed through him. He felt the memory of her touch, the brush of her ghostly lips against his. She was already starting to fade away. He remembered the feeling of her heart beating against him. Whatever spell she had over him, it was a feeling he'd never forget. She stepped back, and that sad smile crept over her face.

Then he watched her walk away into the mist, beyond the barrier, to the place where he couldn't reach her. But the memories of her would be etched into his heart for an eternity.

TWENTY-EIGHT

Suzume felt hollow. It was the only way to describe the empty, wind-blown feeling that swept through her. She was a doll pulled up by invisible strings. She was going through the motions, smiling and acting as if she were fine when she knew deep down she wasn't. But she didn't feel like she had the right to grieve. She and her mother had never been close. There'd always been this yawning distance between them. And for so long she'd formed her life around being enough for her: finding the richest husband, being the perfect daughter and princess. But no matter how much Suzume tried to earn her love, it was never enough. Now that she was gone, she'd never be able to prove she was worthy.

Over and over, Izuki chose herself before Suzume, putting her own ambitions above her children's happiness. Sacrificing motherly love at the altar of power. At the back of her mind, Suzume had longed for reconciliation, or at the least for her mother to act like a mother. Now she was dead, and there were no more chances to heal the wounds between them. No more chances for her to become the mother Suzume needed. She didn't want to grieve, not when her own possible death loomed before her. She didn't want to waste her tears on someone who'd never really cared enough for her. But the grief still sat like a stone on her chest, making it difficult to breathe.

The wind had carried her to the edge of their encampment, where the buzz of everyone else's work faded away, but the grief howled like an angry beast in her breast. A part of her wanted to scream, let out the anger she bottled up, nurtured by injustice, and stoked in the burning fire in her gut. It was Izuki's fault Suzume was like this. Her schemes had thrust this fate upon her. And she didn't even have the decency to look Suzume in the eye and say sorry.

Suzume curled her hand into a fist, a ball of fire burning in her palm, growing in size, fed by her anger until it was large enough to cast long shadows. And then, when she could no longer contain it, she flung it at a nearby tree. She watched as the flames engulfed it, singeing it black and burning hot, and turning green leaves to ash. But as she stood watching the tree burn, she didn't feel satisfaction or relief, just numbness.

This was the end. Wasn't it? Kazue knew her plans. They were probably preparing defenses to stop them, and their plan would fail. Suzume would have no choice but to die to save the world.

"Are you happy now?" she asked the wind.

But of course, it didn't answer her.

Suzume wrapped her arms tight around her torso and watched as the fire burned the tree to black char, and ash rained down at its base. It was foolish to cling to life like a selfish child. The only answer was to run away as her mother wanted. Wasn't it? But she was sick of running. She was tired. So tired.

The forest around the tree was too green to catch, and the single burning tree was already losing strength. The fire was dying down to just a few embers, and then a gust of wind rose up and extinguished it entirely. Still, she kept staring at the smoldering ashes that reminded her of her mother's funeral pyre.

"There you are." Ryuu approached her from behind silently.

She didn't turn to acknowledge his approach. There seemed no point to.

He stopped to stand beside her. She didn't move, but didn't push him away either. They stood in silence, lost in their thoughts. If anyone understood the grief that was crawling up her throat in that moment, it was Ryuu. Only he could understand what it was like to love someone as complicated as her mother. And whose relationship with his parents mirrored hers.

They didn't need to share words or even touch for her to feel comfort from him. It'd been days since the incident. They'd delayed their plans as long as they dared. Kaito wouldn't say it out loud, but he was giving her space to grieve. Waiting for her to get her head on straight enough to face the challenge ahead. If she was going to capture Kazue and force the soul fragments into her, she needed focus. She couldn't be crying over her mother, the betrayer, who'd lured her into yet another trap with a promise of answers she didn't have.

"I followed her beyond the veil," Ryuu confessed.

Suzume's head swiveled in his direction, eyes widening. "Why?" she demanded.

"I had to know the truth." He met her gaze, and the invitation hung between them.

Those same questions burned up in her chest. Why did she do it? Why didn't she love her? Why wasn't she enough for her? Suzume balled her hands into fists at her side and resisted the urge to burn something again.

"Her reasons don't excuse her actions."

"You're right, they don't. And I won't ask you to forgive her. That isn't for me to ask or her. But I think there's something you need to know. She was trying to save you. Hisato wants to bring all the fragments back together."

"I know," Suzume said, her tone flat, emotionless. But her thoughts were anything but. Her mother had known, and she'd stayed with Hisato. How long had she known? Did it matter? Did it change anything? "I don't care whether she was trying to protect me or not. I'll never forgive her." Heat crept into her tone as she said this.

Ryuu nodded. "I understand. That's your choice to make."

"And have you forgiven her then?"

After a long stretch of silence, Ryuu answered, "Yes."

"You still love her."

He swallowed. "Yes."

"Is it hard loving a mortal?" She wasn't asking for her mother's sake, but her own. It was the question that burned in her chest for weeks. If... when things went wrong, death would be an end for her. But Kaito would live forever without her. She knew Ryuu had suffered such losses. But asking him about those he'd left behind seemed too personal.

Ryuu sat down on a nearby fallen tree and patted the space next to him, offering her a place to sit. She did so without a word and picked off a branch to twist in her hands and avoid looking at him directly.

"Loss is never easy, whether you're mortal or immortal. But though I like to tell myself I won't love again, I keep doing it over and over in different ways."

Suzume twisted the branch in her hands until it snapped. "Do you regret it?"

The question encompassed more than past loves. It was about her mother, about her, about Souta, and all the others she didn't know about who came before her.

"Not for a moment. There's lots to regret but never love."

Suzume chewed on the inside of her cheek in an attempt to hold back words that were threatening to spill out of her.

"Are you worried?" Ryuu asked gently.

"I don't want to die." She blurted out the words.

It felt foolish and weak for fearing it. Everyone died eventually. And wouldn't it be a valiant thing to die for the sake of others? The people she loved would be left behind, but they'd grieve and move on. If she were the heroic type, she'd have marched bravely into the White Palace and faced danger gladly. But Kazue was right; she wasn't a hero. She was a coward.

Ryuu took her hand in his. "You may not have to. Hisato wants you to think this is the only way. But your mother believed in you."

"She didn't say that..." but a small part of her wanted to hear that she had, in fact.

"She did." He grabbed her shoulder and squeezed.

Suzume put on a brave smile for him, but on the inside, she knew she was dancing on the blade's edge of disaster. Confidence after death wasn't enough. It couldn't make up for all the wrongs she did. Her mother wasn't here to see her fail anymore, and this time, the stakes were that much higher. Either way, she wouldn't let her make a fool of her from beyond the grave. Suzume was ready to bury that part of her past behind her. It was time she focused on herself and what she wanted.

They returned to camp together. Kaito was talking with Mori of the tengu as they approached. It lifted her spirits to see him. Perhaps the tengu elder had relented at last and sent an army to help them fight. As if their heads were tethered together, Kaito turned and saw her and didn't break eye contact. Even when Mori bowed and retreated, his eyes were only for her.

"Have the tengu agreed to help us?" Suzume asked, forcing herself to sound cheery and excited.

A slight frown marred Kaito's brow as he said, "Not all. Mori managed to convince a few of his clansmen to join him against his father's wishes. They'll be a great boon on the attack on the palace." The "when you're ready" was left unspoken.

"My men are ready whenever you are," Ryuu said.

Kaito nodded at Ryuu. "Good. Almost everything is ready."

"I'm ready. We don't have to hold back on my account," Suzume said.

Another strange look crossed Kaito's face and he was opening his mouth to say something when a commotion at the edge of camp caught all their attention. Yokai were growling and shouting orders. They rushed into the fight and found two monkey yokai lying flat on their backs and Noaki standing over them with his dual blades drawn. His clothes were torn, and there was dirt smearing his face, but otherwise, he seemed unharmed.

"Noaki!" Suzume called his name, but Kaito threw out his arm to stop her from approaching him.

She looked at him with confusion for a moment as he shook his head slowly.

"You've returned, and it seems your journey wasn't easy," Kaito said.

"It wasn't," Noaki replied. His expression was boring into Suzume. It was blank as usual, but there was an almost haunted quality to it. "I've come with important information for Suzume."

Suzume placed her hand on Kaito's arm, signaling him to stand down. She knew Noaki's true name. She could stop him if she must. Kaito stepped back and allowed her to approach Noaki. As she did, he lowered his weapons, and some of the tension in his eyes faded.

"What is it you needed to tell me?"

"Not here." He glanced to his side, where a crowd had gathered.

Suzume nodded and they retreated to a nearby empty tent. Kaito and Ryuu shadowed her the whole way. Once they were alone, Noaki turned to face her.

"I know where the Eight have gone. They're trapped inside the soul fragments. Two per piece," Noaki said.

Suzume pressed her hand over her chest. Four gods were inside her. Somehow that felt like more of a violation than thinking two pieces of Kazue's soul were inside her.

"Killing the hosts weakens Hisato. It's why he's been hiding in the White Palace. If you can get closer and kill Kazue, then it will free the gods, and they'll be on our side," Noaki said.

Suzume wrung her hands together and felt her stomach heave. This was it, confirmation she needed to go ahead with their plan. It aligned with what Kazue had already told her. But why was she so afraid?

"You're sure?" she asked.

He nodded. "Certain."

"We'll need to find Kazue. She knows we're coming. I can't get close to her."

"I can lead you to her. I was captured for a time. I know where the inner sanctum is."

Suzume bit at her lower lip until it bled. There were no more excuses to be made. She said she was ready for action. Now, she had to make good on her word.

"Alright. Let's do it."

TWENTY-NINE

Kaito's army buzzed with anticipation, and he felt their excited energy fizzling against his skin. They'd grown impatient since their last battle, and he'd done his best to keep them busy with drills. Then the tengu arrived and sent them all into a flurry. There were less of them than he'd have hoped, but their excitement burned bright with unrestrained hunger. They'd been caged too long on their mountaintop, and they were out for blood. Even though there weren't many of them, their energy was infectious. It was taking all his skill to keep them from storming the palace before the time was right. Their long-term plans hinged on Suzume capturing Kazue, a task made even more complicated given recent events. She wouldn't say it, but he knew her mother's death had shaken her. Kaito wasn't taking any more chances where Suzume was concerned.

He'd rushed in and luckily managed to defeat Ai. He felt confident that they could conquer the White Palace, and if he wanted, he could kill the emperor and declare himself emperor of all Akatsuki. But brute force wasn't going to save Suzume.

And she was all he wanted. They were staging a coup, trying to rebalance the world, and defeat Hisato. Those goals took more finesse and patience—something he lacked.

When Suzume told him she was ready, he started making preparations. They didn't have the element of surprise any longer, and they had to pivot their strategy somewhat. The bulk of the army would storm the palace gates, acting as a sort of distraction. From their reconnaissance, they'd learned the palace was filled with hybrids, and if Suzume was going to reach Kazue, he'd need to draw them to him. He'd merely need to keep Hisato's hybrid army occupied long enough for Suzume and Noaki to subdue Kazue. Once she was captured, they'd remove her from the palace until they could use her as a vessel to banish the fragments of Kazue's soul beyond the veil. And with the battle won, they'd rebuild the world in a shape of unity and peace. He and Suzume would model the new world of peace between yokai and humans.

A new day dawned as Kaito led his army through the city, surrounding the White Palace. He'd expected resistance, but the streets were empty. It seemed they'd vacated the civilians rather than risk the casualties. It was rather compassionate, seeing as Hisato was the one in charge. They marched in silence, and Kaito and Suzume walked hand in hand. Kaito felt the tension coursing off her and he gave her a reassuring squeeze. She didn't seem to notice as her grim expression was trained on the palace gates looming in the distance. When they passed through them, their paths diverged, and the real work began. Knowing it was coming and living it were two different things. A gnawing sense of uncertainty had been eating at him. Normally, Kaito trusted his gut; it didn't often steer him wrong. But Suzume had made up her mind, and she had Noaki to protect her. There shouldn't be anything to worry about. Should there?

The army came to a halt at the palace gates, and the oni bearing a felled tree marched forward. They'd cut it down outside the city to be used as a battering ram. The groaning oni heaved it into place and then looked to Kaito for his signal. Everyone held their breath in anticipation. They'd made it through the city without incident, but bashing down the gates was a turning point that they couldn't turn back from. And yet he hesitated. This is what they'd come to do.

Suzume looked at him at last and gave him a reassuring nod. He had to trust her. He pushed down his fear and gave the signal. The oni marched forward, their steps shaking the ground beneath his feet. With a flick of his wrist, Kaito ordered his archers ready to shoot down any guards who might attempt to stop them. But the oni reached the gate without a single shout from the walls. They slammed the log into the gates, but though it gave a groaning creak, it held. Kaito waited for a shout from beyond, but no one came, no one attempted to stop them. Everyone paused, holding their breath, waiting for intervention from the palace. When none came, that same uneasy feeling crept over him.

Kaito looked at Suzume, who seemed equally confused. "Do you think they evacuated the palace as well?" Kaito asked.

"They're in there; I can sense them..." Suzume replied.

Mori sidled up next to him, quirking a brow. He hadn't wanted to employ the flying unit so soon into the battle, but they could be walking into a trap. With a nod, Mori instructed his tengu to take flight over the palace walls. They flew at a safe enough distance that arrows could not strike them and circled overhead for a few minutes before fluttering back down to Kaito.

"There're signs of life in the palace, but no obvious ambush I can see. I say we proceed with caution," Mori said.

Kaito dismissed him and returned his attention to the oni, attempting to break down the gate. They rammed it in earnest now, splintering wood and cracking hinges until it collapsed under the strain and left a gap large enough for the forward unit to march through.

The front line advanced, led by the oni and their leader. They were larger and their hides tougher, allowing the smaller, second unit led by Shin to follow behind. The first two units entered on high alert. Kaito, on the other side of the gate, saw them walking into the first courtyard, heads on a swivel. A long, silent moment passed, and Kaito started to suspect they would be able to march straight in and declare themselves the victors.

"Where is everyone?" Suzume asked.

Then the last of Shin's unit passed through the gates, and before he could answer, Kaito felt the hairs rise up along his arms, and the gut-wrenching nausea caused by those false gods. He caught the glimmer of barriers falling. The barriers had hidden the nauseating aura of the hybrids. As the world tilted around him, his vision blurred. The horrid abominations that Hisato had created poured out of the empty city buildings. They'd been flanked on all sides. The surprise attack sent his army scattering and breaking off into chaotic knots of fighting. Kaito had to take control before they were severed further, but his entire body felt as if it were being dragged through mud. His tongue was plastered to the roof of his mouth.

Yokai were screaming, and their organized lines were scattering. Suzume grasped a hold of his arm, and his focus snapped to her.

"Kaito!" She shouted his name, and his vision cleared.

He felt her power flowing into him and wrapping around him like a warm blanket, shielding him from the effects of the new gods. "Should we retreat?" she asked, sounding as if she'd asked several times already.

Noaki was watching Kaito over Suzume's shoulder. This was their chance to save the world. He couldn't let the new gods win. If he pulled back, there'd be heavy casualties. There was no more choice but to continue forward. Gathering his wits about him, Kaito roared and gave a rallying cry to his troops. As if snapping out of a collective trance, they fell back, uniting against the advancing hybrid army closing in around them. They cut through the line that threatened to sever them and continued their push into the palace. He sent the archers to hold back the rear attack and turned his attention to getting Suzume inside the palace walls. Humans battled to hold back the hybrids long enough for the yokai affected by the new gods to recover.

While Kaito and Suzume sliced through the hoard of hybrids. Her fires burned a path for them, and his icy blasts froze others in their tracks. They passed into the inner courtyard, into a protective barrier the priestesses had created to shield against the effects of the new god's magic. But there were too many of them, and he felt their slimy auras creeping through like dark tendrils. They didn't have long before it destroyed all of them.

Suzume's gaze drifted away from the battle to where she knew Kazue, the water of her soul, was hidden. Kaito grasped her hand and squeezed one last time. This was when he knew he had to let her go. He brushed a hand across her face, and she turned to him with a sad smile. Flames were sparking along her hair, and the wind whipped up around him as he leaned in for a parting kiss, sealing their parting with a promise. A promise that no matter what happened today, they would return to one another. They'd find a way forward together. She touched his face before turning, disappearing in the fray. He trusted her instincts and knew she could protect herself. Now, he had to focus on keeping all eyes on the invading army and giving her the chance she needed.

THIRTY

Ryuu was at the rear guard, protecting the young, would-be emperor. The boy sat astride a massive war horse, which dwarfed him and made him seem even younger than he was, rather than a future ruler. Ryuu had argued against bringing him to the battlefield at all, but his concerns fell on deaf ears. The safer route would've been to leave him in hiding with his mother at her clan home. The clansmen that the empress had sent along were insistent that the prince be seen by the army as a symbol and rallying cry. But seeing the way the boy paled, Ryuu didn't think he inspired much devotion. But he also knew how quick a coup could turn. All it took was an ambitious governor with enough royal lineage to usurp a young, absent ruler. The sooner they could get the new emperor onto the throne and enshrined, the less unrest they would have to contend with. If they removed the old emperor and the new one wasn't inside the palace by sundown, enemies would do their best to ensure he never arrived.

A contingent of guards surrounded the prince, and they'd been placed at the very back of the marching column to keep him as far away from the fighting as possible. If anything, him potentially urinate on himself might ruin some of the mystique around the role of emperor. The double guard of soldiers surrounding him would have been better served along the front lines, helping to subdue the hybrids and hopefully saving yokai lives. But the humans were letting them take the brunt of the losses, while they claimed the spoils of victory. Ryuu suspected they feared the yokai would turn on them and try to take the throne from their hands, which is why they were forcing the boy into the fray.

He could have argued, but time was of the essence, and instead, he kept his mouth shut and his eyes on the walls of the White Palace gates. He'd been here before. Marching at the head of various clans, facing off against the most powerful clan, his final obstacle in conquering the island and bringing it under a single rule. He'd been so hopeful back then that he'd be able to create lasting peace. That the island of Akatsuki would only continue to flourish. But he'd been naive to think humans would remain stagnant. Through many battles, plots, and schemes, he'd shaped the country into an empire. Now he was doing it again and he couldn't be certain fate would be any kinder to this boy emperor than it had to his predecessors. The thought made guilt coil in his gut. This was the last time. Once he was a man, Ryuu would retire for good. He'd teach him how to be a just and kind ruler, and then he'd be done with it all. No more court, no more politics. This was the end of it.

Ryuu was consumed by his thoughts of past and future as they inched closer and closer to the palace gates. The city was disturbingly silent, and if he hadn't been distracted, he might have taken note of it sooner. It'd been quickly dismissed as a strategic evacuation to protect the innocent. If he'd taken time to think about it further, he might have seen the signs before it was too late. The spiritual pressure around them changed, like the air before a storm appeared on the horizon. Ryuu's head popped up a moment too late, and the hybrids poured out of the empty buildings, encircling them on all sides. He sprung into action, slashing at the nearest one, but they moved too quick. It didn't take long for them to cut through the outer ring of the prince's guard.

The human soldiers were ill-equipped for battle against hybrids that fought with a mindless, feral abandon. A few held up longer than others, but they, too, were cut down. The inner circle fell back, closing in around the prince. His horse was rearing in a panic, scenting the hybrids and threatening to throw him and bolt. Ryuu surged forward, but the press of bodies was too much, and he watched, powerless, as the young prince was pulled from his horse by the hybrids. The rear guard was scattered and broken up into a myriad of smaller battles. He cut down the hybrids between him and the prince, praying to the gods above he wasn't too late. The prince let out a guttural scream. Ryuu impaled the hybrid in his way and discovered one of the creatures looming over the prince's prone form, its claws dripping in blood.

Ryuu severed the monster's head, but it was too late for the prince. He was dead and so too were the empress' ambitions to control the throne. Ryuu fell to his knees, grabbing the young man in his arms. He was too young to be cut down like this. Cruel fate had thrust him into the center of a battle he did not belong in. Chaos was erupting at the front line. He heard Kaito's roar, and the armies were breaking apart into different factions, human and yokai. The ambush had put them on their back foot, and the tenuous bonds that held them together were threatening to snap. Whoever won today would take control of the palace and plunge Akatsuki into chaos and it had been all Ryuu's fault. He could choose to walk away, or he could continue to fight.

Izuki's last words echoed in his mind. "Protect my son."

She'd known what was coming and hadn't told him to force his hand. A hysterical laugh bubbled up his throat. Either he let another ambitious governor rise and become a tyrant or he searched out Izuki's son and rose him up to emperor. This must be fate's way of punishing him for daring to shape Akatsuki. Because if he walked away and left Izuki's son unprotected, someone would find him and kill him as they had the prince. With no path but forward, Ryuu made a quick decision.

Kaito was rallying the army together, and they'd cut off the hybrids that aimed to sever the two sides as they were all surging through the palace gates. Ryuu led the rear guard into the fray in the inner courtyard. The humans had their own hierarchy of command and didn't need him. Now, he needed to act swiftly to protect the remaining prince and secure Akatsuki's future. As he maneuvered through the skirmishes, he had two goals in mind: find Izuki's son and then hide him. Hisato wouldn't have wanted far beyond his reach, and knowing Izuki she'd have influenced Hisato's choice of hiding place even while her son was held captive. That's why he headed for the place they'd met on their secret rendezvous—an outer palace at the outskirts of the palace grounds. Ryuu headed there as the sounds of fighting faded behind him.

This end of the palace was silent. The shouts and clash of battle felt distant. Several large, old trees shadowed the path and gave the entire place a quiet, serene atmosphere. There were guards at the end of the path, easily dispatched. Their loyalties couldn't be confirmed, and he couldn't risk word getting out to Hisato's other allies that he'd taken the prince. Ryuu strode through the garden he remembered all too well: past the peach tree he and Izuki had embraced one another beneath, where he'd sworn his oath to protect her children. Those memories dug in like a knife to the ribs, but he kept moving. He shoved them down, intent on his task. The building was small, harkening back to a simpler time. Ryuu had built it for himself when he'd first retired as emperor. It gave him a home where he might escape the pressures of court. The floorboards on the veranda creaked, and he heard a shuffle of hurried footsteps within. Ryuu threw open the doors and found the young prince cowering there with a blade clutched in his hands. Upon seeing Ryuu, he lowered his weapon.

"Ryuu?" he asked.

"My prince." Ryuu bowed his head. "I've come to take you to safety."

The prince frowned and looked at him for a moment. "Where is my mother?"

Ryuu's heart wrenched as he held out his hand to the prince. He was older than the second prince—on the brink between man and boy. He'd grown in the past few months, losing some of the coltishness of youth. And while he'd always favored his father in looks, he saw a stamp of Izuki in his cautious gaze.

"Come, it's not safe here," Ryuu said, urging him with a firm word.

The prince slowly took his hand, and Ryuu pulled him into the shadows. It was a sort of in-between space between the world of the seen and unseen. Traveling this way, they could pass through the palace undetected. The strain on Ryuu was high, but he did what he must to keep him safe. They went the long way, traveling beyond the palace walls to the sun temple and his personal rooms with wards he trusted. Ryuu deposited him there, promising to return for him later, and placed even more wards around the place. No one would know the prince was there unless he stepped out of the room. Which Ryuu felt confident he wouldn't. The prince hadn't said as much, but he seemed to know his life was in danger. With the prince secured, Ryuu turned his gaze back to the palace and the emperor he had to force to retire.

THIRTY-ONE

They'd traveled as fast as they could. With every mile, Hikaru grew more and more restless, and his gaze turned to the palace. The dark circles under his eyes were getting bigger, as he hadn't been sleeping. Rin tried to slow their pace for him, stopping to urge him to take a few sips of water and bites of food. But he was a man consumed, certain he had to reach Suzume in time for an event he called "convergence" in an increasingly dreamy voice. Each day, she felt as if more and more of her husband was fading away. Rin was tempted to sever the fragment many times and let it corrupt someone else. But each time the thought overtook her, she dismissed it. Hikaru wouldn't want her to risk Suzume and the others, nor would he want to thrust this burden on someone else. And so, they continued their path to the White Palace.

After another sleepless night, they'd traveled only to find the remnants of Kaito's encampment. By the time they reached the city and the White Palace, it was plunged into chaos. They saw the smoke rising in the distance, and Rin transformed into her kitsune shape and urged Hikaru to climb onto her back. They rushed through the empty streets, past the bodies of hybrids, yokai, and humans alike. At the palace gates, the fighting was thick and chaotic, and bodies littered the ground. Red blood mingled with black hybrid ichor. Rin saw Kaito flying through the sky, shooting icy projectiles down at the ground. It seemed the battle had gone in their favor. There were priestesses and priests fighting alongside the yokai, winning against the hybrids. Hikaru cleared a path through the fighting, shooting arrows at the hybrids, but as they approached the center, Rin felt a strange world-tilting sensation overcome her. She stumbled and Hikaru flew from her back, falling onto the ground.

She tried to stand as the world spun around her. Hikaru was rising to his feet and turned to look at her.

"They're close, I can feel it!" Hikaru shouted, pointing to a group of buildings in the distance.

Rin tried to rise but collapsed to the ground instead. She saw him warring within himself, torn between finding Suzume or coming to her rescue instead. This might be their only chance to perform the spell. And though it pained her, she knew she had to let him go.

"Go! Find her. I'll find you," she roared.

"But you're hurt," he said. She could see the effort it took to fight the pull, calling him to Suzume and the others.

Rin struggled to her feet for his sake and said, "Go!"

Hikaru ran toward her, firing a holy arrow at a hybrid she hadn't noticed creeping up behind her. It struck the hybrid through the eye, and it flailed backward, screaming and clutching at the arrow sizzling in its socket. Hikaru lunged at it and bound it up in vines before piercing it through the heart with one of them. Black blood dripped onto the ground as the hybrid sagged in its bindings and slumped forward.

He reached Rin and grasped either side of her muzzle, pressing his forehead against hers. He was panting from the effort it took to kill the hybrid, and his hands shook. "We are bonded together. I will never leave you behind."

She inhaled his scent, memorized his face. They'd faced so much more together and survived. They'd get through this, too.

"We'll find our way back to one another," she vowed. "Go, find Suzume and come back to me."

Hikaru gave her a sad smile. Then his fingers slipped out of her fur, and he was disappearing through the undulating crowd. They were calling to him, and she wanted to stop him from going before they could bind their souls. Then, before she could second guess her decision, she turned away, throwing herself into the fighting around her. Joining in as they pushed back the hybrids. They would find one another when the battle was over. She knew it, and she just had to believe in Hikaru too.

THIRTY-TWO

With the army at her back and the thread of Kazue's soul guiding her, Suzume rushed through the halls of the palace that had once been her home. The roar of hybrids haunted her steps and sent flames sparking along her skin. As they turned a corner, a pair of hybrids stepped out to block their way, but Noaki made quick work of them. His swords cut them through and left them seeping black ichor onto the ground. He continued on without a second glance. The hybrids' quick, violent end turned her stomach, but she didn't linger over it long.

With each step deeper into the palace, Suzume felt the knot around her heart tighten. The connection she felt to the others beat like a second heart in her chest. She could see Kazue and Hisato in her mind's eye. They weren't cloaking their power any longer; they were calling out to her and Hikaru. She could feel him drawing closer as well, as if their collective magnetic pull was bringing him into them. Preparing them together for their inevitable collision. The sensation made her feel dizzy, and it took all her concentration to keep her focus on the task at hand.

She had to capture Kazue and remove her from the palace. Then find Hikaru and banish the fragments to stop Hisato at last.

The wind whipped around her, tangling in her hair, and fire churned in her gut. She could do this. She had to do it.

They reached the heart of the inner palace where her father resided and held counsel with the governors. She slowed her steps as she looked at the looming, sloped roofs of the main palace building. This was it. Everything she'd worked for had come to this moment. Noaki stopped and waited for her to catch up. She turned away from the palace building and followed him down a connecting path toward one of the adjoining structures. She couldn't sense Kazue any longer, and the loss of their connection felt like she was plunged into sudden darkness. It made her head spin for a moment, and she lost balance. She leaned onto a nearby pillar as she attempted to orient herself.

Noaki held open a door for her and gestured for her to step inside. She trusted he knew where to go. She slid into the room and down the hall, feeling the hairs on the back of her neck standing on end. A silence had fallen over the hall. Without the taut connection she felt between her and the other pieces of Kazue's soul, she felt unmoored, and the urgent certainty she'd felt was turning into doubt. They couldn't have completely severed their connection, not unless one of them perished, and she would have felt if they did. Why had they cloaked their locations? Were they attempting a retreat? Suzume reached out, trying to find them, but all she sensed was Hikaru moving closer and closer to her.

But even without that connection, her gut was telling her something wasn't right. Fire burned on her palms. Suzume lifted her hands and shot it at the closed door at the end of the hall. It caught quickly, burning through the paper screen and incinerating the wood framing. The fire was quickly doused by a rush of water. Kazue stepped out, and as she did, Suzume felt her entire body tilt forward as if pulled by marionette strings. The sensation was more violent than it'd been when she'd last seen her, as if the desire to reconnect was growing stronger with each reunion. The hall seemed to narrow around them until it was just the two of them staring at one another. A smile curled Kazue's lips, as if she, too, was relishing this moment.

"You've come for vengeance?" she asked. New Kazue wanted her to kill her. That was why she'd killed her mother. Rage bubbled beneath the surface of her skin, and it took all her self-control to not act on that killer impulse.

"We both knew this moment was coming," Suzume replied. Then her gaze trailed to the shadow looming behind Kazue. The hybrid she'd made of Akira and Tsuki leered at her maliciously. It made Suzume's heart twist. Their fate was her fault.

She hadn't considered the possibility of fighting her old friends, but she'd do whatever it took. She looked at Noaki, and he nodded in silent agreement. Kazue was for her to deal with. He'd take care of Akira and Tsuki.

Suzume whipped a flaming ball at Kazue's head just as Kazue sent a torrential downpour of water onto her, dousing her flames and sweeping her off her feet. By grabbing onto the wall Suzume saved herself from being pushed out the hall and regained her feet long enough to shove Kazue with a blast of wind. It knocked her back into the far wall, stunning her. Suzume used her advantage to advance on her as her wind pinned her.

Kazue shot another funnel of water at Suzume which she evaporated with a ball of flame. Clouds of vapor haloed her head and obscured her vision. Suzume's heart rattled in her chest, as if the invisible thread that tethered them was growing tighter. Suzume grasped hold of Kazue's neck. She could feel the pulse thrumming there as the fires licked over her skin. Where the fire burned, pain echoed in her flesh. Burning. Her instincts screamed for her to let go, but the fire wanted revenge, wanted to end Kazue here and now, damn the consequences.

"Fate isn't carved into stone, no matter what you may think. You're not owed revenge. Not from me, and not from him," Kazue choked out.

Anger coiled in her gut, making her see red. She was ready to burn them both to the ground in that instant, but Noaki grabbed her by the shoulder, pulling her away from Kazue. At least, that's what she thought he was doing at first. Then his arm wrapped around her neck, and he pinned her hands behind her.

"Noaki, what are you doing?" Suzume cried. "Help me."

But he didn't answer, instead squeezing the breath from her lungs until she nearly collapsed. No matter how she kicked or struggled against him, he didn't lessen his hold on her. Akira and Tsuki's twisted, mixed-up face stood behind Kazue with a gloating expression. This wasn't how this was supposed to go. Why had Noaki betrayed her?

With her concentration restored, Kazue was able to break from the wind holding her in place, and she smiled at Suzume in triumph.

"You were a fool to let him go. You left the sword out of the sheath, and now the blade has been turned against you."

Panicked and terrified, she was losing control of her powers. The flames rose along her skin, burning Noaki, but even the fire didn't deter him.

"He was forged by the sun; your pitiful flames cannot harm him," Kazue crowed.

"Why?" Suzume choked, tears rolling down her eyes as her vision blurred.

This wasn't him. She'd freed him. Noaki wouldn't turn against her after all they'd been through.

"He didn't tell you, did he?" Kazue tilted her head to the side. There was a strange, unhinged look in her gaze. Then, with a flick of her hand, Noaki let her go.

Suzume collapsed onto her knees, gasping for air. She glared up at Kazue.

"You're a fool to let me go." She held up a ball of flame once more, but as she did, Noaki rested his hand on her shoulder.

"Harming me only harms yourself. And he won't let that happen," Kazue said.

"I'm ready to die to stop you. Are you?" Suzume said with more certainty than she felt. Without the heat of battle on her, the throbbing pain of her self-inflicted burns gave her more clarity. Suzume couldn't be the one to kill her, just as Kazue couldn't really harm her.

Kazue leveled Suzume with an unreadable gaze. "More than you know." She stalked closer to Suzume and said, "Noaki will do my bidding and bring you to Hisato. The ultimate sacrifice for love." Her gaze flicked to him once more.

Suzume couldn't see his expression, but she felt his hands tighten on her shoulder.

"Whatever spell you've put him under, I'll find a way to break it," Suzume said.

"There's no spell. The fact is, his love for the Lady of the Moon is stronger than his desire to protect you. He followed me across the island and into the depths of hell to find me again."

What she was saying didn't make any sense.

"Enough monologuing, get to your point," Suzume snapped.

Kazue just laughed as she leaned in close to Suzume. Their proximity left a painful ache, as if her rib cage might split open and rip her heart out of her chest.

Kazue shook her head. "We both wanted power, Kazue and I. And a world where our child could be safe. Our arrangement only made sense."

Suzume heard Kaito's roar in the distance, and she thought he might be drawing closer. She turned the wind up around her, using it to block out the sound. If she could just bide her time, she could find a weakness in Kazue's defense and capture her.

"Who are you talking about?" Suzume asked. Kazue couldn't be talking about herself.

"They're inside you too. The gods she sealed for her own selfish ends. It's why you feel yourself unraveling. Your mortality, your soul, is slipping away as they eat away at you. As Hisato tries to reunite your soul with his. But if you give control to the gods within you, you'll become even more powerful. Join me, and we'll become the new gods ourselves."

Kazue's eyes looked strange, as if she'd seen a thousand lifetimes. As if she were ageless.

Suzume looked inward, imagining she might see the gods within her, that she might hear their voices, but there was nothing but the wind ringing in her ears.

She shook her head. Pushing away the existential thoughts that threatened to overwhelm her.

But she'd never give up herself for some god inside her. "I'll never do it."

Kazue tutted. "Too bad." Then, to Noaki, she said, "Kill her."

THIRTY-THREE

Noaki felt the command ripple through him, and his muscles tensed as he tried to fight it. Though Hisato had invoked his real name and forced him into his servitude, what lingered of his bond with Suzume warred within him. All their wills were a tangled knot inside him. And beneath it all was his desire to fight to free them all from it. The act of disobeying felt like swimming against a strong current, and one misstep could pull him under.

The thing that used to be his children sneered, drawing a sword and threatening to make good on Kazue's demand if he didn't.

"We'll do it if he won't," they said in their strange, echoing voice.

"No." Kazue held up her hand to still them. "Let him." She met his gaze, and for a brief moment, he thought he saw Sayuri beneath the mask of Kazue's face, fighting to get through. That was the crack in the command he felt. The sensation of her trying to take control of the body she was trapped inside.

It was taking all his concentration to stand still. Suzume turned to look at him, her gaze imploring. For all her power, she was still human. Using all his willpower, he removed his hand from the hilt of his sword and grasped Suzume's neck. Her eyes widened, not in fear, but seeming to understand. Her expression was almost peaceful, in fact.

"Nakatomo," Suzume turned to look at him, her voice ringing with the power of his true name. He looked at her. "Don't listen to her."

Kazue's attention sharpened, and he knew Sayuri had lost her small control. "Enough theatrics, do as I command, kill her."

He was caught between two commands as he warred within himself. His children stepped forward, drawing their blade to swing at Suzume. As they did, she blasted them with fire, and they stumbled back, furiously trying to extinguish the flames. They bumped into Kazue, breaking her concentration and her hold on him. In the confusion, Noaki surged forward, slashing at his children, who raised their blade nearly a moment too late to block his strike.

They sneered at him over their crossed blades.

"You weren't able to do what was necessary before; what makes you think you'll do it now?" they said as they struggled against each other.

They circled one another, and Noaki dodged as they struck at him like a venomous snake. Unlike him, they were out for blood.

"I will not hold back. Will you?" they asked.

There was so much anger in them. So much hurt. He couldn't be mad at anyone but himself. He should have been there to protect them, to shield them when they were first born. To prevent this horrid transformation they'd endured. He made a vow then as their blades struck his side, drawing blood. He'd make it right. Even if it took thousands of years, he'd find a way to save them.

"I wasn't there for you, and worse yet, I kept you at arm's length even once we were reunited, and for that, I'm sorry," he said.

They scoffed. "Too late now, old man."

It was his fault. All of it was. He had been born to protect. To serve. But never had he ever gone against the orders of those who held him. Fought for what he wanted. Today, he would do that.

They rushed him again, and he disarmed them by knocking the blade from their hand. But they, too, wrested one of his blades from his hand.

They circled one another. Pacing and testing the limits of each of their power. But more than anything, he had a desire burning in his gut.

Their blade was poised to strike him, and that's when he heard the song of sealing. It tingled across his skin, and he looked down to see the stone on the ground at his children's feet. They screamed as it overtook them, and then there was nothing left but the rock.

Kazue stood across from them, pulling at her hair as if her hands were not in control of her body.

"You were supposed to work for me, not against me!" she cried, looking like a mad woman.

"I'm done being your puppet. And his," Sayuri said.

"No," Kazue moaned.

"Now, Noaki. Do it now." Sayuri looked at him with desperation in her gaze. He knew what must be done, though he didn't relish the task.

Suzume looked at him and started to shout out, but he'd already driven his blade forward, impaling it in Kazue's gut. She grasped hold of the blade, and they were as close together as lovers. She reached out to touch his face, and in that brief moment, his heart was broken into pieces.

"I'm sorry, my love," he said.

She smiled before slumping against him in death.

THIRTY-FOUR

Suzume felt Kazue die. It was like a candle being snuffed out and air stolen from her lungs all in one. Her hope of banishing the soul fragments with her death went up in smoke. The flame fragment and the wind fragment were still firmly planted inside her. And Kazue was lying dead on the ground in front of her. Shock had overcome her, and she didn't know what to think or feel. She felt numb.

Noaki cradled Kazue's body, lowering her to the ground before removing the blade he'd driven through her. The soul fragment was within her, and Suzume needed to absorb it as she'd done the moment Souta died, but she couldn't move. She was frozen in place. Taking that fragment meant accepting her death—walking wide-eyed into the darkness, never to return. It wasn't fair. Kazue had killed Souta, she'd killed her mother, and she'd never had to pay for her crimes. She got to escape into a peaceful death, while Suzume was left to shoulder this burden alone. Noaki scooped up the stone that held his sealed children before turning to face Suzume.

"Why?"

"I had to do it. Either she died or you."

Anger churned in her gut, and she balled her hands into flaming fists at her side. "You've only delayed my death!"

"I'm sorry." Noaki lowered his head, signaling she should toss the burning ball of flame at him in revenge.

But as much as the rage coursing through her wanted her to do so, she couldn't. She extinguished her flames and let her arm fall lamely to her side. She stared at Kazue's lifeless form lying on the ground. Now that she was dead, she could see just how young she was. Not much younger than Suzume. They'd been alike. Mirrors looking back at one another. While she'd grasped for power, Suzume had sought to tear it out at the root. She had to take her fragment. It pulsed within her chest, growing fainter with every second. And something told her if she waited too long, it would fade away into the ether trapped in that world between.

She took a stumbling step forward, her hands and legs shaking. She had to do this. Noaki stepped aside, giving her room. Her heart yearned for that fragment. It tightened her chest to think of it. So close, yet so far. But the moment before she grasped hold of it, a hand appeared out of the shadows, plunging into Kazue's chest and removing a glowing blue aura.

Suzume stumbled back as Hisato emerged in front of her. He pressed the piece of Kazue's soul into his chest, and she watched in horror as blue light suffused his body. It made his body seem even more corporeal. More solid.

"I told you this moment was inevitable," he said, stalking closer to her.

The air crackled as she flung a burning ball of flame at him. But as she did, he extinguished it with a ball of water. With a flick of his hand, he sent another wave at her that knocked her back into Noaki. He recovered more quickly and rushed Hisato, slashing with twin blades, only to be swept aside by another tidal wave. Suzume drew her staff and struck at Hisato, landing a blow that rippled through her body and left her doubled over and wheezing.

Hisato stood over her, smiling in triumph. He had Noaki pinned down beneath his water, cutting off his airflow. Noaki's legs kicked out in a pointless struggle. Hisato moved closer to her, and even though her mind was screaming to back away, she couldn't resist his magnetic pull. He cupped her face, tipping her head up to meet his gaze.

"The time has come. Convergence is here. You cannot deny it, Suzume," he purred.

She felt his slimy arms encase her, cocooning her in his dark embrace. He invaded her thoughts, soothing her and encouraging her to let go. And oblivion sounded good in that moment. Better to let go rather than die. It would be simpler, like falling asleep. Just as she was about to be enshrouded in darkness, the earth shook under her feet, and she was knocked away from Hisato by an overly large boulder that had torn through the floor, leaving a gaping hole in its wake.

Hikaru entered, panting for breath. With his interruption, Suzume was able to scurry back away from Hisato and regain her sense of self.

"Sorry I'm late," Hikaru said, keeping his eyes trained on Hisato.

"Your timing couldn't be better," Suzume replied.

She reached out for his power. It flowed into her as easily as breathing as they found the resonance of their fragments they'd been denying for months. It felt like coming home.

"We can't destroy him. We simply have to trap him long enough to escape," Suzume said.

"We're all together at last," Hisato said with a wicked smile. "We can't end the fun early."

Suzume saw no other course of action other than trying to draw from Hikaru's power before Hisato could. It had been a long time since she'd drawn on his power, but it came to her fingertips instantly. The power thrummed through her.

Inside her chest, the real Kazue's heart burned and thundered. She felt as if it might burst straight out of her chest. She and Hikaru sang together—the song of binding from two mouths.

Hisato realized what they were doing: drawing on the water of Kazue's soul and his own darkness to form their song. He pulled back against them, trying to draw them in with his own power, but they had him outnumbered, and the light coming from them was stronger. And yet the tug of war continued. Each time they gained ground against him, Hisato would regain what he had lost.

This went on for a few more moments. The tide was turning in their favor. They were close. Hisato's strength was lagging, and his color was leaching from him, leaving him pale and gray. His knees buckled, and he fell to the ground, clutching his head. His back arched as if he were in agony.

The pain rippled through her as well, but they had to keep going. Their commingled power was like five glowing ribbons pulled taut, close to snapping. She could feel it. Kazue's soul wanted to be reunited, and the moment Hisato gave up, they would win. They were coming together, and when they did, it would kill.

"You'll kill us all," Hisato roared.

Suzume wavered as she felt the edges of the world around her blur. She wasn't ready to die. She thought of Kaito. Of all the things she still had left to do. She was young. She had so much life left.

And in that moment of hesitation, Hisato pounced. The darkness wrapped around her, pulling at the threads of her uncertainty and breaking the spell that they'd trapped him with.

She shoved him back, but as she did, she could tell she was getting weaker. She could feel Souta draining out of her as fast as the energy was pouring out of Hisato.

She fell to her knees, as did Hikaru and Hisato. She trembled and her vision was going dark around the edges.

Just another moment. Another second.

Then her hand slipped. The power arched, and Hisato's power collided with hers. There was an explosion, and Suzume was thrown backward by the force of it. Her ears rang in her head, and a blinding white light surrounded her. They all seemed to lay stunned for a few moments. No one moved. It seemed as if the world had come to a complete halt.

Hisato's laughter broke the silence, a cold, sinister laugh that chilled her to the bone.

"I knew you weren't brave enough to take it all the way," Hisato said. His voice was shaking, no, shattering, as if he was a piece of glass falling apart.

Suzume got up, but her feet swayed beneath her. NO. NO. NO. They had been so close. She could do this. Hikaru was lying unconscious on the ground. They couldn't resonate. She and Hisato were evenly matched. Both of them injured.

Hisato seemed to unfurl in front of her, growing taller and larger. Large tentacles poured out from his shoulders and shrouded the space in darkness. Suzume willed all her power into her flame, but it was nothing but a meager spark. It felt like she was trying to light a match underwater. No matter how hard she tried, she couldn't get it to light.

"This isn't over yet," his voice echoed around her and through her mind—spearing in, sending pain rippling through her body.

She was frozen in place as his tentacles wrapped around her once again, blocking out all light and sound. This was the end. Wasn't it?

THIRTY-FIVE

Ryuu flung open the doors to the emperor's chamber. The past overlaid the present as he stared at the latest in a long line of emperors. Not the first madman he'd pulled down from his throne, nor the most wicked or cruel. But the weight of the emperor's dead son's sacrifices weighed heavy on Ryuu's shoulders. The killing never seemed to end. No matter if he were present or removed, the cycle of power moved on unending. The emperor cowered, a small, frail human, with his long hair tangled around his face.

The emperor grabbed an ink stone nearest him and hurled it at Ryuu. "Out, spirit. I won't have you come near me!" he shouted.

Ryuu approached him, and the emperor curled into himself, eyes darting wildly around the room. He settled on a brush and then a roll of paper. Ryuu dodged each item and continued his forward march. He backed further into the wall, eyes rolling and unable to settle on anything as if he were jumping at shadows. Dark circles hollowed out his eyes, and his cheeks were sunken, as if he hadn't slept a single night since they'd last spoken.

This was his fault, Ryuu thought. He'd thrust the responsibility on his line, and, through his own machinations, kept him in power. Because his hubris had driven him to found an empire, countless men suffered. This emperor wasn't fit to rule and his son, who he'd hidden away, would succumb one way or another to the corruption of power. If not greed, or madness, then he'd simply wither away, scraped and picked down to bone by his responsibilities. Ryuu's plots doomed them all. No one deserved that fate. Ryuu had already killed two of his sons; could he, with good conscience, destroy a third?

"Come with me. It's time you rested," Ryuu said and held out his hand to the emperor.

The emperor shook his head. "There is no rest. Only darkness. The darkness comes." He folded over on himself, grasping his head in his hands.

Ryuu took another step, hand out as if he were approaching a frightened child. The emperor looked at him with wide, guileless eyes. Whatever had happened here had broken his mind and spirit. But even if he couldn't undo what was done, he could give him peace in his final days.

"Where is Izuki? I need Izuki," he pleaded, grabbing onto the hems of his sleeve.

Ryuu patted his head, even as the reminder of her twisted like a knife in his gut. He couldn't tell him the truth, not in his current state. Instead, he gently guided him to his feet and led him out of the room, down the corridors, and out of the palace grounds. Ryuu pulled the emperor through the shadows of in-between and deposited him safely in the Sun Temple, away from the fighting. And there he would stay for the rest of his days, in quiet contemplation and serenity. The temple was the safest place he could keep him and the prince. When the battle was over, he'd return for them both. But for now, they both deserved a respite.

The battle was nearly over by the time he returned. Kaito's army had overwhelmed and destroyed the hybrids. Bodies were scattered about: yokai, human, and hybrid alike. The stench of ichor and blood clotted the air. It transported him to the battle all those years ago when he'd first taken the palace, and it evoked unpleasant memories. Kaito was flying over the battle, but when he spotted Ryuu, he swooped down to him and transformed back into a human.

"The emperor?"

"Secured and in a safe place only I can reach."

Kaito nodded, then signaled for Rin, who was patrolling the battleground in her kitsune form.

She galloped over to them. Her muzzle was crusted in blood, and she was panting hard. He hadn't realized they'd returned, and as he looked behind her, expecting to see Hikaru trailing after, he was startled to find she was alone.

"Have you seen Hikaru or Suzume? He followed her and hasn't come back yet," she said in a low growl. The hairs along her spine were standing on end.

"She might have taken him to the rendezvous location with Kazue," Kaito said with a furrowed brow.

Before any of them could reply, he'd transformed and taken off into the air once more. Rin resumed her human form and paced around as they waited for Kaito to return with news.

"You seem distraught. Is there something I should know?" Ryuu asked.

"I'd rather talk about it when I know he's safe," Rin said, waving away his concerns.

Ryuu had no choice but to wait. Several minutes passed, and then Kaito returned, diving at them and transforming once again. "There's no sign of either of them."

A chill swept over Ryuu. There could only be one reason they hadn't come back from their mission. Kaito and Rin seemed to have the same thought, and the three of them tore off in the direction Kaito had last seen her. As they ran, Ryuu spread out his senses and felt a black void at the center of the palace. Kaito had sensed it, too, and they redoubled their efforts, running in that direction. When he got closer, Ryuu felt Hisato's power a moment before they saw the clash of power. Suzume and Hikaru were fighting against Hisato, who had Noaki pinned to the ground with a stream of water.

A body lay a few feet away, and Ryuu realized with a sickening drop to his stomach that Suzume had failed to capture Kazue, and now Hisato had absorbed her power. Hisato wrapped his tentacles around Suzume and Hikaru, covering their faces and threatening to swallow them whole.

Ryuu slashed at the tentacles, drawing Hisato's attention onto him, and Rin leapt forward, her jaws angled for his throat. He squirmed out of the way, but she managed to latch onto his shoulder instead, ripping open the flesh. Darkness leaked from the wound. Kaito, in dragon form, blasted ice at Hisato. He flung it back and showered them all with shards of ice.

As Ryuu hacked away at the tentacles, trying to free them, he couldn't help but feel they'd reached an inevitable end. The pieces he'd set in motion were all coming together, and their terrible ending. Ryuu felt the weight of all he'd done bear down on him. The guilt was enough to crush him. Kaito and Rin weren't willing to give up, and they kept throwing themselves at Hisato, slashing more and more wounds into him until he was forced to recoil his tentacles with a hiss.

Hikaru and Suzume collapsed to the ground, free at last, and their partners rushed to their side. Ryuu faced the monster he had inadvertently freed for the first time. And Hisato smiled.

"She loved you," he said, gesturing to Kazue's body. "And I am a testament to that love. Why not join me? We could remake the world as she imagined it." He held out his hand to Ryuu.

For a frightening moment, he felt those slimy tentacles squirming through his mind. Providing a vision of a world where creatures like him could exist without fear. But as soon as the notion took hold, he shook it off. Ryuu instead used the moment of shedding Hisato's influence to rush forward. At the same time, Noaki rose up, finally free of the water that had pinned him. Ryuu swung high, and Noaki swung low. He severed Hisato's head from his body, and Noaki severed him through the middle. Black clouds poured from the wounds.

And Hisato laughed.

"You cannot defeat me so easily." His voice echoed as the smoke dissipated. They'd won the battle but not the war. Ryuu turned from the black smear on the ground and watched as Kaito cradled Suzume in his arms.

She was awake, but just barely. Her eyes were heavy-lidded, and her head drooped as if she were fighting to stay awake. Rin was kneeling beside Hikaru, looking stricken; he'd lost conscious-ness. Noaki lifted the prone form Ryuu had noticed before.

There was a bloody gash in New Kazue's stomach, and her head lolled.

"She's dead," Suzume slurred. "Hisato has her soul fragment. We were too late."

The news dropped like a stone between their group. They'd won but also lost. While they might have captured the palace, it was at great cost. Hisato remained at large, and this war didn't end until he was defeated.

THIRTY-SIX

Rin followed as Ryuu carried Hikaru to their makeshift infirmary, which had been set up in one of the smaller residences within the palace. Cots had been laid out for the injured, and healers, both yokai and human, moved quietly between the rows of wounded and dying. The groans and moans of the infirmary, coupled with the stench of medicinal herbs and blood, made her stomach turn. She held his hand all the while, rubbing circles against his palm as she prayed to each of the Eight that he'd wake up and she wouldn't be too late to save him. They put Hikaru down, and she knelt beside him. The blade the maiden blacksmith had given her was laid out across her lap. They hadn't gotten a chance to perform the ritual or even explain their plan to the others.

If there were any doubts in her mind as to what she'd do next, they were gone now. A life without Hikaru was unthinkable. A priestess came by and offered Rin a bowl of clean water in which she might wash the blood off her face and hands. She took it with a bow, and the priestess drifted off to tend to the other patients. Rather than wash her own body, she washed Hikaru's hands and face first, taking care to wipe away the grit and ichor from him. She'd looked him over several times and had found no evidence of wounds on his body. But she suspected Hisato had taken too much of his energy in that final battle, and it would take time for it to recover.

The others were busy with the aftermath of the battle, but they filtered through one by one to check on him. Ryuu first, and then Noaki, who sat by his bedside without a word before departing just as silently. Kaito came alone. Rin was surprised to see he was without Suzume.

"Where's Suzume?" Rin asked when he took a seat next to Hikaru.

"Resting. I think she's in a bit of shock."

Rin nodded. They all were feeling the strain of the battle. Even if Hikaru woke up and they could successfully bind her soul with his, there were no guarantees they'd win the fight. Hisato was stronger than they realized, and the thought of sacrificing this much and then still losing in the end terrified her.

"How long will he need to rest? I don't know how much longer Suzume can hold out," Kaito said, looking over Hikaru's sleeping form as one would a weapon or some other tool.

It pricked at Rin to see him used. But she buried those feelings. No one understood what she was going through quite like Kaito. He stood to lose the woman he loved as much as she might lose the man she loved.

"I don't know. He's not immortal." The words caught in her throat. She knew what she must say next. What risks they must take. But she wasn't ready to say it. Not until Hikaru woke up, at least.

Kaito stayed a few moments longer, then he too got up and left. The sun was starting to set by the time Suzume arrived. She was bloody and covered in soot, her shoulders slumped in defeat. She kneeled down beside his cot as if a woman giving penance.

"How is he?" she asked quietly, her gaze locked on him. It was the same intense longing she'd seen in Hikaru's gaze as of late. A small part of Rin wanted to shove her away and tell her never to come back again. But that would be petty. She'd already found the answer to their problems. He simply needed to wake up.

"Mostly the same, sleeping, though he doesn't seem to be in pain," Rin said.

"I almost defeated Hisato. But I was too afraid of dying..." Suzume trailed off.

She wouldn't meet Rin's gaze, but she'd known Suzume long enough to guess that guilt was eating her alive. It was too much burden to ask of her.

Rin reached over and grabbed Suzume's hand, squeezing it.

"We might have a solution," Rin said.

Suzume turned to her, hope burning in her gaze.

"What is it?" she asked.

Rin held up the blade the blacksmith had given her, and Suzume's brows furrowed in confusion.

"I found the woman who made your staff, and she made a weapon that reverses what Kazue did with her staff. This blade can sever one soul from another."

"But even if we have the means, won't Hikaru still die if he loses the soul fragment?" Suzume said quietly.

Rin nodded. "Yes, if his soul isn't rebound again. I'm going to bind our souls together. Linking our life forces."

It was a drastic choice, but one Suzume understood. Hikaru and Rin's love was deep and enduring.

"I'm glad you found a way," Suzume said.

"Found what way?" Kaito said, striding over to them with Ryuu right behind him.

"I'm going to sever Kazue's soul from Hikaru's and bind our souls together to save him. I'll give him a portion of my immortality to save his life and to replace the fragment which sustains him," Rin said, meeting Kaito's gaze.

There wasn't a word spoken among them for several long minutes as they all held their collective breaths. Suzume kept her head down and Ryuu was looking at her as if she'd grown a second head. Only Kaito seemed eerily quiet and still.

It was Kaito who spoke first and said, "What you speak of is forbidden." She could tell from the tight grip of his jaw that he was remembering when Kazue had proposed this same plot to him, and he'd turned her away. Only for her to betray him and take immortality without his consent.

"Then will you be the one to drive a dagger through my heart when he dies? Because I will not live a day without him again. I have grieved before. I cannot endure it a second time."

Kaito was silent for a long moment, staring at them both. And then, without another word, he turned and stormed out of the room. Rin watched him go, her chest tight. She knew he'd never approve of their scheme. But they didn't need his approval, just Suzume's consent to free Hikaru of the burden that Ryuu had thrust on them.

Ryuu remained and knelt down between Rin and Suzume. His gaze was on Hikaru, who continued to sleep peacefully. She grabbed Hikaru's hand and squeezed. Even though he might not be conscious, she knew he felt her feelings. And they'd agreed to this plan from the start. If he were awake, he'd encourage her to do it now. As long as they were together, she was at peace. Whatever happened next, Hikaru would be beside her, and they'd faced worse. She'd rather risk her own life than live an eternity without him.

"He cannot stop me," Rin said.

"I don't think Kaito cares about rules. He's worried about me. Once you pass the fragment onto me, I have no other choice than to finish what Kazue started." Suzume was looking into the distance, as if there were no one else in the room.

"Then why—?" Rin asked.

Ryuu shook his head, and she let the question die.

"If you're going to do this, we better get it over with now," Ryuu said with a resigned sigh.

Despite his declaration, another pregnant pause stalled their proceedings. There was something neither Ryuu nor Suzume was saying, and she wasn't sure she wanted to know. Because she had a feeling knowing the truth might shake her resolve. If only a little. Rin held up the blade and felt it grow hot in her hand. Something in her chest pulsed as she brought it closer to Hikaru's chest. Her vision blurred, and Hikaru's form turned into a blend of colors swirling around him. And as she looked down at her hand holding the blade she saw a riot of autumn colors coming from her body.

This was it. A tear rolled down her cheek, and she leaned forward to kiss Hikaru. A kiss that could express her feelings far better than words ever could. She threaded their hands together as she sliced through the green thread which was tangled up with Hikaru's calm blues. As the thread was severed, Hikaru gasped, and she saw his colors fading. Before they could disappear entirely she severed the bright orange red of her own life force. The pain knocked the wind from her, and she felt her magic and life draining from her, sapping her strength. If they were both left untethered this way, they'd die. She reached for the ends of both threads, and tied them together like tying a knot. A full body tingle ran over her body, and a jolt as her heart stuttered before resuming its rhythm, beating in time with Hikaru's.

Distantly, she heard Suzume cry out, and Ryuu was shouting. But their dismay was drowned out by the pain she felt echoing from Hikaru. The blade slipped from her loose grip, its work done. Their souls were now entwined, and she could no longer see the threads of life, but she felt every pain he'd endured echoed in her body. There was a throbbing in her skull, as if someone had stabbed her head. Darkness crept in around her vision, as a voice cackled inside her mind. The last thing she heard was Hisato's voice.

"Fools. Now you are mine."

THIRTY-SEVEN

The earth of Kazue's soul collided with hers. It wasn't like when Souta died or Kazue. It was violent and sudden. One moment, she was upright, and the next, she was knocked back with the wind blown from her lungs and her head spinning. She must have blacked out for a moment because the next thing she knew, Ryuu was leaning over her. She felt incredibly heavy, as if she were being buried in mud and the weight of it was crushing her chest, making breathing difficult. Suzume clutched at her chest and felt the rapid beating of her heart fluttering against her palm. Her other hand fell to the ground, and everywhere it touched vines grew from her fingertips. As soon as they appeared, the vines curled and burned as the fire consumed them.

The yearning to be reconnected was turning into a gnawing in her stomach, and the world seemed to swirl around her, losing all its substance. She could feel her mind fading, overwhelmed by too much Kazue within her. Suzume wrapped her arms around her torso, trying to hold the pieces of her body together before she started to fall apart like a shattered pot. She must have cried out because Kaito came rushing back, elbowing Ryuu out of the way so he could inspect her.

"What have you done?" he whispered as he cupped her face.

Suzume closed her eyes. She couldn't face him in that moment. In her mind's eye, she could see Hikaru, as if he'd imprinted one last message into the fragment before it passed to her.

"We're counting on you," Hikaru's voice whispered. "Make us proud."

Souta's wind ruffled her hair and fanned the flames, which were burning bright in her gut and joined now by a heavy stone of the earth of Kazue's soul. Hot tears pressed at the back of her eyes, but funnily enough, the gnawing feeling was fading, and in its place was serenity and acceptance. The three fragments within her still cried out for the ones inside Hisato. That invisible thread still tugged at her, but she felt more in control of it now. And she also felt as if she were seeing clearly for the first time.

She'd been looking Hisato in the eye, and she'd had his soul in her hands, but when the moment came, her desire to survive had outweighed her desire to destroy him. She thought herself selfish, but she realized now that until this moment she hadn't been ready to face him. Resonance would never be enough to stop him. The will of different minds would always be at odds. She needed to hold them all. That was how this ended.

Suzume sat up, her head spinning, but otherwise, she was okay.

"Say something," Kaito pleaded.

She placed a hand against his cheek. "I'm fine," she said and then she looked over at Hikaru lying motionless on the cot. His and Rin's hands were intertwined. The blade Rin had used to sever her soul and free the earth of Kazue's soul lay on the ground beside her. Suzume picked it up. This blade had severed the soul fragments as her staff had bound them.

Kaito whisked her out of the infirmary and to a private room they'd claimed for their own. He insisted she lay down and urged her to eat and drink. She wasn't losing herself. Not yet. But she felt like she was trying to capture a natural disaster in a jar. Her skin buzzed with want. It was becoming an itch she couldn't scratch. Her fingers sought out the blade, wrapping around it and finding comfort in the feel of it.

"You should get some sleep," Kaito said, tucking her in up to her chin after she'd eaten a few morsels and sipped at some water.

But when he motioned to pull away, she grabbed a hold of his hand and pulled him in close to her. She was terrified of saying it out loud, but this would be their final night together. He looked at her, a question in his gaze, but one he did not speak. He laid down on the cot beside her, his body wrapping around her as if he could envelop her and perhaps hold her there. Maybe he sensed it, too. The coming end. Or maybe it was a beautiful lie she told herself to make it easier. Because she wasn't brave enough to say it. If only his arms were enough to keep her together.

"Hikaru and Rin will recover. They're still breathing, and when they wake, we'll try again," Kaito said.

"His fragment is inside me," Suzume whispered into the dark. "I have three, and Hisato has two. There's nothing left to do but to face him," she said.

"We could bind the soul fragments to someone else?"

Suzume buried her face against his chest and murmured, "That would be too cruel. Besides, what if it went wrong, and Hisato got all the fragments instead? It's too dangerous."

Kaito stroked her face and said nothing for several long minutes.

When at last he spoke he said, "I could do as Rin did and bind our souls together."

Suzume sat up, leaning over him and meeting his gaze. Her chest ached, and she wasn't sure if it was Kazue whose heart was breaking or hers. Maybe it was both of them. Kaito had worked far too hard and long to regain his kingdom to give it up for her. Besides, her duty was to pass the soul fragment beyond the veil. That would mean killing them both, surely.

She shook her head slowly. The words were all tangled up in her throat.

"Then you want me to let you die?" he snarled.

"I want you to live," Suzume said, pressing her forehead to his.

He exhaled raggedly.

"You can't keep me away. I swore to stay by your side and fight for you. If my life is forfeit, so be it." He grabbed a hold of her hands, sandwiching them between his. Her heart swelled at the gesture.

She wished she could make him similar promises. Assurances that they'd have the happy ending they both so desperately wanted. But there was no guarantee other than death. Kazue had confirmed it and now Suzume knew with certainty what she must do. So, she kissed him instead, wanting to feel his body close to hers before the end. They explored one another's bodies, his hand drifting over her hips and the swell of her breasts as if he would memorize her body for when she was gone. And she, too, tried to imprint every part of him onto her. She wasn't sure what death held, but she wanted this night to be the last good thing.

They broke apart, breathing heavily and disheveled. "Tomorrow. We'll bind our souls. Promise me," Kaito said, staring at her with pleading eyes.

"Don't. We don't need to talk about it tonight." She tried to kiss him again to silence him, but he moved out of reach.

"I mean it. I won't let you do this alone."

Suzume started to shake her head, but rather than argue, she said, "I promise."

The lie sank in her stomach, but it was better to give him one perfect night than spend it with bitter tears and have the same outcome.

He kissed her again, nearly lifting her off the ground as he pressed her against him. She felt the sadness and fear in that kiss.

"Suzume." He whispered her name against her skin like a prayer.

There were no more words as he kissed her neck, then rained kisses along her jaw until he caught the corner of her lips and she turned, hungry to feel the warmth of him. To hold onto this moment for eternity. If they never left this place, never let go of one another, perhaps tomorrow would never come, and she'd never have to sacrifice herself to save the world.

She tangled her hands in his haori and pulled him so close that she was afraid she'd suffocate. She couldn't get close enough. She couldn't get enough. It was a need so deep and so raw she couldn't even form it into words. It wasn't physical; it was that old loneliness that crept up. It reminded her over and over that she wasn't necessary, that she wasn't needed. It was the grief for her mother, for herself, and for all of Hisato's victims. Tomorrow, no matter what, she had to make him pay. She ended this one way or another. No matter the cost.

She couldn't fall asleep, and they lay there, limbs tangled together, as she ran her fingers through his hair. Moonlight illuminated his face, and she wanted to remember him just like that. Carve him into her heart and hold onto it. He wouldn't let her go without a fight. And that was why she started to sing, the words came to her from the depths of her soul. Where she'd learned it, she didn't know. All she knew was it influenced Kaito, an immortal who never slept, to relax against her, as his eyes grew heavy. She watched as he fought her song's effect but then slowly succumbed.

Suzume kissed him once more and hoped he had pleasant dreams that might comfort him once she was gone. Then, very gently, she untangled herself from him, leaving him sleeping in their shared futon. There was no more delaying. She couldn't wait for the sunrise. Every minute she stayed like this, she lost a little more of herself to Kazue. And if she was going to die, she wanted to do it as herself. With one last lingering look and the brush of their fingertips, she left Kaito behind and went on her way to end what Kazue started.

THIRTY-EIGHT

The fragments of Kazue's soul hummed in unison beneath Suzume's breast. Her skin felt electric, and yet she was impossibly calm. She'd said her goodbyes, and now it was time to die. The palace was crowded and bustling in the aftermath of their battle. Priestesses and priests were tending to the wounded, and the yokai were establishing clannish campsites in the open courtyards. No one noticed her as she strolled past and out the palace gate.

Kazue's power swelled inside her and she sensed her specter haunting the edges of her vision with each step that brought her closer to Hisato. He hadn't gone far; she'd felt him nearby even as he retreated. As Hisato had warned her, convergence was inevitable, and it was pulling them together. Suzume wanted to keep hold of herself until the end, and to keep the fragments from overwhelming her, she thought of Kaito's smile. His last kiss. The feeling of their bodies intertwined. Those final moments fueled her and tethered her to the past. Tears ran down her cheeks, and even though she desperately wanted to return and fall into his arms, she knew it was too late.

When she was reborn, she would find him again, and in that next lifetime, they'd be happy. She imagined it would be peaceful—no more wars to fight, no more battles to wage, and Kazue would no longer linger between them like a shadow.

In the empty city streets, blood and ichor soaked the earth. She felt it shifting beneath her feet, and flowers bloomed unbidden with each step she took. There hadn't been time to master earth, and she felt each plant and grain of sand. As soon as she felt herself slipping out of control or her mind wandering, she felt Hikaru's guiding hand ghosting over hers as if he were there with her.

The buildings were scorched, and many dead hybrids still lay where they fell. She passed them all by, a growing certainty with each step. By willingly sacrificing herself, she would spare more innocents of a senseless death. She felt Hisato waiting as she drew closer to the center of his spider web, like a foolish fly. He thought he knew her. And maybe once he had. But she wasn't the girl she'd been, selfish and vain. She'd been guided here to this moment. Perhaps not by destiny. But pure dumb luck. She wasn't a hero, and she wouldn't pretend to be one. And it wasn't as if she were ready to die. Damn it, did she want to live. She was selfish at heart, and even now, she wanted desperately to turn away. But there was no more running. She'd done enough of that for a lifetime. The time she'd had in this life was brief. But courage was in facing the thing that scared her the most, and maybe her sacrifice would win her a long and fortuitous next life.

"When I free you from this flesh prison, that's what I want from you, understood?" She spoke to the gods trapped within her, though she doubted if they could hear her. Or if they could, if they'd even grant her last wish.

Kaito, forgive me. I'll see you in my next life, she thought as she raised her sight to the horizon. The sun was rising, and at the top of the hill, Hisato awaited her, hands thrown out in greeting. Her heart was thundering in her chest, and her palms were sweating. But for the first time since her power had awakened, she felt more sure than she ever had.

"You've come at last," he said with a triumphant grin.

She smiled and reached for the staff on her back, though her instinct had been to grab the sword hidden in her waistband. "It's time we ended this game, don't you think?" she said with a false sort of bravado.

She shifted the earth beneath his feet, and for a moment, she had the satisfaction of seeing him stumble. Before he could recover, she shot a fiery ball at his head, which singed a few hairs but not much else.

He smirked at her. "I suppose it is." Then, one of his tentacles shot out at her.

Suzume rolled, dodging it before coming up and shooting more fireballs at him. They crashed into one another, just the staff between them.

He tilted his head down to meet her gaze. "Come to me, Suzume. I can keep you from falling apart. As it is, they're already starting to eat away at you. By sunrise, there will be nothing left..."

She felt it, too, the slow erosion of her mind. She growled, bunching her hands into fists. She thought of Souta dying to give her his soul fragments. Hikaru and Rin on death's doorstep.

And even Kazue, who died in front of her for choosing the wrong side. It was all falling apart around her, and her sacrifice would be for nothing.

His words seemed to drape over her shoulders like a heavy blanket. She felt as if there was nothing she'd rather do than go to sleep right then and there. It was the same spell he'd used to lower her guard last time. She was prepared for it and shook off the feeling before it could sink in. She struck at his tentacles with her staff and felt the pain echo through her limb. They backed up to face one another.

The expression on Hisato's face was at once triumphant and sad. It had been a long time, centuries of loneliness trapped by Kazue's spell. Hisato was Kazue's anger, bitterness, greed, and ambition given form. Either she would destroy Hisato and lay Kazue to rest, or he would absorb her as he had done with the water of Kazue's soul. Either way, Kazue's legacy died today.

He held out a black blade. It shimmered with a blue light, and she felt the soul fragment of Kazue's water pulsing within it. Souta's wind whispered through her, his steady voice guiding her and Kazue's heart beating in time along with hers. Suzume channeled all her energy into the staff and rushed Hisato once more.

As soon as their weapons met, there was a clash and a flash of light. It shook the walls of the buildings nearby and threatened to bring them crashing down. Hisato swiped at her head, and she leapt back, but didn't avoid injury. His blade nicked her cheek, and a single rivulet of blood ran down. Her wind whipped around her, creating a mini typhoon, and water swelled around Hisato to block her fire attacks. She called for the earth power Hikaru had given her, and it came up like fresh, green leaves after the rain. Sharp rocks rose from the ground and pierced through the water, striking Hisato in the chest. The blow sent them both reeling backward and gasping for breath.

Though nothing struck her, Suzume felt the blood trickling down her front from an invisible wound that had nearly pierced her lungs. It pulsed painfully. Meanwhile, Hisato laughed, throwing his head back gleefully.

"Is this how you plan on destroying me? Cutting me so you can bleed?"

"Whatever it takes. I'm not afraid," Suzume said.

Hisato cackled all the harder. And then he grasped a hold of his shoulder, ripping it from the socket with a wet pop and tossing it down on the ground, where it fell in a pile of black goo.

Suzume stared at it in horror.

"You are made of mortal flesh, but I am made of nightmares. You cannot hope to kill me with shallow wounds alone. You'll bleed out long before I exhaust my power." He flashed his elongated needle-teeth at her. "Give up. We both know how this ends."

Suzume balled her hands into fists. She thought she might slow him down long enough to use the sword, but patience had never been her strong suit.

"I know how this ends," Suzume said and drew the sword Rin had used to sever the earth fragment from Hikaru and bind his soul to hers.

She rushed Hisato, who smiled and welcomed her. She buried the sword into his gut and felt his flesh and something else give inside him. The tight coil of his soul was beginning to unravel.

He held onto her as if they were locked in a mockery of a lover's embrace, the dagger still deep in his flesh.

"I always knew it would be you in the end," Hisato said.

"It was always about you and me, wasn't it?" Suzume replied.

Hisato bent forward, and his mouth pressed to hers. As their skin touched, she felt longing for convergence shoot through her body like an electric spark, and their souls hummed in resonance. Desperate for reunification, Suzume let him inside her and pulled on the threads that were unraveling from them both. It was impossible to say where one started and the other ended. They were united—two halves of a whole. She wasn't sure Hisato understood what was happening at first, or maybe it was the relief that made him hesitate. As if, at last, he could set down the glowing coals of anger that had been holding him together. Then she pulled out the dagger and plunged it into her own heart.

"You've killed us both," he cried.

"I know," Suzume said, or maybe she had merely thought it. A single tear ran down her cheek.

The world around her was losing all meaning. The pain was beyond explanation. Hisato's eyes widened in surprise, but by the time he realized what was happening, they were already entangled beyond unknotting. Yet he still tried to free himself, tugging and pulling. The fragments swelled inside her, growing in size, and filling her body. Earth rolled under her feet; fire set the hill ablaze, fanned by the wind, and extinguished by the water. The material world around them seemed to fade away as she looked into Hisato's black eyes one last time. She saw her own face looking back at her, and it was the last thing she saw before she died.

THIRTY-NINE

Kaito was awakened by an explosion. He hadn't meant to fall asleep, and his first thought was to reach for Suzume, but she was gone. His stomach sank. Damn her. He burst out of their room and tore through the palace grounds, ignoring the startled questions of yokai and humans alike. He knew where she'd gone, and why she'd sung him to sleep. He would forgive this betrayal if only she lived. Kaito transformed and took to the sky, searching for her. Her path was obvious from above. There was a line of new growth that marked her steps and a ring of scorched earth where she and Hisato had collided.

She lay in the center, black ichor staining her clothes. It was all that remained of Hisato. She'd done it; she'd absorbed him. But not only that, a sword was embedded in her chest to the hilt. Kaito approached, his eyes unwilling to believe what he was seeing. He approached slowly as if sudden movements would shatter the illusion. As he crouched down beside her, he brushed a hand against her rapidly cooling skin. She looked peaceful, as if sleeping, but no breaths rose and fell in her chest. Kaito scooped her up, pulling her to him. She was cold. Too cold.

"No!" He roared. "Noooo."

His howls filled the night air. She wasn't breathing. She couldn't be dead. They'd promised. She'd promised.

"You promised me!" he shouted. He clutched her close to his chest, cradling her limp body. He was ready to sever his immortality in two for her. They'd sworn they'd be together no matter what. But she had left first. Now, he only felt hollow. Suzume was gone.

A crowd filtered out from the palace, having heard the commotion. They circled around him, but no one approached, and he was too lost in his own grief to care. He stroked her blood-splattered face as tears fell freely down his own. He'd never known loss so profound; no wound could ever have gutted him as her death had.

Only Shin dared approach him, placing a hand on Kaito's shoulder, but he knocked him back, growling like a feral beast. Then, one by one, they left him alone to grieve. Suzume, his spoiled priestess, his headstrong, reckless woman. She had given up her life. For what? To let him keep his kingdom? None of it mattered without her. He'd sacrifice his own immortality, his life, to have her back again. His gaze fell onto the sword embedded in her chest. The same weapon Rin had used to sever her soul and bind it with Hikaru's. Perhaps it was delusional, but he grasped hold of its hilt, and as he did, he saw the threads of power emanating from his own hand. Mixed in with them was a single red thread—one that traveled from him to Suzume. On her end, it was fading, nearly gone.

"A little bit of her spirit must remain tethered to this world," Ryuu said, coming up from behind Kaito.

"Then there's a chance she can be saved?" Kaito asked.

It was difficult to believe, holding onto her cold, lifeless body. But hope ignited in his chest. If there was a way he could save her, he'd pay any cost.

"A small one. She used that soul blade to sever her and Hisato's souls from their bodies. A blade that is not meant to wound but which might have origins in the spirit realm itself. Her spirit will be passing through the veil. Normally, it would be impossible to find her and bring her back, but your bond connects you, and that same blade could save her. There is a way you could find her, sever her bond to Kazue, and bring her back, but to keep her tethered to this flesh, you'll have to bind her soul with yours."

Like Rin had done for Hikaru and as he had wanted to do from the start.

"Tell me how to find her," Kaito said. He'd never walked in the realm of spirits.

Ryuu knelt opposite Kaito and Suzume and laid his hands over Kaito's. Kaito upturned his palm, grasping his son's hand tightly. Ryuu looked at their joined hands and frowned slightly before meeting his eyes.

"I must warn you, there is a chance that this won't work; I don't know if this blade will even travel with you to the spirit realm, or you could become lost beyond the veil searching for her."

"I don't care. Whatever it takes."

Ryuu nodded.

"Listen to my song, and as you do, pull upon that thread that connects you."

Kaito closed his eyes and listened as Ryuu's song washed over him. It reverberated within him. Echoing and filling every fiber of his being. He reached into the void, the world of spiritual energy. To the innermost reaches of his own mind, pulling tight the thread that bound them together.

What he found as he closed his eyes wasn't her but the smallest flickering flame. It glowed orange in the dimness of the inner world and bounced about. He tried to grasp it, but it flittered away from him. Going deeper through the darkness of the void, he followed after it. It led him further and further from where he started.

Ryuu's voice became distant, and the fog grew thicker. As he wandered, he found himself in front of a large doorway, the spirit sword in his hand. Kaito's grip on it tightened as he stared up at the door between life and death. It seemed to be made up of a multitude of doorways nestled into one another, and in each were a myriad of keys, both big and small, made of metal, wood, and improbably water and flame. Etched into that door were symbols he could only guess at.

"You're not supposed to be here, immortal," an echoing voice intoned.

Kaito turned to see the small, bald man who floated on a cloud just before the doorway.

"I came for someone."

"Now that is strange indeed." He tilted his head to the side. "Who is it the Great Dragon hunts for?"

"Suzume."

"Ah. She and Kazue are preparing to pass through."

He gestured at the door, where he saw them standing hand in hand. Kaito lurched forward to reach out for her, but the man floated in front of him, preventing him from getting closer.

"Suzume!" he shouted, but even when he called her name, she didn't seem to hear him.

"It is not you who chooses whether she lives or dies," the floating man said.

"Then who does? I will face them and take her back by force if I must."

"It's me," Suzume said. She turned to him at last, and so did Kazue. Her unblinking stare bore into him and set him ill at ease. There was something uncanny about both of their stares.

He reached out to take Suzume's hand. He tried tugging her away from Kazue, but she held firm, dragging Kazue behind her like a doll.

"Come back; this doesn't have to be the end. I'll save you," Kaito pleaded.

"I have to go. The road calls me." She turned to the door looming before them. Her gaze was distant, as if she were staring at a far-off horizon only she and Kazue could see. Kazue tugged on her, urging her to step beyond the door creaking open. A bright light poured out from within.

Kaito grabbed Suzume's other hand, which held onto Kazue, and brought them both to him. The pair faced him, blank-faced and pale.

"I can't let you go."

"Which one of us?" Kazue asked.

And he looked at her for the first time. If he was being honest he'd been avoiding her gaze because he was afraid of how he would react facing her again. He thought if he were confronted with her again, he'd want to speak with her or feel some tugging at his heart. But when he looked into Kazue's face once more, he felt nothing. Because she wasn't her anymore and hadn't been for a long time. Kazue died the moment she tore her soul apart. Now the person standing in front of him, shifted and changed and flickered. It wasn't just Kazue anymore—she was Hisato, Souta, Kazue, and every other part of her that had been reborn and reformed. Even Hikaru and Suzume were there in her ever-changing face. Their time was over, but it wasn't the end for Suzume. This person, who was a combination of so many people, was ready to start over.

"Goodbye, Kazue," he said and drew the sword, severing the ties that tethered Suzume and Kazue together.

"Thank you for loving me, and for letting me go." She bowed her head and then turned and walked into the mist.

He watched her go. His first love, his first heartbreak. If she was reborn, he hoped she would be happy in her new life.

Suzume blinked, and then her eyes widened. She was floating listlessly now that she wasn't attached to anyone. He saw the bright red glow of the thread that connected them and led him to her. He severed one of his threads, a blue one for his soul, and bound it where he'd cut Kazue free. She drifted nearer to him, looking more corporeal with every step.

"Come back, and let us live as two halves of one soul, Suzume," Kaito said.

A smile spread across her face as he took her hand and squeezed.

"Let's go home," she said.

FORTY

Suzume awoke with a gasp. Her lungs ached, as did the rest of her body, and there was a strange thumping in her chest as if her heart had two beats instead of one. Kaito was hovering over her with a smile on his face, and that's when it hit her. She hadn't been having a strange dream; she had died, and Kaito had brought her back to life.

"I'm not sure whether to strangle you or hug you, maybe both," she said as Kaito slowly eased her into a seated position.

"Would you rather I left you dead?"

"I have to agree with Kaito here," Ryuu interjected.

She scowled and stuck out her tongue at them. "Since when are you both on the same side?"

They shared a look. "When it comes to keeping you safe, we've always been on the same side," Ryuu said sagely.

Suzume rolled her eyes, which elicited a laugh from Kaito. The sound seemed to reverberate through her. Their bond echoed with his pleasure. Then she threw her arms around him, reveling in the feeling of their two hearts beating as one. She couldn't believe she was alive. Just to be certain, she reached for Kazue's flame and found nothing. The power was gone, but she felt something new in its place—a cold burn that she assumed must be Kaito's power halved between them both. This would take some getting used to. Good thing she had an excellent teacher like Kaito. Kaito wrapped an arm around her, anchoring her in a way she hadn't known she needed. She was feeling overcome by her emotions and Kaito's. And from the way his eyes seemed to sparkle, he was feeling much the same as her.

What happened next was a series of chaotic moments, too confusing to fully comprehend. Suzume, having been reborn, felt as if she were being swept up in a giant current. The Eight returned, having been freed when Kazue's soul passed beyond the veil, and their return caused quite a stir. Yokai and humans alike came to gawk at them. Suzume wanted to slip away amidst the chaos of it all, but they noticed her trying to escape and summoned her to them. The crowd parted, and she had no choice but to approach. One couldn't ignore a god's summons, after all.

They were almost too beautiful to look at, even more radiant and glorious than artists' renderings could ever capture. Kaito held her hand as they approached, and she was grateful to have him close by and to feel the steady rhythm of his heartbeat. He'd faced them and won before, but she hoped it wouldn't come to violence. They'd had enough of that for a lifetime.

The Sun Emperor stood at the center, and the others flanked on both sides of him. He wore a golden crown with wrought metal beams that reflected the light and made it difficult to look at him directly.

"Thank you for freeing us. I feared this day would never come. For your sacrifices, both of you, we owe a great debt of gratitude," he said in a booming voice.

She accepted the thanks with the bow of her head, not sure if it was appropriate to speak back to a god. She'd be lying to say it didn't stroke her ego to be acknowledged in such a way, but it also pricked at her that she didn't deserve such praise. Many people had sacrificed to get them here, and while she had died temporarily, she hadn't stayed dead.

"We would grant you a boon for what you've done for us. Anything you want is yours," the Sun Emperor intoned.

Suzume looked at Kaito, unsure what would be appropriate to ask for. She had everything she could want.

"I'll have to consider your offer," Suzume said, thinking it would be the most diplomatic answer.

They let her slip away graciously. After that, they spent time freeing the hybrids who'd survived the battle. The spirit blade allowed them to separate the yokai from the humans, but more importantly, she was able to free Tsuki and Akira. They'd been incapacitated and then captured, and when she arrived to free them, they were snarling and stalking the inside of their prison cell. With the sword in hand, she could see where their souls had been tangled up and how she might sever them.

She cut those ties, and they fell backward as if stunned. Then, after several long, anxious moments, they rose again as two different people. Even though she'd freed them, Suzume had to do a double take because she couldn't quite trust her eyes that she'd succeeded.

When the cell door opened, Tsuki ran out, and Akira followed at a sedated place. Tsuki picked Suzume up and twirled her around in circles, laughing all the while.

"You did it," he crowed.

"You've done a wonderful job," Akira said in her cool way. Suzume took it as high praise.

Before Tsuki's hands could linger too long on her, Kaito put his arm around her shoulder and brought her closer to him. She merely chuckled at his jealous display, but inside, she was swelling with pride. She feared they'd never get here and though there had been sacrifices made, at least she'd kept Kazue's promise and her own and righted most of her wrongs.

FORTY-ONE

As soon as Noaki heard the Eight had been freed, he went in search of Sayuri. He found her surrounded by a crowd of worshippers and her fellow kami. But for him, everything faded away but her. She turned, eyes locking on him. He stared into her eyes, gazed upon *her* face and not some imposter. He feared it was all a cruel dream. His entire body was held tight as a bowstring, fearing the slightest wrong move of his hand would break the spell that had settled over them, and she'd disappear back into his memories once again. Then ran to him, without her usual unhurried elegance. Her pale skin was flushed, and the long trail of her white hair fanned out behind her like a banner. And the tether that was holding him in place snapped.

With arms his arms outstretched to embrace her, she slid into them, and they fit together like two puzzle pieces. Her head slotted under his chin, and her hands wrapped around his back, bunching in his blood-splattered haori. He never wanted to let her go again and never wanted to stop touching her. Because he feared the moment he let her go, all of this would burst apart like the mist in the early morning.

"I'm sorry," Sayuri started to say, but he cut her off, capturing her lips in a bruising kiss the way he'd dreamed about for centuries. Her lips parted, allowing him to pour years of longing and love into her in a way that words would never be adequate.

Noaki could have spent an eternity locked in her embrace, foregoing sleep, nourishment, and any other comfort. But someone cleared their throat insistently, and Noaki looked away from Sayuri long enough to see two familiar faces staring at him uncertainly. Noaki held onto Sayuri's hand as he turned to face his children and then kneeled to bow in front of them in penance. He'd failed them in many ways, as a father and as a warrior who should have protected them from harm.

They stood on opposite sides of him, and in unison, as if still tethered by invisible strings, they placed their hands on his shoulders.

"We were the makers of our own undoing. Do not blame yourself," Akira said.

"And it wasn't your fault that you didn't know we existed," Tsuki said.

Noaki raised his head and met his children's gazes for the first time. After centuries bound to one body, they were individuals again.

"We can be a family," Akira said.

Tsuki let out a whoop of excitement and ran for his mother, gathering her up in his arms before twirling her around. Sayuri laughed at his antics and then motioned to Akira, who was watching solemnly. Akira approached her mother and reluctantly folded herself into her arms.

"You're well again?" Akira asked.

"Can't you see the color is returning to her cheeks," Tsuki said.

He turned to look at Noaki, who felt like an outsider looking in. Then Tsuki slapped him on the shoulder and brought him in for a family hug. Noaki had never known anything like a family before, and the feeling was as warm as it was foreign. There was so much to say and not enough time because even as they rejoiced in their reunion, Noaki felt the tug of the Sun Emperor's presence. Facing his old master couldn't be avoided forever. Sayuri and his children weren't the only ones who'd been freed by Hisato's end. The rest of the Eight had escaped their bindings as well, and he knew his former master well enough to know centuries of imprisonment wouldn't have softened the Sun Emperor, nor would he willingly give up the moon to his son. Noaki tightened his grip on Sayuri. Their battle wasn't quite won yet.

As much as he'd missed Sayuri, as desperate as he was to hold onto her, Noaki was also realistic about their difference in stations. For the first time in his long lifetime, he was untethered and belonged to no master. But Sayuri was different, she belonged to the moon, and she'd always be destined to reflect upon the sun's light.

"Your plan failed. What happens to us now?" Noaki asked.

A slow smile spread across her lips. "Did it?"

He knew that cryptic smile all too well, and seeing it play across her lips made him even more nervous than before, and he frowned.

The playful smile faded from her face, and she cupped his cheek with her palm. "We've all been changed by our time inside human hearts. We might be gods, but we're not as we were before. Trust me when I say, I know what I'm doing."

She leaned forward and pecked him on the lips. A crowd had surrounded them, yokai and human alike, basking in the glow of the Eight's presence. The Sun Emperor turned his gaze to them, though Noaki was certain he'd been aware of them for some time. Noaki had yet to let go of Sayuri's hand, and even beneath that heavy stare, he refused to budge. Tsuki and Akira also hovered on either side of them. Akira's hand brushed against his, and Noaki took it. They stood united against the emperor, and he trusted Sayuri's instincts would keep them together.

His instinct before would have been to bow to their supreme ruler. Sayuri's tight grip kept him from doing so. They approached the Sun Emperor, and the rest of the Eight flanked them on either side, looking a combination of amused and horrified.

"My Lord," Sayuri addressed the Sun Emperor, her chin jutted out proudly.

The Sun Emperor shone as brilliantly as a bright summer day, and looking into his face might have blinded him, but Sayuri was not afraid. If anything, she reflected that same light back at him. A hush had fallen over the gathered crowd as if the rest of the Eight and the onlookers were holding their collective breaths, waiting to see what he would do.

"It was a clever trick. Sealing me in a human's heart," he said. His voice carried over the crowd without any real effort on his part.

"I did what was necessary to claim my freedom," she replied.

"And yet I could claim you again, as is my right. And this time, destroy all you love." His voice boomed with his threat.

Akira tensed and Tsuki grasped for the blade at his hip. Noaki lifted his hand, signaling he should stand back. Sayuri didn't flinch, and he loved her even more for her bravery in that moment. His knees felt weak, and it was her grip upon him that kept him standing.

"But now you know what it is like to love and lose. Would you do it again?" she asked him.

Then something happened that Noaki never thought he'd see in a thousand lifetimes. The Sun Emperor's expression softened as he looked over to Suzume, who'd just arrived. It was, as Sayuri said, his time trapped had changed him. It rounded out his sharp edges and made him, if only a little, human. He'd lived a human life through Suzume: seen what she had seen and endured every loss and triumph.

"It was a bold gambit, but one that has paid off for you. I free you to live your own life, Sayuri. May you find happiness with it."

She bowed her head, and they turned to walk away as calmly as they could. But as soon as they were out of sight of the Sun Emperor, his attention was on other matters. Sayuri had started to weep, and her body was shaking. Noaki turned to embrace her, holding her as she buried her face into his chest. She was good at pretending to be brave, but he knew how much she feared her one-time captor. But at last, they were free.

"Then where do we go next?" Tsuki asked.

"Home," Sayuri said with a wistful sigh.

Sayuri grabbed his hand, threaded their fingers together, and looked up at Noaki with a watery smile. "We're going home. All four of us."

Home sounded wonderful for a man who'd never had one. He felt secure and perhaps not so unattached as he thought. The bonds that were tied between the four of them couldn't be severed, and he looked forward to a life in which he chose his own destiny.

Forty-Two

The battle was won, the gods had returned, but the war was only just beginning. This one wouldn't be fought with swords and armies, but through manipulation and cunning. Ryuu saw the power vacuum forming. Despite losing both the princes to the fight, the empress' clan wasn't willing to give up their control of the throne. And those who'd fought on the side of the emperor and Hisato needed to be brought under control before they could prop up their own puppet emperor. Rightfully, the next emperor should be Izuki's son. Now, Ryuu needed to win allies to his side if he wanted to put him in control. He knew who he must speak to straight away.

The retired governor and his clan had arrived at the tail end of the battle. And it was to them that Ryuu approached with plans for a future, one he had initially scoffed at when the former governor had first suggested it. But he was surprised to find that the governor had a guest. The former empress was seated at the head of the room, the former governor kneeling in front of her as she sipped her tea. Dark circles shadowed her eyes, and she'd grown wan and thin.

"My son is dead," she said without looking up at Ryuu. "Is my husband as well?"

Ryuu knelt down before her and bowed his head. "Forgive me for not protecting him."

The boy's death weighed heavily upon him and would remain like a wound in his chest for many years to come. She studied him without speaking for a long while.

"It is the price we pay for power, I suppose." Her voice caught, and Ryuu thought she was doing a terrible job of convincing even herself.

"Whom shall be the new emperor?" the governor asked.

"There is one candidate. Izuki's son is in the palace," Ryuu said.

"You cannot be serious. You'd put that woman's son on the throne?"

"I would, and with me as regent," Ryuu said.

The empress slammed her hands down on the table in front of her. "You are a liar and a deceiver. Do you truly believe that I cannot see through your duplicity? You killed my son to make yourself emperor."

"I think we should let Ryuu explain himself," the governor said, stroking his long beard.

Ryuu lifted his head to meet her gaze. No amount of penance would repair the damage he'd done. But for the lives lost in this endeavor, the kingdom had to change.

"The boy is in my care, and he will be emperor whether you choose to join me or not." He let the subtle threat linger between them. If he wanted to avoid years of bloody battle, he needed their support.

The empress puckered her lips but said nothing. She was wise enough to not challenge him. That was a good start.

"We are entering a new age. The yokai are coming out of hiding, and the time of emperors is coming to an end. I will rule as regent only long enough to tear down this empire I built. And either you shall help me make this new world. Or you will get out of my way."

The empress paled at his threats, but the governor smiled as he tugged on the end of his long beard.

There wasn't much more discussion to be had after that. Ryuu felt confident that they wouldn't challenge his authority, and he moved on to other pressing matters, like earning the support of the rest of the palace government. And it wasn't just the humans that needed to be reconciled. The yokai had entered the fray very publicly. They couldn't go back to the shadows. And the gods were back walking among mortals.

He spent days sending messages to local advisors and government officials. Many had fled at the impending threat of war, others had died in the battle, and some simply disappeared. While they waited for their arrivals or swift replacements, Ryuu met with Kaito and had him gather his trusted advisors.

But finally, they reached their assembly day. Seven of the Eight kami presided over the hearings, seated side by side at the head of the room. Yokai filled one side, the humans on the other. Both sides watched each other warily. Ryuu was one of the first to speak with the crowd.

"We are in unprecedented times. Humans and yokai worked together to fight a greater foe. But this tenuous peace cannot last forever, not without old resentments coming to a head. We must find a way to coexist. I suggest on this day we begin negotiations to balance our world."

Kaito was the first to step forward. "I agree. I say we all come to the negotiation table for peace."

More yokai voices agreed, and then the humans hesitatingly added their agreement. Progress was moving forward, but it would take days, weeks, or years to mend the wounds that lay between the different factions. Ryuu was willing to put in the work for the good of all peoples, and as he looked out at the crowd at the two halves of himself: human and yokai, he realized this was what he'd been born to do. Not to bury his immortality and yokai nature in shame but unite the two worlds in harmony.

With his help, they could set the gears in motion to reform the island of Akatsuki in the new age. The other half of his plan hinged on the prince's cooperation. He would be crowned emperor in the interim as a new government was formed. But Ryuu did not want to thrust another child into power without his consent first.

He'd checked in on the boy periodically, but their interactions were tense. The would-be emperor didn't trust him. He'd assigned priests he trusted implicitly in watching over him and hoped with time, he'd learn to trust him.

The young prince was seated in his room when Ryuu entered, and he rose to greet him. His expression was filled with fiery indignation. He reminded him painfully of Izuki. So, like his mother, but there were hints of his father, the late emperor, there, too. He was painfully young, a boy, really, caught up in his mother's ambitions. He'd have spared him the coming burden, but he could not see the governors and leaders agreeing to his ideas for a democracy without some sort of bridge between.

"Come to kill me at last?" he sneered, and Ryuu noticed how his arm tensed as he reached beneath his haori. Perhaps for some hidden weapon.

He moved faster than the boy's eyes could perceive and disarmed him. The young emperor stared wide-eyed at Ryuu as he placed the weapon on the table in front of him and motioned for him to sit.

"Take a seat, please," Ryuu said.

He stared at Ryuu with defiance. But hesitatingly, he sat down and proceeded to scowl in Ryuu's direction.

"May I ask what prompted this sudden burst of violence?" Ryuu asked.

"Your servant came and warned me," the prince sneered.

"My servant—" then he shook his head. The neko was growing more and more bold as of late. Perhaps their long bond was starting to wear thin. He'd always been defiant, but it seemed his defiance was reaching beyond simple acts of rebellion. He'd have to banish him until a more permanent solution could be reached, he supposed. He put it from his mind and focused instead on the young man in front of him.

"I have no ill intentions. Indeed, I've not come to kill you but to discuss the future of Akatsuki with you," Ryuu said.

The boy blinked at him, his mouth opening and closing in apparent confusion.

"Why would you discuss it with me?"

Ryuu suspected he'd never been consulted before, and his mother and the elders around him had likely made all the decisions for him. He'd been a pawn on the game board of politics, but soon, he'd have to learn how to move the players and control the game himself.

"Because this is your life we are discussing," Ryuu said.

The boy nodded. His expression was earnest and open, hungry even. Not for power, but for some measure of control over his own life. It was a promising start.

"I am going to share with you a secret I shared with every emperor who came before you."

The boy nodded his head again.

"I am the first emperor."

His eyes widened, and his mouth flopped open like a fish. Ryuu let the silence hang between them as the boy processed what he was telling him.

Then he said the more difficult part. "And you shall be the last."

The young man eyed the dagger on the table between him as if he hadn't quite given up on the idea of slashing at Ryuu. To avoid any such reckless behaviors, Ryuu laid his hand over it. The boy looked at him sheepishly before replying, "If I am the last, does that mean you're going to kill me?"

Ryuu shook his head. "Not at all. I've had my fill of bloodshed. But as I said, I've come here with a choice for you."

"What is that?" That stubborn streak was glinting in his eye again.

It would be difficult to guide the child, but Ryuu knew that he must. For the sake of the empire he'd created and for the future of Akatsuki.

"You will either become a tyrant, or you will be the savior of Akatsuki."

His eyes widened as he looked at Ryuu, and he saw the light dawning in his expression. Ryuu breathed a sigh of relief that he'd judged the boy correctly. He didn't want to be wicked. With the right guidance, he could help usher in a new age of Akatsuki, one that was both just and fair.

"What must I do to save it?" he asked Ryuu.

"Before I tell you, you must agree to trust me and no one else. For there are those at court, who would use you to their own wicked ends. Do you believe me?"

He nodded his head slowly.

"Then good. Together, we will prepare Akatsuki for a transition. We will change from an empire ruled by one man to one where each state has its own say. And their own right to choose how they live."

"You're talking about a democracy."

"Just so."

The boy nodded.

Ryuu felt the knot in his stomach lessen. This he could do, both for Akatsuki and for Izuki. She might not be here to see her children grow, but he would protect them both just the same. And when they met beyond that veil someday, he hoped she would greet him with a smile and a warm embrace.

It was just a spark, the merest start of a thing, but Ryuu felt confident this would be the thing that changed the island for the better—bringing them into a brighter and better future for everyone.

FORTY-THREE

Kaito hadn't expected his reward for helping save the world would be the boredom of being chained to meeting rooms for days on end. It shouldn't have come as a surprise. The human world and the yokai world had well and truly collided. The capital city and White Palace were in shambles. Workers were pouring in to help with the reconstruction effort. And the government was struggling to hold everything together in the post-coup storm. On top of that, the Eight had returned, and as was their way, they'd decided to insert themselves into the middle of everything.

In the large audience room, voices, snarls, and growls overlapped as the two uneasy sides sized one another up. Kaito and Suzume sat near the front of the room. Ryuu sat on the other, and the seven of the Eight sat above them all. The moon goddess and Noaki had removed themselves from the proceedings. If Kaito thought the human governors and advisors would be humbled by the presence of literal gods, he was wrong. One elderly man with a long, thin, white beard, which trembled when he spoke, addressed them in a thin, reedy voice high enough to puncture eardrums.

Suzume's eyes were glazed over as she watched the old man prattle on about tradition and borderlines.

Nothing would go back to the way it had been before. Yokai had too long been pushed out of their ancestral lands, dwindling in population as human populations expanded. Humans and their farmlands, towns, and cities had hacked away at the forests and sacred lands where the yokai and lesser kami dwelled. For the kami's part, they listened to the droning of the old men and stepped in to maintain order, when yokai called for bloodshed by having them removed from proceedings. The tengu elder arrived, looking even more skeletal and translucent than before. He spoke eloquently about divisions of land, which clearly favored the yokai over the humans. This assertion caused fractures in thin alliances and set them back in weeks of negotiations.

As weeks turned to months, boring meeting bled into the next boring meeting. It was the part of being a ruler that Kaito hated the most. In fact, the longer he spent in these onerous meetings, the more he reflected on how much of rulership he disliked. When he'd first conquered the island, it had been for glory and honor. To give yokai greater independence from the Eight. But not long after, he grew bored of the day-to-day ruling of the island and left it to his advisors and generals to handle and spent much of his time away from court looking for diversions. As the months wore on, the idea of going back to that life was starting to wear upon him.

They were reaching the end of deliberations and official leaders were going to be declared soon. Concessions were made, and as with any fair negotiation, no one walked away entirely happy. It was assumed he and Suzume would be ruling the yokai together as a sort of symbol of peace between the humans and yokai. But when he thought about being a ruler again, it just filled him with dread. It wasn't just the tedium. His life was bound to Suzume's, and if anyone were to challenge him for the position, which was likely despite all their talks as yokai did not change easily, his injury would harm Suzume. And if his enemies discovered her death would cause his, they'd use her against him. Besides, she'd never be happy living as the sole human in a court of yokai.

On the last day of their negotiations, Kaito woke up with Suzume in his arms. They'd fallen asleep too exhausted to talk. She stirred against him as if she would rise and dress for the day, but Kaito pulled her in tighter around him, preventing her from getting up.

She laughed as he nuzzled against her. "Stop. We're going to be late at this rate."

"I'd rather stay in bed with you all day," he said, nipping at her earlobe.

She gave him a slow, seductive smile. "Finish today's negotiations, and we won't have to get out of bed for weeks."

Kaito nuzzled against her neck, inhaling the scent of her, feeling the cascade of her hair fall against his face as he breathed her in. They were still learning the nature of their bond, but she must have sensed some of his reticence because she twisted around in his grip to turn and face him fully.

"Something wrong?" she asked.

"I thought all I wanted was to rule. That getting my kingdom back was all that mattered. But after watching you die and bringing you back, those goals feel petty. We'll never be happy as rulers. I don't think I ever really was."

"And?" she prompted.

"What if we ran away from it all?" Kaito said.

"You're joking." But she didn't really think that. She could feel his sincerity as he could feel hers. She sat up to face him, and Kaito followed her.

They both knew neither of them could go back to the way things were, and neither of them wanted them to.

"I want to step down as the ruler of Akatsuki," Kaito said

"Will they let you? It hasn't been said yet, but I think everyone assumes we'll rule together," she said.

"Is that what you want, to rule?"

Suzume was silent for a long beat, and her reply was almost too quiet to hear. "No."

Kaito cupped her cheeks in his hands and tilted her head up to face him. "Our hearts beat as one, and I cannot imagine a life where our mutual happiness doesn't come first. We did what we set out to do. We stopped Hisato, and we brought yokai and humans to the same negotiation table. Maybe this is where our story ends."

"What will we do then? The kami and the governors will be displeased."

"I have an idea for how we can fix this and keep the peace."

Suzume didn't question him further, and they quickly dressed and prepared for another day of meetings. When they entered, the remaining seven of the Eight, were already seated and speaking amongst themselves. Most of the clan representatives and leaders hadn't arrived yet, and Kaito thought it best to bring up the topic of his retirement before things got underway.

"May I speak with your holiness?" Kaito asked.

The Sun Emperor narrowed his eyes at Kaito as if suspecting he was already up to some mischief, but gestured for him to step closer.

"I am planning to step down as leader of the yokai. I would have your blessing to make the announcement before the meeting starts."

The Sun Emperor frowned at the declaration, and the fellow kami flanking him also seemed puzzled by the turn of events.

"You fought so hard to win back your rule; are you certain?" The Sun Emperor wasn't the merciless god he'd been before. A part of him was indelibly marked by Suzume, which forced him to favor Kaito in some ways. Were it not for that Kaito wasn't sure he could walk away so easily.

Suzume was standing beside him, and he reached for her hand giving it a squeeze. "I'm certain."

"Very well," the Sun Emperor said, inclining his head slightly.

The crowd filed in, and Kaito waited to address them until they were settled.

"I have an announcement I'd like to make," Kaito said once everyone was settled into place.

Curious gazes stared up at him. Ryuu, in particular, looked torn between amusement and curiosity. Perhaps he had suspected, or maybe it was his influence, that led Kaito to this decision. They'd spent many hours in counsel together, finding the strain on their relationship eased without the threat of destruction looming over them both. Whatever it was, he knew he had his son's support.

Kaito smiled at the group in front of him, then said, "I was gone for five hundred years."

The words lingered in the air, and then words were muttered amongst the yokai. "Before that, I was your ruler. The one who brought the yokai together. And once again, you joined me in battle. But I've realized something in the past few years. You don't need me to rule you."

There was more murmuring and a few shouts of displeasure, but Kaito held up his hand to quiet them once more.

"I propose a counsel. Leaders of all yokai and humans." He looked to the human side. "Shall come together as we have here. To make decisions for our island. To guide and make decisions for the good of us all. Not just human or yokai."

There was a ringing silence after his proclamation, and for a moment, the world seemed to teeter on the edge of chaos once again. Then Ryuu stood up and clapped his hands together.

"I, for one, welcome the discourse of a counsel. It is the glue that would unite the kingdoms together."

And then the elder tengu stood. "I, too, agree to this idea."

More and more humans and yokai spoke up in support of the action. Not everyone, of course, but it was a start. The rest of the meeting proceeded much as the ones before had, with an endless string of debates and an inching progress toward amicable resolution. Everyone gathered was beyond exhausted, but they'd reached agreements on almost everything. Leaders of each yokai territory had been established, and a new counsel of representatives selected. The dawn of a new age was upon them.

By the time the council meeting ended, the sun was starting to set. Normally, he and Suzume would head back to their room and collapse into bed, only to rise and do it all over again. But after making his declaration, Kaito was feeling lighter than ever, and he took Suzume to a secluded part of the palace gardens that hadn't been destroyed in the battle as others were.

The moon was full in the sky as they strolled together in amicable silence. They stopped beneath a cherry tree covered in tight buds just days away from bursting. Suzume stopped to look at them before Kaito grasped her chin and turned her to face him.

"There's something I've been wanting to ask you. But I wanted to wait until everything was settled," Kaito said.

He felt the echo of her heartbeat racing alongside his. Suzume's lips parted slightly as if she could anticipate the words he'd say next.

"Yes?" she asked.

"Will you become my wife?" he asked.

She flung herself forward into his embrace. They kissed with urgency and renewed passion.

"Third time's the charm, I suppose?" she teased.

"I always knew it would be you in the end."

They kissed beneath the full moon, his heart full, and for the first time in a long time, he was at peace.

FORTY-FOUR

The temple hadn't changed while they'd been away. New, green shoots shot up in the garden beds, and the ancient gingkoes were covered in fresh branches covered in tight, green buds. Rin strolled along the familiar pathway, half in a dream. They'd nearly died when she'd bound her and Hikaru's souls together. She hadn't realized how close they'd been to death until she woke up feeling Hikaru's heart beating in time with hers. Rather than stay and help rebuild the new society Suzume, Kaito, and Ryuu aimed to found, they returned home. When the proceedings between humans and yokai had started, Kaito offered her a place at court and a spot at the table to help decide the future of the island. She and Hikaru had talked it over and decided to forego the political machinations for good.

Kaito didn't need her anymore, not really. She'd left her shrine behind out of a sense of obligation to him, but he let her go with a smile.

Rin and Hikaru could have gone anywhere, but in her heart, she knew their temple was where they belonged. Starting over where they left off was more than she could have hoped for. They headed for the main shrine building and pried open the swollen doors. During the wet season, the wood absorbed extra liquid that made them stick. The doors opened with a groan and released the strong mildew scent from the interior. There was work to be done to bring their home back to its former glory. Even when Rin had been an active resident, she'd let repairs and upkeep slide; her grief had swallowed her whole back then.

"I wanted to redo the interior of the shrine. And with Akio dead, we'll need to erect a new idol. Maybe the Lady of the Forest. I think she'd like that," Hikaru mused to himself as he surveyed the faded paint and cobwebbed interior.

Rin smiled at his enthusiasm, and he looked back at her with a cheeky grin. "What's that look for?" he asked.

"It's good to have you back here," she said.

"It's good to be back." He held out his hand to her, and she took it as they faced their dirty temple.

"Should we get started?"

She nodded, and they dove into the work, clearing out the rotted pieces of wood and sweeping up the debris. They fell back into their centuries' old routines. Cleaning, organizing, and making lists of items they'd need to repair the shrine buildings. It might take years to fix it back up, but she relished the work. As they worked, the temple bloomed under their careful ministrations, awakening with light and color, as they rang in spring and then summer.

It was a blisteringly hot summer day. Rin was wiping down one of the verandas when she felt Hikaru's heart racing. She dropped her rag and raced to where he was across the temple grounds. Hikaru was standing at the foot of the shrine steps and staring up at the torii, his gaze a thousand miles away. She reached out for him, placing her hands on either side of his face and turning him to look at her. His vision cleared but the color had drained from his face, as if he'd seen a ghost.

"What's wrong?" she asked, though her bond told her what it was. Another waking nightmare.

"Nothing." He patted her hand. "Just remembering..."

Hikaru, realizing he couldn't lie, not really, brought her into the circle of his embrace and held her closer to him. She'd always been aware of him before. Her senses were keener than his, and she constantly worried about his well-being, knowing that her life was infinite while his life was transient and fleeting. Now, their lives were linked. Irrevocably intertwined for all time. And it was a relief to know she'd never have to live a moment without him. But it was also a burden to him. She'd lost him once, and after years of grief and longing, she knew it wouldn't be easy to shake the ghosts that haunted her. The fear would continue to linger at the edges of her mind—waiting for the enemies to return and strike.

"It won't be like it used to be, will it?" she asked.

"Nothing ever truly stays the same, does it?"

Rin sighed heavily and relaxed against him. "But we'll have each other?" she prompted.

"Always us. Forever."

With time, the memories of their near-death experience began to fade. Though there were times the nightmares woke him in the dead of night, and his fear bolted her upright in bed. They would hold one another in the dark, waiting for their linked hearts to slow their beating. And when her fears of Hisato returning paralyzed her and sent her into a spiral, Hikaru felt the echo of those worries in his own chest.

In time, they found ways to balance their fears and to regain a sort of semblance of control over their minds and hearts. It would be a long road, and perhaps they'd never truly heal from all they'd been through, but whatever road lay ahead, they'd walk it together.

FORTY-FIVE

Suzume's headdress chimed with every move she made. It was a bright and lively sound. The sun shone overhead, and she couldn't think of a more perfect day for a wedding. Her wedding procession was led by Hikaru and Rin, each carrying symbols of both yokai and human. At the end of the long pathway, Kaito beamed, looking handsome in his sky-blue hakama and haori. Her heart swelled at the sight.

The wedding march was agonizingly slow as she was weighed down by her layers of kimono and extravagant headdress. But she'd wanted to savor this moment. After war, loss, triumph, and falling in love, she and Kaito had gone on a wild journey together. His heartbeat echoed in her chest, matching her rhythm. Nothing about their lives had been simple or normal. Their first meeting had been their wedding day, and it felt fitting to recreate that moment in happier circumstances. The wedding, like Kaito's proposal, was more symbolic than necessary. Their souls were forever entwined. She considered their wedding more a celebration for their friends and surviving family.

As she walked down the aisle to Kaito, her friends watched with ecstatic smiles. Akira and Tsuki stood side by side with their parents, Noaki and Sayuri, holding hands. Ryuu and Suzume's younger brother, the interim emperor, stood nearby, grinning up at her. The world had changed, and they'd all suffered immense loss. But the future was bright.

They moved forward another step, and Kaito impatiently tapped his foot at the end of the aisle. Another inch forward, and his patience broke. Suzume felt it a second before he brushed past Rin and Hikaru to scoop Suzume up into his arms.

She gave a surprised yelp as he carried her to the temple altar, where the new head priest waited to officiate.

"Impatient to have the ceremony finished?" Suzume teased.

"Yes, I'm eager to skip to the wedding night, my bride," he whispered into her ear.

A pleasurable chill ran over her skin as she smirked at him. After he set her down, the head priest cleared his throat, and the ceremony began. Kaito broke tradition and let his hand linger on the small of her waist. The head priest gave them a narrowed-eyed look of disapproval but said nothing. When your wedding was attended by oni and tengu, along with the most influential government officials in Akatsuki, and after saving the world, you got away with a lot. The ceremony was quick, and despite Kaito's teasing about rushing to the wedding night, they joined their friends for a celebration feast afterward.

They sat at the head of the group while sake flowed, and laughter filled the room. Sumptuous dishes were served, but Suzume felt full just from watching all her friends celebrate. She rejoiced in their good fortune and the fact they were all alive, vibrant, and well. Yokai and humans filed past their table to congratulate her on her wedding. While humans and yokai sat on opposite sides of the room, the dinner was tense at first, Shin went over and mingled with the humans, quickly followed by Tsuki and others, and some of the tension eased.

Eventually the humans went over to mingle with the yokai, and the room was a blend of their different peoples all together. It felt surreal to see it. But this truly was a new age of humans and yokai. One where they could coexist peacefully.

Kaito reached for her hand under the table and squeezed.

"A drink, my bride?" He offered her a cup of sake. She took her time drinking, watching as his eyes darkened. He was seconds away from taking her from the feast and back to their private room; she was sure of it.

Then Tsuki approached, and they looked away from one another, blushing. "I can't believe it. You two stopped bickering long enough to marry," Tsuki said.

Suzume stuck out her tongue at him.

"Brother, really, we all knew they were meant to be from the start." Akira glided up next to her brother, looking beautiful and deadly all at once. It was still strange to see them standing side by side. She had actually grown accustomed to them sharing a single body. But she was happy to see them free to live their own lives.

Noaki, and their mother, Sayuri, came by with warm greetings as well. Noaki, as usual, didn't say much, but he gave her a rare half-smile.

"Let's leave the happy couple be," Akira said and shooed away her family.

More guests came through, making their greetings and offering their allegiance to Kaito should he change his mind about ruling over Akatsuki. He gracefully denied their pledges. That was in the past now. They were free to make their own future.

When the night started to wind down, Kaito grabbed her by the hand, and her skin burned at the touch. She'd been waiting for this moment since she'd dawned that heavy kimono. They went back to their room, which overlooked the ocean, and their very large futon awaited them.

She stared out at the water, reflecting on the long road that had brought them here, and let out a sigh. Kaito came up behind her and wrapped his arms around her. She leaned back into his embrace.

"Just think, my bride. This is only the beginning of our very long lives together."

She turned in his embrace and kissed him in response. She hoped they would spend centuries together. But no one really knew what it meant for a human and a yokai to bond as they had. It was a relief to know neither would spend a moment without the other in the future.

Kaito's hand ran along her arm, and goosebumps pebbled her skin. He tugged loose the sash of her obi and, one by one, let each piece fall to the ground. This time, on their real wedding night, she wasn't afraid. Because they'd been through fire and ice, even through death, and come out stronger.

He kissed her again, and she opened herself up to him, wrapping her arms around his neck.

"I love you," she whispered.

"And I you, forever and beyond."

"And through death and back."

"And in immortality." He smiled against her mouth before pulling her down onto the bed.

"Now that we're free of meetings and rule. What do we do now?" she asked.

"Whatever we want." He smiled.

This is the end. Thank you for joining me on Suzume and Kaito's journey.

This is the end. Thank you for joining me on Suzume and Kaito's journey.

Acknowledgments

Four years ago, I canceled the pre-order for the Immortal Vow. I feared I'd never complete the series. I was determined to write an epic conclusion, but I wasn't sure I was talented enough to realize my vision. I paused working on it after writing a messy first draft. With time and space, I realized I was on the verge of burnout.

I rested a while (thanks to a worldwide pandemic) and slowly clawed my way back to writing by working on other books, but before I knew it, I'd finished a trilogy and launched another. All that time many lovely readers gently inquired: where's book 5? After a long rest and a few Kickstarters in between, I returned at last to a sloppy chaotic first draft I'd abandoned four years before. Untangling the plot threads and tying them together was a challenge, but also extremely gratifying.

The Dragon Saga has been a career changer for me. It helped me become a full-time author, and it's the world I've spent the most time writing in out of five different series I've published. It's bittersweet to be finished with this world. But this is the end. As I'm writing this, I have no plans to return to Akatsuki. And since this is the "finale" I wanted to thank a few people.

Thanks to my husband, Andrew, for the words of quiet encouragement. Thank you for listening to me talk about dragon shifters and elemental magic. Thanks to my sister, Mel, who's my biggest cheerleader and first fan. Thanks to my best friend,

Nicole, you're always there for me in my time of need and first introduced me to fantasy novels via the Unicorns of Balinor in the 7th grade. Technically, this is because of you. Charity, my second hand and ride or die. You're always so patient, no matter how many times I change my mind. Thank you, you're never getting rid of me. Katie, my editor, who's been editing this series for ten years and is always patient and kind in her feedback no matter how confusing and chaotic some of my drafts might be.

There's so many others I'm probably forgetting to thank, but thank you as well. I'm lucky to make writing my job and to have connected with so many incredible readers. Each of you makes my life that much richer!

ALSO BY NICOLETTE ANDREWS

Moonlight Dragon

Empress Ascending (Newsletter Exclusive)

Dragon's Deception

Dragon's Temptation

Thornwood Series

Fairy Ring (Free)

Pricked by Thorns (Free)

Heart of Thorns

Tangled in Thorns

Blood and Thorns

World of Akatsuki

The Dragon Saga

The Priestess and the Dragon (Free)

The Sea Stone

The Song of the Wind

The Fractured Soul

The Immortal Vow

Tales of Akatsuki

Kitsune: A Little Mermaid Retelling (Free)

Yuki: A Snow White Retelling

Okami: A Little Red Riding Hood Retelling

<u>**Diviner's World**</u>

Duchess (Free)

Sorcerer (Free)

Diviner's Prophecy

Diviner's Curse

Diviner's Fate

Princess

<u>**Witch of the Lake Series**</u>

Feast of the Mother

Fate of the Demon

Fall of the Reaper

About the Author

Nicolette is a native San Diegan with a passion for the world of make believe. From a young age, Nicolette was telling stories whether it be writing plays for her friends to act out or making a series of children's books that her mother still likes drag out to embarrass her with in front of company. She still lives in her imagination but in reality she resides in San Diego with her husband, children and a couple cats. She loves reading, attempting arts and crafts, and cooking.

You can visit her at her website: www.nicoletteandrews.com or at these places:

facebook.com/nicandfantasy

x.com/nicandfantasy

instagram.com/nicolette_andrews

amazon.com/author/nicoletteandrews

bookbub.com/authors/nicolette-andrews

goodreads.com/nicolette_andrews

pinterest.com/Nicandfantasy